International Acclaim for *Fernando: Beethoven of the Guitar*

Beautifully written and meticulously researched, this biographical novel is a fascinating account of the amazing (and amazingly unknown) life of Fernando Sor, the greatest virtuoso and composer in the history of music for guitar.

— Santiago del Rey
Editor and Translator, Barcelona

This extraordinary trilogy on the life and times of Fernando Sor is a rare triumph that combines historical fiction with philosophical romance. Lou Marinoff offers us a virtuoso performance, entwining music, mystery, and metaphysics in a gripping tale whose motto may well be summed up in the author's own wise words—"truth is stranger than fiction, and fiction is nothing but truth in disguise."

— Makarand R. Paranjape, Ph.D.
Professor of English Literature, Jawaharlal Nehru University
Director, Indian Institute of Advanced Study, Shimla

The secret to any great book is a great story. Lou Marinoff's historical novel about the life of Fernando Sor is exactly that. All classical guitarists know how important a figure Sor was and is to their world, but this book goes far beyond that. Rich in Spanish history, its monarchy, and the Napoleonic Wars, it will be a most enjoyable and informative read for people from all walks of life.

— Peter McCutcheon
Honorary Professor of Classical Guitar, The University of Montreal

Lou Marinoff's latest book, *Fernando: Beethoven of the Guitar,* is a *tour de force*, written as a novelized history of the great Catalan composer and guitarist Fernando Sor (1778-1839). Marinoff conjures up in great detail the intrigues and politics of the rulers of Spain, England, France, and Russia, who employed Sor to entertain and instruct their families, and who favored Sor above other composers. The Catalan's life intersected with leading artists of his time including Paganini, Berlioz, Goya, and Goethe. So vivid is the style with which he re-creates the episodes of the composer's life, the author has the knack of causing the reader to feel present in each scene. A guitarist himself, Marinoff's great love and affinity for Sor are evident throughout this three-part opus. Bravo on an engrossing account of this fascinating genius!

— Maestro Cesare Civetta
Founder and Music Director
Beethoven Festival Orchestra, New York

Lou Marinoff's *Fernando: Beethoven of the Guitar* is many things. It's a historical novel, and most readers will find the 'historical' aspect the prominent one, but they'll keep reading because it's not just a history but a delightful embroidering of a history few of us knew much of. We are taken not only—and very thoroughly—through Fernando Sor's remarkable life, but also through the tumultuous history of Europe forming the stage of that life. I'm sure that almost all readers will be hugely informed, and completely fascinated by this book, which is so beautifully written that it will seem a lot less lengthy than it is. Its three parts are devoted to Early, Middle, and Late Sor, as it were, and having read the first you will be unable to resist going on to the second and then the third. The last chapter is devoted to his legacy, which amounts virtually to the christening of the classical guitar as a serious instrument, an employment that had been essentially unheard of before Sor's day. The book is not only a history but a romp, following its eminently likable as well as extremely gifted hero through a Europe you probably didn't know much about, and doing so with a level of gusto that is unlikely to be equaled. Hats off to Marinoff for this astonishing book!

—Jan Narveson, Ph.D., O.C.
Professor Emeritus of Philosophy, University of Waterloo
President, Kitchener-Waterloo Chamber Music Society

History simply tells us about facts. The historical novel, though, is an instrument that allows readers to relive important events by introducing us into the intimate lives of great historical figures. This is exactly what Lou Marinoff does in recreating the life of an extraordinary but mostly unknown Catalan musician of the XVIII and XIX centuries: Fernando Sor. Marinoff says, "My main literary goals in writing this trilogy were to resuscitate dry bones of facticity by adorning them with human flesh and blood; to animate desiccated dates with a pounding heartbeat and a surging pulse; to restore remote events to an all-embracing immediacy; and to revivify long-dead names with vibrant personalities and vivacious passions."

Marinoff transports readers to another time and place, both real and imagined. As we know, writing historical fiction requires a balance of research and creativity; Marinoff expertly handles both elements in a masterful way. This cast of real people living the events of their time has given the author rich territory to tell a wholly distinctive story; creating this fantastic literary piece required a profound knowledge of the genre and unique music appreciation, both of which Marinoff possesses. By reading this book, the reader can relive many historical moments, including the unique encounter and conversations held at the Duchess of Alba's Palacio de Liria; of note, she was also the patron of Francisco de Goya. There are many more important and significant historical events such as Sor and the Inquisition, Napoleon's Invasion of Spain, the Battle of Bailén, the first defeat for the French invaders, and the execution of Madrileños at the '2 de Mayo' by French firing squads (as portrayed so majestically by Goya in his series called 'The Disasters of War'). Marinoff conveys the spirit, manners, and social conditions of a past age with realistic detail and fidelity, framed in beautiful prose. This is a very enjoyable read on many fronts.

A colleague of mine who serves as a professor at a very prestigious Spanish university told me that if we want to truly know Spanish history of the last centuries, it is fundamental to read literature pieces instead of only history books. I believe this to be absolutely true in the case of

Fernando Sor. Marinoff has given us a welcome and exceptional gift to better understand the life of this extraordinary musician.

—Juan Carlos Mercado, Ph.D.
Dean of Interdisciplinary Studies, Center for Worker Education
The City College of the City University of New York

Few biographers tell the story of a life as compellingly as Lou Marinoff. In creating a 'romantic historical' novel about Fernando Sor, we *live* 'Fernando's' life step-by-step; we don't just know about his movements, we *feel* them. We experience his challenges as both guitarist—fighting to give his very instrument the recognition it so deserved and, indeed, deserves—and as a man. We feel both his losses of loved ones and the sense of bereavement when forced by circumstances to leave his native, beloved Spain. We feel his loves, too; even, or perhaps especially, when they are conflicted. And as we follow Fernando across Europe to Paris, to London, to Russia via Cologne, Bonn, Brussels and other cities, we see him in the arms of fame and fortune. And as we 'travel', we encounter a multitude of familiar figures, from Cherubini and Clementi to Méhul to Goethe.

In allowing himself space over three volumes ('Youth, Celebrity, and War'; 'Exile, Favor, and Triumph'; 'Glory, Finale, and Legacy') Marinoff allows for huge elucidations on historical context, politics and war. In so doing, not only do we feel enriched, but we also feel inspired to investigate further, just as one is inspired to seek out the music of the illustrious 'Fernando' (a highly recommended endeavor, incidentally). One of Marinoff's specialties, philosophy, also finds its place in the discourse. And by using fiction to create bridges between the facts we do know about Fernando, we come out with a satisfyingly complete picture of the composer.

An uncanny prophesy of Sor's greatness by a gypsy palm reader sows the seeds as Fernando frees himself from his father's restrictions, has his education at Montserrat and goes on to have a momentous meeting with Goya, a great man who towers over Sor's life, inspiring him to his best.

The gypsy prophesy returns time after time, like a supernatural thread through his life.

"In short, music gushed out of Fernando like water from a modern fire-hose," says Marinoff. It shot out of him in a multitude of directions, from Somers Town in London to deepest Russia. It is a pleasure and a privilege to live Sor's life in these pages, to rejoice in his triumphs, to feel his heartaches. An extensive bibliography and webography complete the picture.

Over a decade in the making, Lou Marinoff's *Fernando* is a work of passion that leaves one energized and, notwithstanding the length, eager for more.

— Colin Clarke

International Classical Music Critic, London

Fernando: Beethoven of the Guitar is an incredible historical novel of a Spanish musician-composer caught up in the upheavals of the Napoleonic Wars. It is simply extraordinary that Marinoff uses the medium of a historical novel to paint the relationships between the protagonists of this Napoleonic period. And for me, particularly important were the friendships between many engaged 'liberals', who were also artists of one kind or another: writers, composers, performers, dancers, poets, painters... artists who were not just 'artists for the sake of being artists'!

I have never learned so much about European history in all my life! In Book II, I experienced Fernando's grand tour voyaging toward Russia like a series of literary jewels, which permitted me to 'meet' some of my greatest 'heroes' including Goethe, and never in frivolous ways. At the same time, Professor Marinoff lets us see that such exemplary personages were also human beings, yet in contexts that were complex and often dangerous. I learned implicit lessons on courage here. History *lives* through the pen of this author!

After reading all three volumes, I feel that Marinoff's message of demonstrating the horrors of war was as intentional as the decision of the great

Spanish artist Goya to visually depict the realities of that horrible era. And although Marinoff does not express this in so many words, or hit us over the head with his own convictions, I felt perhaps his underlying message was in fact, through the voice of Fernando, that war and violence are not the solutions to resolving problems among human beings.

These books are also a treat for the senses! Cuisine from all over Europe is described to the point where your mouth waters, and it's a delight for those who want to discover such things. In the same way, the wonders seen from a traveling carriage, including the countryside, are depicted until we actually feel the breeze, see the sun's rays in changing seasons, hear the different birds ... And of course, there are also exquisite details of all the palaces Fernando visited.

There is obviously the inestimable gift the author gives Spain and its artists and musicians, in restoring Fernando Sor to his rightful position as a 'son of Spain' who took the guitar to unimaginable heights. This was so very long in coming, because Fernando was the victim of the era and its contradictions, and of the jealous, power-hungry leaders who governed nation-states and empires—not the least being Napoleon. In this context I was delighted to find references to Beethoven and his longing for a new Humanism to take hold in Europe.

During this historic COVID-19 pandemic, Professor Lou Marinoff has given us an enormous gift in numerous ways, not the very least being the ability to travel without getting on a plane. And learning critically important lessons of history that will stand us in good stead in the coming years. Anyone who felt that history in school was a bore, this is your antidote!

Some of the *most* impressive things for me were the anecdotes we discover about Fernando's approach to education. First of all, he never stopped teaching. And he did not position himself as someone to be adored and mimicked. Professor Marinoff shows us that Fernando believed it vital to boost the confidence of his students, to the point where he even proposed to perform with them, with the student playing the first part and Fernando the accompanying parts. What generosity of heart!

There are connections between things alluded to at the start of the novel and taken up again near the end, which convey a tremendous sense of 'coming full circle'. Gives one the marvelous impression that life is one enormous continuity. Is this not in several ways an autobiography, dear Professor Marinoff? Those parallels between that young man in Canada (late in Book III), and the life of Fernando, are absolutely astounding despite obvious differences in place and époque. What a labor of love by this guitar-playing philosophy professor-author, to come up with this precious life story!

— Michèle de Gastyne

President, Musique Universelle Arc-en-Ciel, Paris

Fernando

Beethoven of the Guitar

Lou Marinoff

Cover designed by Lou Marinoff and Ken Fraser.

ISBN-13: 978-1-954968-06-6 print edition
ISBN-13: 978-1-954968-07-3 ebook edition

Waterside Productions
2055 Oxford Ave
Cardiff, CA 92007
www.waterside.com

Dedicated to the unique artistic spirit of Catalonia
and to the great musical traditions of Spain

Table of Contents

Appendices

Acknowledgements

Thanks to my late parents, Rosaline Tafler and Julius Marinoff, for strongly encouraging my literary and musical interests from an early age. Thanks to my late parents' cultured friends, Violet and Eric Shaw, for gifting me at a very early age with long-playing records of classics by Grieg, Mendelssohn, and Tchaikovsky.

Thanks to all my devoted guitar teachers for their exemplary private lessons, inspiring public performances, and invaluable recordings: Miguel Garcia, Florence Brown, and Peter McCutcheon in Montreal; Harold Micay in Vancouver; and David Leisner in New York. Thanks additionally to those virtuoso guitarists in whose master classes I was fortunate enough to participate, including Alexandre Lagoya, Leo Brouwer, Scott Tennant, and David Russell. Thanks also to Jeunesses Musicales Canada at the Orford Arts Center, for idyllic summers of total immersion in music. Thanks as well to Maestro Moshe Denburg, composer, conductor, and performer, for many decades of friendship, encouragement, and fruitful musical collaboration.

Thanks to Brian Jeffery for his decades of painstaking work in researching, writing, publishing, and updating the most historically authoritative biography of Fernando Sor, in addition to Sor's complete oeuvre for solo guitar and guitar duets, and for his long-time friendship and encouragement. Thanks to Joel Flegler, editor of *Fanfare*, for publishing laudatory reviews by Colin Clarke, Maria Nockin, and David Saemann of my CD *Classical Journey*, as well as an extensive interview with Colin Clarke (*Fanfare*, September/October 2016). Thanks to Irvin Yalom for writing wonderful historical novels about Nietzsche,

Schopenhauer, and Spinoza, and for the inspiring example he thereby set. Since the psychiatrist Yalom had so successfully fictionalized the lives of these important philosophers, it loaned credence to the hope that a philosopher could attempt to do so for an important guitarist and composer.

Thanks to the Division of Humanities at The City College of New York for providing the seminal impetus for the scholarly research underpinning this trilogy, by means of a Humanities Enrichment Grant. Thanks to Monica Agrest and Antoinette Williams-Tutt for translating selected texts. Thanks to Father Daniel Codina for his private tour of Montserrat Monastery, enabling me to view parts of it through the eyes of Fernando Sor. Thanks to librarians at the British Library in London, the Montserrat Monastery Library, the Morris Cohen Library at The City College, the National Library in Madrid, and the New York Public Library, for their expert assistance.

Thanks to many family members, friends, colleagues, fellow artists and fellow travelers based chiefly in the Americas and Europe, who encouraged me musically and/or literarily, both in general and also with respect to the conception and completion of this project. They include Giselle Monges and Ray Dalton in Argentina; Paulo Coelho in Brazil; Sonny Stone, David Fink, Jay Iversen, Gail Richardson, Bernard de los Cobos, Jean and Jan Narveson, the late Howard Abracen, the late Michael Godfrey, and the late James Matheson in Canada; Cristian Warken in Chile; Anette Prins, Isabel and Oscar Brenifier, Albert Werckmann, Mieke de Moor, Jean Christophe Iseux von Pfetten, John Kidd, and Michèle de Gastyne in France; Johannes Thome, Horst Gronke, and Dominique Hertzer in Germany; Evi Choutou in Greece; Makarand Paranjape, Balaganapathi Devarakonda, Ashwani Kumar, Sundeep Waslekar, and Ilmas Futehally in India; Ida Jongsma in Holland; Lydia Amir in Israel; Giancarlo Marinelli, Lino Missio, Luca Nave, and the late Salvatore Geraci in Italy; David Sumiacher, Hugo Pereyra, and Horacio López Córdova in Mexico; Jorge Humberto Dias and Francisco Mendonça in Portugal; Beatrice Popescu, Vasile Hategan, and Florin Labont in Romania; Alexey Pushkov, and Sergey Borisov in Russia; Aleksandar Fatic in Serbia; Santiago del Rey, Ana Lafuente, Silvia Fernandez, Mercè Diago, José Barrientos Rastrójo, María Victoria Caro

Bernal, Michael Thallium, Louis Grané and family, Berta Noy, and Lucia Luengo in Spain; Richard Levi and Claes Hultling in Sweden; Rolf Dobelli, Lory and Guy Spier, and Nadja and Frank Richter in Switzerland; Sonja Abracen, Patrick Curry, Clair and Tim Beardson, and the late Paul Robertson in the UK; Martha and Gustavo Colominas in Uruguay; Vaughana Feary, Paula Miksic, Pierre Grimes, Valerie and J. Michael Russell, George Hole, Andrew Fitz-Gibbon, Stacy Kenworthy, Ana and Andrew Twarden, Frederick Collier, Bethany Mutone, Phil Bulla, Steven Gimbel, Cesare Civetta, Juan Carlos Mercado, the late Paul Almond, and the late Thomas Humphrey in the USA.

A special thanks to Daisaku Ikeda in Japan, for his inspiration and encouragement of literary and musical projects too numerous to name, including this one.

Thanks moreover to all my readers of previous books in many lands, for laying the foundation for this trilogy.

Last but far from least, thanks Alexandra Davidson for her meticulous copy-editing, and to Bill Gladstone, Kimberly Brabec and Josh Freel for their encouragement, collaboration and facilitation in matters of publication.

Author's Preface

This is a work of historical fiction. First conceived in 2009, it gestated for nine years, its development abetted by intermittent intervals of intensive research, regular episodes of eclectic reading, and frequent periods of protracted reflection. The lengthy labor itself began in May 2018, culminating in the trilogy's birth almost three years later, in March 2021.

The main figure and primary focus of the work is Fernando Sor, a prodigious Spanish guitarist and composer. He led a remarkable life and left an enduring legacy. The background to his story, and the historical context that shaped his trajectory, encompasses the tumultuous era of the French Revolution, the rise and fall of Napoleon, the Europe of Bonaparte's aftermath, and the struggles for political and social reform that pervaded the entire period.

Fernando experienced the painful birth of one of Spain's most bitter internal conflicts. As a liberal-minded artist, he embraced the values of the enlightenment, and wanted Spain to reform herself politically and socially. But as a patriot, monarchist, and Catholic, he resisted Napoleon's attempted imposition of such reforms by invasion and coercion (1808-1813). An ugly rift soon opened among the Spanish people themselves, such that anyone who identified with enlightenment values was deemed a traitor to Spain and branded an *afrancesado:* a Francophile in the most pejorative sense. There was no middle ground. Anyone who desired that Spain liberalize and democratize on her own terms, even if he ardently supported the monarchy and the Church, became unjustly but irrevocably associated with the Jacobins, and thus was demonized. This conflict bitterly divided Spain. It eventually drove Fernando, along with tens of thousands of his liberal compatriots—not only artists and intellectuals, but also politicians, soldiers, engineers, bankers, and merchants—into exile.

Even two centuries later, embers of that conflict still smoldered. When I found myself in Madrid's National Library in 2012, pursuing research on Fernando Sor, the librarian in the Music Department shot me a disapproving look, scowled darkly at me, and hissed "*afrancesado*" under his breath. While that surprised me at the time, it became all too comprehensible as my research progressed. I gradually discovered how Fernando himself was internally torn by that very same conflict, and how it would haunt Spain over and over again, re-manifesting in her subsequent Carlist Wars, and even (if not especially) in her traumatic Civil War. A dear Spanish friend prevailed on me to mention this anecdote, because he said that relatively few Spaniards today know what '*afrancesado*' means. If only more Spaniards knew, they might finally douse those embers with reconciliation and understanding, preventing them from ever flaring up again. Maybe this novel can help assuage these deep historical wounds.

Literarily, this portrait of a heroic artistic figure against a turbulent background strives to accomplish two related goals.

First, it attempts to weave, as seamlessly as possible, factual events of Fernando Sor's biography as reliably documented (most authoritatively by Brian Jeffery) with plausible fictional threads that bridge the many tantalizing gaps of missing data between and among known facts—connecting the dots, as it were, to fabricate a continuous tapestry of his life. Ideally, someone who knows nothing about Sor before reading this trilogy will be unable to disentangle fact from fancy, and will simply enjoy the tale.

Second, from the vast mountain of documented historical material on the age of Napoleon, this work endeavors to mine the richest veins of events in which Fernando himself became caught up, once again embellishing his romances, friendships, and relationships with historical figures, or indeed inventing plausible encounters that dovetail with established facts. Ideally, an historian who knows much about the era yet little about Sor will find nothing in the story that is contrary to history, neither in its selected events nor in its fictional forays. Thus even such an historian will be unable at first sight to distinguish fact from fancy, and may likewise simply enjoy the tale.

A third and relatively specialized readership consists of those who already know something, if not many things, about Fernando Sor's music, life, and times. Such readers are especially well-placed to discern where fact leaves off and fiction begins, yet hopefully they too will appreciate that wherever literary license is invoked, its purpose is to enrich the narrative with plausible invention. Where history is mute, creativity can speak.

In Spring 2020, I sent a draft of this trilogy to Brian Jeffery for his inspection. As mentioned, his biography of Sor is the 'gold standard' for accuracy and completeness, and I had been consulting his second edition (1994) all along, as the veritable 'bible' of known facts about Fernando Sor's life. Among many things unknown to historians during more than two centuries were: the name of his first wife, how and where they met, the exact circumstances of their departure from Spain, the precise date in 1815 of their daughter's birth, and the place, date, and cause of her mother's death. Those details, among others, being still unknown when I wrote the trilogy, my creativity rose to the occasion.

Then Brian Jeffrey dropped this bombshell: as fate would have it, while I had been fully absorbed by writing, busily inventing missing dots and their plausible connections to known facts, new historical data had meanwhile surfaced. Unbeknownst to me but simultaneously in 2020, Jeffrey had just published a revised third edition of his biography of Sor, revealing new data concerning a few (but not all) of these aforementioned long-missing bits and pieces. Some new facts had been unearthed by the diligent labors of Josep María Mangado; yet others had been provided to Jeffery in dribs and drabs, as various scholars encountered them fortuitously during historical researches in far-ranging subjects. Indeed, when Brian and I had last met in London, in 2016, he shared with me details of Sor's brush with the Inquisition, which he had published in a separate paper in 2012. That episode had been long unknown to him, and thus was not mentioned in his 1994 edition of Sor's biography. Thanks to his 2012 article, the episode is woven into the fabric of this trilogy (in Book I).

So in May 2020, desirous of honoring Jeffery's third (2020) edition within the context of my literary tale, I felt compelled to do some additional 'invisible weaving' for general readers, updating the tale in light of some, but not all, recent disclosures. Jeffery, Mangado, and a small handful of experts will recognize the very few places where this trilogy deviates from newly revealed historical details. Sticklers for history and Sor alike should read Jeffery for themselves. Even so, there still remain inevitable gaps in factual knowledge of Sor's life, to be bridged, if at all, by future historians and biographers. But since this trilogy is historical fiction, it is also, and by definition, informed yet not embalmed by facts alone. We can demarcate between these two genres as follows: history strives for perfect accuracy but never tells a complete story; historical fiction strives to tell a complete story but never claims perfect accuracy.

My main literary goals in writing this trilogy were to resuscitate dry bones of facticity by adorning them with human flesh and blood; to animate desiccated dates with a pounding heartbeat and a surging pulse; to restore remote events to an all-embracing immediacy; and to revivify long-dead names with vibrant personalities and vivacious passions. *Fernando* invites the reader on an artistic, political, and romantic thrill ride, seamlessly weaving biography, history, art history, literature, musicology—and a few touches of philosophy—with inventive literary fiction.

During the trilogy's lengthy gestation and laborious birth, a number of friends inquired as to my motive for writing it in the first place. "Why a novel about Fernando Sor?" they asked. Given that the work has consumed so many years and not so little effort in the making, it seems a fair question. To answer most generally: Fernando Sor is a great musical treasure of Spain, interred under many layers of forgotten events, neglected achievements, and divisive conflicts. Relatively few contemporary Spaniards even know his name. Out of gratitude to the Spanish people for their enthusiastic reception of my popular philosophy books, I decided to unearth this buried treasure of their nation, polish it, set it like a precious gem, and offer it to Spanish readers—and beyond them, to aficionados of the Spanish guitar and music lovers everywhere— as a token of my esteem.

Beyond this, a more personal answer to the question is given during the course of the final chapters, which treat Sor's legacy and its impact on my own life, and which may serve to remind the reader of two rather oddly conjoined propositions: first, that truth is stranger than fiction; and second, that fiction is nothing but truth in disguise.

Lou Marinoff
Monroe, NY
March 2021

Introduction

Many readers of this splendid biographical novel will be amazed, for at least three reasons. First of all, for the exceptional magnitude of the character it portrays. To a vast majority, Fernando Sor is just a name glimpsed in some program of pieces for classical guitar. Few people could imagine that this barely-recognizable composer, born in Barcelona in 1778, was a celebrity in his day: a virtuoso acclaimed all over Europe, in constant demand in London and Paris, adored by ladies of the aristocracy, fêted in Weimar by Goethe himself and appointed, at the summit of his career, Concert Master of the Imperial Court of Tsar Alexander I. His compositions for piano and orchestra, as well as his ballets, were resounding successes, and his pieces for guitar earned him the distinction of being the first to elevate this instrument from taverns and street corners to concert halls. In sum, to form an idea of his huge fame, it suffices to know that among the guests at a dinner party held in Paris on his fiftieth birthday were musicians like Niccolò Paganini, Luigi Cherubini, Hector Berlioz and Franz Liszt, artists like Eugène Delacroix, and writers like Victor Hugo and George Sand.

The second reason for amazement is self-evident. How can it be that such a character is nowadays so little known in his own country? Certainly not because his music has fallen into oblivion. On the contrary: pieces by Sor are still regularly performed and can be found in the repertoire of any classical guitarist; in fact, performances of his master works are still required to graduate from some conservatories. Why, then, has such an extraordinary life for an artist of his time remained so obscure? Sor committed an apparently unforgivable sin: he was an *afrancesado*. Although he initially fought against the Napoleonic invasion and composed patriotic songs of immense popularity, afterwards, once Joseph Bonaparte was installed on the throne, he reckoned (as did many other liberals) that Spain would be better off under an enlightened monarchy than with the restoration of the corrupt and inept Bourbons. History, however, ruled against him. Fernando VII regained the throne, reinstated absolutism and the Inquisition, and cruelly expelled all *afrancesados*, who were outlawed, condemned to exile for life, and branded traitors to the country. It can now be said that they were rather patriots of another Spain: of a very different Spain, whose eventual birth would require much more time and suffer yet more labor pains. Even so, what is surprising, and what really makes one pause to reflect, is that such condemnation has persisted up to this very day.

The third reason for amazement, of course, is that this vindication of the figure of Fernando Sor has been written by an author like Lou Marinoff, whom many readers know by his books of thought and philosophy, like the famous *Plato Not Prozac!*. While it is by no means a novelty that a foreigner comes to show us our own history, such a thing could hardly have been anticipated from an author like him. Even to myself, who was for many years his Spanish editor and traveling companion on extended promotional tours, the prospect of a biographical novel about Fernando Sor struck me as a perplexing idea (if not an alarming one: it is known that editors prefer that the author of a great success subsequently write a book nearly identical or very similar to the previous). Fortunately, he was carried away by his characteristic passion, a passion that runs through all his books, and confirms in these pages that he is a more multifaceted author than might be expected: a 'Renaissance Man', as he has sometimes been described, with an endless range of interests and a soft spot for the classical guitar, which he has played since his youth.

Driven by this all-encompassing spirit, and following the principle that each man is a child of his time, Marinoff offers an ambitious panorama of the age that came to shape the destiny of Fernando Sor—the age of the Napoleonic campaigns, of *El Dos de Mayo* and the Peninsular

War, to begin with, here conjured with stunning liveliness—as well as a portrait of the great figures that would mark his career, starting with the Duchess of Alba, who welcomed him in her Liria Palace, and continuing with Francisco de Goya, who honored him with life-long friendship. All this is recreated with careful accuracy and a surprising command of Spanish history, whose paradoxes, nuances and contradictions, far from intimidating the author, seem to spur his omnivorous curiosity that much more.

No less meticulous descriptions follow, during Sor's period of exile, of the sophisticated circles and concert halls of London and Paris, where Sor strengthened his reputation, and in the sumptuous account of the years spent in the Imperial Court of the Tsar, where he resided, surrounded by luxuries and admiration, with his second wife and his beloved daughter Carolina. These successive stages of this Grand Tour, which to a great extent comprise the biography of Fernando Sor, are peppered with deep reflections, wherein the reader will recognize the proverbial insight of Marinoff, and which are written with a charmingly old-fangled language that conveys a fine irony, especially in describing such characters as Godoy and Napoleon.

On a personal level, the life of Sor was marked by great loves and great tragedies; also by the hard experience of exile, by the longing and constant desire to return to Spain; but above all by an endless devotion to music that impelled him to compose without respite, to perform in public with the guitar and other instruments, to explore the most varied genres—from boleros and popular songs to operas, ballets, symphonies and pieces for piano—and to write a *Method for Spanish Guitar* that is still considered one of the most remarkable books on the technique of playing this instrument. This kind of passion is always infectious: firstly, as explained at the end of the trilogy, it was transmitted to his great successors, Francisco Tárrega and Andrés Segovia, and later on to the author himself. I have no doubt that it will transmit itself to the reader too. After witnessing in these pages so many rehearsals, so many performances and concerts, and so many standing ovations from thrilled audiences, I think that no reader will fail to feel an urge to listen—maybe for the first time—to Sor's *Variations on a Theme by Mozart* or his *Studies* for guitar. If the author's ultimate goal was to rescue Fernando Sor from oblivion, that is the greatest compliment that can be paid to this magnificent book.

Santiago del Rey
Editor and Translator, Barcelona
March 2021

Artistas españoles, que sentís en vuestras mentes la llama del genio, si llevados de un noble amor á la gloria, aspiráis á conquistar las palmas y coronas que sois acreedores, pasad las fronteras de vuestra patria; las recompensas que esta os destina, son la indiferencia, el desaliento y quizá la miseria.

Artists of Spain, who feel in your spirits the call of genius, if you are inspired by a noble love of glory and desire to conquer the laurels and crowns which you deserve, cross the frontiers of your country; for the rewards which your country destines for you are indifference, discouragement, and perhaps penury.

—Eusebio Font y Moresco
La Opinion Publica
Barcelona, January 1850
(English translation: Brian Jeffery)

Fernando: Beethoven of the Guitar

Book I: Youth, Celebrity, and War

Part 1. Fernando in Youth, 1778-1800

Chapter 1. Barcelona: The Prophecy

"Where are you, Fernando?" his mother's voice rang out, echoing down the sleepy alleyways of Barcelona's Dry Quarter. The late August heat of 1783 had turned it into the Baked Quarter, the locals jested, and her every step churned up a little cloud of desiccated red dust.

"Fernando, do you hear me?" she persisted, "It's time to come home!"

The women of the quarter had grown accustomed to these frantic forays of Isabella de Muntada Sor, and there was no telling where young Fernando might be found. They shook their heads in silent sympathy with his mother. Many of them believed the young boy to be possessed by a musical devil who lured him all over the city at ungodly hours—to what end no-one could fathom. That made them all afraid: some for the boy himself, others for his family, and not a few for their own sakes.

They all remembered when Isabella was carrying that baby. One day in late 1777, maybe six or seven months into her term, Isabella had confided in her best friend, Sofia Aviñó, that she was hearing music "inside her head".

"What do you mean?" asked Sofia, "You and Joan make music all the time! And don't we all hear music in our heads?"

"Of course we do," Isabella had exclaimed. "But this music is being sung by my unborn child! I *feel* him exuding it at times, and when the feeling reaches my inner ear I can *hear* it."

"And what does it sound like?"

"Divine, like a choir of angels."

"If I were you," cautioned Sofia, "I'd be careful who I told this to. There are rumors that the Inquisition is active again."

"But this is surely a blessing, not a curse," said Isabella, just as any expectant mother would say, only more so.

"Maybe, but blessed souls have just as surely been cursed, and put to death, by sinners—starting with our Lord and Savior."

At this, the two women paused to cross themselves.

Soon after, Sofia told a few close friends about Isabella's choir of angels, having first sworn them to secrecy. Naturally, they followed suit. Before long, the whole quarter had learned of this woman possessed by a musical demon. And since no-one as prodigious as Fernando soon turned out to be had ever sprung from their midst, they can all be forgiven for having confused his rarest of gifts with a curse. When Isabella gave birth to him, on Saint Valentine's Day 1778, she and Sofia and the midwife all heard him singing, not crying, as he entered this world. February 14th is a day that celebrates love, and indeed Fernando would be beloved on this day, as on every day of his life, by all who eventually heard him sing or play, or even beheld his beaming countenance.

In the next few years, as the neighborhood grew accustomed to seeing and hearing Isabella chasing after Fernando at all hours, they conceded that while the boy was not exactly cursed, he was certainly a handful—that is, if one could ever manage to get hold of him. They did not envy Isabella and Joan, for Fernando's parents were ordinary middle-class people just like themselves, except that their firstborn son—musical prodigy or not— had introduced extraordinariness into their lives. This Dry Quarter of Catalan civil servants and merchants had carved out a quiet niche for itself in the grand, decadent, unproductive, yet remarkably stable scheme of Bourbon rule over Catalonia, and these middle classes did not want anything—or anyone—to rock their happily dry-docked boat.

Little did they concern themselves, at least in that sullen, heat-baked Barcelona August of 1783, that democratic forces unleashed by the Thirteen Colonies in 1776, in far-away America, had precipitated a bloody War of Independence from England. But they would experience its impact soon enough.

And perhaps less prudently, they remained unconcerned that kindred yet different democratic forces were being uncorked in next-door France. Like a fraternal twin of American democracy, these forces would soon enough foment the French Revolution. Little did these Catalans suspect that Iberia would be swept up in a floodtide of catastrophic events of truly historic proportion, and that it would become a ghastly but decisive theatre of cataclysmic European war among catharses of political and cultural transformation. But as many mildly comfortable people worry mostly about what is under their noses at any given moment, so Barcelonans who knew the Sors, or who were the Sors, merely worried innocently about the predicament of Fernando's parents and their musical child.

With the clarity of hindsight, it is easy to observe uncanny parallels between young Fernando's strivings for musical liberty, and of young America's and older France's yearnings for political liberty. After all, the natural authority of one's parents to a five-year-old child must seem as absolute as the Divine Right of monarchs to their subjects. Defiance of either authority is not to be undertaken lightly, and requires resolute adherence to principle along with unshakeable courage of conviction.

Meanwhile Isabella had left her quiet neighborhood and entered the crowded plaza, still intoning, "Fernando, where are you?" Isabella had a fine soprano voice, untrained but instinctively musical, and she sang often, sometimes accompanied by her husband Joan on guitar, at house parties and community events. So her voice carried brightly across the plaza, past merchants and hawkers in their shaded stalls, around jugglers and buskers in the sunshine. As many of them knew her well enough, they pointed in the direction they had last seen Fernando wander.

This led Isabella to a side street on the far side of the plaza, on which a band of gypsies had camped to hawk their wares—and inevitably, to play and dance. As she homed in on the swirling sounds of the accordion and violin, and the colorful ring of clapping and stamping and dancing gypsies surrounding the players, to her enormous relief she spotted young Fernando perched on a barrel, his countenance radiant with joy, his whole being immersed in the wildly cavorting melodies that filled the air.

Isabella saw too that Fernando was being watched over by an elderly gypsy woman, with a leathery complexion wrinkled like a prune, but with a heart of gold and an aura of light. She smiled at Isabella's approach. Fernando was still transfixed by the music, and did not notice her.

"He is a special child," the old woman declared.

"Yes," sighed Isabella. "Very special."

"Maybe even more than you know, Señora. I took the liberty of reading his palm."

With some relief, Isabella began surreptitiously rummaging for a coin, happy to pay a modest ransom for her invaluable son.

"And what did it say?" asked his mother. As she was paying for it, she might as well know.

"Your son will give the world treasures it never before possessed. He will be regaled by royalty, and adored by the masses. Women will find him irresistible. And how he will travel! Like a wandering star! If I may say so, you are fortunate, Señora, and your child is blessed."

And just as she had finished speaking this prophecy, as if on cue the music and dancing paused. Only then did Fernando turn his head, and his countenance beamed when he saw his mother. Of course her heart invariably melted at such moments, and she could never bring herself to scold the boy for running off in the direction of whatever passing music caught his ear. So she snatched him off the barrel and hugged him instead.

"Mama, this music is beautiful! And the dancing too!" Fernando exclaimed.

He always said this, no matter who played what or how they danced. At five he was unaware of this particular facet of his gift: the ability to immerse himself in the spirit of the music being played, no matter what the style or genre. A little later in life, he would utilize this talent deliberately, and to great effect. Just as Johann Sebastian Bach had done before him, Fernando Sor would mimic in a most authentically charming way the styles of myriad countries and cultures. He was at times a near-pure spirit, who could therefore enter into the spirit of things themselves and mirror them in their best light. No wonder everyone loved him.

"Yes, it is beautiful, and so are you," his mother fawned. "But now we must return home. Your father will be waking soon from his siesta, and I must prepare tapas, and we have company coming, and there will be more music for you to enjoy!" And that was an offer Fernando could scarcely refuse.

The elderly gypsy woman, however, politely and somewhat indignantly refused Isabella's offering of a coin. "His is the most remarkable palm I have ever read in all my years," she declared. "That experience is beyond price. Let us not tarnish it with money, Señora."

Much later that night, really into the next morning—long past tapas, and wine, and home-made music, and supper, and more wine, and after all the guests had departed and Fernando was finally asleep—Isabella and Joan resumed their argument.

"The boy will commence his studies soon enough," Joan reminded her. "And he must be able to apply himself primarily to Latin, and not to music! Otherwise I fear for his future."

Fernando's father was a talented amateur guitarist, and generally a music lover, but he never conceived that any son of his loins could be other than a military man or a civil servant, if not both. As a former army officer himself, Joan had wrangled a sinecure as deputy superintendent of the Department of Roads. He had attained a comfortable and reasonably secure station in life, and could provide for his family, as long as Spanish Bourbon rule remained stable. A staunch monarchist, notwithstanding inevitable flashes of Catalan contempt for these foreigners from Madrid who had imposed the Castilian language and laws upon them, Joan had even named his first son after King Ferdinand VI (and would soon name his second son, Carlos, after the current King Charles). The road to this 'good life' led through grammar school, followed by either the military or the civil service or both, and to cultivating the political and social connections necessary for a commodious posting.

This road to security, and Joan Sor knew it well, most assuredly did not lead through gypsy flea-markets. Joan had become incensed when Isabella related Fernando's latest adventure, and he appeared determined to clap the boy in irons rather than let him pursue his Muse all over town.

"But what about the gypsy woman's prophecy?" Isabella countered.

"Men maintain the roads so that women can socialize in the plaza and share female superstitions," declared Joan, squaring his jaw.

Isabella saw that she had reached the bedrock of his resistance, and would have to take another tack. "Didn't Fernando amaze our guests tonight?" she reminded him.

That was undeniable. Just a few months ago, when he had turned five, Fernando had asked permission to play his father's guitar. "Wait a few years, my son," Joan had chuckled. "You need to grow much bigger just to hold it!"

"No, I mean like this, Papa!" Fernando then mimed a kind of keyboard position, and his father saw immediately what he intended.

"OK my boy, let's try it." And with that Joan took his guitar down from the wall, where it was hanging by its strap of finely-tooled Barcelona leather, and laid it flat upon the kitchen table, strings facing up. Fernando stood on a chair and began plucking the open strings with his right hand. Soon he began pressing his left-hand fingers down on the fretboard, as though it were a keyboard. Before long he could pluck clean notes and, soon after that, simple harmonies. Soon he could carry a tune. Within a short while—a matter of weeks—Fernando was plucking some of the popular melodies that his parents sang at home.

Perhaps understandably, at this stage Fernando's father mistook this gift for mere promise as an amateur musician like himself. But he and Isabella thought enough of it to invite Fernando to perform at the party of that very evening. And so Fernando made his musical debut, most appropriately on the guitar, and at a house party. Unbeknownst to the boy, he had started rehearsing for the salons, concert halls, and palaces of Europe's leading cities. This was a harbinger of many such events to come.

His mother was absolutely correct to observe that Fernando had indeed amazed the guests, and moreover had inspired them, to the extent that they joined in a rousing chorus with the melody he plucked, and applauded and yelled for an encore, which he gave them. Après-concert, they handed him around the room for hearty congratulations, choice tidbits from the table, and perhaps even a sip of wine before his mother carted him off to bed. He slept like a proverbial charm.

One of the Sors' guests at that party, and a longtime friend of the family, was a certain Chevalier de Sabater, the Marquis of Campany.

Even though Joan Sor occupied a relatively middling post in the civil service, his father had been a Doctor of Medicine, and had tended to the Chevalier's family, and to Sabater himself as a youth. Isabella de Muntada's family, for their part, also maintained aristocratic connections, especially since her father had been a Doctor of Laws, and had rendered legal services to various provincial administrations. Such connections in Catalonia indubitably led to more powerful ones in Castilia, as we will see manifestly in Fernando's case.

So it would be a mistake to suppose that Fernando's middle-class parents lacked friends in high places; on the contrary, it was their families' reputable services to friends in high places that had granted them a relatively secure and modestly comfortable lifestyle.

This much was true throughout European society, but only in Spain did the classes also mingle socially. France and England maintained much more rigid social lines, but could afford to do so because they were that much more progressive politically. The French, in particular, were about to become perhaps too progressive for their own good, while the American revolution had provoked a profoundly anti-democratic backlash in England. American Yankees, of course, lacked both an *ancièn régime* and the class distinctions it spawned, so gregarious Americans of the northern colonies were willing to mix socially at almost any occasion, with more distinction of wealth than of class. This, among other things, had endeared Benjamin Franklin to French nobility and commoners alike: he was at once uncommonly sophisticated, yet at the same time completely unpretentious. Fernando had this gift too.

On a European continent still ruled by class distinctions, Iberia was a political animal of a species that defied classification. Her classes were real but their differences were often inconsequential, except at the very apex of the pyramid, which floated above the masses, separated by a gulf through which money flowed up and policy rained down. Beneath that thin and narrow apex, in which scandalously few families owned almost all the nation's wealth, Spain had legions of *hidalgos*: impoverished nobles who paid no taxes but owned no land. They consorted much more often with commoners than with royalty. Yet that was merely a norm. If you went to the Basque country, where they considered both Castilian and Catalan to be barbaric foreign tongues, everyone was deemed to be of noble birth. So, among the Basques, deep poverty was a sign of high nobility. Such was the topsy-turvy nature of Spain. But it hardly ended there. More widespread in Spain was something else which the rest of Europe lacked: the *majos* and *majas,* who likewise stood class distinctions on their heads, but in a different way.

And as the Chevalier rode home on his fine Arabian horse, he continued to be amazed by the performance of young Fernando. The Chevalier had dabbled on guitar for years, and many a time had played and sung along with Joan, and Isabella, and others. Their repertoire ranged from rustic folk tunes (suitable for the entire family) to popular Baroque and classical airs (for more formal gatherings) to ribald ditties (at drinking parties for the men alone). But never before had Sabater seen anyone play the guitar like a zither! And play it so well, at such a tender age. He made a mental note to encourage the lad, and more importantly to impress upon Fernando's parents that the boy's unusual talent warranted formal music lessons, without delay.

As we have seen, Isabella would need little persuasion, and the Chevalier suspected as much. But Joan remained divided, and therefore intransigent. He was beginning to believe that Fernando just might be as talented as Sabater soon never tired of observing, but this only deepened his concerns that the lad would end up as a 'one-trick pony', not much different from those guitarists who busked in the plazas. Their music was generally liked by laborers, housewives, and vendors, and sometimes even by jugglers, conjurors, and card sharps, who tossed them coins enough to keep them playing. But in more cultured circles their genre was more often derisively dismissed as '*frons-frons*', which onomatopoeically mimicked their continuous and frequently raucous strumming of the strings. So Joan insisted the boy study Latin first and foremost, but consented to exposing his son to grander musical experiences than could be encountered in plazas, flea markets, taverns and house parties. Thus coaxed by the Chevalier and cajoled by Isabella, Joan agreed, not without some reluctance bordering on trepidation, to take Fernando to the Italian opera.

Chapter 2. Barcelona: The Italian Opera

As the week of the opera approached, young Fernando could barely contain himself. Not that he ever contained himself much anyway, at least where music was concerned. Just as one cannot keep music in a jar as though it were olives, similarly one cannot imprison musical prodigies in a box hewn from middle-class aspirations. At this stage Fernando did not know, nor could he have known, the extent of his gifts, and of the magnificent journey on which their expression would lead him. He thought he was 'normal'—that is to say, he imagined that everyone heard and retained music just as he did, more or less. 'Everyone' being grown-ups with grown-up things to do; he being a child with child-like things to do, Fernando simply assumed that they all heard music exactly as he did, but that they were too busy with other matters to give it as much attention as he, Fernando the child, was still at liberty to do.

This misconception is carried for a time by almost all gifted children—whose young minds are still so full of curiosity and wonder, whose tender beings are still so malleable and impressionable—that everything amazes them except their own genius, which they do not yet recognize as special. The Italian opera would shortly cause these scales to fall from Fernando's eyes, and even from his father's.

When finally the appointed evening arrived, the Sors rode in Sabater's carriage, and were guests in his box. Joan and Isabella also held season tickets in the loges, which on this occasion they gave to friends. As they approached the opera house square, Fernando caught glimpses of the diverse throngs flocking their way toward the entrance, from seemingly all quarters and classes, and displaying an astonishing variety of attire.

Fernando's eyes grew wider than saucers as he took in the sights, starting with the stocking-legged men in embroidered coats and flamboyant hats, and their women in swirling layers of translucent gowns bedecked with glitter and lace: and these were the *majos* and *majas*, the coarsest of the poor, but with the swagger of peacocks, the audacity of princes, the ferocity of pirates, and the leather accessories of fetishists. They occupied the cheapest seats, at the back.

The merchants arrived in their shirts of spun Egyptian cotton, and ornamented vests of fine wool or cashmere, while their wives were far less gaudy than the *majas*, but covered in more delicate attire, adorned with gold and silver jewelry. They sat in the front half of the house. Above and around them, the *hidalgos* and professionals and senior civil servants occupied the lower balconies, clad in fine frock coats and ruffled shirts and bright silk scarves, while their wives flaunted fashionably layered gowns, and festooned themselves with family heirlooms.

The uppermost balconies, framed by finely carved and highly ornamented balustrades, were reserved for royalty and high nobility. They alone stood empty tonight, as they often did, in an otherwise packed house. Perhaps the theme of this night's opera was too alien to resonate with the ruling classes. Giuseppe Sarti's *Giulio Sabino,* set in first-century Gaul, then under Vespasian's rule, celebrated—of all things!—conjugal love. Whatever else they were, these ruling classes of Spain, like their Bourbon cousins across Europe, considered themselves exempt from the seventh commandment, among several others. After all, their marriages and conjugations were political, from first to last. They had heard of conjugal love, and they strongly supported the Church's relentless enforcement of it on everyone but themselves. At the same time they harbored no particular desire to hear its praises sung in Italian, however ardently and sweetly.

Besides, the Bourbons had several reasons to dislike this particular opera. Not only was it Italian—and therefore, by definition, an affront to French taste—it also reminded them that Rome had civilized Gaul, and with it their own forebears. They also despised Vespasian, a money-grubbing emperor who would stoop to anything for lucre. He was the first to impose a tax on public urinals, and when criticism arose he remarked "*Pecunia non olet*" ("Money doesn't smell"). At this the Bourbons held up their noses, and they could well afford to do so. In their family's hands, and in those of their most noble allies, was concentrated 95% of the wealth of Spain. Everyone else fought over the scraps, like so many dogs under the table.

The ruling classes, like everyone else, had house parties, except they took place in palaces. Notwithstanding their differences, French and Italian rulers alike had expanded their respective audiences, and gave ever-larger command performances, at which important new symphonic or operatic works were premiered. But the court in Madrid had not yet succumbed to this 'progressive' fashion; it clung to High Baroque house parties in a country estate, with perhaps a hundred guests. And their music came from France, and northern Europe. It was the same with fine art. They had Goya on the payroll, and would soon appoint him court painter, but they still sent their most promising youths to study with David, in Paris. They loved but one Italian, namely the late Domingo Scarlatti, who alone had demonstrated the good sense to flee Italy and make his home in Madrid, where his exquisite sonatas were composed, and still played regularly, for small gatherings of perhaps a few dozen royals and nobles.

By contrast, Barcelona's new opera house held seven hundred souls, though even more were packed in that night. The old opera house had burned down a few years previously, whether from a candelabra or a careless smoker no-one knew. So the leading citizens had raised subscriptions (and not from public urinals, either) and commissioned an even grander building, in the Rococo style, to suit the age. Italian opera was all the rage around Europe—France and Madrid excepted—and had even warmed the cold-blooded English. The hot-blooded Catalans had embraced it wildly.

And it was about to embrace Fernando. He had taken in the whole spectacle as the house filled up, and his excitement quickened as the orchestra tuned up. So many voices! He was already enthralled. When the curtain rose, Fernando was transported. His mind immersed itself in the colorful music and flowed along with it, as an iridescent rainbow trout drifts down a singing stream. When the final curtain descended Isabella had to rouse him, as though from a trance. Everyone loved the performance, and the hall seemed to ring with their applause and cheers even as the contented throngs filed out to drinks and supper, and then more drinks, and more music of course. In Barcelona, music poured out of windows, echoed down alleys, flared up in plazas, and coursed along avenues: rising, ebbing, and swirling in unending tides.

Perhaps uncharacteristically, the Sors were mostly silent in the carriage on the way home, each lost in his or her own reverie of the performance. Isabella involuntarily hummed a few measures of one of the arias—or thought she had, anyway. Suddenly Fernando awoke from his trance, and tugged at her sleeve. "Not like that, Mama," he corrected her. "Like this": whereupon he hummed the measures correctly, as though he had been reading the score.

When they arrived home, Fernando taught his father the tenor's harmony to his mother's soprano part, while he himself hummed the first violin melody. That turned out to be the last song of a long musical evening, and also a watershed moment in Fernando's euphonious career. For once they had put their young prodigy to bed, Joan did not wait for Isabella to start the conversation. Instead, he declared "We must get Fernando some music lessons. Will you ask around for a suitable teacher?"

"Of course," beamed Isabella. He had just made her happy beyond words. Henceforth she beheld him again in that wonderful light in which she had first loved him, and conceived Fernando. Bathed in that light again, they would soon enough conceive Fernando's younger brother, Carlos.

But, for now, Isabella wisely let her husband have the last word:

"Just make sure he doesn't neglect his Latin!" Joan threw in, along with the proverbial towel.

Needless to say, that evening marked a turning point, and a timely one. Joan, Isabella, and Fernando performed their 'trio' at a few house parties, where all were astounded by the lad's adaptation, by ear, of that aria from the opera. It did not take long for word of his gifts to circulate, nor did his mother miss an opportunity to let it be known that she was seeking a music teacher for her prodigious son. The Chinese have a saying 'When the student is ready, the teacher will appear', and this rang as true in Barcelona as in Beijing.

One day soon after, a note was hand delivered to Isabella by a special courier, who drew up in a small but well-appointed carriage.

Esteemed Señora Isabella de Muntada Sor,
Your son Fernando's brilliant reputation far exceeds his modest age, and it has reached my ear that you seek musical instruction for him. Please consider me at your complete disposal in that capacity. It would be a signal honor to help illuminate the coming stage of his extraordinary path.
I beg to remain,
Your most humble and obedient servant,
Arnau Narcis Pla
Director and First Violin of the Orchestra of Barcelona

Reading this, Isabella practically wept for joy. Her prayers had been answered! Of course she had not prayed explicitly for this man, for she did not feel qualified to know who the right teacher would be. She simply asked The Virgin to send the right one. And She did! Isabella would never have dared approach the orchestra's director on such a mission, but she could not imagine a more ideal teacher for her son.

When Joan came home for a siesta, she shared the letter with him. Deeply honored and impressed, he nodded his assent. "Just make sure he keeps up with his Latin."

To himself, Joan wondered how he'd keep up with the payments. The maestro was reputedly the best private teacher of music in all Barcelona, a city that teemed with professional musicians. The maestro was so good, in fact, that he chose his own private pupils exclusively. He would refuse a fortune rather than accept a student of insufficient promise. The rumor was that he had already refused one such offer in Madrid and had to flee for his life, because the family in question felt he had dishonored their daughter by rejecting her hand in music. It was far more unusual for the maestro to approach a student, and unheard of at

Fernando's age. Joan smelled the influence of Sabater behind this. Well, he mused, drinks would be on the Chevalier for a while, at least as long as Joan was footing the music bill. So Joan resolved to squeeze a few more reales out of the network of dusty roads he superintended, whose diverse commercial travelers paid an array of duties, taxes, tolls and protections for the merchandise they ferried to and fro.

Corruption was the order of the day in Spain at that time, but the Catalan civil service prided itself on the integrity with which it kept its own vices to an absolute minimum. Years in the civil service had taught Joan that corruption came in two varieties: benign, and malignant. Benign corruption merely greased the economic wheels, whereas malignant corruption made the wheels come off. The French would soon prove this conclusively.

Fernando now entered a different familial orbit, with the old maestro in the role of a wise and loving grandfather—which, musically speaking, he was. He knew that Fernando was still a five-year-old, in age and at heart, and that five-year-old boys like playing with toys. So for their very first lesson, he brought him into a practice room used by a chamber orchestra. One by one, the maestro introduced the boy to his own favorite instruments. First he showed him a cello, and bowed on it a prelude from a Bach suite. At that, Fernando's jaw dropped. Next he sat at a harpsichord, and fingered a Scarlatti sonata. Fernando's ears opened even wider. Then he sat on a piano bench and motioned Fernando to join him. He tinkled the theme and a few variations from Mozart's *Twinkle, Twinkle Little Star.* Fernando's fingers danced in deftly in the air, miming the maestro's motions. After this the maestro picked up a violin and intoned the opening measures of a Haydn symphony. Fernando could smell the resin and the French polish, and his synesthesia allowed him to hear their music too, somehow in sync with Haydn. For an encore, the old maestro picked up a lute and plucked a popular Spanish folk-dance by Gaspar Sanz. At this Fernando's heart opened, for he suddenly knew two things at that moment, and forever. First, that he loved Spanish music even more deeply than all the great music he already loved; and second, it had to be played on a lute or, even better, a guitar.

This first official music lesson of Fernando's still-young life served to open his mind to the veritable galaxy of astounding composers who had emerged since the death of the High Baroque, with J.S. Bach, in 1750. Mere decades later, twin revolutions in both composition and instrumentation—which somehow anticipated the twin democratic revolutions of that period—reversed the entire trajectory of noble and popular music alike, by fusing them with a sound so powerful that it drowned out class distinctions. The common people's folk music was perennially pervaded by gaiety and levity, perhaps to afford them escape from the sordidness and harshness of their lives. By contrast, the music of aristocrats was introspective and intricate, often tinged with sadness if not tragedy. Freed by birth or achievement from mere ordinary strife and expected sorrows, the ruling classes and their court artists encountered strife extraordinary, and sorrows unexpected. High Baroque had offered them a sanctuary, a privileged mirror in which to behold their noblest reflections and deepest affectations, and also to have them sanctified. For High Baroque merged seamlessly with the Church, as the sacred music of its greatest composers attested weekly. But this new-fangled music, which some called 'classical', had somehow blended the sacred with the profane: it was music for *everyone.* Goya would soon pioneer the same transformation in painting. And Fernando's open mind was immediately captivated by it too, although he would not have been able (if asked by some wizard) to explain this fuller effect of the old maestro's first lesson upon him.

Even so, Fernando was unconsciously aware that he had already formulated a cardinal rule for his life, at some deep and pre-linguistic level. It had emerged from his frequent struggles to free himself from his father's anxieties and restrictions, especially those which sought to rein in Fernando's experiences of music. Many years later, as an adult, in his timeless *Method for the Spanish Guitar*, he would formulate this rule in one elegant sentence: "Blind submission of the reason [to authority] degrades the human mind, when it occurs in other instances than those of religious faith." For Fernando this was an artistic principle, but the unfolding age of reform had adopted it for political purposes, too.

Meanwhile Fernando was speechless after his first music lesson, but not for long.

The old maestro asked the boy: "Which instrument would you most like to play?"

"All of them, like you," said Fernando.

"So be it," approved the maestro, delighted with the boy already.

So, having found for their extraordinary son a superb music teacher, Isabella and Joan got back to the ordinary business of being middle-class parents: Joan found a way to make more money, while Isabella—encouraged by his success—soon found a way to make another baby. Carlos Sor was born in August 1785, and this pregnancy (she thanked the Holy Mother) had been normal. It was a relief to them all, for it gradually became clear that Carlos was his father's son, with a similar temperament and musical talent, and so would lead an enviably normal life. They couldn't be blamed for thinking this, based on the evidence that confronted them at the time. Yet soon enough nothing would be normal, and the two brothers would be swept into a vortex of cathartic change, yet singing and playing guitars all the while.

Fernando loved his baby brother Carlos, who from his first months showed the usual Sor precocities: he babbled musically, clapped or kicked rhythmically, and before long he could even sing tunefully. By the time Fernando turned ten Carlos was only three—a sizeable gap for brothers at that age. They would eventually grow closer than Fernando could have imagined, but meanwhile he remained the prodigious son; Carlos, the toddler.

Fernando's sunlit childhood ended rather abruptly one afternoon, in late August of 1788. As he arrived home from Maestro Pla's music studio just in time for tapas as usual, Fernando saw that a crowd had gathered outside their door, and spilled into the yard. The next-door neighbor was comforting his brother Carlos, while a priest was consoling his mother. There was great lamentation, and much weeping. Fernando did not see Joan anywhere, and his agile mind conceived a possibility that all this commotion had something to do with his father, so conspicuously absent.

Isabella suddenly caught sight of Fernando, detached herself from the priest, and ran to embrace him.

"My dearest and most beloved son, I cannot find the words to tell you, but you must know it from me first, that we could not awaken your father from his siesta."

"Is he sleeping, then?" asked Fernando, perhaps the last innocent question of his childhood.

Isabella smiled through her tears. "Yes, dearest boy, one could say that. To us he appears to be sleeping for all eternity, but his soul now lives forever in Heaven."

Now Fernando's tears welled up, as he began to understand what his mother meant. It soon became clear that Joan had died peacefully, during his siesta, of some foul humor that had suddenly stopped his heart. He had still been warm to the touch when Isabella and Carlos had come in to rouse him, and at first they thought he was only playing. But Joan grew quickly colder, and as he would not (because he could not) respond even to her most strident prodding, Isabella grabbed Carlos and dashed off to find help.

But Joan now lay beyond the help of mortals, and in the hands of Providence alone.

So Fernando joined the small but swelling assembly of mourners—friends, neighbors, distant relations—who gathered as word spread like wildfire around the social tinderbox of the Dry Quarter.

Fernando felt a strange sensation inside, like a force that was stretching and twisting him into a different shape, while simultaneously transporting him to an unknown inner place. He had no name for this feeling, which at times was so powerful that it scared him.

"What is happening to me?" he wondered. "Is this death? Is this what Papa felt before he died?"

Fernando did not know that his thought of death was not entirely improper, for Joan's demise had indeed signaled the death of Fernando's childhood. But this figurative death also had heralded a kindred birth, namely that of his late boyhood. And the boy—no longer a child, yet nowhere near a man—thus became eligible to be transported, as though on a magic carpet, to a place so wonderful that it had lain beyond even his most fanciful boyhood dreams.

Chapter 3. Montserrat: The Magic Mountain

Fernando and Isabella wound slowly up the serpentine dirt track that hugged the mountain in dizzying switchbacks. Bounced by boulders and jostled by ruts, they hardly noticed the lurching and pounding, so taken in were they by the spectacle that gradually unfolded on their ascent. The Monastery itself had been visible from the valley floor. It perched high on a wide ridge near the summit, as though carved from the very cliffs that jutted two thousand meters nearly straight up, culminating in a giant jaw of toothy peaks that bit through the misty clouds, and pierced the azure sky. The austere, mysterious, and beckoning buildings of Montserrat Monastery nestled under those peaks, and rose toward heaven with their own man-made grandeur. And from the Monastery, since the eleventh century, music of a divine quality had emanated at regular intervals in perpetual offerings to God, whose wisdom had charged the Order of Saint Benedict with the custody and instruction of Europe's finest choir school: the Escolania.

Fernando could scarcely believe the good fortune that had transported him here. He had been overcome with excitement as Sabater's carriage conveyed him and Isabella from Barcelona to the sleepy village of Manresa, at the foot of the great mountain, where a donkey cart from the Monastery awaited them. Indeed, Fernando's excited state of mind was well justified, as he correctly intuited that a life-changing experience now awaited him. This journey was no mere interlude with novelty; it betokened a summons from the Almighty. As the donkey cart slowly wound and lurched its way up the switchbacks, revealing ever-more-expansive vistas below, and fantastically carved protuberances above, Fernando felt, with justification, that he was ascending toward Heaven itself.

Their driver—a congenial local man who daily ferried people and supplies up and down the mountainside—added a piquant flavor to their ascent, as he pointed out this or that famous landmark, above and below, in a thickly-accented local patois, which he deemed to be Catalan, but of which Fernando and Isabella understood perhaps one word in five.

Isabella herself was a bundle of mixed emotions. She felt boundless joy for her beloved Fernando, who by God's grace had now been favored beyond even her immodest dreams. She felt unassuageable anguish, for her family had been torn apart by the sudden death of Joan, now followed by the swift departure of Fernando. She felt soothing relief, since only young Carlos remained at home, and caring for him alone would neither strain her slender means unduly, nor make her widowhood a mortal threat to motherhood. And as the donkey cart ascended higher, she felt abundant hope that Divine providence was keeping them all safe, in its inscrutable yet loving embrace.

Isabella's hope had tangible roots. This journey to Montserrat had been initiated at the invitation of Father Josef Arredondo, a Benedictine monk and the newly installed abbot. Given the illustrious history of Montserrat—a geological wonder, a spiritual oasis, a Christian sanctuary, and a musical Mecca—it was incumbent on its abbots not only to preserve and protect the monastery, but also to further its tradition. Perched remotely and on high, the abbots of Montserrat needed keen eyes and long ears to fulfill the full measure of their duties, and in these capacities Father Arredondo was not lacking. The winds of political unrest in France had reached even these austere Catalan peaks, while fears of insurgency had already prompted the flight of several prominent monks of the French Benedictine order, and their installation, for safety, in Montserrat itself. As these expatriate musical mentors infused the community with current French themes, the abbot wisely sought to draw fresh choirboys from the region—new raw talents who might become polished vessels, to contain and mature the musical ferment of the times. As Father Arredondo's inquiries reached Barcelona, one name above all coursed back through every channel: that of the young prodigy Fernando Sor. And so the invitation, timely from everyone's perspective, was duly issued.

The choir school at Montserrat had upheld this mission for centuries. At any given time, and for as long as anyone could remember, sixty boys were maintained and educated in residence, all expenses borne by the Order, until they reached sixteen years of age. At such time they were returned to their villages or towns—some to become choirmasters, others to take up military or civil service posts, a few to profess religious vows and enter holy orders. In any case their education and training in Montserrat liberated most of them from hard agricultural labor, and kindred peasant occupations, even though many of them sprang from these rougher classes. Thus a boyhood sojourn at Montserrat conferred a gift for life, even to the relatively ungifted. To a gifted child like Fernando, Montserrat represented rebirth into a higher realm from which he would never fully depart. Much later in his extraordinary life, when he sat down to write his memoirs for Ledhuy's *Encyclopedia of Music*, Fernando would devote one third of them to his six years on Catalonia's 'Magic Mountain'.

So, after stops at various altars and shrines spaced at intervals along the winding ascent, at each of which Isabella insisted on offering a prayer of thanks to the Virgin Mary, the donkey cart arrived at the reception house in late afternoon. There a young monk greeted them warmly, and conveyed Isabella and Fernando to their guest quarters, where they would spend their last night together *en famille*. They were invited to stroll around the public gardens, and take their evening meal in the pilgrims' refectory, a smaller hall off the main refectory, where silence during mealtimes was not mandatory.

Fernando, however, was too excited to eat. He wanted to hear Compline sung, and so the young monk obligingly escorted him to the Church. From the opening verse of the first psalm, *Cum invocarem*, Fernando was dumbfounded with delight. The cantor began solo, then was joined by the organ, and then by the choir, all voices distinct yet interwoven into a flowing contrapuntal canon. Fernando later learned that this plainsong had been composed by Father Céréols, one of the resident music masters. But two things struck him immediately: first, this sublime music was a far cry from the lusty choruses of the Italian opera; and second, all the singers were children more or less his own age. Returning to his quarters, Fernando picked up his guitar and sang the plainsong faithfully from memory, but failed completely to recreate the counterpoint of Céréols. Having ascended on high, the child prodigy was suddenly brought low to earth. He still had much to learn, and was so enthralled at the prospect that he could barely fall asleep.

Isabella, by contrast, slept like a baby, comforted by dreams of Mother Mary, in whose divine embrace she felt truly at peace, for the first time since Joan's untimely passing.

The next morning, Fernando and Isabella were taken to meet the abbot. Father Arredondo cut an inspiring figure: his tall and angular torso, hawk-like countenance, and piercing eyes conveyed strong leadership, while his soft voice revealed a compassionate demeanor; and his wry expressions, a sense of humor. One needed a sense of humor to be an abbot these days, he mused in the privacy of his thoughts. But truly, he had been elected for these very qualities. The French Benedictines were sensing dire premonitions, and so their Catalan brethren were preparing to gird their own loins, lest some foul French breeze surmount the Pyrenees.

So Father Arredondo had been elected to protect the monastery from dangers that had as yet neither a face nor a name, but which were palpable nonetheless, as are the signs of an imminent thunderstorm well in advance of its torrential rainfall. Father Arredondo not only took the usual defensive precautions—such as fortifying the walls and quietly preparing for a siege—but also undertook some proactive political ones. These included recruiting prodigious sons whose presumed future influence in corridors of power would redound to the monastery's credit, thus affording future political protection if not patronage. Among other things, Montserrat was known to house the best choir school in Christendom. Now Father Arredondo sought to improve on this, by recruiting *virtuosi.* A lifelong adherent to *Matthew 7:16* ("by their fruits shall ye know them"), he wanted Montserrat to be known for as many delectable fruits as possible.

The abbot warmly greeted Isabella and Fernando, and led them by stages toward the sacristy and the chapel, so they could admire its abundant riches by the light of day. En route they passed a softly lit corbel which contained a worn stone sculpture dating from the fourteenth century, depicting two angels holding Montserrat's coat of arms: a mountain crossed by a saw. It was impossible to describe the feeling of reverence that overcame them both at this sight. Indeed, another century would pass before the celebrated Catalan poet Jacint Verdaguer would express it thus: "With a saw of gold, the angels hewed twisting hills to make a palace for you."

For the full name of this palace was not simply Montserrat—serrated mountain though it was. That name referred well enough to the monumental massif and its jutting crown, a menagerie of sculpted figures all created by that ultimate sculptor, geological time, under the unflagging patronage of the Almighty. More recently, under human occupancy, within a few centuries of Iberian history, this magical place had become a prize contested by various versions of several deities, and occasionally none at all. Following centuries of intrigue and conquest, counter-intrigue and counter-conquest, the serrated mountain had settled in the temporal custody of the Benedictines, and their divine music. The monastery was consecrated to Mother Mary; its proper name was Santa Maria de Montserrat.

Deep within its physical and spiritual heart, the monastery housed one of the most magnificent Madonnas in all of Christendom: *La Moreneta*, a Black Madonna, an obsidian pearl of rarest beauty. No sooner was she installed in the old Romanesque church than she began to attract the faithful in such numbers that King James I called Montserrat a place "which God embellishes and illustrates with continuous miracles". It was at this time, in the early thirteenth century, that the Brotherhood of Our Lady of Montserrat was founded, and soon afterwards the choir school to which our Fernando was about to be enrolled.

The abbot led them past the door to the old Romanesque church, and into the Gothic cloister. Fernando noticed that the columns were festooned with fanciful sculptures: here a man with the body of a bizarre creature, there a circle of men and women dancing naked. The significance of these things would be revealed to him in time. Then they reached the Church—later to become a Basilica—and all the wonders it contained. Their eyes grew wider than plates as they beheld the stained glass, sculptures, frescos, altars, chapels, and magnificent vault over the nave. At the back of the Church, they ascended a marble staircase that led to the Niche, in which *La Moreneta* had been re-installed in 1599, adorned by richly embroidered fabrics. Her renown had simply outgrown the tiny Romanesque church.

As soon as Isabella beheld *La Moreneta*, she was transported by such divine rapture that she fell into a dead faint. The abbot dispatched an attendant to fetch medicinal brandy from the refectory, gently admonishing him not to spill any (down his own throat) en route—and she was soon revived. But to the end of her days, the feeling of rapture never left her. Anesthetized by her encounter with *La Moreneta*, Isabella was spared the immediate pain of separation from her son, whom the abbot led away to join the company of the choir school. A nun took Isabella on a leisurely walk along one of the many pilgrim trails that carved its way among the serrated peaks, and they stopped at every shrine to offer prayers.

Meanwhile the abbot and Fernando reached the second floor of the monastery itself, where the school was located. A crowd of children awaited them, and flocked around the abbot to receive his blessing. One of their principal teachers, Father Anselmo Viola, then appeared and bowed, and Father Arredondo blessed him too. He reserved his final blessing for young Fernando, who felt grace beyond even music. Then the abbot spoke:

"I present to you a new student whose recommendation is unnecessary because of your kindness for all students. He has a good heart, and the mind of a little devil."

As Father Arredondo himself had a good heart, he knew whereof he spoke. Even so, one could not become an abbot, and especially not an abbot of Montserrat, without having encountered and overcome quite a number of devils, ranging from little to large, who appeared in a vast variety of guises. As for Fernando, he was by this time so accustomed to being associated with devilry on account of his talents, even at a still-tender age, that he accepted the abbot's assessment as a kind of benediction.

The method to this madness was evident enough. As if on cue, the boys stepped forward one by one to welcome Fernando with warm hugs, thus weaning him from the embrace of his mother, from whom his parting was now imminent. A boy of ten was neither a child nor a man, and was therefore bound to miss his mother and suffer the pangs of homesickness, even in this blessed place amidst such steadfast company. Their welcome made Fernando realize that although he had lost one father, he had gained several; that although he was parted from one brother, he had gained many; that although he was deprived of his mother's care, he was delivered into the arms of the Divine Mother. Thus Fernando felt overwhelming joy, and surprisingly little sorrow. Even the pangs of homesickness that would assail him in the wake of this relocation, replete with pains of separation from his dear mother, would be diverted by near-total immersion in music, distracted by daily study and practice, and sublimated by his own budding talents.

In the midst of this transition he experienced a delicious yet fleeting moment of limbo, in which he belonged to no-one. Then Father Viola led him off to another building where the sacristan, Isidore Capdevila, gave him a haircut and fitted him out with a uniform, taking great pains to find garments and accoutrements of exactly the right proportions. The uniform was quite handsome. It consisted of a pair of short trousers made of dark, soft suede (called a *gamouza*), violet stockings, ankle boots fastened with a copper button, and a small jacket with black woolen sleeves, worn over a linen shirt. On top of these he donned a black twill cassock, open at the front up to the belt. The cassock was trimmed with a blue silk collar, while the sleeves had deep elbow pockets. One pocket held a handkerchief; the other, a book of the Office of the Virgin Mary. Finally, a black strap with a yellow buckle served as a belt.

Fully attired, Fernando rejoined his classmates, with whom he now felt he belonged, and they greeted him accordingly. To welcome him officially, and to humble themselves all before God, they sang Benet Julia's *Parce mihi Domine,* led by Father Viola. The sacred *a cappella* strains washed over Fernando, immersing him in waves of gratitude, and stirring tears of joy that coursed down his cheeks. Then, as the choir took a recess, he was led outside to bid farewell to his mother. As soon as Isabella beheld him attired in the workaday garb of the choir school, her eyes filled with tears of pride, which she tried but failed to conceal. They said their fond good-byes, but even as she embraced and kissed him she sensed his eagerness to rejoin his new-found family, and so she relented and turned him loose. Fernando scampered into the schoolroom, and did not look back.

For Isabella, the journey home seemed long and lonely. She was drowning in a turbulent sea of mixed emotions. She felt desolated by the sudden disintegration of her family, precipitated by the death of her husband. She felt the heavy burden of a widow's solitariness. She felt pangs of maternal guilt for having abandoned her older son. She felt anxiety for the welfare of her younger son, Carlos, for whom she would now have to fend single-handed. Yet she also felt nervously hopeful, for she was already planning to open a music and dance school for children, with the help of her friend Sofia.

Like Isabella, Sofia Aviñó was a widow. Her deceased husband, captain of a fishing boat, had been lost with all hands at sea a few years before. Their daughter, Joaquina, was the same age as Carlos. It was not easy for a widow with a child to make ends meet without remarrying, so Sofia was eager to open the school of music and dance with Isabella. She danced boleros, among other traditional forms, sufficiently well to teach small children, and Joaquina was proof enough of that.

For her part, Isabella now felt some relief, as Fernando would be well looked after, and so the prospects for Carlos were already brighter, or at least undivided—albeit in her sole care. She felt joy in Fernando's acceptance to the Escolania, where his musical gifts would be well received and superbly honed. She felt blessed and protected by the Holy Mother, who would stand loving and abiding watch over them all. She felt pride in her son's newly elevated station in life, for he was clearly inhabiting a kind of palace, whose eternal Queen was the Holy Virgin—so much pride, in fact, that she felt bound to confess it. Indeed, Montserrat was but the first of many palaces that Fernando would come to call home, but of this he had no inkling at the time.

Chapter 4. Montserrat: The Escolania

As there are never enough hours in the day for the deeply devoted, the Benedictines were early risers. At Montserrat, at least one of them remained awake during each watch of the night, offering vocal prayers or soulful chants so that no second would elapse without a musical gift wafting over the serrated peaks and beyond the swirling clouds that draped them like a shifting veil, toward the ear of She who ruled and protected them.

Aside from those who stood the watch, the main body of monks arose at 3:00 a.m., but permitted the boys to sleep in until 4:00 a.m., whereupon most of them hopped to it with a will. Fernando did not yet realize that many of the lads—perhaps a majority—were the sons of poor farmers from the agricultural villages in the valley, and so were accustomed to rising even earlier. It was all the same to Fernando: awake or asleep, or day-dreaming in between, he lived and breathed music.

They assembled in the Church by 5:00 a.m., where mass was accompanied by a small orchestra of violins, cellos, double basses, bassoons, horns, and oboes, all played by the children, and conducted by Father Viola, who was to become Fernando's principal teacher. The first mass was one Fernando would never forget: at the offertory the orchestra played the prelude and allegro of one of Haydn's symphonies in D; at the communion they continued with the andante; and they concluded the final gospel with the allegro. This was Fernando's first complete exposure to Haydn and, drowning in seas of delightful harmonies, he wanted to play all the instruments at once. For now he merely listened, with as many inner ears as there were outer voices.

After mass they had some recreation time, and then were taken to a room filled with clavichords, some of which were set with tablecloths, on which freshly baked rolls and ham omelets awaited their eager appetites. After breakfast parts were distributed, they began rehearsals, then continued with lessons of many and varied kinds. Thus the day flew by, on the wings of Muses.

At last the dinner bell rang, whereupon the boys made their way to the refectory. Father Viola seated Fernando between two of the oldest boys, who showed him the etiquette, as they consumed a hearty meal with great gusto. Father Viola sat at a solitary table, eating in silence while presiding over the decorum of the boys. Under his loving yet stern countenance, all boyish inclinations toward prankish misbehaviors seemed stifled before they arose. After dinner the boys repaired to the school and donned their surplices, making ready to descend to the Church to sing Vespers and Compline of the Little Office.

On this first day Fernando stayed with Father Viola, who questioned him generally about his health, and education. It did not take long for Fernando to confess that he had shirked his Latin studies, neither out of rebelliousness against his father nor owing to congenital independence of mind, but simply because of some strange repugnance he felt—not so much toward the Latin tongue itself as toward the uninspiring technique of brute recitation imposed upon the lessons.

"So you will not be able to sing in Latin, because not knowing what you would be saying, you would express yourself poorly?" asked Father Viola. He deliberately posed this as a question, not a judgment nor an accusation.

"I will observe the phrasing and I will sing at least as well as the soloists that I heard this morning," replied young Fernando, not at all boastfully, merely matter-of-factly.

Father Viola smiled: "You do not know that the majority of these children are born of poor parents, living in villages and countryside. Since it is necessary to teach them everything, they cannot achieve perfection so quickly. Therefore your criticism is not completely fair."

At this, more scales fell from Fernando's eyes. For perhaps the first time in his young life, he suddenly realized that his birth into the Sor family had been fortunate indeed. He also understood something that Father Viola had (perhaps intentionally) failed to conceal behind this thin facade of class distinction, namely that Fernando's unusual ability to "achieve perfection so quickly" had nothing to do with his station of birth: it was a gift from God. Yet this exchange thoroughly humbled the boy, and disposed him thereafter toward undying gratitude for this gift, and endless patience with others less gifted. Never would Fernando display that arrogance, and intolerance of others' imperfections, for which so many otherwise gifted composers and conductors were justly disliked, if not reviled, by their peers. And the immediate consequence of this conversation was the very effect that Father Viola had desired from the outset: Fernando suddenly began to apply himself to Latin, so that he could sing with complete comprehension, and express himself as richly as possible. Unlike his biological father who, despite his good intentions, had foisted upon the boy a false dichotomy of choice between Latin and music, Father Viola—not only a music master but evidently also a master psychologist—had fused the two in young Fernando's mind. Thus inspired, Fernando quickly caught up on his Latin studies, so that nothing could hold him back from singing with the choir. And from his very first note, Father Viola realized that this boy was not only gifted *by* God, but was himself a gift *from* God, as though on loan to the Escolania from a heavenly choir on high.

As his first days at Montserrat flew by in a whirlwind of enchanting sounds, Fernando's total immersion in music—which also played on his feelings of reverence for the place itself—spared him any pangs of sadness at the enforced separation from his mother. At the same time, his sense of joyful novelty at this chapter of his life, the delicious newness of belonging to this blessed community, and the unmistakable air of promise it allowed him to imbibe day and night, never deserted him. In all his years to come in Montserrat, every morning there would dawn as freshly inspiring as his first, as every evening would carry him to bed on a tide of unsurpassed fulfillment. And when asleep, he did not dream of music so much as he became music, merging his slumbering consciousness with that of the singing and dancing cosmos, which never sleeps. He often awoke before first light, not to the tinkling bell rung by the father on duty but to the sound of his own voice, humming an air he had composed—unknowingly but unerringly—in his dreams.

Nor was every day dictated by inflexible musical ritual. While some recreation periods were necessarily devoted to rehearsing orchestral parts, others saw the students take to their various instruments for practice. At such times Fernando relished the racket. As in the conservatories of Italy, everyone was practicing different things at the same time. Rather than disturbing his composure, the cacophony titillated his soul. And when Father Viola asked Fernando which instruments he found most attractive (aside from the voice itself, a given thing at the Escolania), the boy immediately inclined toward violin, cello, and clavichord. Before long he was practicing them all, with surprising dexterity in addition to his innate musicality.

Even so, Fernando had much to learn, especially when it came to musical notation. Music can mean many things to many people but, whatever else it may be, music is also a language. And however expressive and beautiful a language, as long as it remains rooted in an oral tradition it cannot progress beyond a certain stage. To develop most fully its powers of expressivity, complexity, and beauty—not to mention reproducibility, appreciability, and longevity—music must be written down by composers, so it can be disseminated, read, and performed by other musicians. While audiences can afford the luxury of relying upon their ears alone, classical musicians need their eyes as well.

Seeking to lengthen and broaden the musical horizons of his young charges as far and as wide as possible, Father Viola instructed them daily in *solfège*, teaching them to recognize pitch, melody, and harmony from notation alone, thus enabling them to sing from scores written on the page. Of Father Viola's lessons, which touched on aspects both theoretical and practical, Fernando understood next to nothing. He was a babe in these woods of notation, yet his ignorance served to deepen his respect for his fellow students, who despite being less musically gifted than he, had progressed far beyond him in *solfège*, by virtue of persistent effort and diligent practice. Fernando resolved to catch up with them. This would require some time, but meanwhile, he could enlist his prodigious musical memory to good effect. And indeed, to the very end of his days, he never forgot the enchanting music and sense of wonder summoned up in this place by the grace of the Madonna, the devotion of the Fathers, the magic of Montserrat itself, and the chaste hearts and pure sopranos of these still-innocent young lads.

Two emotions above all animated Fernando's blessed years in this company: love, and reverence. He loved music without reservation, and music requited his love in equal measure. He revered every moment in Montserrat, and was soon enough revered at all moments. Every time the choir filed into the church, two abreast in a column that separated along the nave and rejoined in front of the high altar, the lads revested in their surplices adorned with lace, and tasseled at the collar, he rejoiced in the reverence of the occasion. He loved the Benedictine style of singing, the elegance and clarity of the plainsong, the gentleness of the breathing, effortlessly rising and falling on the turn of each phrase, and the purity of the pre-pubescent voices themselves, devoid of the shrieking and vibrato to which female sopranos sooner or later fell prey. He loved Father Casanova's accompaniments on the organ, and how elegantly his bass lines underpinned the plainsong. He loved the compositions that they sang after Compline, called *gozos* (joy), in honor of the Virgin Mary, alternating solo voices with refrains in unison, with all the lyrics in Spanish. He loved the canticles composed by Father Viola, and the compositions in the Gregorian mode by Father Céréols. He loved the morning masses sung in the lower chancel of the Church, flanked by massive mahogany stalls with wondrous engravings. He loved the lingering moment of anticipation as Father Capdevila went up to the altar, whereupon the choir sang the Introit, followed by the Kyrie, and he loved the sensation of novelty as these unfamiliar genres immersed him in warm waves of vibrant reverence.

In those early days Fernando dared not sing, as he was quite unable to read the music, but he followed the notation as best he could, immersing himself in the divine sounds that somehow arose from these indecipherable squiggles on the page. He made his first friend in this way, a boy of his age named Pablo, who stood next to him in the choir and, perceiving his puzzlement, tried to give him hints for singing the correct notes. Even though Pablo hailed from a village in the valley, and aspired only to taking the frock one day and leading a local church choir, Fernando was forever touched by his generosity of heart, and boundless good cheer. Even so, Pablo's hints did little to help him decode the scores.

Reduced to listening carefully, Fernando formed the enduring impression, later reinforced by experience in the wider world, that under the sagacious guidance of Father Viola the boys never tried to prove their talents or display their artistry by straining a tempo, or forcing a cadence. No symphonic allegro, and no delicate minuet, was ever defaced by them. It did not even occur to them that they never performed a piece; rather—by means of love, reverence, and a complete lack of pretension—they elevated it to sublime heights. And to Fernando, this represented ideal musicianship, in both attitude and performance. By cultivating this ideal himself, Fernando would never fail to enchant audiences large and small, common and noble alike.

As autumn receded and winter approached, the atmosphere at Montserrat grew increasingly festive in preparation for Christmas. Decorations festooned the public areas in anticipation of the arrival of seasonal pilgrims. Even the rugged, saw-toothed peaks for which Montserrat had been named were softened with sprinklings of light snow, which dusted them like icing sugar. The upper peaks became frosted like Christmas cakes during December's chilliest nights. Within the monastery, solemnity in the inner sanctums gradually gave way to mirthful celebration.

Fernando's heart warmed to all of this, as he had been on a mission. Determined not to have his voice silenced while his eyes learned (ever so slowly) to decipher squiggles, he had quietly but faithfully memorized all the parts of a *responsorio* and a *villancico* composed by Father Viola, along with several solos from midnight mass. As soon as he revealed this, and sang a few parts, the kindly maestro suggested that he sing the lead voice. Thrilled to sing at all, let alone as a soloist with orchestral accompaniment, Fernando prepared for his debut by using a method he had learned from an actress in the Italian theater, who had taken a shine to the young prodigy in Barcelona.

Fernando had no idea that, immediately after hearing his voice and offering him the role of soloist, Father Viola went directly to Father Arredondo, to make a report.

"While we all know how musically gifted Fernando is…" began Father Viola.

"By the grace of God," intoned the abbot.

"Just so," continued Father Viola, "but now that I have heard him sing, I declare before God that he belongs in a choir of angels!"

"Perhaps he is on loan to us from just such a choir," mused Father Arredondo, "with the blessing of Mother Mary."

"Amen to that," said Father Viola. "But you must come and hear him yourself!"

"That I shall," promised the abbot, "at the appointed time. And I will also bring special guests."

"We will all be greatly honored," said Father Viola, before kissing the abbot's hand, and taking his leave.

When at last the hour arrived for the Christmas concert, Fernando could barely contain his excitement. He permitted himself a momentary indulgence in pride, at singing with an orchestra, but did not allow this sin to diminish his performance. On the contrary: he rose to the occasion as he was apparently born to do. And just as Fernando stood to sing his opening lines, the abbot entered in the company of the Governor and other dignitaries. Inspired by the realization that they had come to hear him sing, Fernando's solos were magnificent. Less clear in his own mind, and thus in his voicing, were his deliveries in the ensemble and in the three-part lines, but afterwards Father Viola had praised his solos and applauded his overall efforts. Fernando's singing pleased everyone, and from that time on he occupied a kind of center stage in the attentions of the ordinary clergy as well those of *la paternité*. There followed a succession of gifts, mostly sweets, which Fernando unfailingly shared with his classmates. All of them being rewarded, none succumbed to envy of his talents, and of the special attentions they attracted.

After Christmas, Father Viola began to intensify Fernando's instruction, through both learning and teaching. He positioned him neither in the most experienced rank of seniority (which Fernando's talents merited) nor at the rear of the queue of priority (based on the rule of order of arrival, the newest being last). Rather, Father Viola situated him in the middle. He also put him to work, naming him primary reader for the refectory. There Fernando gave the youngest students reading and writing lessons, consisting of sermons by Blasius and the *Flos Sanctorum* by Villegas. Fernando immediately proved to be a kind, patient and effective teacher—a skill that would later serve him in great stead, and also draw him into peril—and he was also quick to realize the extent to which one invariably learned new things by teaching familiar ones.

Father Viola also initiated Fernando's in-depth study of music, ingeniously by positioning himself as one who possessed no prior knowledge of music. Rather, he treated it as a science of sounds.

"You know music," he said to Fernando, "like you know how to speak. You also know how to read and write words, but you do not yet know how to read or write music."

Fernando then demonstrated to Father Viola the crude tablature he had invented for notating music. The kindly monk was surprised, and not a little impressed. "You are a harmonist without even knowing it!" he declared.

Yet soon enough, under Father Viola's sagacious tutelage, Fernando came to know it, and much more besides. Sitting with the youngest students in *solfège* class, his slate tablet perched on his lap, absorbed by the daily exercises drilled into them, Fernando began to experience a luminous understanding of the significance of relative versus absolute pitch, of how the scales were represented on the various staves, of the reason for the presence or absence of accidentals (sharps and flats), and of the correspondence between tailed and dotted notes and their respective durations according to the meter. Without even realizing it, he was becoming literate in music. One day it simply astonished him that they were able to sing without a key, and yet he completely understood Father Viola's explanation, of which he would scarcely have grasped a word in his first hours at Montserrat:

"In order to sing *solfège* musically," the monk patiently explained, "there must be a symbol designating the name of the pitch that belongs to the scale of the tone moved anywhere. In the pieces where there is no longer a sharp, here is the rule to recognize it: the last sharp, which is the highest to the right, is the seventh note of *ut*, which is the next pitch going up. With that positioned, one can easily find the rest of the scale. The sharp is even something other than the symbol that indicates the pitch: it is the pitch itself. This pitch is the sharp of the scale that you must call *si*. This designation proves that your first instructor was unaware that the signature is only a caution giving character to the note that that separates it from the new *la*, as much as the construction of the scale demands it, and as a result, moves this note closer to the end of the scale as necessary."

In tandem with their increasing mastery of pitch, they began to study intervals, which opened Fernando's eyes and ears to the deeper structures that underpinned melody, engendered harmony, and informed composition itself. His progress was so rapid that before long he could not only sing what was written, but also write what was sung. Now he could practice all the instruments efficiently, not only as an increasingly accomplished player, but also as a budding composer. While organ remained compulsory for all the boys, Fernando was encouraged to experiment with his musical ideas on the clavichord and the violin.

While music is a playful vocation—a veritable labor of play as well as of love—periodic respites from routine are refreshing to the mind and soul alike. The Benedictines knew this well, and so granted the boys seasonal vacations. When the winter holiday arrived, they were divided into two groups, which took their turns on leave, so that there would always be sufficient voices in residence for daily singing: from morning mass and *gozos,* to Magnificat and Salve. Fernando found himself in the first cohort for departure and, as they passed the guest house where he had first stayed with his mother upon arrival—mere months but seemingly a lifetime ago—he suddenly remembered his guitar, which he retrieved at once. Given that they were on vacation, Father Viola permitted Fernando this boyish indulgence. But he himself had little regard for the instrument, from which emanated raucous sounds that hardly qualified as music; rather, as mere '*frons-frons*'. Nonetheless, Fernando gratefully greeted the guitar like an old friend, and slung it happily over his shoulder by its strap of hand-tooled Barcelona leather.

Their path wound around a huge precipice, on whose opposite edge they glimpsed the windows of their Great Hall, from which, to their immense delight, wafted the sounds of a minuet from a Haydn symphony, performed by their classmates as a farewell chorus. This charming custom would be repeated on their return. Then Fernando and Father Viola deviated from the main company, and arrived at a small chapel consecrated to Saint Michael, where two riding horses awaited them. "What new adventure does this betoken?" Fernando mused to himself, and the answer was not long in coming. Father Viola took one of the horses, while Fernando was hoisted onto the other by a valet, who led the docile mount by its bridle.

They were then treated to a leisurely tour along some of the main paths that skirted the edges of the undulating monastery property, and on side paths that traversed narrow passes in the serrated peaks. At regular intervals they passed brightly decorated shrines, or spied secluded hermitages dotting the higher reaches of the hills, perching precariously upon exposed ledges or nestling at the bases of towering, tooth-like peaks. Fernando marveled, not only at the expanse of the sprawling estate, but also at the vast variety of the rock formations, many of which were fancifully named for their suggestive shapes, which had given rise to local fables concerning their origins. Father Viola called out some of their names, or pointed to more distant ones: "La Nina (the Doll), El Bacallà (the Cod), El Lloro (the Parrot), El Camell de Sant Jeroni (Saint Jerome's Camel), El Cap de Mort (the Death's Head), El Cavall Bernat (the Horse Bernard), La Gorra Marinera (the Sea Cap), El Faraó (the Pharaoh), Els Frares Encantats (the Enchanted Friars) ..." and more. Soon Fernando's head was swimming with names and shapes and local lore.

As they approached one particular formation—a tight cluster of tall, tapering pinnacles—they dismounted and scrambled closer on foot. Suddenly Fernando began to hear strange music, of a genre unknown, made by nature herself. "Els Flautats (the Pipes)," Father Viola explained. Indeed, the petrous stack resembled nothing if not organ pipes, but even more remarkable was the sound of the wind whistling through their fissures—a veritable chorus of unpredictable if not unearthly cadences and harmonies. Els Flautats echoed in Fernando's head ever after. Throughout later life, he sometimes dreamed of them— as if they serenaded him in his sleep—to the point of awakening, writing down an approximation of what he heard, and adapting it to a composition. On this mystical mountain of Santa Maria de Montserrat, Els Flautats were the organ pipes of the Sacred Mother's outdoor chapel.

Remounting their horses and continuing their journey, Fernando also noticed a surprising abundance of flora and fauna. The rocky massif's soil was thin and windblown, yet rich in minerals, and so a variety of flowering plants, hardy shrubs, and even somewhat stunted trees—mostly oaks, yews, and pines—clung to seemingly bare outcroppings, or sheltered in shady ravines. These in turn shaped a habitat for a menagerie of animals that roamed everywhere except within the confines of the monastery itself, which is why Fernando had not spotted them until now. The higher cliffs were dotted with sure-footed wild goats, while majestic Bonelli's eagles soared above the narrow valleys and perched their eyries out of sight, atop the tallest cliffs. Denser tracts of brush concealed badgers, boars, and foxes, while the trees were home to owls, ravens, and blackbirds. Vipers nested in crevices between the rocks, but in this Eden men and serpents kept to themselves: in the absence of Eves and apples alike, temptation could not take root.

Eventually the switchbacks spilled onto the valley floor, and not long afterwards they reached their destination, a farm called Vina-Nueva. There the abbot awaited them, along with three other clergy. They proceeded to the chapel and sang a *gozos* to the Virgin Mary, followed by the hymn *Ave Maria Stella*, in four parts. At this moment Fernando felt himself so touched by reverent emotions that, years later, when he heard the hymn again at the Barcelona cathedral, he could not hold back his tears.

After supper they went to the abbot's apartment and made more music. At first Fernando had been surprised to see that Father Arredondo maintained such quarters at this distance from the monastery, but he had yet to realize that Montserrat extended far and wide, reaching incomparably further into the City of Man than its altitude approached the

City of God. Given the expense of its upkeep and the abundance of alms it distributed, the monastery could not have survived, let alone flourished, without substantial private donations along with regular revenues from properties. Later, in France, Fernando would learn that the abbot was also seigneur of several villages in the valley, whose stewards he himself selected, and beyond this that the monastery owned houses and appointed administrators in virtually every city and town in Catalonia, and even in Castilia, including Madrid. But for now Fernando was still a boy, whose luxurious horizons were yet untroubled with mundane matters of material wealth, and were defined primarily by immaterial delights of music.

So, encouraged by the abbot, Fernando sang part of a well-known trio he recalled from the theater. The company applauded him, and so he tried another that no-one knew. He then suggested to Father Viola that he dictate the three parts of this song while his teacher compose the bass line. Noting the approving smile of the abbot, the kindly monk was happy to do so, and sat next to Fernando, and asked him what the tone of the trio was. But Fernando did not know how to respond.

"I am not angered by your ignorance," said Father Viola. "Some people think they are musicians because they figure out how the auditory production of a sound corresponds to a key on the keyboard. But they are deceived: their way of designating sounds destroys any musical idea, since it applies only to the mechanism of instruments. In proper music theory, there are no absolute sounds, only relative ones, and these sounds do not indicate the keys of a keyboard, but the true intonations of the scale of the mode."

Fernando understood this no better than the good father's original question, and so following their brief sojourn in the valley, when they returned to the monastery, Father Viola intensified the boy's studies. Fernando's natural gifts were as wild as the eagles that soared on the whim of swirling updrafts, perceiving what only their keen eyes could detect from the lofty heights to which their expansive wings so effortlessly bore them. But such a noble bird, to be made useful for the hunt, must be trained to the jess, the creance, and the hood, for only then can its talents be focused on a single purpose: quarry destined for the royal table. This training is the falconer's art. Similarly, Father Viola's mission was to train Fernando in *solfège*, harmony, and counterpoint, for only then could his musical talents be focused on a single purpose: compositions commissioned for the royal ear. And since Fernando still had no inkling of this, his innocence only enhanced his aptitude as a pupil.

Chapter 5. Montserrat: From Boy to Young Man

Because Fernando's congenital independence of mind, along with his free spirit, made him averse to musical formulas and rote learning of every kind, the resourceful Father Viola often devised games instead of drills, amusements instead of methods, and diversions instead of repetitions. All of these had the desired effect of stimulating Fernando's interest in mastering musical theory, without in the least inhibiting his creativity. Before long he had absorbed fugues and variations, which he rendered artfully on the organ. And so the months at Montserrat passed agreeably yet steadily, each day an apparent eternity as a child experiences time, yet all the years flashing by in the blink of an eye, as an adult later recollects them.

One morning Fernando awoke and, as was his habit, hummed softly to himself as he dressed, giving voice to whatever transient air had just serenaded his pre-dawn dreams. But his sweet soprano tones were suddenly displaced by hoarse croaks, as if someone were throttling a frog. He cleared his throat to no avail; the harder he tried to sing, the more his voice cracked. Fernando was not particularly alarmed by this sudden change, for he had known that it would come. The older boys had all passed through it. When their pure soprano voices suddenly cascaded down the muddy stream of puberty, their once-unblemished complexions erupted with acne, their once-smooth skins sprouted patches of tell-tale stubble, and their bodies elongated awkwardly in all directions, like gangly weeds. They experienced stronger, deeper urges too, which for a time remained nameless, and which they sublimated into music.

The onset of adolescence signaled their enforced graduation from the choir, but needless to say the Escolania anticipated and accommodated this transformation.

They shifted from singing to helping the younger boys with *solfège*, and focused their own expressive energies on instruments other than voice. Fernando not only flung himself into fugue and counterpoint on the organ, but also developed an avid interest in the violin. One of his older friends, Sunyer, was lead first violinist. Noting Fernando's talent and fascination for this instrument, Sunyer gave him advice that greatly enhanced his practice. Before long he attained sufficient competence to play with the second violins, and was made head of that group. This only whetted his appetite for first violin, which became his new heart's desire. Sunyer and most of the best violinists—also older boys—were going to take the frock on graduation from Montserrat, and so Fernando saw his chance looming in the near future. Thus spurred on by mere possibility, he intensified his zeal and perseverance, and soon met with crowning success.

Not long after Sunyer had entered the novitiate, a strenuous competition was held for the new lead first violin. All the contestants had to play a rehearsed piece, followed by a sight-reading test, and finally a multi-part piece containing deliberate errors (unbeknownst to the contestants) that had to be corrected without stopping. Fernando so excelled in all three stages that he was named principal first violin and conductor of the strings. His natural voice having deserted him for a time, the violin became his newly adopted voice, and proved just as triumphant in performance.

Fernando's transition from boyhood to young manhood was marked by other kinds of lessons as well, to which he applied himself with a newfound seriousness that only budding manhood could confer, and whose rewards in later life would prove more bountiful than boyhood's fleeting laurels. Most important among these lessons were catechism (which would later save his life at the hands of the Inquisition), and French (whose acquisition would catalyze future successes, beyond imagination, in France and Russia).

Since Saint Benedict's Rules for the conduct of monastic life pertained initially to men and not to boys, the monks at Montserrat had to devise their own ways of confronting and punishing lads who transgressed communal norms. 'Boys will be boys' rang true no less on the holy mountain's peaks than on Barcelona's streets. Rather ingeniously, and with their usual admixture of sagacity and compassion, the monks devised their remedy for transgressions in the context of religious instruction. Each Sunday the boys assembled in the master's room, or else in the room of the head sacristan priest, where they were questioned on the catechism. At the same time, four student leaders were chosen from among the eldest boys, and their mandate was to observe whether any of the lads had strayed beyond the rather strict confines of monastic rules. If so, they would accuse the lads who had so transgressed. The accused were then obliged to prostrate themselves and, faces pressed to the ground, absorb the master's verbal exhortations, addressed personally to each in turn. Instead of inflicting a punishment, the master then compelled each lad to embrace his accusers.

Following Sunyer's departure, Fernando was appointed one of the student leaders, and so he received instructions from Father Viola on fulfilling the duties of this position. The good father, being no less skilled at teaching this than music, soon made Fernando aware of his own transgressions. Father Viola complained, in general, about lads who tuned their instruments, or who amused themselves by playing this or that passage in the wings while the chorus itself was still singing. Thus Fernando's pride at this new duty was swiftly, if not too subtly, tempered by an indirect reproach, for he admittedly had a bad habit of playing concerto themes, fantasias, or improvised harmonies on his violin during the plainsong that preceded the orchestra's appearance. Placing Fernando in a position in which he was supposed to accuse others aloud had the desired effect of making him accuse himself silently, and of quickly correcting his own behavior. Then again, he never intended to interfere with the chorus, nor for that matter with anyone else's performance at any time. One could simply not put an instrument in his hands and expect him not to make music with it. If one gave wood to a fire, it burned; similarly, if one handed an instrument to Fernando, he played. He was like a force of nature, obeying laws ordained by a higher power than mere men, even holy ones.

Beyond Fernando's lessons in catechism, Father Arredondo wisely exploited the turning tide of history to imbue the prodigious youth with a knowledge of France, both its music and its language. As the horrors of the Revolution began to unfold on the other side of the Pyrenees, French Benedictines sent a number of their brethren to temporary safety in Montserrat. One of them, a certain Father Coste, wanted to teach Fernando some romances and arias from *Belle Arsène.* At first Fernando proved surprisingly resistant to this genre, perhaps partly because the scores that Father Coste showed him were notated in a much more primitive way than that to which—thanks to Father Viola's sophisticated methods—Fernando had grown accustomed. But Father Viola stepped in yet again, and successfully weaned Fernando from this prejudice by playing for him magnificent fugues composed by Charpentier and Séjan. So Fernando began to acquire a valuable taste for French music too.

His instruction in the French language began soon after that. An illustrious prelate, namely the Archbishop of Auch, Monsieur de La Tour du Pin, took up residence at the monastery, having fled France a step, a wing, and a prayer ahead of the guillotine. The Jacobins had already beheaded a number of his relatives, some of whom had been intimates of the Versailles Court. His sister, Henriette-Lucy, had also made a hair-raising escape from Robespierre. Eventually, Napoleon would elevate the Archbishop to Cardinal. Meanwhile, Fernando was charged with delivering a welcome speech—in French, of course—on behalf of the choir and orchestra. Father Coste taught him to pronounce the words correctly, and so he took his first confident strides toward acquiring fluency in yet another Romance tongue, and an important one at that.

Being an aficionado of music, the Archbishop regularly hosted small concerts in his quarters, and could not fail to notice Fernando's virtuosity, which sparkled even on the highly polished veneer of Montserrat's best chamber ensembles. He took a shine to the Catalan prodigy, and commenced instructing him in the French language, three times per week. Fernando's astounding auditory memory, and his chameleon-like ability to mimic sounds, turned out to be as well-equipped for assimilating spoken language as they were for music. Moreover, he enjoyed speaking and reading French, and took to it like a proverbial duck to water. Delighted with his pupil's rapid progress, the Archbishop extended and intensified his lessons.

Father Viola, who noticed everything, saw that Fernando had begun to neglect the violin to make sufficient time for French, and this perturbed him enough to seek the abbot's counsel. After gaining an audience with Father Arredondo and explaining the dilemma, he asked "My Lord, is this the wisest course for Fernando to pursue?"

The abbot held Father Viola in the highest esteem. No-one was better qualified than he to know exactly what each boy needed to learn and practice, and at every stage of his development, in terms of music itself. Yet Father Viola held no less esteem for Father Arredondo, as no-one was better qualified than he to know how each boy's musical ability could be most strategically deployed beyond the monastery, when the time came, and for the benefit of all concerned. So he was more than happy to defer to the abbot's advice. Father Arredondo's hawk-like countenance flashed this way and that as he spoke, his far-sighted eyes seemingly fixed unerringly on a sharp yet terrible image of the future.

"Beloved Father Viola," he said in a kindly voice that belied his raptor-like gaze, "you are surely aware that evil times are almost upon us. An unspeakable terror has been unleashed in France, whose ignorant Jacobins are merely its unwitting slaves. In truth, they know neither what they do, nor whom they serve. The distinguished French brethren flocking to our gates as honored guests are regarded as vile criminals by those minions of Satan, who would put them to death for exemplifying any and every virtue that we prize. While we can offer them temporary shelter from that heinous storm, know that those tempestuous clouds will soon enough gather over Catalonia—indeed, over all Iberia too—and will let loose a deluge in their coming season. As always, we rely on the protection of the Holy Mother, blessed be Her name, and trust to Divine Providence for our Salvation. But the very best thing we can do on this mortal plane, to combat such implacable evil, is to send forth from our gates the greatest musical talents we can muster, to celebrate in Her name, and in ours, the boon of melody in days of anguished cries, the balm of harmony in nights of discordant strife, and the godsend of song in weeks of woeful lamentation. Let the soothing grace of music charm the hearts and calm the minds of ravening beasts in every land, restoring humanity to their souls.

"For that very mission was Fernando born, and bred, and trained. He does not know it yet—nor need he know, for he is still a boy but teetering on the cusp of manhood. Although you have taught him surpassingly well, you also know that if he stayed much longer he'd soon become our instructor; and we, his pupils. So let him learn French, for Frenchmen sorely need his musical gifts. And for that matter let him learn a dozen tongues of men, to serve as emissaries to his musical majesty. This is our devoutest way, and our best hope, to do Her bidding."

"So shall it be, my Lord Abbot, by the grace of She who watches over us," said Father Viola, and kissed his Master's hand.

Thereafter he allowed Fernando as much latitude as the boy desired to devote to French, and never once reproached him for neglecting to practice an instrument. That said, the good Father could not resist supplementing the boy's education with further analyses of classical works, melodic patterns, and harmonic rules, all of which pleased Fernando's mind and ear alike. Father Viola also acquainted him with musical literature from the works of Nasarre, Kircher, Soler, and Cerone, all drawn from collections in the Monastery's marvelous library.

Soon enough Fernando turned sixteen—a man by the standard of those times, and thereby fit for adult employment. But now his mother Isabella found herself on the horns of a new dilemma. On the advice of several friends, including Sabater, she wanted to take him out of Montserrat and place him in a comfortable commission with the army which, thanks to her reliable social connections, had awaited his coming of age. Then again, out of profound gratitude to Father Viola, with whom she corresponded regularly, she did not wish to interfere with Montserrat's internal workings by withdrawing him prematurely, or at least before they could recruit a younger boy to replace him, as they routinely did with all their graduates. The Benedictines greatly appreciated Isabella's respect, and considerateness. And as usual, Fernando's case was most unusual. So they deferred to her, and responded:

"According to the statutes of the monastery, we do not dismiss any student without securing him a place in a chapel that would provide for all his needs, unless his family claims him. Since your family has found him a commission, we do not see any point in assessing him for placement via our channels. So he will be permitted to depart at your convenience."

Their response also reflected their awareness of the world beyond the monastery's walls, and their willingness to serve Fernando's better interests in it. In the topsy-turvy ethos of Spain, his musical career would encounter more opportunities for advancement through service in the army rather than via the seemingly more obvious route, as organist and choir-master of a chapel. Father Arredondo was supremely mindful that Fernando's family, although of the bourgeoisie and not the nobility, maintained social and political contacts in the military and civil sectors that simply outclassed the monastery's musical network. The abbot knew full well that an officer in the contemporary Spanish army, having at this time no wars to fight, would find sufficient leisure to pursue other interests—particularly and peculiarly in Spain, if said interests were musical. And so he let Fernando go, confident that the young man could embark on a path no more suitable than that arranged by his devoted mother.

At this, Isabella breathed a great sigh of relief. But this resolution of her dilemma imposed a different dilemma on Fernando, namely one of mixed emotions. While he had experienced deep sadness at the sudden death of his father, and had felt profound joy at his immersion in the Escolania, he had never until this moment been buffeted by both emotional extremes at once. So profound was his love for Montserrat that even the thought of departing wounded him grievously; yet his inner voice, which he trusted above all else, now joyfully proclaimed that a new and wondrous road lay open before him, ready to receive him. So Fernando shed tears of grief and joy all at once, as he bundled his few belongings and girded his loins for the imposing departure ceremony. He had witnessed this ceremony many times before, but needless to say had never been its focus.

So, when the appointed day arrived, all the students assembled in Father Viola's chamber, where they stood upright awaiting the graduate's arrival. As custom dictated, Fernando then kneeled at the door and recited the standard supplication, by which the student begs forgiveness of the Master and all his classmates, for the wrongs that he might have done them. Father Viola then delivered a very touching speech, and embraced Fernando with great tenderness. He then led him away, to the abbot's chamber, where Father Arredondo adorned him with a black cloak and hat resembling those of a priest, and blessed him. Thus attired, Fernando made the rounds and visited all the clergymen who had shown him kindness, and gave them thanks. Finally he was taken to a place where a horse, saddled and slung with his baggage and guitar, was waiting to bear him away. There too awaited the head sacristan priest, who handed him a gold coin worth forty francs. At first Fernando refused it, but the priest explained that they did this for each departing student returning to his family. This bounty was conferred for the purchase of an object that would recall the memory of Montserrat. So Fernando accepted the coin with gratitude, although he needed no such souvenir: he himself was that very object, who would recall the memory of Montserrat with a fondness no quantity of gold could ever buy, and until the very end of his days.

And with that, Fernando rode slowly away, winding down the switchbacks, overcome as always by the magnificent vistas, now newly tinged with bittersweet nostalgia. He knew that he would never pass this way again. Yet he also knew that Montserrat would never leave him, as he would never leave the memory of those who inhabited this sacred mountain. Humming a cheerful air from Haydn, Fernando rode resolutely back to Barcelona, which he had not seen for what seemed like many long years, and to his family, whom he had not embraced for what felt like an eternity.

Chapter 6. Barcelona: Il Telemaco

The Sor household, and indeed their neighborhood, rejoiced at the return of their prodigious (not prodigal) son. Isabella was beside herself with joy, and gave bountiful thanks to the Holy Mother for the safekeeping and homecoming of her precious Fernando. As soon as he crossed the threshold of their abode, she was caught in a seemingly interminable cycle of hugging him, admiring him, and hugging him anew. His younger brother Carlos, now ten years old, was also overjoyed to see him again. Although Carlos had relished the undivided attentions of his mother all these years, without interference from sibling rivalry, his elder brother had taken on a kind of legendary status during his absence, and so Carlos could not help but revere Fernando, at least in his imagination. Now that the flesh-and-blood version suddenly stood before him, beamed lovingly at him, then hoisted him playfully into the air, Carlos let out an involuntary shriek of delight. Fernando was also old enough to represent a kind of father figure to his younger brother, who was still sufficiently tender in years to prefer, quite sensibly, to remain a child. So when Fernando crossed the threshold, he immediately relieved Carlos of the burden—partly imaginary but also partly real—of being the eldest male in the household. Carlos happily relinquished it, and in its place rekindled his love, which at times verged on worship, of his older brother.

Barcelona's Dry Quarter soon ran wet with liquid libations, which were copiously poured and enthusiastically quaffed at Fernando's homecoming party. Not that Barcelonans required much of an excuse to celebrate; but this was truly a festive occasion. Plenty of food accompanied the drink. Isabella and Sofia had cooked up a veritable storm of tapas delights, roasted choice cuts of pork *al horno*, and topped that off with a paella. Sabater remarked jocularly that they had prepared for either a large celebration, or else a long siege. In fact, Isabella's and Sofia's school of music and dance for children had prospered during Fernando's absence, and they were only too glad to share their bounty with a throng of invited guests, as well as with neighbors who had simply dropped in.

Sofia's daughter Joaquina, the same age as Carlos, was also his classmate in their mothers' music and dance school. Joaquina and Carlos were soon ushered onto a makeshift stage (really a platform of crates emptied of wine bottles, which in turn the guests were now emptying), and sang together some charming duets they had rehearsed for the occasion, well coached by their mothers. Then Carlos played a bolero on his child-sized guitar, to which Joaquina danced, as if on air, like a hummingbird. This was their warm musical welcome for Fernando, and an obvious prelude to his expected performance. He did not disappoint. He played some classical keyboard pieces, then sang some popular songs, accompanying himself on the guitar, and inviting all to join in on the choruses. Fernando's voice had finally metamorphosed into its adult form, a rich and mellifluous tenor that charmed all ears, and made female hearts flutter in the bargain. Fernando was a huge success, and gossip from those at the party soon circulated throughout the city. He had left Barcelona as a child prodigy, and returned as a virtuoso performer.

Within a few days Fernando was introduced to his new master, General Juan Miguel de Vivès y Feliu, who commanded the Catalan army corps at Villafranca, which Fernando joined as a provisional sub-lieutenant. The General rode with him to Villafranca, just two or three hours by horse from Barcelona. To Fernando's delight, the commander devoted most of their conversation to music and, when they arrived, presented him to the company at large. They immediately demanded that he give them a concert that very night. He played with such skill and panache, on both piano and guitar, that not only the soldiers but also notable public figures from the city were enthralled with him. Soon after, when the armament committee sent in a list of officers for appointment, he was promoted to lieutenant, and was given every encouragement, in addition to liberty, to pursue his musical interests. His military duties at this time consisted of nothing more than light drills with horse and saber, and negligible paperwork. To his pleasant surprise, he was able to devote as much time to music now as he could at Montserrat—if not even more. On top of this, and by contrast with the rigid regime of the monastery, his musical hours were largely unstructured, and so became guided more by inner creativity rather than by outward constraint.

Spending as much time as he pleased in Barcelona, Fernando fell in with a group of Italian musicians whose passions infected his own with renewed ardor, and thanks to whom he made a breakthrough on guitar. One day he heard General Solano's brother play a piece which, embodying both melody and accompaniment, made the guitar resemble a piano. This struck Fernando like a thunderbolt. He learned that the composer of this piece was Federico Moretti, originally from Naples and now a fellow officer in the Spanish army. Moretti was perhaps the first to understand the true nature of the guitar—as a simulacrum of a small orchestra. Sor's knowledge of harmony, so diligently acquired at Montserrat, now combined with Moretti's revelation that the guitar could be an instrument of composition no less effective than the keyboard. Thus inspired, Fernando began composing and performing pieces with true multiple voices—melody, harmony, accompaniment—whose overall effect was indeed that of an orchestra in miniature. These early compositions proved so popular that guitarists began asking Fernando for the scores. A music publisher in Barcelona caught wind of this, as several guitarists had come into his shop asking for various scores by Sor. So he struck a deal with young Fernando, who began to derive a modest income from the sale of sheet music. His compositions first went into print in 1795, and have never been out of print since.

At the same time, he made another breakthrough, in a direction that no-one, including himself, could have predicted. Browsing one day in the musical library of Monsieur Caetano de Gispert, administrator of the Theater of Barcelona and godfather to his younger brother Carlos,

Fernando happened upon an old libretto by Maestro Cipolla: *Telemaco, opera in due atti.* The cast comprised four characters, and a chorus of nymphs. Italian opera still dominated Barcelona's musical scene, as it had when Fernando was yet a child. It suddenly dawned on him to set this opera to music. He completed it within three months, and showed it to Monsieur Gispert, who immediately contacted his friend Tozzi, musical director of the theater's resident Italian troupe. Tozzi perused the score, and was impressed. He first complimented Fernando: "At your age, I was not capable of doing so much." He then shocked him by declaring that he wanted to perform the piece, and requesting that Fernando write the overture. Sensing some inexplicable hesitancy on Sor's part, Tozzi became insistent.

In truth, Fernando was temporarily overcome by the momentousness of the occasion. In his wildest dreams, he had not imagined that his maiden opera would be instantly accepted for performance by the Theater of Barcelona. Temporarily daunted by the magnitude of this triumph, he conceived—but dared not write—an allegro in the style of Haydn or Mozart. Reverting to the modesty of his cherished mentor Father Viola, Fernando instead wrote a less ambitious but entirely satisfactory overture.

And if another truth be surmised, it was neither the ongoing popularity of this genre in Barcelona, nor the fond memory of his transformative first exposure to it as a child, that had fueled Fernando's inspiration to write *Il Telemaco.* It may well have been the libretto's chorus of nymphs that caught and held his fancy, like so many Sirens luring him with their song. His innocent boyhood years in Montserrat, where his mind's ear was devoutly attuned to choirs of angels, were now behind him. Suddenly a charismatic, adventurous, and amorous guitarist of seventeen, his mind had become fervently, if not feverishly, aware of bevies of beautiful young women, of which Barcelona boasted more than its fair share. In turn, one look at him, either promenading handsomely about town in his smart lieutenant's uniform, or performing brilliantly on stage with his sonorous guitar, left droves of young (and not so young) beauties either swooning in his wake, or contriving to be noticed by this youthful Catalan avatar of a Greek god.

Once he left the protective cloister of Montserrat, it had not taken Fernando long to become infatuated with the opposite sex, both in general, and in a succession of particular cases. Of course boys his age were desperately driven to sow wild oats, while young girls just as badly wanted their furrows ploughed. But whereas boys were rarely constrained by consequences, girls were constantly—and rightly—concerned about their reputations, and above all afraid of untimely pregnancy, which in those days could spell their utter ruin. Even so, just as the wrinkled gypsy had predicted to Isabella a dozen years beforehand, women found Fernando irresistible. They fluttered toward his flame like helpless moths. This was more on account of his innate charms than his uniform or musicianship, yet both contributed heavily to his allure.

And women seemed especially attracted to guitarists, as every guitarist surely knows. The instrument itself is a hermaphrodite: an enchanting blend of a woman's curvaceous torso, and a man's rigid phallus. The female part (accurately called 'the body') is replete with an orifice surrounded by a floral rosette, which decorates this portal leading to a dark virgin womb, guarded by a lattice of tight strings, through which nothing penetrates but from which intimate sounds are born. The male part (politely called 'the neck') is permanently erect, and its enlarged tip is studded with knurled tuning keys. The player's left had caresses it smoothly and skillfully up and down, along its entire length, while the right hand delicately titillates the lattice of strings, never straying far from the aperture, strong yet gentle fingers plucking and strumming the region in pulsating rhythms that gradually build to a crescendo. If playing the guitar is a metaphoric *ménage-à-trois*, then playing it on stage conveys an invitation to an orgy, which apparently few women can resist. The guitar casts a veritable spell on females, compelling them to throw their habitual caution to the wind, and consign their prudential inhibitions to the tide. And by some happy mutual coincidence, just as a good many women never tire of guitarists, so a good many guitarists never tire of women.

Fernando proved willing to play his role in this state of affairs, and seemed altogether satisfied with the arrangement. A lover of popular Spanish music in all its forms, as well as of popular Spanish women in all of theirs, he soon found himself writing and performing *seguidillas*, one of which reflected this comparison:

Las mujeres y cuerdas
De la guitarra,
Es menester talento
Para templares.
Flojas no suenan
Y suelan saltar muchas
Si las aprietan.

(Women and guitar strings: you need talent to tune them. If they're slack they don't sound, and they usually jump if you squeeze them.)

While women began to weave themselves, in their inimitable fashion, into Fernando's tapestry of affairs, he continued to devote himself first and foremost to music. His opera *Il Telemaco nell'Isola di Calipso* premiered in August 1797. On the day of its opening, *El Diario de Barcelona* announced it with great fanfare, emphasizing the youth of its composer. Subsequent issues of *El Diario* published poems praising both the work, and Sor himself. The opera enjoyed a successful run of performances throughout the 1797–98 season, and made Fernando's name a household word throughout Catalonia, and beyond. Upon hearing of his former pupil's rapid acclaim, Father Viola obtained a copy of the orchestral score, which remains preserved to this day—like a sacred relic—in the music archive of Montserrat.

To his credit, Fernando hardly rested on these laurels. Complacency never numbering among his faults, each new musical success spurred him on toward the next. His boundless creative energy of youth, and the unflagging encouragement he received from all quarters, inspired him to try his hand at every genre he encountered. In turn, his performances of original compositions were greeted with unending enthusiasm, and relentless demand for encores. In the flamboyant Italian idiom, with proven success, he wrote cavatinas, arias, and recitatives. In the native Spanish idiom, which he loved best and most truly, he wrote seguidillas, tonadillas, and boleros.

Sad news reached Fernando from Montserrat one cold December morning near the close of 1798. Father Anselm Viola, beloved teacher and musical mentor of so many boys for so many years, had gone to his reward. Fernando was temporarily overcome with grief, and composed a lugubrious tombeau in the French style. All who heard it were instantly reduced to tears. As Fernando's shock and sadness at his great teacher's death gradually subsided, he renewed his determination to honor Father Viola's memory by applying himself not only to composing and performing music, to also but to studying it. Not quite ready to compose in the pure classical idiom, and yet in awe of its incomparable maestros, he methodically analyzed the quartets of Haydn and Pleyel, and the concertos of Mozart. During that period he often carried on imaginary conversations with Father Viola, to see whether his dearly departed mentor would approve of his analyses.

Thus four years passed swiftly in Barcelona, as if in a whirlwind of inspiration, composition, performance, and adulation. Now the close of the eighteenth century drew nigh, and with it the opening of yet-unimagined horizons for this recently risen star of Catalonia. One evening, late in 1799, a uniformed courier from Villafranca brought Fernando a letter. It had been sent to him from Madrid, by special messenger, addressed to his military post in care of General Vives. The courier had tracked Fernando down to Isabella's abode, where he was visiting his dear mother and brother Carlos, who at age fourteen still lived at home. Isabella had prepared Fernando's favorite tapas, and the Sor family had been joined by Sofia and Joaquina. They had just opened a bottle of wine, and were about to propose a toast to Joaquina and Carlos, who had recently performed a bolero (written for them by Fernando) at a local recital, when the courier knocked on the door. He silently handed the envelope to Fernando, saluted him, bowed to the others, and departed without ado.

They handed the envelope around before opening it, somewhat agog with suspense, for its sealing wax bore the unmistakable imprint of the Dukedom of Alba de Tormes. The House of Alba was one of the richest and most important in the realm. Its heirs were Grandees of Spain. The current heiress, Doña María Cayetana de Silva, the 13th Duchess of

Alba, was by repute the most gorgeous, and also most notorious, woman in Iberia. The company gingerly passed the still-unopened envelope back to Fernando, and Isabella silently intoned a Hail Mary as he slit the seal and withdrew its contents—a single sheet of exquisite paper, bordered in gold leaf. Isabella nearly fainted at the whiff of perfume that suddenly permeated the room.

The recipient's cherubic countenance lit up as he scanned the scented missive. The gathered company, unable to hold back their excitement any longer, importuned with one voice, "Read it to us aloud, Fernando!" And so he did.

"It is written and signed by the Duchess's Secretary," he began, "but clearly it emanates from none other than Her Grace." (No one harbored any reason to doubt this, as the scent of her perfume still lingered heavily.)

"It is addressed to Maestro Fernando Sor, Lieutenant in the Army of General Vives, and Renowned Composer and Performer of Barcelona." (Here Fernando bowed gravely to them, in good-natured mockery of the salutation's adulatory tone.)

The 13th Duchess of Alba, Doña María Cayetana de Silva, hereby extends to Maestro Fernando Sor her most cordial and personal invitation to join the distinguished retinue of the House of Alba, as a resident teacher, composer and performer of music under the patronage of Her Grace. Anticipating the favor of your affirmative reply, a coach-and-four will be at your disposal in Villafranca during the first week of January 1800, to convey you in safety and comfort to Her Grace's Liria Palace in Madrid.
I beg to remain,
Your most humble and obedient servant,
José Sanchez
Secretary to the House of Alba

At this Isabella indeed fell into a dead faint, but was caught by Carlos and Fernando, who eased her into her chair, while Sofia hurried off to fetch medicinal brandy. Amidst all this sudden commotion, Joaquina alone remained motionless, although far from expressionless. Fernando alone caught a glimpse of her visage. She was staring at him unabashedly, with wide and shining eyes that unmistakably betokened two things: love, and admiration. He acknowledged her gaze by flashing her a warm smile, but when their eyes met it seemed as though everyone and everything around them temporarily vanished. He briefly lost track of time, or perhaps time itself had stopped, until Sofia bustled in with brandy, and Isabella was revived. No-one else appeared to have noticed the look that passed between them, and indeed transfixed them, although Fernando would dream of it, from time to time, in the coming years.

Until that moment he had never thought of Joaquina—nor indeed of any girl—in the light of love, and in point of fact had scarcely thought of her at all. Whenever he did so, it was always in the company or context of his brother Carlos. For Joaquina and Carlos were long-time neighbors, friends, playmates, classmates, and duet partners, and it always seemed a given thing that they would one day marry. And as they were now both fourteen, 'one day' was surely not far off. In that era, girls routinely wedded at fourteen or fifteen, to boys either not very much older—sixteen or seventeen—or older by as much as a factor of two or even more. In those days nobody raised an eyebrow if a girl of fifteen married a man of thirty, as long as he provided for her and their offspring.

As Carlos had matured into a young teenager, Isabella noted, with satisfaction and relief, that he was every inch his father's son. Sensible, methodical, and worldly, Carlos had learned his Latin without demur, and was preparing to enter the army or the civil service, thanks to the Sors' reliable contacts, by the age of sixteen or seventeen—now on the visible horizon. Of course, and again like his father, Carlos was also a talented amateur musician, who moreover loved music passionately, but who entertained no ambition greater than playing his guitar as a hobby, and for fun. One prodigy per household being more than enough, Isabella never neglected to give as much thanks to God for Carlos's normalcy as she did for Fernando's gifts. She and Sofia also assumed, without really discussing it, and without ever suggesting it to the children, that Carlos and Joaquina might one day wed. The two mothers were both content to let nature take its course, under the unerring guidance of the Holy Mother.

And what of Joaquina? Outwardly a quiet and obedient daughter, who made no trouble and encountered none, Joaquina guarded her inward life with understandable secrecy. She was growing into a great beauty, not of the shallow sensational kind that arrests men in the street and sprains their necks, only to be forgotten once out of eyeshot, but rather of the subtle yet deeply penetrating variety, barely noticeable at first—like the first pale light of dawn—but then gradually evanescing into a blazing luminosity that outshines every other star in the sky, rendering them all invisible. This was the beauty that Fernando had beheld, for the first time, when their eyes had locked.

Like all girls her age, Joaquina had wondered whom she would marry, and when, and how. Many of her friends had already embarked on that path, some with older men, and a few were even carrying their first babies. Joaquina was not in a particular hurry, for her full radiance was yet a few years away, and meanwhile she was trying to decide exactly what kind of love would claim her matrimonial heart. It seemed to her that she had only two choices in matter: ordinary love, or extraordinary love. Ordinary love was safe, secure, predictable, and—even if boringly domestic—the surest path to family, stability, and decency. By contrast, extraordinary love was dangerous, wild, unpredictable, and—even though exhilaratingly romantic—a rocky road to scandal, instability, and tragedy.

And while all girls her age at least fantasized about extraordinary love, many were willing or simply obliged to settle for ordinary love. But to the end of their days, these girls would always harbor some private regret at never having experienced the extraordinary. It would secretly torment them to the end of their days. Then again, those who dared to wade into the hazardous river of extraordinary love ran the risk of being swept away by its raging currents, and of drowning in them, never regaining the solid banks of the ordinary—or even worse, after having been saved from drowning by some ordinary gallantry, of craving the river's perilous rapids to the point of leaping back in. This only brought them regret of a different kind, but regret nonetheless. To make matters worse, each regret envied the other. Was there any escape from love's regrets? Or an antidote to them, other than death?

Yes, there was. A few fortunate girls had brief flings with extraordinary love, immersed in it up to their necks, then came to their senses and managed to extricate themselves before going under completely, scrambling back to the safety of the ordinary, and remaining there for the duration of their lives. Having experienced the best of both worlds, they had alone no regrets, or almost no regrets, of love.

And as Joaquina pondered her fate, she felt paralyzed by indecision, and pierced by daggers of dread. For it was her tragic destiny both to love Carlos in the ordinary way, and to love Fernando in the extraordinary way. She planned sensibly to marry and raise a family with Carlos, secure in his ordinary and protective embrace; yet she dreamed wildly of eloping with Fernando, even if it meant being consumed by flames of reckless rapture.

Joaquina hid this secret surpassingly well, in plain sight, for she made no effort to conceal it. Carlos simply assumed he would propose to her one day soon, and that she would accept; and she gave him no reason to doubt it, for the ordinary part of her heart indeed belonged only to him.

As for Fernando, he had harbored no thought of love for girls, who struck him as deeply mysterious, unpredictably moody, and exquisitely pleasurable playthings. To this point he loved only music, with all his heart, and music requited it. Girls provided sex, which had nothing to do with love. But all that had changed in an instant. Turnabout being fair play, the Duchess of Alba had suddenly invited Fernando to be *her* plaything, at least musically. At the very same moment, that shining look in Joaquina's eyes conveyed a radiant love, which Fernando had never before felt. When their gazes locked, he realized that an extraordinary part of her heart belonged only to him.

Perhaps fortunately for all three of them—Fernando, Carlos, Joaquina—the cathartic implosion of this impossible triangle would be brought about by a cataclysm of incomparably greater tragedy, as the plague of war would soon enough ravage Spain with a fury that would transform love of every kind to unadulterated madness, and would try their souls by ordeal in the crucible of a world gone mad.

Of this they had no inkling at the time, and so can be forgiven and endorsed for proposing a toast to Fernando's newest and literally crowning success; that is, once Isabella was roused from her swoon by brandy, and so made ready again to raise a glass of wine. As the full force of the letter sank in, it occasioned the proudest moment of her life. The hand of Divine Providence and the grace of the Holy Mother had raised her son to the threshold of ascendancy, to a station not even she had envisioned (although the gypsy fortune-teller had foreseen it). Fernando, not yet twenty-two, would shortly exercise his talents for the ears of Grandees! Isabella's bosom swelled with gratitude, and her soul lit up with joy. If she permitted herself a single unselfish regret, fleeting like the merest wisp of a cloud across an otherwise unblemished azure sky, it was the forlorn wish that Joan could be present to share in this moment of triumph, to rejoice in their son's success as much as she did. Isabella consoled herself in her faith that the angels could not fail to convey these glad tidings to her late husband on high.

For his part, Fernando learned a double lesson that evening; namely, what was true of love was equally true of patronage. For patrons also came in two varieties: the ordinary, and the extraordinary. Until now Fernando had been a beneficiary of the ordinary patronage of his fans: they could safely, dependably, and predictably be relied on to buy tickets to his performances, and to performances of his music by other artists. Ordinary patronage had been, and would never cease to be, the bread and butter of Fernando's musical career. But now he was on the verge of sampling the champagne and caviar of extraordinary patronage, a taste for which he acquired with ease. And luckily for Fernando, a future succession of extraordinary patrons would just as readily acquire a taste for his talents.

So there was never any question about accepting the Duchess's invitation, which was really more of a command. General Vives was enthralled to learn of it, and he immediately released Fernando from his military duties (which in truth had been largely fictitious anyway), listing him as 'inactive' until further notice, thus permitting him to retain his rank (without pay, of course) while keeping open the possibility of reinstatement at the same or higher rank, should future circumstances warrant it (as they soon enough would). He requested only that Fernando give a farewell recital for the troops at Villafranca, and Fernando was only too happy to oblige. His performance began with the usual popular Spanish forms, and lasted long into the night with a Bacchanalia of barrack-room ballads, in whose bawdy choruses the inebriated troops lustily joined.

It was just as well that the Duchess had sent a conveyance to Villafranca, for Fernando was too wobbly next day to mount a horse, let alone ride one. So he clambered gratefully into the cushioned coach and—alternately dozing and dreaming—gradually recovered from the previous night's revelry as the coach-and-four traversed the sun-baked interior plateau en route to Madrid, flanked by outriders courtesy of General Vives.

Traveling at a steady but far from brutal pace, it took a few days to reach the Duchess's palace in Madrid. Thus Fernando had plenty of time to ponder his farewell conversation with Sabater, over dinner in Barcelona, prior to his departure to Villafranca. The stately Catalan aristocrat had aged well, and still had all his wits about him, but even so time had taken its inevitable toll. Sabater had been compelled to sell his fine Arabian horses, for his gout made riding impossibly painful. His eyes were now clouded with cataracts but, as Fernando would learn, his political vision remained as acute as ever. Though he now carried a cane, Sabater still bore himself upright, and his words of advice to his godson were similarly forthright.

"My dear Fernando," Sabater began, as their supper's first courses were served to them, "you are about to enter a world as corrupt and profane as Montserrat was pure and sacred. You were well protected and well schooled in those holy Benedictine cloisters, but those now charged with protecting you in the slippery corridors of political power—starting with the Duchess of Alba—can scarcely protect themselves. And you will have to school yourself in the ways and wiles of royalty, for none of it is what it seems.

"Outwardly, these noble lords and ladies are paragons of politeness, epitomes of etiquette, and quintessences of charm. But that is merely paint and varnish. Inwardly, they are treacherous, self-regarding predators, ever-ready to promote anyone or anything that serves their momentary interest or instantaneous caprice; yet even readier to do away with anyone or anything that hinders their grander designs. Never have such power and wealth been concentrated in fewer hands, yet always are such hands prepared to wash one another in blood.

"While sycophantic ministers and their unctuous underlings attend to the hatching of political plots, the King and his lords hunt beasts of the field, while the Queen and her ladies hunt men of the court. Their majesties watched in abject horror as criminal rabble lately beheaded their cousins in France, yet continued their hunting as though Spain were immune to such murder, mayhem, and madness. Their majesties left it to the upstart opportunist Godoy to make a most unfavorable peace. But mark my words, dear Fernando: it will not long endure. While our King is content to hunt beasts, and his Queen to hunt men, a yet more formidable monster is rising in France, who will soon hunt them, and all the Kings and Queens of Europe to boot. From this monster Spain will not be spared, and may even be used to set an example to the others.

"So although you are patronized to make music and nothing else, pray be mindful of everything else. Trust no-one except yourself, and doubt even yourself at times. And if you seek advice, look chiefly to Goya, whom you will soon meet, for he too is patronized by the Duchess. Goya is a titan whose works will long outlive this age, for he paints to witness enduring truths, and not to whitewash expedient lies. Like you, Goya is a prodigy. And just as Father Arredondo once said of you, Goya also has a good heart, and the mind of a little devil—except in his case, if only half the rumors are true, a not-so-little devil.

"May God continue to protect and preserve you, my beloved son, and inspire you to make ever more magnificent music to His everlasting glory, and to the greatness of Catalonia, and of Spain."

Fernando committed these pearls of wisdom to his capacious auditory memory, and mulled them over on the road to Madrid. They would come to serve him well, and not only in Spain. Meanwhile, wherever they halted for the night, be it in a city like Zaragoza or a smaller town on their route, they were welcomed, fed and quartered at one or another of the Duchess's seemingly countless properties, be they palaces, villas, or country estates. So Fernando began to believe what was said of her vast wealth: that if she walked the length and breadth of Spain, from one end to the other, she could stay every night at one of her homes, and need never set a foot off her land throughout the entire journey.

Part 2. Fernando in Celebrity, 1800-1808

Chapter 7. Madrid, and Goya

Fernando's excitement mounted as they reached the outskirts of Madrid, and approached the city center. When at last the coach entered Calle de la Princesa, drove through the gilt gates of the Liria Palace, passed along its immaculately manicured front gardens and by its sculpted fountains, and halted in the forecourt, it was met by none other than the Duchess's Secretary, José Sanchez, who bowed and greeted Fernando as though he himself were royalty.

"Welcome to Liria Palace, Maestro Sor. You honor us immeasurably by your presence. Permit me to escort you to your quarters, and orient you to your new home." A footman shouldered Fernando's guitar, toted his luggage, and followed them at a discreet distance.

José Sanchez then guided the young maestro through the ornate portals of the main palace, where a pair of liveried sentinels saluted them, and into what seemed to Fernando a labyrinth of lavish corridors giving onto countless sumptuous rooms—designed for every occasion, furnished with luxurious decor, strewn with priceless heirlooms, and festooned with rare antiquities. The floors and Greco-Roman pillars were of finest Italian marble; the tapestries, of Gobelins Manufactory; the porcelains were Sèvres; the furniture, empire style. Archeological collections included painted ceramics from ancient Greece, and armor and weapons from every period.

Liria's art treasures alone were simply mind-boggling. The walls were hung with masterpieces by Pietro Perugino, Titian, Palma il Vecchio, El Greco, Anthonis Mor, Murillo, Zurbarán, Rembrandt,

Jacob van Ruisdael, Ribera, Rubens, Francesco Guardi, and, needless to say, Goya himself, who was then in residence. These were interspersed with engravings by Dürer, Mantegna, Lucas van Leyden and Van Dyck. Elegant pedestals boasted marble and bronze sculptures from early Roman through late Baroque periods. The library housed some nine thousand volumes, including a first edition of *Don Quixote*, the *Alba Bible*, an assortment of *Papal bulls* from the Vatican, letters by Christopher Columbus and Rousseau, and musical scores by Scarlatti.

José Sanchez led Fernando through the music room, an intimate Baroque recital hall that could comfortably seat one hundred guests. Among other instruments, it held a double-manual harpsichord by famed Hamburg builder—and friend of Bach's—Hieronymus Albrecht Hass, along with a pedal harpsichord built by Zacharias Hildebrandt, and a Viennese fortepiano. Its stringed instruments included both a violin and a cello by Stradivarius, and an assortment of Spanish laúds and bandurrias. Fernando was especially excited to see several brand-new Spanish guitars patiently waiting upright on stands, their varnish still gleaming, silently begging to be picked up and played. His own guitar, inherited from his father, was a serviceable but quite weather-beaten instrument made by Nicholas Duclos in Barcelona.

"The Duchess took the liberty of procuring for you some guitars from leading luthiers," José explained. "Please try them at your leisure. If they prove unsuitable, others can be found."

Fernando could hardly contain himself. For the moment, he simply ogled the beautifully polished woods and peered through the sound-holes to read the makers' labels: Lorenzo Alonso of Madrid, Joseph Martinez of Málaga, Juan and Joseph Pagés of Cadiz. The Duchess's agents had scoured Spain, and had rounded up these instruments from the best luthiers of the day. Indeed, their quality would not be exceeded by any in Sor's lifetime, though they would later be equaled by the Parisian luthier René Lacôte.

At last they reached Fernando's quarters, a suite of well-appointed rooms in a secluded wing of the palace, reserved for residents of grace and favor. The footman deposited Fernando's baggage, bowed, and took his leave. José pulled a bell cord, and in a few moments a butler arrived.

"This is Miguel," said José. "He will attend to your every need. He will show you where meals are served and, if and when you prefer, will have them sent to your rooms. He will orient you to the palace, and to its many activities and diversions. He will also arrange for a tailor to fit you out with a wardrobe—suitable attire for various functions such as high teas, formal dinners, and your own recitals of course. Her Grace will return in a few days, and will lunch privately with you then."

Reaching into his waistcoat, José drew out a small silk purse that rattled with coins, and handed it to Fernando.

"Here is your monthly pension from Her Grace. Should you require anything else whatsoever, Miguel and my humble self are at your service." With that, José prepared to bow and take his leave.

"Please forgive me," he added, "I almost forgot... Señor Francisco Goya would like to meet you this evening, for tapas, in his studio. Miguel will escort you there at 6 p.m. Now with your kind permission, I must attend to other duties." With that, José bowed and departed.

Fernando reposed briefly on a plush brocaded divan, admiring the sweeping vista of manicured lawns and splendid gardens, curved with flagged paths flanked by shapely trees that twittered with birdsong. He took in the princely decor of his own rooms, and gave bountiful thanks to God for his ongoing magic carpet ride from the saintly Escolania, to the bawdy barracks, to this heavenly abode of grace and favor. Only one thing was needed to complete these new surroundings—namely music. Immediately inspired, and ever mindful of his purpose in being transported here, Fernando pulled the bell cord to summon Miguel, who appeared forthwith.

"At your service, Maestro."

Fernando had counted the money in the purse, which held one thousand reales—five times his former monthly salary as a Lieutenant. So he had removed that modest amount, a mere two hundred, and pocketed it. Then he handed the purse, which still rattled with eight hundred reales, to the butler.

"Can you arrange to have this sent to my family in Barcelona?"

"But of course, Maestro. Please write down their name and address, and it shall be done forthwith."

At that, Fernando seated himself at the ornate writing desk, drew a sheet of exquisite hand-made paper from the stack in a drawer, dipped a swan quill pen into the glittering crystal ink bottle, and penned a note to his family:

Beloved Mother and Dearest Brother,
Trusting in Providence that you are both well, I am comfortably ensconced in the Liria Palace. Her Grace having provided for all my needs and wants, the enclosed portion of my pension will hopefully help provide for yours. A like amount will be sent to you monthly. Please forgive the haste of this note, as my mind is overcome with inspiration and fevered with excitement. New guitars impatiently await my playing, and Goya has invited me to meet him this very evening. I promise to write you every month, and keenly look forward to your replies and news. May God keep you both safe and sound.
Yours, with undying love and boundless devotion,
Fernando

Fernando folded the note and sealed it in a matching envelope. The seal was not that of the House of Alba itself but rather a handsome bas-relief of the palace, bearing the inscription 'From Liria, in Residence'. He addressed the envelope and handed it to Miguel.

Miguel bowed and asked "Will there be anything else, Maestro?"

"Yes: please bring me a guitar from the music room, along with its stand."

"At once, Maestro. Is there a particular instrument that you favor?"

For a fleeting instant Fernando felt like a Sultan being asked to choose a concubine from his harem. He mulled it over momentarily.

"Kindly bring me the Alonso of Madrid," he responded, in a show of loyalty toward his new city. He never regretted the choice. It proved to be the finest guitar he had ever played, and would ever play to the end of his prodigious days, rivaled later only by Lacôte. He became so absorbed in the new instrument, exploring its contours and savoring its colors, that he completely lost track of time. Although several hours passed, it seemed like only an instant later that Miguel was at his door again, pulling a silken cord that rang a small silver bell in his anteroom, signaling that the hour of tapas had arrived.

Miguel wordlessly guided Fernando through yet another labyrinthine wing of the palace, to a ballroom that had been converted into Goya's studio.

Never before had Fernando witnessed such a spectacle: the fashioning of immortal art from mundane material, the wresting of sublime order from utter chaos, and the ever-active portrait of the incandescent artist himself. It seemed as though Goya were dancing like a dervish from one easel to another, among tables laden with paints, pigments and jars, strewn with palettes, brushes and rags. His activities swirled from completed sketches to half-finished rococo cartoon tapestries to majestic portraits in progress, touching up this and refining that and painting over something else, beholding things first close up then from afar, squinting from every angle and glaring in every light, muttering to himself all the while, seemingly oblivious to Miguel and Fernando, who had paused at the threshold of the wide-open ballroom doors. Although meticulous to a fault, and willing to agonize for days or weeks over the merest dab of a brush or tint of a hue, Goya nonetheless conveyed the impression of a crazed conductor of an orchestra, trying to play all the instruments himself and at once, yet somehow succeeding. Fernando's eyes were soon drowning in symphonies of form and color, figure and ground, light and shade, likeness and distortion. Taking all this in, Fernando felt a surge of familiar delight, for Goya somehow reminded him of himself. Indeed, this first impression soon proved well founded.

Goya suddenly arrested himself in mid-brush-stroke, swirled to face the entrance, and beamed at Fernando. "Welcome, little brother! Do come in, sit down, and let us quaff a toast." He motioned toward a tapas table for two, under a capacious window through which the south-western light warmly bathed the setting. Laid with linen and silver, crystal and china, it was the only table in the room free of paints and brushes and other accoutrements of Goya's art. A bottle of Palomina fino sherry stood at the ready, from which Goya poured two generous libations into cut crystal goblets. "Here's to art," he proposed, and the pair emptied their glasses.

Once seated, they were served exquisite culinary art, an assortment of tapas whose recipes were gathered from every region of Spain, including gazpacho, tortilla española, pan amb tomàquet, croquetas with serrano ham, Andalusian calamari, patatas bravas, Manchego cheese with assorted olives and pickled garlic, all washed down with tempranillo from Ribera del Duerno.

As they ate and drank with gusto, Goya asked Fernando about the path that had led him from Barcelona's Dry Quarter to the Liria Palace. Fernando briefly summarized the highlights of his young life to date, and as he did so Goya's blazing eyes widened with amazement.

"You have already eclipsed me, Little Brother," complimented Goya. "For I am more than twice your age, and moreover had to struggle for more than half of my life to reach the path which you have apparently trod since birth."

"But Señor Goya," protested Fernando, "you are the most important painter in all of Spain, and—so it is widely said—famous throughout Europe besides! The highest and mightiest rulers would barter their realms to have you paint their portraits. My small accomplishments are nothing beside your great ones."

"First of all, Fernando," countered Goya, "you must call me 'Elder Brother' or 'Francisco'. For we are truly brothers under the skin, both progeny of the Muse, as well as old friends meeting for the first time. Second, your birth has been more fortunate than mine, for you were born under a happier star, and so your future will be that much brighter. And third, my best works already lie behind me, while yours yet await you. Mark well my words, Little Brother, for I am as gifted with sight as you are with sound. And my gift is not only vision of persons and events, but also vision into and through them, and on occasion even through time itself. And beholding you just now, I see greatness in early blossom, greatness which will flower most fragrantly in its time. Of course the Muse will exact a steep price for this, as She always does, even from a cheerful sort of genius such as yourself. Enjoy your innocence and youth while they last, Little Brother, for they will not last long."

And precisely because he was still young and innocent, Fernando can be forgiven for not entirely understanding what Goya was trying to tell him. Nonetheless, he felt that a deep bond of friendship had already formed between them, or, as Goya intimated, had somehow pre-existed their actual meeting. Fernando sensed, and correctly, that Goya was an intensely lonely man, isolated from the world by the very gift that had propelled him to this lofty station, and needing a friend of comparable talent with whom he could share his deepest experiences of life. That Goya had singled him out for such a friendship both flattered and awed Fernando.

"No-one can doubt your penetrating vision, Elder Brother, but at times it sounds quite daunting," replied Fernando. Wishing to learn more about his new-found old friend, he invited him: "Pray, tell me something of your early struggles."

At that, Goya's eyes misted over with remembrances, both of things worth recollecting and of things better forgotten. He had been born in 1746, in the Aragonese village of Fuendetodos, in the modest brick house of his parents, who belonged to the lower middle classes. His father was a gilder, earning his bread through decorative craftwork, mostly for religious purposes. At age fourteen, Francisco studied with the painter José Luzán, under whose tutelage he copied stamps for four years. Seeking more creative scope, he moved to Madrid to study with Anton Raphael Mengs, a German transplant who had become popular with Spanish royalty. But their fiery temperaments soon clashed, and Francisco was twice denied admission to the prestigious Real Academia de Bellas Artes de San Fernando. Goya was now twenty-two years old, and without further prospects in Madrid for the time being.

(Here he paused for effect, which was not lost upon Fernando who, now twenty-two himself, had virtually every prospect in Madrid laid at his very feet. Goya narrated without rancor, but this present irony was inevitable.)

So in 1668 Goya had set out penniless for Rome, a perennial Mecca for aspiring but impecunious artists. En route he fell in with a gang of bullfighters, which set the tone for a series of improbable adventures. He busked on the Roman streets, as a mediocre acrobat and an even worse guitarist, until a Russian diplomat hired him for a variety of nefarious purposes. He fell in love with a beautiful young nun, whom he attempted to seduce and plotted to abduct from her convent. He painted Greco-Roman mythology, and some of those early works had survived. But had not the divine hand of Providence held him in reserve for an incomparably grand role in art history—the last Old Master, the first modernist, and a peerless portraitist—Goya himself might not have survived.

(Fernando took in this rollicking autobiography dumbfounded beyond words. For the first time he now appreciated what a sheltered life he had led by comparison.)

Goya's artistic fortunes improved in 1771, when he won second place in a painting competition held in the city of Parma. This prize enabled him to return to Zaragoza and study with the well-connected Aragonese artist Francisco Bayeu y Subías. This time he befriended his master, and for good measure married his sister Josefa. Their long-suffering union gave rise to seven children, six of whom died in infancy. His portrait of her reveals a hopeful, doe-eyed young brunette, whose pale, almost translucent skin, rouged cheeks and white dress stand out bravely, if somewhat futilely, against an opaque background of impenetrable blackness. As with all of Goya 's portraits, this one too loaned itself to varying interpretations. No-one could be sure whether the starkly black background represented the dark side of their marriage, made sunless by the loss of so many offspring, or the dark side of the artist himself, which began to encroach on the very heels of his success.

Goya 's true trajectory revealed itself in the ripeness of time. Francisco Bayeu, a long-time member of the Real Academia de Bellas Artes de San Fernando, became director of the Royal Tapestry Factory in 1777. He arranged for Goya to receive commissions for a series of tapestry cartoons, which were used to decorate the royal palaces of El Escorial and the Palacio Real de El Pardo. Although this work was arduous, time consuming, and not particularly well paid, it made Goya's name known to the Spanish monarchs and their court. His decisive breakthrough came in 1783, when José Moñino y Redondo, the first Count of Floridablanca and chief minister to King Charles III, commissioned Goya to paint his portrait. In the process, Goya befriended the king's half-brother Luis, the Infante of Spain, and painted portraits of him and his family. These works were so well received that they led to a flood of similar commissions from

Spanish nobility. During the 1780s Goya painted portraits of the Duke and Duchess of Osuna, the Marchioness of Pontejos, and the Duke and Duchess of Alba, among other Grandees of Spain. In 1789—the ominous year of the French Revolution—Goya was appointed a court painter to Charles IV. The following year he attained the apogee of this inner orbit of select artists, being named First Court Painter, which carried an annual salary of 50,000 reales plus an allowance of 500 ducats for a coach.

"So you see, Little Brother," Goya observed, "your path has been like an arrow shot from God's own bow: flying swiftly and directly toward its target, unwavering and unerring in its flight. Whereas mine," he added wryly, "has been more like a half-blind drunkard climbing a steep mountain: prone to staggers, slips and tumbles."

Nonetheless, Fernando remained awestruck by Goya's ascent to artistic prominence, emanating as he did from such humble origins. "However did you sustain the resolve to triumph over adversity?" he asked.

"Ah, Little Brother," replied Goya with a twinkling eye, "that art lay in never experiencing adversity at all, at least in my youth. I merely wanted to paint, and never harbored any expectations of success or recognition. So I just painted, and lived to paint, and loved to paint—as I do to this day. Whether I had enough to eat, or a roof over my head, or a few coins to jingle in my pocket, were matters of small moment compared to painting. In 1778 (the year you were born, if I have it aright), I painted 'The Blind Guitarist', a merry but sightless busker who unfailingly attracted an admiring crowd. Most people do not realize that it was a metaphorical self-portrait of an artist who could not envision his own path. True adversity came only with success itself, when the jealous and petty-minded community of established painters perceived and sought to sabotage my rise."

"And how did they attempt that?" asked Fernando.

"In all the usual ways, plus some unusual ones," said Goya. "Typically, they circulated baseless rumors, salacious gossip, and malicious lies, hoping to discredit a competitor's character, thereby alienating his would-be patrons. But this rarely succeeds, since the lives of the patrons themselves are often more truly depraved than any of these fictions. So when those machinations failed, they preyed upon my less-than-robust physical and mental constitutions, which are prone to bouts of illness, and fits of melancholy. They claimed that I could never survive the rigors and demands placed upon a court painter ... But I proved them wrong!"

Here Goya made a sweeping gesture, indicating the depth and breadth and variety of masterpieces that he churned out of his studio with seemingly boundless energy.

At this Fernando nodded, in both appreciation and understanding.

"Perhaps, Elder Brother, this is our common bond: for I live to perform, as you live to paint."

At this Goya raised a glass, and toasted "*Vita brevis, ars longa.*"

While Fernando had swiftly identified his common bond with Goya, it would take him somewhat longer to discern the fundamental difference between them, namely one of temperament. Fernando's perpetually sunny disposition radiated an infectious *joie-de-vivre*, making people happy in his company. But Goya's darker and more sardonic side—which he tried but often failed to conceal—could make people distinctly uncomfortable. So when periodic bouts of melancholy overtook him, Goya usually went for long, solitary walks in forlorn or forbidding places, whether in reality or in his dreams. Then he secluded himself in his studio, shunning human company, keeping his demons at bay by painting them. He painted prisoners, lunatics, lepers, and witches. Evidently, his demons were at least as numerous as his patrons. Needless to say, these works did not adorn royal palaces; rather, they were closeted for posterity.

The hour of tapas having passed, Fernando made ready to take his leave. "Will you permit two parting questions, Elder Brother?" he inquired.

"Of course," said Goya.

"First, having attained the absolute summit of your art, how have you managed to remain so long at such a lofty yet doubtless precarious peak? Do you paint as you please, or to please your patrons?"

"An excellent question, Little Brother," complimented Goya. "And a pertinent one, as you will soon enough be commissioned to compose and play for them yourself. My answer is: neither. Above all, I paint to please my Muse. When She is pleased, everyone is pleased. Or at least, everyone who aims at pleasure and not displeasure. If I painted merely to please my patrons, they would soon distrust and even revile me, for they are surrounded by throngs of fawning sycophants constantly seeking to curry favor. They trust no-one, and with good reason. They possess such inconceivable wealth, and wield such unimaginable power, that their lives consist largely of interminable periods of utter boredom. These immensely boring existences are punctuated by inconsequential intrigues, or excited by ill-hatched plots, but are only rarely threatened by usurpation or dispossession. At such moments they experience terror beyond imagination, for they have far more to lose than anyone.

"Art affords them an entertaining escape from boredom, and a kind of second-hand immortality. For even their incomparable wealth and power cannot purchase time beyond that allotted them by Providence. Mortality weighs heavily on them. But when I paint their portraits, they know that they will live on, long after death. However their deeds are recalled or forgotten by history, their visages will endure, because Goya painted them.

"And why should they care who paints them (you may well ask), when they have at their beck and call the best portrait artists in Iberia, and for that matter Europe? Ah, Little Brother, I will share my secret with you. They want Goya to paint them because my portraits are mysterious to them, and to the art critics. No-one knows exactly what my likenesses intend, and so they foment debate and even controversy. This serves well to alleviate royal boredom, and also to titillate royal speculation. For if no-one can decipher my portraits, then they might mean anything, including whatever the subjects want them to mean. So by not seeking to please them, I end up pleasing them even more."

At this Goya suppressed an ironic chuckle.

"But why don't they simply ask you what your portraits mean?" inquired Fernando, straightforwardly if somewhat naively.

"Because, Little Brother, they are mostly afraid to know. At times I perceive my subjects more clearly than they perceive themselves. I see what I paint, and paint what I see. And sometimes I dream what I paint, and paint what I dream. My subjects are contented that Goya paints them. That in itself gives meaning to their lives. What the paintings actually mean is quite another matter, and of far less moment to them. And they are also wary of asking me because they do not wish to tax my impaired hearing. That disability has spared me from answering a good many questions." At this Goya smiled toothily, like a crocodile.

"But you seem to hear me fine, and are answering all of mine," Fernando said self-evidently.

"That is because we are brothers," said Goya.

At this, tears welled up in Fernando's eyes—tears of love and gratitude for being worthy of having such an elder sibling in spirit.

"Come, Little Brother, let me show you an example." Goya took his arm, and led him to the center of the studio, where a grand work in progress sat on an easel, shielded by a curtain. Goya flung back the curtain, revealing a near-completed portrait of the Royal Family. It was his inaugural major work as First Painter of the Court, and it would provoke centuries of heated debate.

"Pray, what is your initial impression, Little Brother?"

"To be perfectly candid, Elder Brother, they do not appear so very regal to me."

Goya laughed aloud. "Exactly right! Apparently your eye is as acute as your ear."

"But I do not understand," said Fernando."Will not they be insulted by such a plebian portrayal?"

"On the contrary," Goya replied. "They will adore it. They would be insulted by being over-regalized. Remember, Little Brother, this is Spain, where things are topsy-turvy. Flamboyant attire and arrogant demeanor are signs of vulgarity, reserved for *majos* and *majas*, whereas simplicity and modesty are signs of nobility. On several occasions I painted the current monarch's father, King Carlos III, a man much beloved for his piety. By far his favorite portrait depicts him in rustic hunting garb, not mounted but on foot, leaning on his musket like a country squire, a hound curled at his feet. He loved it because it made him look plain and pious, almost like a priest (aside from the gun).

Here Goya laughed again. "His children and their cousins are much more pretentious, and far more impious, so they will feel that much more flattered by my 'plebian' depiction, as you so justly call it."

And Goya was right. This painting would cement his position as First Court Painter for as long as he cared to hold it. Its treatment of the Royal Family would confer immunity even from the malignant monster who would succeed Charles IV, namely his son Ferdinand VII. He was still a youth at the time of this painting, and Goya made him appear benign, unremarkable, and almost likeable. This was Fernando's first glimpse of the future tyrant, who was to become his lifelong nemesis.

Goya's plausibly irreverent treatment was later vindicated by an incurably romantic Frenchman, a bohemian critic named Théophile Gautier. When he laid eyes on the painting, Gautier proclaimed that it looked like the picture of a corner grocer who had just won the lottery. This solecism swiftly made the rounds of the French salons, and from there all the courts of Europe. When the Spanish Royals heard, it, they immediately raised Goya's salary. In a normal monarchy, Goya might well have been clapped in irons, tortured, and sentenced to a dog's death for humiliating the Royal Family; only in Spain could he have been rewarded for it.

Goya alone had the temerity combined with the genius to portray his patrons as possessing the one thing they could never own, namely 'the common touch'. This was especially important to them in the wake of the French Revolution. Although they had never seen a corner grocer in their lives, and although winning a lottery would have added as much to their wealth as a thimbleful of sand to a beach, it nonetheless flattered their self-images, however ridiculously, to be portrayed as if somehow in solidarity with 'the people'. Goya was the only painter in Spain, and for that matter in Europe, who was capable of such a feat.

By now Fernando's head was spinning, not only from the sherry and wine, followed by port and single-malt whiskey, but also from these lessons in the politics of art, taught by a consummate master. Yet his curiosity was piqued.

"And one last question to round out this delightful evening, Elder Brother: what can you tell me of Her Grace, the Duchess of Alba, who favors us both in this magnificent abode?"

"Ah, Little Brother, now you are fishing in deep waters. She is my favorite subject: I have painted her more often than anyone, and in a vast variety of moods and settings. Every time she sits for me, she appears in a new light. Each portrait of her is complete in itself, yet each one captures only a facet of her character. If I painted her from now until Doomsday, I might never come to know her fully. She is mysterious and perhaps unknowable, even to herself. She is a veritable Grandee among Grandees: beautiful, cultivated, and wise beyond her years; a woman of charm, wit, and impeccable taste in all the arts—which is why she brought us here. You will meet her soon enough, and form your own impression."

"I can hardly wait," replied Fernando.

"She will not keep you waiting long," affirmed Goya. "But, all that said, she is also in grave danger."

"But why?" Fernando asked.

"Because, Little Brother, women have three ways of endangering themselves: either by throwing themselves at men, or by attracting the wrong sort of men, or by attracting too many of the right sort of men. By virtue of her station and condition, Her Grace is immune from the first two ways. But by the same token, she is unfortunately more vulnerable than most to the third. She had made a perfect match in 1776 when, at age fourteen, she wedded Don José Álvarez de Toledo Osorio y Gonzaga, 11th Marquis of Villafranca, Grandee of Spain, *jure uxoris* Duke of Alba de Tormes. He was only twenty at the time, but their union made them the wealthiest couple in the kingdom, rivaled only by the Duke and Duchess of Osuna. You would have admired the Duke of Alba, and he you, because he was (among other things) a great lover of music, and a fine amateur violinist. He commissioned me to paint him thus: at leisure, clad in hunting attire, but in a pensive air, perusing a score of Haydn's songs.

"Unfortunately, the Duke died in 1796, leaving their marriage without issue and heir. Whereupon the widowed Duchess, without conspicuous effort or deliberate intent, succeeded in attracting virtually every man of substance in the realm, and beyond. It is not the quantity of such admirers, but rather the jealousy of their lovers and consorts, which maintains her in constant peril. And of all jealous women (and they are all jealous, more or less) no woman is more dangerous to her rivals—be they real or imagined—than a jealous Queen ... Enough said. Just keep it under your hat."

And with that they hugged, and parted company. Miguel escorted Fernando back to his quarters. His excitement was so great that he could barely fall asleep. He replayed the grandeur of the evening over and over, setting it to music in the orchestra of his dreams.

Chapter 8. Madrid, and Godoy

During that winter of 1800, while Fernando settled in at Liria, His Majesty King Charles IV, according to his daily wont, was out on the hunt. He deemed hunting to be the proper pursuit of sovereigns, if not their God-given duty. He felt that politics and other sordid affairs of state lay far beneath the dignity of a monarch, and were best attended to by ministers and other servants, both public and civil. In any case, His Majesty had no aptitude for politics, whereas he was—at least according to everyone at Court—a most accomplished hunter. Once he had finished hunting for the day, he habitually repaired to the palace to arrange the next day's hunt. Later in the evening, over long and lavish dinners, while entertained by French musicians, he and his royal company regaled one another with memorable tales of past hunts, and plans for future hunts. A veritable army of servants had to be enlisted, trained and organized for a successful hunt, ranging from hounds and their keepers, to horses and their handlers, to beaters for flushing the quarry, to chasers for rounding up lost dogs, to tailors for crafting equestrian garb, to cooks for rendering the bounty fit for the royal table. Only a King could command such a complex undertaking with a suitable degree of aplomb, and His Majesty devoted himself to it with a will. Moreover, he knew that as long as Godoy was managing the political affairs of the realm, His Majesty need never trouble himself on that account.

While the King was busy hunting in the winter months of 1800, Manuel Godoy was indeed attending to political affairs, in the company of none other than his closest confidante, the Queen Consort, Maria Luisa of Parma. Daughter of the Duke of Parma, and grand-daughter of King Louis XV of France, she had been born and bred to this station.

While she encouraged her husband and cousin, the King, to indulge the fantasy that it was manly of him to hunt, in fact he was a weakling, and completely subservient to her whims. In contrast, her companion at breakfast that morning (and most mornings, if the gossip was only half-true) had been born Manuel Godoy y Álvarez de Faria, a *hidalgo* in remote Badajoz, of noble but impoverished lineage, and had been bred as if by surrogate parents: undisguised audacity and naked ambition.

In 1784, at age seventeen, Godoy had moved from Badajoz to Madrid, where he joined the Royal Bodyguard. His singing, guitar playing, and womanizing soon brought him to the attention of the Court, where he became an improbable favorite of the Queen. Her Majesty fell hopelessly in love with him, and immediately prevailed upon the King to shower him with seemingly endless promotions, titles, and powers, and ultimately with duties which—tragically for Spain—he was remarkably ill-equipped to discharge. Godoy's main qualification was, and would remain, that the Queen loved him without reservation, and would do all in her power to grant his every wish, particularly if it would keep him too distracted by pomp, circumstance, and affairs of state to pursue his apparently insatiable appetite for women. Thus abetted by the Queen's unremitting favor, Godoy was promoted in 1788 to Cadete Supernumerario of the royal palace, in 1789 to the rank of Colonel and a knight of the Order of Santiago, and in 1790 to Commander of that Order.

Having thus whetted Godoy's appetite for power, the Queen proved only too eager to permit this improbable upstart to play upon her misplaced affections in exchange for yet more power. In January 1791 Godoy was promoted to Adjutant-General of the Royal Bodyguard; in February he was named Field-Marshal; in March, Gentleman of the Chamber. There followed a brief lull, to give the tailors time to fit him out in all the required uniforms. Once suitably attired for these occasions, Godoy resumed his meteoric career. In July 1791, he became Lieutenant-General and Knight Grand Cross of the Order of Charles III. Yet even at this juncture he was barely getting started.

Later that year, the Count of Floridablanca—Spain's most able statesman of the eighteenth century, Goya's first royal patron, and at the time Prime Minister—accused Godoy of carrying on an adulterous affair with the Queen. It goes without saying that royal marriages were arranged for political reasons—to cement relations between sovereigns and to produce legitimate heirs—but that every gentleman of condition kept as many mistresses as he could decently (or, come to that, indecently) manage. The more prominent the mistress, the greater his reputation as a philanderer. Ladies of condition, obedient to the double standard dictated to them by Nature, first fulfilled their marital obligations by bearing heirs to their line, and only then took a succession of lovers, but always more discreetly, as modesty and reputation demanded. Devout Catholics one and all, they nonetheless considered themselves exempt from the seventh commandment, as a birthright. So Floridablanca did not object to the tryst between Godoy and the Queen per se; but rather to their complete lack of discretion, which at times appeared embarrassing to the King, and therefore to the throne.

But owing to Her Majesty's relentless machinations and total power over Charles IV, the accusation backfired, and Floridablanca was obliged to resign from the office of Prime Minister in 1792. This opened the door to Godoy, who seized upon the opportunity and, abetted by the Queen's influence, persuaded the King to appoint him to the office. Godoy's first term as Prime Minister proved to be an ill-starred prelude to the complete disaster of his second term, but by now he had a virtual stranglehold on power. In that same year he was named Duke of Alcudia, which also carried a Grandeeship. Soon after he became a Knight of the Order of the Golden Fleece, *and* Captain General. Then he acquired the titles of Duke of Sueca, Marquis of Alvarez, and Lord of Soto de Roma, along with the office of Minister for Foreign Affairs of Spain. By now Godoy had taken up quarters in the royal palace in addition to his own nearby palace, where he occupied not only his own spacious apartments but also kept another capacious suite merely to house his uniforms, and all their accoutrements.

Godoy's policy of neutrality toward France did nothing to spare King Louis XVI from the guillotine. But after that King's head rolled in 1793, a general protest erupted in Madrid's noble circles, and Spain was obliged to join the alliance against the French Republic. This resulted in the War of the Pyrenees, in whose aftermath Godoy negotiated two unfavorable treaties with France. The second of these, signed in 1796, supposedly guaranteed Spain's border with France but compelled Spain to declare war on Great Britain. Although this would lead to nothing but more conflict, Godoy was given the ironic title 'Prince of Peace'.

Next, the Queen made a serious attempt not only to curtail Godoy's amorous affairs, but also to divert attention from their own scandalous relationship. Her strategy of distracting him from women by conferring titles and associated duties on him had completely backfired, as the more important he became the more women threw themselves at him. She found herself increasingly jealous of her two main rivals: Josefa Petra Francisca de Paula (Pepita) de Tudó y Cathalán, and the Duchess of Alba, whom the Queen hated with a special passion.

Josefa was the daughter of Antonio de Tudó y Alemany—Brigadier of the Royal Spanish Armies and Governor of the Royal Palace of Buen Retiro—and a Noble Dame of the Royal Order of Queen Maria Luisa herself. When Godoy persuaded the King to grant Josefa the titles of 1st Condesa de Castillo Fiel, and later the 1st Vizcondesa de Rocafuerte, the Queen flew into a rage. She was already in a perpetual fury over the Duchess of Alba, not only because of her amorous flings with Godoy, but also because Godoy had just commissioned Goya to paint a nude of her for his secret collection, to which the brazen hussy—Duchess or not—had actually acquiesced. Godoy kept these nudes locked away in a concealed room, and showed them only to trusted male friends (with the exception of the Duchess herself, who had insisted on seeing them); but the Queen had spies everywhere, and Godoy's gaze could not fall upon anything—especially a woman, whether in the flesh, painted on canvas, or beheld in a dream—without it being reported to the Queen.

Future historians of art would credit Goya as the first modernist for painting this nude, at the time a highly risqué undertaking that would soon enough attract the Inquisition's enmity, but they would never agree on the identity of the model for *La Maja Desnuda*. Opinion would come to be divided between Josefa, and the Duchess. As the Queen passionately hated them both, she didn't particularly care which one Goya had painted nude. She now laid intricate plans to divert Godoy's attentions from both of these mistresses, and onto herself.

In 1797 she arranged for Godoy's marriage to Doña María Teresa Carolina de Borbón y Vallabriga, Farnesio y Rozas, the 15th Countess of Chinchón, and a cousin of the King. Maria Teresa agreed to this marriage because it restored the family's fortune, which had been confiscated in a scandal involving her uncle, the 13th Count. This marriage not only distracted Godoy from Josefa, but also obscured his affair with the Queen. Her plan to eliminate her other chief rival, the Duchess of Alba, was more intricate, and would take longer to bring to fruition.

So during those winter mornings of 1800, while the King was out hunting, the Queen and Godoy habitually breakfasted together, and plotted their next political moves. Just now, the Queen was about to prevail upon the King to reinstate Godoy for a second term as Prime Minister. He had been removed from that office in 1797, and relieved as Foreign Minister in 1798, on account of his unpopular handling of ongoing troubles with France, and persistent rumors of his affair with the Queen. They had finished their breakfast of candied oranges, pickled quail's eggs, and jellied lark's tongues, and had dismissed the food-tasters and the servants. Thus they were free to speak openly, and intimately.

"Dearest Manuel," the Queen began, "We see that your brow is knitted with more than usual concerns this morning. Pray, what troubles you, my Prince?"

Indeed, Godoy's title 'Prince of Peace' was unusually pretentious, considering that he was neither a member of the Spanish royal family nor heir to any throne. Nonetheless, he was permitted to utilize it officially, although the Queen called him 'My Prince' as a term of endearment. Everyone else, members of the royal family and intimate friends excepted, was obliged to address him as 'Your Highness'.

"Dearest Maria Luisa," Godoy replied, "you are unfailingly perceptive. It seems to me that the title 'His Highness, The Prince of Peace' is somehow lacking in distinction. I am vexed by an inability to decide which improvement would be more suitable: either 'His Highness, The Most Excellent Prince of Peace', or 'His Highness, The Most Serene Prince of Peace'. What do you think, my Queen?"

"We can think of no reason," the Queen replied, "why you should not employ both. It strikes us that 'His Highness, The Most Excellent and Most Serene Prince of Peace' is more suitable than either improvement alone."

"A thousand thanks, my Dearest! So shall it be done. Your wisdom is truly unsurpassed, except of course by your beauty."

At this Her Majesty blushed visibly, despite her several thick layers of white pancake makeup and rouged cheeks. It always warmed her heart to be flattered by Godoy, and by Godoy alone. Others who complimented her were mere fawning sycophants seeking to curry favor, untrustworthy in precise proportion to the degree of their unctuous adulation.

His Highness, The Most Excellent and Most Serene Prince of Peace, smiled at her. It was a thin smile, made difficult by his own thick layers of white pancake makeup and rouged cheeks, even thicker than the Queen's. The pair of them looked like fragile porcelain dolls; had either smiled too broadly their faces might have cracked like eggshells.

"And which affair of state compels your first attention this morning, My Prince?" the Queen inquired.

At this Godoy's pancaked brow furrowed narrowly anew. "That remains to be seen, My Queen… Perhaps I should summon the tailor, to design a Most Excellent and Most Serene Princely outfit?"

"A brilliant idea," said the Queen approvingly, "and while you're thus occupied, don't neglect your new Prime Minister's attire. His Majesty will re-appoint you any day now, and it would never to do re-assume that office in your former costume."

"So shall it be done," Godoy asserted. "But enough of these boring affairs of state! Let us contemplate the arts. Will you attend the upcoming Madrid debut of the young Catalan guitarist Fernando Sor? I am informed that a date will soon be announced. Rumors compare his artistry to sheer wizardry."

"We should like to hear him," the Queen replied, "but you know full well that we shall never set foot in any palace belonging to that strumpet, the Duchess of Alba. You yourself must go hear him play, My Prince, and bring us back a report. If he lives up to the gossip, we will arrange a command performance. And pray go accompanied by your wife, and not your mistress!" she gently admonished, but with a trace of rancor.

"So it shall be done, My Queen."

Their breakfast conversation concluded, they resumed their onerous affairs of state. His Highness, The Most Excellent and Most Serene Prince of Peace, returned to his apartments and summoned the royal tailor. Meanwhile Her Majesty the Queen schemed to manipulate King Charles IV into expediting Godoy's re-instatement as Prime Minister, just as soon as His Majesty returned from the hunt.

Chapter 9. Madrid, and the Duchess of Alba

Fernando had been in residence only for a week or so when, as Goya had intimated, the Duchess of Alba returned and invited him to lunch privately with her. Anxious to make a good impression, Fernando wore some of the new attire the shoemaker and tailor had run up for him: leather riding boots, knee-high stockings, skin-tight breeches, silk blouse with ruffled collar, and embroidered velour jacket. Indeed, the gentlemen of condition of the day were more vainly dressed than their ladies, who had to be strapped into whalebone corsets, layered with lacy petticoats, and buttoned into long silk dresses adorned with sashes and bows. Only the ladies' jewelry revealed the marks of their station, just as men's military insignia revealed their rank. Compared with the ladies, the men appeared as vain as peacocks, even though their clothing was on the whole reserved compared with the sheer gaudiness and ridiculous flamboyance of the *majos*.

Although Fernando was by now familiar with the main highways and byways of Liria Palace, on this day José Sanchez led him into *terra incognita*: the Duchess's wing, and her private dining room. There she received him, at a table laid for two. José made the formal introduction:

"May it please Your Grace, it is my privilege to present Maestro Fernando Sor… Maestro Sor," he continued, "please meet Her Grace María Cayetana de Silva, the 13th Duchess of Alba."

The Duchess extended her arm, offering the back of her perfumed, jeweled hand, which Fernando bowed and kissed.

"At your service, Your Grace," he offered.

"Maestro Sor, you do us great honor with your presence at Liria," replied the Duchess, well pleased at his appearance and demeanor. "We hope that your sojourn here will prove inspiring and fruitful."

"Your Grace affords inspiration beyond words," Fernando said, "whose fruits, it is hoped, with prove delectable to Your Grace's esteemed palate."

The Duchess smiled sweetly at him. She then dismissed José, asking him to have their lunch sent in. José bowed, and took his leave.

"In private, I shall call you Don Fernando," the Duchess said, "and you may call me Doña María."

"Very well, Doña María."

"Is everything to your liking here at Liria, Don Fernando?"

"'Liking' is too modest a word, Doña María. Everything is simply magnificent."

"You are too kind. If a truth be told, I maintain this palace mostly for show. One must always keep up appearances in Madrid. But one day you must visit my favorite palace, the seat of the House of Medina-Sidonia (of which my late husband was also Duke) in the Andalusian seaside town of Sanlúcar de Barrameda. The air is invigorating, the light enchanting, and the sherry second to none. Goya also loves the place, and has painted some of his finest portraits there."

"Thank you. I greatly look forward to it."

"You too will love it... But first things first: we must arrange your debut recital here in Madrid. I can hardly wait to hear you play, and sing. And I want to introduce you to the ruling circle. If you are even half as accomplished as your reputation proclaims, the Grandees of Spain will clamor for encore performances, like *majos* and *majas* at a bullfight, and will keep you well heeled with commissions besides.

"It will be a signal honor to play for you, Doña María... and for your circle. What are your preferences for the program?" asked Fernando.

"It is well that you ask. For quite some time, our Bourbon court has been under the spell that only the music of France is fit for royal ears," the Duchess replied, "even though the ears of their French cousins have been rendered permanently deaf by the guillotine" (this she added *sotto voce*). "Pray, give us a program of Spanish music, and nothing else.

Nothing French, nothing Italian, nothing German. Remind us of the greatness of our own traditions, and the grandeur of our own styles."

"It will be a joy to do so," said Fernando.

"Are the instruments suitable?" she asked.

"More than suitable!" declared Fernando. "Doña María, you have provided the finest guitars this side of paradise."

"Wonderful! Then I look forward to hearing them played by the finest guitarist this side of paradise."

At this Fernando blushed, and the Duchess smiled at his modesty.

"And to assist your preparations," she added, "I have placed at your disposal a suite of rooms at a well-appointed hotel on the Gran Via, called the Excelsior, quite close to here. You may repair to this hotel at any time, and remain there at your leisure, whenever you require absolute privacy, and complete liberty from the commotion of the palace."

Now it was Fernando's turn to smile, in appreciation of the Duchess's thoughtfulness. While strangers to the daily routine of a palace might deem it a tranquilly spacious and serenely cloistered abode, nothing could be further from the truth, especially when its proprietor or proprietress was in residence. At such times it became a hive of interminable hustle and bustle, especially in a capital city like Madrid. Even Fernando's brief experience at Liria attested to this.

Breakfasts were served at a huge octagonal oaken table seating up to twenty-four guests, in a cork-paneled breakfast room adjacent to the capacious kitchen. Here one rubbed elbows with nobles, ministers, diplomats, generals, admirals, judges, and artists. The guests lingered over endless cups of café *cortado*, catching up on all the latest salacious gossip, social rumor, or political scandal. They maintained a perfect double standard: it was understood on the one hand that every word was uttered in utmost confidence, while on the other hand that every word worth repeating would somehow be spread far and wide by midday, throughout the populace, right down to the buskers in the Plaza Mayor.

After breakfast guests engaged in a variety of activities, from riding to hunting to court tennis to croquet, or simply strolling in the gardens. Lunch was generally served in the conservatory, where guests were surrounded by exotic flowers and plants, with views onto the lawns and ponds and beehives. After lunch it was time for a siesta, and for reading or catching up on correspondence. By late afternoon tapas would be on offer, usually in the games room, where guests could play cards or billiards, or perhaps be amused by a travelling gamesman who set up a portable casino and proceeded to fleece them in a highly entertaining style. Soon after tapas it was time to dress for supper, a formal affair held in the main dining room, with lords and ladies attired in all their finery, attended by swarms of servers bearing endless exotic courses, prepared and plated by a corps of sous chefs, chefs de partie, and commis chefs, assisted by platoons of kitchen porters and dishwashers, all under the exacting command of the head chef, who would take either all the credit or all the blame for every tidbit of each course placed before the discerning diners.

After supper, the sexes were customarily segregated. The men repaired to the library to imbibe digestives (Cognac, Armagnac, Calvados, Grappa, or single-malt whiskey), and to smoke cigars, a new-fangled habit lately arrived from Cuba, and—free of the clinging and cloying company of women—to engage in unadulterated man-talk, mostly about politics, hunting, and bullfighting. The women, pretending to pout at being excluded from the man-talk, were ushered into a plush salon, and soon busied themselves sipping tea and putting on airs and engaging in girl-talk—mostly about fashion, decor, society, and all the latest gossip since breakfast.

By the wee hours it was time to retire, to collapse into a plush, four-poster canopy bed, and to sink into well-sated slumber, recuperating sobriety and energy for the next day's relentless round of activities.

Fernando had swiftly realized that living in a palace left little time for solitary devotion to one's art, unless one wanted to risk being branded an anti-social misfit: not a good idea among a throng of potential patrons. Only someone like Goya could get away with it. Walling himself off behind canvasses and behaving like an ogre when strong-armed into genteel company seemed to enhance his reputation. By contrast, Fernando's vivacious personality and convivial demeanor made him the life of a party, at which he could have made a living had he not been so musically gifted.

Thus he was thrilled to hear that the Duchess had so thoughtfully provided a secluded retreat on the nearby Gran Via. She had truly afforded him the best of both worlds: immersion with the ruling class, along with insulation from the corrosive effects of over-exposure to it.

"However can ever I thank you, Doña María," Fernando inquired, "for such incredible largesse?"

"You will thank me many times over, Don Fernando, merely by being as talented as you are," replied the Duchess. "Ultimately, it is Spain herself that will owe *you* a debt of gratitude. But meanwhile I ask you to promise me just one thing."

"Pray, name it. Your wish is my command, Doña María."

"Very well. It is only this: you must never refer to yourself as a musician, nor even think of yourself as a musician."

"Consider it done—or rather, not done," Fernando promised. "But if it pleases you, Doña María, kindly explain why."

"Because, Don Fernando, to the ruling class a musician is no different than any other servant, be he a tailor, a gardener, or a butler. The nobility's social world is governed by three simple relations: greater, equal, or lesser. Since you are not their peer, you cannot be an equal. Therefore you must be either a greater, or a lesser. If you self-identify as a musician, you will be regarded as a lesser, and moreover as least among lessers, since what you provide is ephemeral rather than tangible. To them, a musician is only a busker, while a patronized musician is merely a successful busker who has contrived to busk with a roof over his head."

"Then how should I refer to myself, and conceive myself?" Fernando asked.

"Always and only as a *composer*," said the Duchess emphatically. "For then you will be regarded as an immortal, and therefore as a greater. Haydn, Mozart, and Beethoven were all child prodigies (as you were, it is said), and phenomenally accomplished pianists (as you are a guitarist). But they were, and are, and ever shall be known as composers, not mere musicians. They are immortals (as you shall be). And that is why they were patronized: to confer a touch of immortality upon their patrons, by virtue of composing for them. Musicians come and go; composers are forever. Be forever, Don Fernando! Promise me this, and I shall be forever with you," the Duchess implored.

At this, several scales fell from Fernando's eyes, and he suddenly beheld the Duchess in a new light. To be sure, Goya was correct about her visage, and her character. Her eyes glittered when she spoke, and as she inclined her head this way and that, her beauty gleamed and sparkled like the facets of a priceless gem. Fernando formed the distinct impression that he was beholding not one Duchess, but many, each of which revealed herself in a different pose, just as Goya had painted them: here the White Duchess, there the Black Duchess, now la Maja Vestida, then la Maja Desnuda. Fernando also understood why so many men were attracted to her: she was not simply a beautiful and brilliant woman, but rather several beautiful and brilliant women, all rolled into one.

Fernando also realized that the Duchess was not merely his patron; rather, a kind of mother, mentor, and guardian angel, Heaven-sent to guide him on this stage of his exemplary path. And he was not wrong. The only thing he missed, or rather heard but did not fully understand, was the note of urgency in her voice when she spoke of immortality. She must have had a premonition that her life was destined to be cut short, and it consoled her greatly to know that Fernando would dedicate compositions to her. For his part, Fernando's heart was made so glad by this conversation with the Duchess, and all the developments it portended, that he was overcome with gratitude and overwhelmed by inspiration.

"So it shall be done. I promise never to be a musician, Doña María, and always to be a composer—and moreover to dedicate my most heartfelt compositions to you. I yearn to begin! Shall we set a date for the recital?"

"Indeed we shall, Don Fernando. Let us say in six weeks hence, to coincide with the Spring equinox? Let the season of rebirth and your blossoming career reveal their abundance together. I will make all the arrangements. You need only ready yourself to enchant the Grandees of Spain. I see that you are keen to begin your preparations. José will escort you to the Gran Via, and to your suite of rooms in the Excelsior Hotel, where your privacy is assured. Know that I own the hotel, and that its manager and all his staff are my trusted servants, who will attend to your every need with utmost discretion."

Fernando bowed, and kissed her hand, and José appeared on cue. They took their leave of this remarkable woman, and straight away Fernando returned to his quarters to pack up some clothes and other essentials, along with his Alonso guitar, all of which Miguel toted to a waiting carriage.

"The hotel is only a few minutes from here," assured José. "Once you are installed there, you may prefer to walk back and forth from Liria, at your leisure. Or, at any time, you can summon a carriage to convey you in either direction."

"Thank you, José."

"At your service, Maestro Sor."

Thus completely liberated from the daily routine of the palace, provisioned to a fault by the hotel staff, and highly motivated by his upcoming recital, Fernando threw himself into preparations with a will. He composed and rehearsed like a man possessed. The Duchess had thoughtfully installed a piano in his suite, which facilitated composition. Between periods of intense immersion in his planned program, he took solitary walks around Madrid, imbibing the music that poured from every tavern, church, plaza, and alleyway. For this was Spain, where music was in the very air. From the buskers in the Plaza Mayor to the revelers at the Puerta del Sol, from the Italian opera house to the Flamenco clubs of the theater district, from the devotional music in houses of worship on seemingly every block to the *pasodoble* of the bullfighting arena, Fernando absorbed and re-synthesized it all. His ear even took in the exotic birdsong in Retiro Park.

In 1800 Madrid was much smaller than it is today, and Fernando could cross the city in any direction, on foot, in little more than half an hour. For a carefree young man with a famous patron and burgeoning social connections, in the capital of a former empire whose immediate horizons were still unclouded by war, in a city rich with arts and cultures and handicrafts, at once decadent and vibrant, life was truly magnificent. Fernando often caught himself singing aloud on these walks, out of pure joy.

As the vernal equinox approached, and with it the evening of his recital, Fernando sensed himself on the cusp of momentous change. Everything would hinge on this maiden performance at Liria—but to such occasions was he born, and would never fail to rise. Now dressed to the nines, fingers warmed up, and instrument tuned, he waited alone and excitedly in a small salon adjacent to Liria's music room, which was packed with a highly expectant and most distinguished audience. At the appointed hour, José Sanchez came in to fetch him.

"At your pleasure, Maestro. Her Grace has introduced you, and the audience awaits you."

Fernando followed him through a short adjoining corridor, to the connecting doors. José flung these open, and Fernando strode into the music room to a standing ovation. He bowed deeply, and the patrons retook their seats.

Their chairs had been arranged in three banks. Directly facing him were several Grandees of Spain. The Duchess of Alba sat in the front row, beaming at him. On her right sat her close friend the Duke of Medinaceli, and on his right the Duke and Duchess of Osuna. To her left sat His Highness, The Most Excellent and Most Serene Prince of Peace, along with his new wife, the Countess of Chinchón. Beside them sat Luis María de Borbón y Vallábriga, formerly Archbishop of Toledo, newly elevated to Cardinal of Spain. Several rows behind were occupied by a variety of lesser nobles.

To their left, another bank of chairs was reserved for leading public intellectuals, especially the most prominent exponents of the Spanish Enlightenment, many of whom were also Goya's friends. The front row included the reformist statesman, judge, philosopher and author Gaspar Melchor de Jovellanos, and beside him his close friend, the poet, dramatist, man of letters and royal librarian Leandro Fernández de Moratín. Next to them sat Goya; behind them, an array of other liberal intellectuals and reformists.

To the right of the nobles, another bank of chairs was reserved for leading composers and performers of the day, at least those sympathetic to the Duchess of Alba's taste for Spanish music. In the front row of that bank sat Girolamo Crescentini, the celebrated Italian castrato (sopranista), composer, and singing teacher. In his current post as Director of the Teatro Nacional de São Carlos, in Lisbon, he often travelled to Madrid. Beside him sat the young Spanish opera singer Isabella Angela Colbran, a mezzo-soprano of extraordinary range and promise, who had studied with Crescentini in Paris. She would later relocate to Naples as the prima donna of the Teatro di San Carlo company, and there wed the famous operatic composer Gioachino Antonio Rossini. To her right sat the virtuoso cellist and composer Ridolfo Luigi Boccherini, who was writing concert pieces for the Marquis de Benavente. Just behind them sat a sixteen-year-old Madrileño guitarist and aspiring composer named Dionisio Aguado y García. He and Fernando were destined to become close friends for life—really more like brothers.

As mentioned and witnessed thus far, Fernando had a knack of rising to important occasions. Although the importance and altitude of this particular one far outstripped anything in his still-tender experience to date, he succeeded without hesitation or difficulty in mesmerizing even this discerning audience with his copious talents. At the Duchess of Alba's specific request, Fernando had prepared a program exclusively of Spanish music. He began with some charming Catalan folk songs—which he never would have insulted his family and friends in Barcelona by calling 'Spanish', but which these Castilians in Madrid accepted as their due. He continued with more purely Spanish forms, including boleros, seguidillas, and tonadillas which he had adapted or composed. The audience was enchanted by the richness of his voice, and dazzled by the virtuosity of his playing. To the appreciation of the cognoscenti, he had even embellished this traditional repertoire with subtle classical flourishes and operatic touches, which hinted at the range of his broader musical palate.

One hour and two encores later, Fernando Sor was a 'made man' in Spanish musical circles and, by virtue of the inevitable gossip that soon circulated far and wide, he became an increasingly known quantity—at least by repute—in Portugal, France, and Italy. For his maiden recital in Madrid not only had a transformative effect on his career; it also transformed the audience itself. They were not only mesmerized by his playing, but were also cheered by his infectious joy, and afterwards, at the reception, uplifted from their worldly cares by his buoyant personality.

Had electricity been invented, they would have described the entire soirée as electrifying. As foreseen by both Goya and the Duchess, the nobility responded in like manner: Fernando soon found himself inundated with commissions, along with invitations to perform, and his purse accordingly recharged with currency.

The Duchess herself, whose failings had never included modesty of taste in art or men, wanted him to compose a symphony for her, for full orchestra, in the Spanish style. Fernando agreed at once. Upon hearing of this, and not to be outdone, the Duke and Duchess of Osuna likewise commissioned a symphony for themselves, and once again Fernando agreed. Both these works were performed in Madrid, and to great acclaim, but unfortunately the scores were not preserved for posterity to relish. The Duke of Medinaceli, more rustic and nostalgic by temperament, commissioned a cycle of seguidillas and boleros. The Most Excellent and Most Serene Prince of Peace, a music lover and a patron of all fine arts, including (as we have seen) the art of love, drew Fernando aside during the reception.

"Maestro Sor, would you do us the signal honor of accepting a commission?"

"Your Highness's request favors me beyond measure," Fernando replied. "What kind of composition does Your Highness have in mind?"

"Can you write us a sonata in the style of Haydn?"

"Most assuredly, Your Highness. For which instruments would Your Highness wish it to be scored?"

"Everyone at Court these days is infatuated with the violin," Godoy sighed (meaning, of course, that it was King Charles IV's favorite instrument). "But we find ourselves rather charmed by the guitar, at least in the way that you play it, Maestro. Can you score a sonata for solo guitar?"

"Consider it done, Your Highness."

"Excellent, Maestro. We will try to prevail upon the King to invite you to premiere it for him."

"Your Highness is too kind."

"Not at all, Maestro. Your talent is worthy of the Royal Ear."

Thus Godoy revealed a certain precocity in his artistic tastes, not only in painting, but also in music. Although well beyond risqué at the time, and bound to attract accusations of obscenity from those charged with laundering the soul, his private gallery of nudes anticipated the future widespread demand for eroticism. Similarly, his then-eccentric notion that the guitar was a suitable instrument for rendering an unaccompanied sonata in the classical style vaulted it into a league with the piano itself. Until this moment, not one star in the blazing galaxy of Baroque and Classical composers, who regularly churned out sonatas for solo keyboard, and for violins and flutes and oboes and a plethora of other instruments accompanied by keyboard, had ever deemed the guitar worthy of such empowerment. So credit Godoy for realizing that the guitar—at least in Fernando's capable hands—could reproduce any form that graced the concert stage.

And to this challenge Fernando responded magnificently, composing one of his most endearing virtuoso pieces in what would become a vast catalogue of works: his Grand Sonata in C Major for solo guitar, in four movements: Allegro, Adagio, Minuet, and Rondo. This oeuvre he dutifully dedicated to His Most Excellent and Serene Highness, The Prince of Peace. Godoy was mightily pleased with it, and remarked rightly that it made the guitar sound like a small orchestra. This too proved precocious, for around a century later Debussy would provide the continuation: after hearing Segovia perform this piece, among others, he remarked that the guitar is not a small orchestra; rather, the orchestra is a large guitar.

While the Grandees of Spain showered Fernando with commissions, his fellow composers and musicians sought eagerly to collaborate with him. Crescentini invited him to perform in Lisbon; Angela Colbran wanted to sing duets with him, accompanied by his guitar, and also take some voice lessons from him; a youthful Dionisio Aguado wanted to play for him, and receive his guidance. Fernando said yes to them all, although the fates would keep him from Lisbon, and reserve him instead for a hundred other compass points.

At the same time, notable public intellectuals wanted to sound the depths of Fernando's political views and, if necessary, afford occasions for their elaboration. For in his day as in ours, and in all other eras for that matter, the masses were influenced by important artists: not just artistically, but also politically. So Jovellanos and Moratín conspired with Goya to invite Fernando to a dinner for four. As for Goya, who had already painted most of the audience at this recital, some of them several times over, he invited Fernando to sit for a portrait, guitar in hand. This was perhaps the most unlooked-for honor bestowed upon Fernando that day. It was no longer easy, and no longer even a matter of money, to commission Goya to paint a portrait; after all, he was First Court Painter to the King. It was almost unheard of for Goya himself to invite anyone to sit for a portrait. Only someone of transcendent—or better, immortal—promise could ever hope to receive such an invitation. Goya's eventual portrait of Sor counted among his greatest masterpieces but, like Fernando's symphonies from that period, were ultimately lost to posterity. But even the loss of this portrait, as we shall see, bestowed upon Fernando another gift of incalculable value.

Even so, while Fernando's maiden recital in Madrid was undeniably an unqualified triumph, it is also a truism that no man can have everything his heart desires. There is always some pleasure, some treasure, or some honor that is denied him, either in spite of or even because of his accomplishments. In Fernando's case, even as he became the new musical darling of the ruling class, the literal and figurative jewel in this crown—as it were—would be withheld.

True to his word, Godoy had wasted no time conveying tidings of Fernando's talents to the King, and suggesting that His Majesty host a command performance in the royal palace. Unbeknownst to Godoy, however, Sor's reputation had long-since reached Charles IV's ear, via the Queen's spies planted in Liria Palace. This regal Bourbon huntsman and amateur violinist (with an emphasis on *amateur*) fancied French composition above all, and took his musical advice solely from his chief of chamber music, a mean-spirited Castilian sycophant whose primary talent lay in sabotaging all potential competitors for his position. He considered Catalans second-class citizens, and deemed the guitar barely an instrument at all. While this genre of sabotage had long ago failed dismally to exclude Goya from the inner circle of Court Painters, this time it succeeded tragically in excluding Fernando from the inner circle of Court Musicians. For when His Majesty had inquired of his Chief

Musician whether he ought to invite Sor to perform, the saboteur had already prepared some venomous advice to pour into the Royal Ear:

"May it please Your Majesty, I have it on good authority that his talents are grossly exaggerated. Besides which, he strums the guitar, an instrument itself unworthy of a royal chamber. This is not really music; it is only the *frons-frons*."

As far as His Majesty was concerned, that ended the matter. So when Godoy came running to him, breathless with excitement over Fernando's performance at Liria, the King had merely humored him.

"Our Dear Prince, that witch of a Duchess must have cast a spell on you." (This idea had come to him from the Queen.) "Let us rely on our chief of music to attend to royal concerts, as we rely on you, esteemed Prince, to attend to affairs of state." (For the Queen had by now convinced him to reinstate Godoy as Prime Minister.)

Undoubtedly, both Fernando and Spain herself would have fared far better had His Majesty more closely followed Godoy's musical advice, and altogether disregarded his political counsel. But Spain was a topsy-turvy place, and nothing was more topsy-turvy than the mind of its current King. Thus one may begin to appreciate the method in Goya's madness, and why he experienced no contradiction alternating portraits of Spain's royalty in their palaces with sketches of Spain's lunatics in their asylums. Needless to say, this mad state of affairs could not, and would not, endure much longer. It would become even madder.

Chapter 10. Madrid, and the Last Supper at Liria

One balmy summer evening in July 1802, four distinguished friends gathered for dinner, cards, and conversation in Goya's apartments at Liria. As artists in residence, Goya and Sor jointly hosted the get-together, but since Fernando was not only younger than Francisco but also the youngest of the foursome, he happily followed Goya's lead. After a sumptuous dinner in Goya's private dining room, the quartet repaired to Liria's games room for cognac, cigars, whist, and political conversation. The cognac was French; the cigars Cuban; the card-game English; the politics Spanish, with a focus on the future of the Spain's Enlightenment project, which at that moment looked fairly bleak.

The senior member of this far-sighted foursome, who led the conversation, was a man of incredible accomplishment and longevity in the political arena: none other than José Moñino y Redondo, the First Count of Floridablanca, and (it may be recalled) Goya's first noble patron. José Moñino had served as Prime Minister for fifteen years running (1777-1792), and was the undisputed leader of the Spanish reformist movement. Under the benevolent reign of Charles III, who had tolerated both considerable reform as well as talk of more to come, José Moñino (or 'El Conde', as he was popularly known) had reformed virtually every institution he had touched. Among other things, he established an actual cabinet, the Supreme Council of State, to advise the King, initiated free trade in Spain's American colonies, founded the Bank of San Carlos, modernized university curricula, and expanded freedom of the press.

Under his able guidance, Madrid itself was rebuilt, enlarged, and adorned with public works. Spain having been dragged into the American War of Independence on the side of the rebels and their French allies, El Conde nonetheless reaped gains in Spanish prestige, and saw both the Balearic island of Menorca and the territory of Florida returned by Great Britain and restored to Spanish rule. He also settled long-standing colonial disputes with Portugal, acquiring some minor possessions in the bargain.

But everything had changed in 1789 with the outbreak of the French Revolution. The new Spanish King, Charles IV, who had succeeded to the throne only one year before, in 1788, was absolutely horrified by the Jacobin terror unleashed in neighboring France. Having no idea what to do when not at the hunt, but seeking to keep his royal head squarely on its shoulders, and his royal bottom glued to the throne, he instructed his Prime Minister, El Conde, to bring Spanish reform to a halt and preserve the status quo. In truth, El Conde needed little command from the King: his own vision of reform had never entailed abolishing the monarchy, let alone handing the reins of political power to a spiteful mob of *sans-culottes*. As the leader of Spanish reform, El Conde had been placed in an impossible political position by the events of 1789: he was obliged to perform a *volte-face* and support the outraged but ineffectual First Coalition against the French Revolution, and meanwhile to shelve his own agenda of moderate reforms. But at the same time, all Spanish reformists—of whom he was the ideal personification—were forever tarred with the Jacobin brush, deemed guilty by mere association with any of the lofty ideals that had impelled men in America and France to establish governments by consent of the governed. Because of the Jacobin extremists, and the terror they soon instituted, any Spanish aristocrat who harbored liberal tendencies was immediately, if unjustly, accused of sympathizing with these devils. The guillotine soon separated not only heads from torsos in France, but also moderate reformists from political influence in Spain.

Thus El Conde soon enough fell prey to the relentless machinations of Queen Maria Luisa and her lover, Manuel de Godoy. They unhorsed him as Prime Minister in 1792, on trumped-up charges of embezzlement, and had him imprisoned in the castle of Pamplona. Godoy took over as Prime Minister, while Spanish reform languished in prison with El Conde. He was eventually acquitted in 1795, but remained disempowered, and retired to his rural estates, near Seville, to lick his political wounds in seclusion.

El Conde returned periodically to Madrid, to sniff the political air and weigh his chances of regaining high office. On this balmy summer evening in July 1802, however, he deemed his odds of winning at whist better than those of recuperating political favor. Indeed, his foremost protégé, Gaspar Melchor de Jovellanos, who had worked long and hard on agrarian land reform, seeking to unchain Spain's dormant economic potential by incentivizing private agriculture, had just fallen literally from grace. Jovellanos had been Minister of Grace and Justice under Godoy, whom he conspired to unseat as Prime Minister in 1797. But now the political tables had turned and, not long after Fernando's inaugural recital at Liria, which he attended and admired, Jovellanos had been imprisoned in Majorca's Bellver Castle in a counter-plot hatched by the Queen and Godoy. Needless to say, his reformist agenda was locked down with him.

Jovellanos's foremost protégé, Leandro Fernández de Moratín, was still at liberty, but no-one could say for how long. Moratín's work focused on literary culture, and its ability to shape popular opinion. A gifted linguist, he had translated for Spanish audiences classic English works by Shakespeare and Sheridan, and classic French ones by Molière and Voltaire. He also wrote plays of his own in similar veins, criticizing, satirizing, or ridiculing reactionary mores that militated against liberalization and emancipation. Thanks to the patronage, promotion, and friendship of politically influential men such as Moñino and Jovellanos, and thanks also to the mistaken notion—held by the Royal family—that literature, like music, constituted entertainment only, but was of little political consequence, Moratín had risen to the post of Royal Librarian, which he used as a platform from which to disseminate liberal values (and chastise conservative ones) to an increasingly literate public. But seeing his two chief sponsors—first Moñino and then Jovellanos—disempowered and carted off to prison, Moratín could feel invisible irons gradually tightening around his limbs as well. He sensed that the Spanish backlash against the French Revolution would soon enough turn on him, and he was not wrong.

So it was Moratín who posed the essential question to Moñino: "Excellency, what are we to do? How can we proceed to liberalize Spain when our two greatest reformists have fallen out of political favor? Your Excellency has been rusticated to his rural estates, while Jovellanos languishes in prison. How can a painter, a composer, and a librarian—although yet at liberty and still in favor—further your Herculean accomplishments? Pray, enlighten us."

At this El Conde lit a cigar, and collected his thoughts. Goya poured another round of cognac, while Fernando, all ears, sat silently and listened. The youngest of this august quartet, he had no idea that he was about to be nominated to play a pivotal role.

The Count of Floridablanca puffed on his cigar and exhaled a billowing cloud of blue smoke, through which his piercing eyes penetrated far beyond—not only through space, but also through time—as he prepared to answer the librarian's essential question.

"My esteemed Leandro, if you will pardon an apparent contradiction, you are both right, and wrong. You are right that a painter (even an immortal one like Francisco), a composer (even a scintillating one like Fernando), and a librarian (even a gifted *literatus* like yourself) cannot directly further the necessary political work. But never forget that there are two ways to foment political reforms: either from the top down (as Jovellanos and I, among many others, have striven to do in Spain); or from the bottom up (as in the recent populist revolutions in America and France). In my view, the 'top-down' model of gradual but steady reform, supported by an enlightened monarch, is the most pacific and least unpredictable path. Under the benevolent reign of Charles III, we made considerable progress on this path. But when a monarch remains intransigent in the face of necessary reforms (as was George III in England), or worse, oblivious to their necessity itself (as was Louis XVI in France), recent history teaches that men may feel driven by desperation to take matters into their own hands, and opt for the 'bottom-up' model. That path is revolutionary, not conciliatory, and its consequences—whether intended or not—may be dire.

"One cannot fail to notice a common denominator in both the American and the French revolutions; namely, a political activist who fires popular imagination, and ultimately ignites populist uprising. In America, it was not the framers of the Declaration of Independence who impelled homesteaders to pick up their muskets and risk everything for liberty; rather, it was the pamphleteering of Thomas Paine that spurred them on. And in France, it was not the caustic wit of Voltaire that spearheaded the storming of the Bastille; rather, it was the utopian nonsense spouted by the imposter Rousseau that inflamed the *sans-culottes*, and engendered the guillotine.

"And what of Spain, you ask? Should statecraft continue to fail, as it seems to be failing now, and should we follow instead the revolutionary path toward which we seem to be heading now, then who will play the vital role of populist? And will it be played successfully, as with Paine, or disastrously, as with Rousseau? How it will be played remains to be seen. But the person who shall play it may well be seated at this very table tonight. That person cannot be me, as my métier is statecraft. Nor can that person be Goya, for he is no populist; rather, he is the sole reliable witness, before God, of all that shall transpire in this era. Should a revolution succeed, his paintings will one day hang in public rather than private galleries, and the future masses will duly marvel at his testimony. Nor can that person be you, dear Leandro. For you are Spain's Voltaire, and not (thank all our lucky stars) its Rousseau. The inescapable conclusion is that this vital role of populist will be composed and played by someone who is already a brilliant composer and virtuoso player."

At this, all eyes fell upon Fernando, who had been listening attentively without expression, save nodding in periodic agreement with their political mentor, and likewise puffing on a cigar. (He had swiftly acquired this habit, and liked to indulge it after dinner. He discovered that as long as he did not inhale the acrid smoke, his voice did not become hoarse, nor his breathing congested.) Now that everyone was suddenly looking at him expectantly, Fernando's jaw dropped. He had had no inkling of this new role. Yet he rapidly collected his wits, and spoke:

"Excellency, please rest assured that if this duty falls to me, I shall do my best to discharge it faithfully. But pray expand upon your vision of this role, and how it is to be played in Spain, for I am only a babe in these political woods."

At this El Conde smiled. Like everyone, he was charmed by Fernando's cheerful innocence.

"Maestro," he replied, "it cannot have escaped your notice that the American soul is stirred foremost by liberty, whatever the cost; the French soul by philosophy, whatever the absurdity; and the Spanish soul by music, whatever the occasion."

"Excellency," responded Fernando, "your profound understanding of American and French political cultures surpasses, I daresay, that of ours combined," at which both Goya and Moratín nodded in agreement, "but yes, even my youthful inexperience confirms that the Spanish soul is forever musical, and at all hours."

"Then, Maestro, should that hour arrive when you are called upon, whether by muse or man, to write patriotic songs, in popular idioms, pray assure us now that you will not fail to stir the souls and animate the hearts of our people," implored El Conde.

"I solemnly swear to do my musical duty," answered Fernando, "but once again, I fail to grasp what kind of occasion would necessitate that call. For, if I may boldly speak for the present company, neither the First Court Painter, nor the Royal Librarian, nor this fortunate composer, would ever conceive of biting the hand that feeds us. And you yourself, Excellency, have served two Kings as Prime Minister, always for the mutual benefit of the Crown and the people, and never to my knowledge has a word of sedition ever escaped your lips. Under what conditions, then, would I be serving Spain by writing songs to agitate the populace?"

"That is a prescient question, Maestro. Allow me to attempt an answer. Indeed I do foresee a coming time, and that right soon, when patriots will be needed—but not to foment revolution against our own sovereign. Everything in Spain is upside-down. Because of the villainous excesses of the French Jacobin radicals, we moderate reformers in Spain are unjustly equated with them by our mutual enemies of change. Liberal reforms are now deliberately confused with treasonous executions. Our patriotism is denounced as sedition. Whereas our current King and Queen, long may they reign, consider it patriotic to empower Godoy to make Spain a vassal state of France, in their vain attempt to preserve an untenable status quo. Spain is in an impossible position: it cannot move forward, and most assuredly cannot go back. Neither can this political paralysis long endure, and I fear that it will be alleviated only by sudden upheaval.

"A monster of historic proportions now determines, by his will alone, the fate of France, and through it of Europe in its entirety. His name is Napoleon, and that name will define our era. He is a force of nature, which cannot be stopped by man alone. He will one day blow himself out, as a hurricane exhausts itself by furiously expending its own power, or as a volcanic eruption ceases once its pent-up molten matter is violently ejected. Yet unlike these purely destructive forces of nature, this monster is also capable of benevolent acts of justice and far-sighted social reforms. Just this year, he established a new French constitution, and restructured their education system—thus accomplishing in mere months missions that I could not complete in fifteen years. How? Because I was a dutiful public servant, while he is an absolute dictator. Just two months ago, the same mob that gleefully decapitated their entire ruling class has happily elected him First Consul for life. Were I a philosopher or a poet, I would despair at human nature.

"But never forget that the price of this monster's justice, which he so generously dispenses with one hand, is interminable war, which he needs to wage without surcease to regularly bathe the other hand in blood. And he thirsts not only for the blood of Europe's monarchies, which one by one he will bring to heel, but also for the blood of England, and beyond that even of Russia. His overweening ambition will certainly make an end of him, but not before he will have made an end of many.

"And what does this mean for Spain?" asked Fernando, awed by the scope of El Conde's vision.

"We Iberians occupy a unique place in European geography. The 'back door' of Iberia is the Pyrenees, which separate us from the continent, and give us a measure of privacy, as a great wall at the rear of an estate grants privacy from neighbors. The 'front door' of Iberia is the Atlantic Ocean, a vista that has always afforded us a very different view of the world than other Europeans. Most people set out from their own front doors on foot, or horseback; we Iberians, of necessity, set sail in ships. So we were the first to explore as seafarers the far reaches of the earth: the first to navigate to the Americas, and around the Horn of Africa to the Indies, and beyond that to the Orient. But our Spanish and Portuguese empires have waned over time. England's navy now controls the sea lanes, and their empire is still waxing in its might. This Napoleon cannot countenance.

"From Napoleon's point of view, Iberia is merely the rump of Europe. But his dire enemy, the English, have a beachhead on this rump: a safe harbor in Lisbon, thanks to their ally, Portugal. To Napoleon, the English presence in Lisbon is like a flea on his backside: it irritates him, and he needs to scratch it out. Will he do so by sea, or by land? Napoleon is a land-monster, not a sea-monster. A formidable general on *terra firma*, in 1798 he wrested Egypt from the ferocious but degenerate Mamelukes with an army of fewer than 40,000 men, but at the same time saw his supply lines cut off by the British navy, whose Admiral Nelson destroyed the French fleet in the Battle of the Nile. Mark my words: Napoleon will march an army into Portugal, to chase the English out, and in that process, he will endeavor to subdue the entire Iberian peninsula. With his rump secure, and rid of fleas, he can turn his unslakable thirst for blood northward, southward, and ultimately eastward. Therefore at present, Spain lies directly in his path. And it is against that tyranny, Maestro, that we may soon need patriotic songs to mobilize resistance."

Fernando bowed his head in acquiescence, and the company fell silent, digesting El Conde's foreboding political forecast.

The hour was growing late, even for Madrileños. So as not to end the night on such a somber note, Goya injected some levity into the gathering.

"Shall we play one last hand, and quaff a final toast, before disbanding?"

The company proved amenable. As they tallied up their net winnings and losses, it became clear that they had played cards according to their characters. Goya gambled as he painted: boldly, and heedless of consequences. Moratín was a man of letters, not of numbers. Fernando's fortunes were best described by the adage 'unlucky at cards, lucky in love'. The only winner had been Moñino: he was as shrewd a card player as he was a political visionary.

At last, around four in the morning, as they rose to bid their final farewells, they were abruptly and unexpectedly interrupted. José Sanchez virtually burst into the games room, without so much as a by-your-leave. He looked as though he had just been roused from slumber, and had hastily dressed. His countenance wore an expression beyond distraught.

"Excellencies, please forgive this untimely intrusion," he began, "but I bear tidings that cannot wait. Her Grace always insisted on hearing bad news at once, and to honor her preference I must tell you that a terrible fate has befallen her. María del Pilar Teresa Cayetana de Silva-Álvarez de Toledo y Silva, 13th Duchess of Alba, is dead."

"What?!" "When?!" "Where?!" "How?!" exclaimed the foursome, incredulous at this news.

"As your Excellencies know, Her Grace was in Seville, attending the wedding of a cousin of her late husband. A messenger just arrived on horseback a few minutes ago, having ridden non-stop for days, pausing only to change mounts. He reports that right after the wedding feast, Her Grace fell suddenly and violently ill, and took straight away to bed. She endured high fever with agonizing convulsions and, despite the constant attentions of Seville's best physician, she expired after three days of unremitting suffering. Her body is being transported to Madrid for the funeral. I apologize again for interrupting your Excellencies, and for bearing such tragic tidings."

"Did anyone else fall ill after the feast?" El Conde inquired.

"Apparently not, Excellency, or it would have been reported."

"Very well, José, you may be excused."

The Secretary of the late Duchess of Alba bowed and took his leave.

The foursome tarried a few minutes longer, but an uncomfortable and indeed unbearable silence descended on them, for no-one dared to voice aloud the thought they all had in mind: that the Duchess of Alba had been poisoned. They did not even dare to voice silently, in the privacy of thoughts alone, the obvious question—who had poisoned her?—for the most plausible answer to that question, if unprovable, constituted high treason. This chain of thought served only to reinforce El Conde's astute analysis: if it were treasonous to seek justice, then Spain was indeed politically upside-down.

Immersed in such thoughts as were thinkable, the quartet dispersed into the sultry gloom of pre-dawn. El Conde repaired to his estates in Aragon, to gather strength and to pray he would still be vigorous enough to help defend Spain once the monster invaded. Moratín returned to the Royal Library and penned a merciless satire on the counterfeit manners of the ruling class, no more than a thin veneer concealing their savage bestiality. Goya wandered among asylums, painting lunatics. Fernando composed a lugubrious mass in honor of his dearly departed, much-beloved, and never-to-be-forgotten Duchess.

Chapter 11. Barcelona, and Joaquina

The Duchess of Alba's funeral was attended by a pack of Grandees, and a herd of lesser nobles. Only the King was absent, for that day found him on a particularly important hunt. Queen Maria Luisa came with her retinue, heavily veiled not only to display her profound degree of mourning, but also so that no-one could detect the triumphant smirk she wore under the disguise. Prime Minister Godoy came with his tearful wife, and exerted himself so as not to betray a single emotion, not even the hint of a glistening eye, as he knew that the Queen was closely monitoring his every expression through her conveniently multi-purpose veil.

But many at the funeral, who had loved the Duchess one way or another, and who moreover were unafraid to show it, wept openly and copiously, especially during Fernando's heart-wrenching mass. Only someone who knew the delirious heights of joy, as he did, could also plumb the abysmal depths of sorrow. This mass resulted in yet more commissions, which could not have been further from his intentions in composing it, yet which subsequently distracted him from the irreversible loss of the Duchess. He had known her only for two and a half years, but would remember her fondly for the rest of his life. Indeed, history would never forget her either, and not just because Goya never tired of painting her; rather, because she was an extraordinary woman. And perhaps, in last analysis, her very extraordinariness—as contrasted, for example, with the altogether ordinary, albeit murderous, jealousy of certain Queens—had also been the cause of her untimely death.

Shortly after the funeral, Fernando was approached by the Secretary to the 8th Duke of Medinaceli, Luis Fernández de Córdoba y Gonzaga, and invited to an audience the following day. This Duke, whom Fernando had met several times at concerts and other functions, had been a close friend and confidante of the Duchess of Alba, almost like a brother to her. They shared the same circles of faithful friends, and needless to say of mortal enemies. The Duke informed Fernando that the Duchess had made ample provisions for him in her will: he would continue to receive a pension from her estate, and would continue to have at his disposal the suite of rooms on the Gran Via. Moreover, he would be patronized anew by His Grace, The Duke himself, who was honored to assume that role, no matter how clumsily he might play it compared with the incomparably refined but now departed Duchess. The Duke wanted to render the maestro every conceivable assistance, and so offered him a commission in the administration of his estates in Catalonia. It was the usual sinecure, a way of assuming a position and keeping up an appearance of employment, but in fact Fernando would be free to compose and perform as he wished.

Fernando jumped at this chance, for it meant that he could return to Barcelona, and spend time with his dear mother and brother, and—at this thought his heart skipped a beat—with Joaquina. And so the prodigious son came home once again, to the Dry Quarter, and found it a welcome relief from the lavish lifestyles and incessant intrigues of Madrid's inner circles.

Isabella and Carlos were overjoyed to see him again, after a two-and-a-half-year absence, and apparently had endless appetites for hearing of the ins and outs, the scandalous antics, and the devious machinations of daily life among the Grandees. For his part, Fernando sank gratefully into the simple comforts and familiar pleasantries of his childhood home and neighborhood. He found the quotidian concerns of the Dry Quarter a welcome relief from the high offices and debased vendettas of Madrid's ruling classes. Compared to the burdens of state, wealth, and history borne by his patrons in Madrid, Fernando deemed the middle classes of the Dry Quarter fortunate indeed to be preoccupied by mundane matters, ranging from the weather to the price of ham. They had no idea how fortunate they were; or then again, perhaps they did. Isabella cooked and baked for him, and neighbors dropped over with homemade wines and tapas, and nobody took anything too seriously aside from the business of relishing each moment. Carlos, now seventeen, and a sub-lieutenant under General Vives in Villafranca, came home on weekends as he pleased, and nothing pleased him more than playing guitar duets with his older brother.

On the very first Saturday morning that found the family thus reunited, they had lingered over coffee and pastries and conversation, until Fernando went into his bedroom to fetch the gifts he had brought them from Madrid. To Carlos he presented a guitar from the collection bequeathed him by the Duchess, namely the Pagés from Cadiz. This was the finest gift that Carlos had ever received. He almost wept for joy, and immediately loved playing it, and would treasure it until the end of his days. To Isabella, Fernando presented what looked a like a large scroll, made of rough, cotton-fibered paper, bound up with a silk ribbon. She wondered what it could be, and unrolled it at the table.

"Oh look!" she exclaimed. "It's a charcoal sketch of you, Fernando, playing a guitar. What a wonderful likeness! Thank you so much, dear son... Pray tell us, was it done by a street artist in Madrid? It has an authentic rough-and-ready look. And the signature is smudged, so the artist's name is illegible."

Fernando smiled at his mother's reaction, and saw that much of his own child-like innocence had been inherited from her.

"You are most perceptive, dear mama. Yes, it was sketched by a *former* street artist, upon whom fortune subsequently smiled. And the signature was deliberately smudged—at my own request— to protect you, and it, from prospective thieves. For the artist's name is Goya."

At this Isabella almost swooned, and Carlos and Fernando each took an arm to steady her.

"But this is incredible, Fernando! Isn't he busy painting all the Grandees of Spain?"

"Yes, mama, as First Court Painter, that is Goya's duty. But he is also a pure spirit, and so he paints as he pleases, or else to please his Muse. And among other things, it pleases him to paint his friends, among whom I count myself fortunate to be numbered. This is only a sketch, with which I persuaded him to part as a gift to you. He is working on a full-blown portrait in oils, which may be completed next year. The sketch is yours to frame, to hang, and to enjoy... but keep well the secret of the artist's name. Do not reveal it to the framer, nor even to your friends and neighbors."

Isabella laughed. What a world her son had come to inhabit! Here was a treasure, to be hung in plain view, only disguised as a trinket.

In Fernando's case, his music was also in plain view, or rather plain earshot, and needed no disguise. His compositions were treasures, and were likewise treasured. Following the lead of his dearly departed patron, the Duchess of Alba, he rented a loft near Barcelona's Opera House, and had a piano installed. Whenever inspiration struck, usually on a daily basis, Fernando closeted himself there, and immersed himself in creativity. He had begun an opera in Madrid, having composed some movements for a classical libretto, *Don Trastullo*. But this oeuvre progressed more slowly than he would have liked, as he soon found himself besieged by local commissions. The master of the cathedral's chapel, Monsieur Quéralt, consulted with him on many works. The chapel master of Santa-Maria-del-Mar, Monsieur Cau, commissioned him with the orchestration of movements from his oratorios. Commissions from Catalan aristocrats and well-heeled private citizens flowed in as well. And often Fernando composed out of pure joy, with no thought whatsoever of remuneration.

In short, music gushed out of Fernando like water from a modern fire-hose. In a matter of nine or ten months he had composed two symphonies, three quartets, a hymn, five or six *rosarios*, and many distinctively Spanish airs. Beyond this, his knack of hearing music everywhere and in everything remained acute. Inspired by the street sounds that assailed him on his walks about Barcelona, he fashioned a beautiful piece called *Draps i Ferro Vell* (*Cloth and Old Iron*). Owing to the carelessness of the period, precious few of these compositions survive. At the same time, Fernando remained open to musical influences from abroad, in particular to the Italian melodies that continued to captivate the Catalan heart. Little did he know that in years to come this Italian influence would serve him surpassingly well.

Far less frequently, but unfailingly at the death of dear friends, Fernando also composed out of sorrow. And so he did after the demise of Sabater, who had declined with alarming rapidity following Fernando's departure to Madrid some three years earlier. The Chevalier had summoned Fernando to his bedside, requesting that he bring a guitar. When Fernando arrived, he was dismayed at Sabater's condition. The Chevalier was now bed-ridden and blind. The gout that had formerly merely debilitated him was evidently only a symptom of a far worse illness, which was now causing his kidneys to fail. In addition, his cataracts entirely obscured his vision, clouding his eyes with a thick milky film. There was nothing wrong with his hearing, however, and his mind was still as sharp as a rapier. Fernando could not contain himself, and began to weep at the sight of this once-magnificent but now decrepit figure of a man, lying sightless on his deathbed.

"Now, now, my boy," Sabater gently chided him, "pray steel yourself. We all must pass this way, first through the gate of life, and—sooner or later—at last through the gate of death. No-one escapes this fate: the young, the beautiful, the gallant, the learned, the rich, the royal, and the masses alike. We all share this passage, and we all must submit to Divine judgment. There is no cause for tears, nor for regret. I have lived a marvelous life, filled with blessed years, and replete with beloved friends. Now I go to my reward, with a willing heart.

"But first, pray tell me of your time in Madrid, and of what tragedy (or treachery, more like) befell the Duchess. Did Goya befriend you? I heard that Godoy himself commissioned you. What did you compose for him? Share with me your tidings, for now you have outdistanced me in all the topsy-turvy goings-on in our magnificent but troubled nation."

Fernando did his best to summarize his recent life in Madrid, and to sketch the doings of all the improbable characters that populated its most lavish stages. He also confirmed how sagacious the Chevalier had been with his advice, some three years before, and how invaluable that counsel had proved, time and again, in the palaces of the mighty. He described his friendship with his 'elder brother' Goya, which made Sabater smile. He told of his encounters with Godoy, and of the Grand Sonata he had composed for the Prince of Peace.

"Pray, play it for me," asked Sabater.

Fernando did so, and afterwards the Chevalier found strength enough to give him a resounding ovation.

"Bravo!" he applauded. "Bravissimo! You are one with Haydn and Mozart. Moreover, you and Goya are the voice and the vision of Spain. If anyone wishes truly to understand our nation, they need only look at Goya's art, and listen to Sor's music."

Fernando felt deeply grateful. The Chevalier has been the first, after his dear mother, to recognize his musical gifts, and now, at the last, Sabater exuded a deep satisfaction at their flowering. Dying or not, blind or not, he smiled happily on his deathbed.

"One final request, my dear boy: play for me some Catalan folk songs, like those we used to play and sing together in your home when you were but a child. For although anyone can taste the flavor of Spain by sampling her arts, none but a native Catalan can ever know the true essence of our culture."

Fernando did as he was bidden, and soon the Chevalier's frail voice joined his in singing the Catalan melodies of their long-lost youths.

"And now I must rest, dear boy," said Sabater. "But know that your visit, and your music, have given this worn-out body wings to fly skyward." He smiled deeply and contentedly.

Fernando kissed his godfather good-bye, and wept silently despite the old man's joy. It would be their final meeting. The Chevalier sank into a deep slumber that very night, from which he awoke, if at all, in the embrace of life everlasting. Overcome by sorrow at the news of Sabater's passing, Fernando composed a lugubrious yet uplifting *tombeau* for his godfather. All who heard it were compelled to shed tears of sadness, and yet also of hope. This *tombeau* was also lost to posterity in the carelessness of the day, but perhaps the angels are still singing it in the next world, to mourn—and yet celebrate—the passage of good souls from this worldly vale of tears into the divine embrace of eternal light and love.

While Fernando busied himself with music, mostly joyful but occasionally mournful, others whom he knew quite well concerned themselves with equally pressing but far more mundane affairs.

By the standards of the day, his dear mother Isabella had reached an age (around forty) at which most women were already grandmothers, and could happily spoil their grandchildren with unconditional love. Although she desired this avidly, Isabella never broached the subject with her sons. After all, she temporized, Carlos was only seventeen, had just left home to pursue a career, and was free to sow wild oats for years to come before claiming a bride. Men were so lucky, she ruminated, for they felt no pressure to marry, and could always find eligible young women half their age when their time came to raise a family. As for Fernando, she fully understood that his musical gifts had transported him to an even loftier plane, which lay well beyond the ken of her experience and the limits of her imagination alike. She could not conceive whether or when or whom he would ever marry, but dared not bring up the subject with him. And while Carlos and Joaquina had been inseparable childhood friends and neighbors, such that Isabella and Sofia had both hoped they would wed, there seemed to be no sign of this on the immediate horizon, even though most girls of seventeen were already wives and mothers. So Isabella merely sighed, knowing it was not her business to intrude on Joaquina's life, but secretly hoping that Sofia would. For while mothers had no real authority over their grown sons, they could certainly attempt to influence, if not manipulate, their daughters of marriageable age.

Isabella need not have worried on this score. In fact, Joaquina's apparent indifference to the question of marriage was driving Sofia slightly crazy. Like her best friend Isabella, Sofia longed to become a grandmother, but given that Joaquina was an only child, her urgency was that much greater. All her eggs were literally in one basket. Thus Sofia was not shy to broach this with her daughter. Being a woman, she did not confront Joaquina directly, but rather spun a delicately sticky web that eventually snared her daughter in the question.

"I bumped into Estel in the market yesterday," she casually mentioned to Joaquina over tea one morning.

"And how is she?" asked Joaquina. (Estel was an old friend of her mother's, and Joaquina knew her daughter Marta.)

"She is overjoyed," replied Sofia, "because Marta is getting married! Estel was shopping for fabric and lace. As she is an excellent seamstress, she will make the wedding dress herself."

"How exciting!" replied Joaquina. "Who is the groom? And when is the wedding? I have not yet heard about it from Marta."

"It is very fresh news. The groom is Arnau Bauza. You know, he's a good friend of Carlos, and the same age. He just proposed the other day. Marta accepted at once. She always had a crush on him. And besides, she is already sixteen, and most of her friends are married by now."

Of course Joaquina saw where this was leading, and tried to deflect the conversation. "What kind of fabric did Estel buy?" she asked.

"She was trying to make up her mind, but I couldn't stay long enough to find out. They will let us know soon enough, as I'm sure you will be a bridesmaid... And by the way, I still have my wedding dress, and it's a perfect fit for you too," Sofia added. "Would you like to try it on?"

"Of course!" Joaquina replied. "But not right now. I must go and see Marta at once, to congratulate her, and ask her how he proposed, and find out when the wedding will be."

"Of course you must," Sofia acknowledged. "That's the right way to treat a friend. You have always been such a considerate girl. No wonder you are so well liked. I only wish, sometimes, that you treated your mother as considerately."

"What do you mean, mother? I am helping you and Isabella teach in your school. Is that not considerate?"

"Of course it is!" Sofia exclaimed. "You are a wonderful helper at the school. Yet Barcelona is full of young music and dance teachers; such help can be found on every corner. But I have only one daughter in this world, and only one family wedding to look forward to, and only one way to become a grandmother. Have you given that any consideration lately?"

"Of course, mother!"

"Well, maybe you should give it more. At your age I was already married, and carrying you. So what are your plans?"

"Nothing definite yet."

"Isabella told me that Carlos had proposed to you. How embarrassing that I should have to learn it from her!"

"I'm truly sorry, mother! Had I accepted, of course I would have told you at once."

"You mean you refused him? You two grew up together. He loves you. And now he has a career in the army. What more do you want?" Sofia asked incredulously.

"I did not refuse him, mother. I love him too, at least in a certain way. I told him that I do not feel ready to marry just yet, and that is the truth."

"Well, I hope that your feelings change soon. If you wait much longer, you will be an old maid." That was also true. In those days, if a girl was not married by nineteen, she would be deemed an old maid at twenty, and perhaps thus obliged to marry someone three times her age, instead of the customary two.

"Please don't worry, dear mother. I know in my heart that I shall marry, and bear you a grandchild," Joaquina tried to reassure her.

"But you do worry me, dear daughter. When we were at dinner with the Sors last weekend, I saw you steal a glance at Fernando. That look in your eyes truly frightened me—a look of almost sacred devotion. Has he reciprocated this in any way?"

"Yes he has, mother."

"How?"

"With the same look."

"Be that as it may, his devotion, however sacred it may be, is to music."

"Yes, it is. But he also loves me as I love him. I just know it." It was a woman's way of knowing, by mysterious and inexplicable intuition alone, and not demonstrable by any proof. But suddenly Joaquina could no longer contain herself, and burst into tears. At this, tears welled up in Sofia's eyes too, and she comforted her only daughter.

"May Mother Mary watch over you, dear child. For this way lies only madness. Carlos awaits you; you await Fernando; Fernando awaits his destiny. Without a doubt his destiny will be great, but it will also leave a trail of broken hearts, starting on his own street. Our Dry Quarter will be well watered by tears."

And on that ominous note, Sofia and Joaquina dabbed their eyes, and finished their tea in silent sadness. Although mothers and daughters are wont to endure such episodes of strife, Sofia and Joaquina genuinely loved each other, and so each felt sadder for the other than for herself.

Fernando and Carlos genuinely loved each other too. Now both young adults, their age differential of seven years, which had been necessarily momentous in childhood, had gradually receded into insignificance. These days, whenever Carlos came to Barcelona for a weekend, they invariably made music not only at home with Isabella, but also in Fernando's loft, where they rehearsed new pieces—principally guitar duets—that the elder Sor had composed to play with his younger brother. This delighted them both.

One Saturday afternoon, around the time that Sofia and Joaquina had their mother-daughter confrontation and heart-to-heart talk over the subject of these brothers, the brothers themselves saw fit to broach the subject of Joaquina. Carlos had rather timidly initiated the conversation, partly because of his relative inexperience with women compared to that (or so he imagined, and not injudiciously) of his illustrious brother.

"Pray tell me, elder brother," began his gambit, as they had lain down their instruments to light cigars and quaff wine, "have you given any thought to marriage? You must be the most popular bachelor in the realm, and can have your pick among the bevies of ravishing young beauties who adore you."

"To be truthful, younger brother, I do not yet feel ready for marriage. Of course I encounter temptation at every turn, and confess that sometimes I succumb to it. But marriage is a far more serious matter than rolling in the hay, and you know that I am serious about music above all else. So while I can envision taking the matrimonial plunge one day, I do not yet perceive the path that leads to such waters ... And what of you, dear Carlos? Does your heart belong to someone special?"

"Indeed it does, Fernando. And I have even proposed to her."

"How marvelous! Did she accept? And do I know her?"

"Alas for love's marvels! Indeed you know her surpassingly well, for she is none other than Joaquina. But she neither accepted, nor refused. Her young heart is apparently torn between two suitors—one steadfast, the other wild. She desires a normal life, but is in thrall to an abnormal one. She fears she cannot be satisfied by sane love, owing to some unrequited appetite for mad love. Her poor heart is impaled on the horns of this dilemma, like a matador gored by both horns of a bull. She feels paralyzed, and so does nothing, hoping her situation will resolve itself in time. She wept with gratitude when I proposed, but also with torment at being unable to say yea or nay."

"What a diabolical conundrum," said Fernando, shaken to the core, for this was his first inkling of the impossible love triangle that bound them.

"Yes, it is," Carlos agreed. "Pray tell me, elder brother, are all women so frightfully complicated? It seems as though nothing whatsoever is simple for them."

"I do not pretend to understand women," said Fernando. "But it seems to me that where men see black and white, women see endless shades of grey. I only wish, dear brother, that Joaquina had accepted your proposal. It would have simplified things for sure."

"Yes, it would have: and for us all."

At this Fernando suddenly realized that Carlos knew full well that he, Fernando, was the object of Joaquina's mad love, as she was of his.

"Dear younger brother, my heart is now in torment too! Above all, I want you, and she, to be happy. If only she had accepted your proposal, I would have rejoiced."

"Dear elder brother, I understand, and reciprocate, your noble sentiments. Likewise, I want you, and she, to be happy. If only she had rejected my proposal, then I too, albeit in a different way, would have rejoiced."

"Yes, I understand that too. And of course you realize that she, for her part, wants us both to be happy, yet is incapable of making a choice, any choice, that either way would release us both from torment."

"Pray tell me, dear Fernando, whatever are we to do?"

"My dear Carlos, although Fate has placed us in this predicament (for clearly none of us would have chosen it), we can save ourselves only by unselfish love. So first, let us embrace each other as loving brothers, and swear to one another, before God, that no woman will ever come between us, to divide our brotherly love."

"My dear Fernando, so do I swear." At this they drank a libation, and embraced.

"Second," continued Fernando, "since we both love the same woman, we must swear before God to place her happiness above our own, come what may."

"My dear Fernando, so do I swear." At this they drank another libation, and embraced anew.

"Third, since the same woman loves us both, we must pray to God to heal her fractured heart, and not to rend it further in twain."

"My dear Fernando, so let us pray." At this they fell on their knees.

The bond of love that these remarkable brothers had sworn to, and deepened, and sanctified that day, would indeed withstand the terrible trials that Fate would soon hurl at them, and would remain unsundered by the coming ordeals of love and war alike.

But Joaquina's divided heart inevitably exerted a similar effect on them. Each loved her in his own way, and they loved one other as brothers, and from this triangle there was no escape. Sometimes Carlos wished more than anything that she would accept his proposal, so they could marry and lead a normal life; while at other times he wished as ardently that she would reject him and marry Fernando, which at least would alleviate the terrible tensions among them. But he knew that Fernando was not yet ready to wed her, and might never be, so he also hoped that Joaquina would eventually give up on his untamable brother, and settle for the domesticated one. For his part, sometimes Fernando wished above all that Joaquina would accept Carlos's proposal, which at least would resolve the terrible tensions among them. But Fernando also knew, from the unspoken things that passed between Joaquina and him whenever their eyes met, that their souls were bonded to some other purpose, whose time had not yet arrived. And poor Joaquina was perhaps in the direst straits of all, since she yearned both for domesticity with Carlos and for adventure with Fernando, and could not relinquish either desire. She felt herself pulled in two opposing directions at once, by two brothers—both of whom she loved, albeit in different ways—which left her completely immobilized. Although she herself seemed unable to move any which way, the merciless river of time continued to flow by her, leaving her terrified, at times, that it would completely pass her by, and leave her stranded on the barren banks of things that once might have been, but never would be.

At last, one day, unable to bear this burden any longer, she confessed her predicament to the priest. He was a wise and kindly man, and he offered her a way out.

"My child," he began in a deeply compassionate tone, "there are but two ways to satiate carnal desires, without incurring sin. One way is to confine them to the sacrament of marriage. The other way to is renounce them by professing vows in a holy order. Since the prospect of marriage confronts and tempts you so cruelly, like the forked tongue of a serpent, perhaps you should consider taking refuge in a convent, with a view to becoming the bride of Christ."

Merely contemplating this option immediately eased Joaquina's anguish. It soothed her like a balm. It opened a door to a comforting fantasy, into which she could escape whenever it suited her. It did not derail her desire to marry and bear children, but it offered her a temporary respite from her tormented triangle of love.

Wanting to be considerate, as always, Joaquina did not dare disclose this fantasy to Sofia. While it brought temporary solace to her own troubled heart, it would only wound her mother more deeply, and torment her with the thought that she might never have a grandchild to spoil.

Chapter 12. Madrid: Insouciance, Inquisition, and Intrigue

For his part, Fernando contrived an escape to Madrid, where commissions were fortuitously pilling up. He requested and received leave from the Duke of Medinaceli, and reimmersed himself in the hubbub of the capital city. Liria Palace was now occupied by the Duchess's heir, Carlos Miguel Fitz-James Stuart, the 14th Duke of Alba, but Fernando's suite of rooms at the Excelsior remained at his disposal, as did his pension, thanks to the Duchess's posthumous provisions for him.

Fernando got to down to work with a will. Still reeling from the intense and heartrending episodes of his embroilment in the love triangle, he departed from his usual joyful demeanor and composed a melodrama, *La Elvira Portuguese*. Then, much as Joaquina had found refuge in religious fantasy, Fernando likewise comforted himself with sacred music, composing a motet (*O crux, ave spes unica*) and an *Ave Maria*, for four voices with orchestra, for the Church of Merced. This catharsis helped him to recover his naturally cheerful disposition; after this he became himself again, and composed a good many boleros.

As we have seen, Fernando was gifted with a playful demeanor that colored his character as well as his performances. His natural ebullience being hardly confined to music, it expressed itself in a constant stream of words and deeds as well. At the same time, being completely unpretentious, he enjoyed teasing or poking fun at those who took themselves too seriously, or were wont to put on airs. Because he usually did so in a good-natured way, with spontaneity and not premeditation, this tendency usually made him even more endearing.

Sometimes his jests were so sublime that they went over everyone's head except his own. Take, for example, the episode with the guitarist who busked in the Plaza Mayor. During his perambulations about Madrid, from his suite on the Gran Via to and from his favorite haunts, Fernando often found himself crossing the Plaza Mayor in one direction or another. Because little escaped his eyes and nothing evaded his ears, he always took note of the guitarist who huddled in one corner of the Plaza, propped up against a column, sheltered from the sun just inside a colonnade, busking for maravedies from passers-by. His repertoire consisted of traditional Spanish airs, and these days included one of Fernando's boleros, which were becoming increasingly popular. He was dressed flamboyantly, like a *majo*, and played that way too, long on élan but short on refinement. Spain being Spain, he drew a good many "Olés" from pedestrians, but not many coins. In sum, he was an embodiment of Fernando's late father's worst fears of his own boy's fate had he neglected his Latin for the sake of the guitar.

While Fernando's heart went out to this busker, so that he never failed to part with spare change, his temptation to tease the undiscerning passers-by soon got the better of him. So one day he approached the guitarist and struck up a conversation with him.

"You play very well," said Fernando.

"Thanks for your kindness, Señor," replied the busker.

"Not at all," said Fernando. "Pray, what is your name?"

"Jésus Garcia."

"Pleased to meet you, Señor Garcia. I am Juan Muntada," said Fernando. To conceal his identity, he used the Spanish version of his father's first name, plus his mother's last name.

"The pleasure is mine, Señor Muntada. Can I play something for you?" Jésus inquired hopefully, noting Juan's casual but well-heeled appearance.

"Normally yes, but today I have a more unusual—but also more rewarding—request to make of you."

"And what might that be, Señor?"

"If you will lend me your cape, your hat, and your guitar, and let me sit in your place for an hour or two, I will give you a silver reale." Here Fernando proffered a coin. It was more than Jésus earned in a fortnight of busking.

At this Jésus Garcia proved himself at least as enterprising as he was musical.

"Very good, Señor Muntada. But what about a security deposit on the guitar? It is worth more than one silver reale."

So Fernando handed him ten more silver reales. "You can give these back to me when you return. Don't worry, I will be here."

Jésus only half believed him, but fully believed the handful of silver reales. So they stepped into the recesses of the colonnade, where the shadows concealed the remainder of their transaction. Jésus Garcia, now wearing Juan Muntada's frock coat, scurried off to his favorite tavern, while Juan Muntada, now clad in a *majo*'s gaudy cape and a large-brimmed hat that sported an outsized imitation ostrich feather, took Jésus's place in the plaza and began to strum his weather-beaten guitar.

Passers-by, on the whole, took very little notice of him. And there was no apparent reason why they should have. Guitarists busking in public places were a dime a dozen in Spain. Fernando had listened to Jésus play before, as he often crisscrossed the Plaza Mayor, and so he effortlessly imitated the busker's style and repertoire. Only a few passers-by stopped momentarily to listen, and of these only a few in turn mildly applauded, before tossing him a maravedie and going on their ways. So with good-humored mischief, Fernando began to introduce little flourishes into his playing, 'spicing up' the repertoire with touches that no ordinary busker could manage. To his surprise, displaying these flashes of virtuosity did not increase the size of his audience, nor the length of time they spent listening, nor the thin trickle of maravedies into his tin cup.

One passing fellow, who evidently fancied himself an aficionado, listened intently for a few minutes, then asked the busker whether he could play any boleros by that famous guitarist Fernando Sor. To his credit, Fernando stepped up to this challenge, and began to play one of his more popular boleros, almost as well as he might have rendered it at a private recital for the Grandees.

"Bravo!" said the passer-by, dropping a few maravedies into his cup. "You play very well, for a busker," he added.

But his companion, who had hitherto remained silent, offered the final pearl of wisdom. As the two went on their way, Fernando heard her mutter "No, no, it is only the *frons-frons*".

In due course the real Jésus Garcia returned, to claim his outfit, instrument, and perch on the colonnade. He peered into the cup and, noting that it contained a few fresh maravedies, remarked "Well done, Señor Muntada—you obviously have some talent, and might even earn a living at this, if you applied yourself".

Fernando merely smiled at him, and handed Jésus his weather-beaten guitar, whereupon Jésus attempted to return the security deposit of ten silver reales. "You may keep them, Señor Garcia, as a token of my thanks for allowing me to take your place, and of my admiration for your daily efforts to fill this public space with music."

At this, Jésus Garcia's eyes fairly bulged out of his head, and he replied: "For this unsolicited generosity, Señor Muntada, I can but offer inadequate words of thanks. I have been busking in this plaza for nearly a decade, and this marks the greatest day of my musical life. May God always be with you, Señor."

Fernando shook his hand, and went on his way. In truth, he thought, ten silver reales was a small price to pay for the ironic lesson he had just learned. It both amazed yet also dismayed him to behold that the public at large, who adored his popular music, and who paid a pretty penny to scalpers for tickets to his public performances, which always sold out quickly, lacked the discernment to realize that this self-same artist, however thinly disguised, had just been playing for them for free in the Plaza Mayor. Most people are so easily fooled by mere appearances, he concluded, that only with great difficulty, if at all, can they penetrate even the thinnest of veils, and apprehend reality.

This shocking realization bordered on an epiphany: that the entire world of man was but a welter of illusion, that only a fine line separated Fernando Sor from Jésus Garcia and a thousand other buskers, and that—but for the grace of God—Fernando could otherwise have been born as Jésus, and Jésus as Fernando. This revelation that the real world could only be sustained by the grace of God, and never by the illusions of man, disabused Fernando permanently of any possible delusions of grandeur that he might be tempted to harbor, especially in the wake of his meteoric rise to fame.

At the same time, however, Fernando's love of good-natured mischief, his ironic sense of humor, and his torrential stream of thought to which he gave uninhibited voice, would now draw him into potentially mortal peril at the hand of a dread force that also claimed to be doing God's work: namely the Spanish Inquisition.

The Tribunal of the Holy Office of the Inquisition had been established in Spain in 1478, by Catholic Monarchs Ferdinand II of Aragon and Isabella I of Castile. Operating in conjunction with the Roman and Portuguese Inquisitions, the Spanish version had permeated the far-flung empire. Its original mandate was to weed out Jewish and Muslim heretics who had falsely converted to Catholicism in attempts to save themselves from persecution or expulsion. But since its authority extended over all Christians, the Inquisition also busied itself investigating those professing any heresy whatsoever, including Anglicanism and Protestantism. Needless to say, the Inquisition also zealously investigated anyone suspected of witchcraft, sodomy, Freemasonry, or any other kind of blasphemy—including that harmless sort of which Fernando would shortly find himself accused.

In fact, the Spanish Inquisition's reputation was far more insidious than its actual catalogue of horrors. Over almost four centuries during which it held sway, the Office had investigated perhaps 150,000 suspects, of whom no more than 5,000 were ultimately tortured and burned at *autos de fe*. This was a relatively small number indeed, compared (for example) with more than 50,000 women burned for witchcraft alone in the rest of Europe, among tens of thousands of other heretics. Meanwhile infant mortality, disease, plague, and warfare carried off far greater numbers of pious souls. But owing to relentless propaganda by Spain's political enemies, notably England, fables of the 'Black Legend' had spread far and wide, inspiring terror far out of proportion to peril.

This legend would echo down the decades, even after the final waning of the Inquisition's power, immortalized for example by the English poet laureate Tennyson's foreboding verse 'Fall into the hands of God, not into the hands of Spain!'

The Spanish Inquisition's power had greatly diminished during the reigns of Charles III and Charles IV, as enlightened breezes from Europe gradually wafted over the Pyrenees. Yet the Holy Office was still a force to be reckoned with. Godoy hated the Inquisition, which in turn hated his collection of nude paintings with equal fervor; yet neither could manage to get rid of the other. While the *auto de fe* was a terror of the past, the Holy Office could still fling suspects into prison during or following its investigations, and in those days paupers' prisons were as good as a death sentence. But for the most part the Spanish intelligentsia endured no worse than the inconvenience of seeing their books banned. Yet this measure was just as likely to backfire, since a banned book immediately took on the aura of 'forbidden fruit', and became that much more sought after. An underground industry of banned books flourished in Spain, whose sales were often brisker than those of legitimate booksellers. And the Spanish index of banned books could be just as topsy-turvy as its homeland: Machiavelli, for example, had been a strong proponent of the Roman Inquisition, owing to its utility in keeping the populace in a state of fear, but his writings had nevertheless been banned by the Spanish Inquisition.

Not only painters and writers but also musicians ran the risk of being accused of heresy. For example, a busker in Cádiz was hauled before the Inquisition for singing a rather risqué song about a friar and a young girl. The girl had confessed some romantic dalliance to the friar, who had pressed her for more intimate details than the protocols of the confessional required. While this made for a bawdy ballad, it mightily offended a devout passer-by, who promptly denounced the busker to the Inquisition. Once it was established that not he but rather the guitarist Moretti had written the song—apparently during a fit of drunken revelry—the busker was acquitted with an admonition to mend his heretical tendencies, and strengthen his resolve to resist the malign influence of foreign heretics.

So however did Fernando fall afoul of this unholy Holy Office? It came about through a combination of his usual playful fun, and an unusual bout of feverish delirium. In June 1803, Fernando had been visiting Dionisio Aguado's country estate in Fuenlabrada, around fifteen miles southwest of Madrid. Dionisio had by now blossomed into a fine guitarist, and the two often wrote and played duets together. During this visit Fernando fell ill with a high fever and Dionisio conveyed him to the nearest reputable doctor, a man named Vicente Álvarez, who lived in the nearby village of Casarrubios. In those days anyone could be carried off by fever at any stage of life, and doctors could do little but put their patients to bed, keep them hydrated, dose them with foul-tasting but largely ineffectual tonics, and pray that they would recover. Fernando remained delirious for several days, during which time he muttered to Dr. Álvarez that it was impossible to prove that hell or angels or demons actually exist; that although there is definitely a Supreme Being, Moses and Jesus Christ were *politicones* ('big politicos'), and that all the rest was invented by friars.

Dr. Álvarez did not take these feverish ravings too seriously, for he also heard Fernando call on '*Jésus mio*' and the Holy Virgin, repeatedly and with fervor during his delirium. Moreover, the well-connected Álvarez family knew Fernando rather well, and so Vicente also knew that Fernando went unfailingly to mass on prescribed days, and had even heard him complain about certain lazy priests who gave insufficient devotion to the sacrament. After a lengthy convalescence under the good doctor's care, Fernando eventually regained his health, and returned to Madrid in September. Matters would have rested there, except that Dr. Álvarez happened to mention the episode during one of his own confessions, and the confessor told him to report it to the Inquisition, which he did in May 1804. This initiated an investigation that was to last more than two years, during most of which time Fernando remained unaware that Inquisitors were interviewing cadres of witnesses, and were meticulously recording every playful jest that he was careless enough to make, whether within earshot of his many friends, or his few detractors.

The Inquisitors began at the source, interrogating both Dr. Álvarez and his wife, Doña María Esteve. While the couple confirmed the things that Fernando had muttered during his delirium, they made sure to mention his fervent prayers to Jesus and Mary. For good measure, Dr. Álvarez added that he and Fernando had gone to the nearby village of Chozas for the fiesta of Santa María Magdalena that July, where Fernando had played the organ and the violin in the principal mass. Dr. Álvarez emphasized that Fernando had insisted on remaining in Chozas to attend a second mass, because his playing of the instruments during the principal had diverted his full attention from the sacrament.

The Inquisitors began to form the opinion that Fernando was pious but loose-tongued, and this view became reinforced when they interrogated Doña María Esteve's sister, Doña Tomasa Esteve, in Madrid. Doña Tomasa was married to Augustín Esteve, a friend of Goya's and a Court Painter to His Majesty Charles IV. Since Fernando was frequently in their home, Doña Tomasa was able to confirm that she had heard him say similar things, especially after taking a few glasses of wine. He said, for example, that if he ever had children he would never teach them the Christian doctrine as currently taught, forcing them to learn 'like parrots'. He spoke, she said, "with the loquacity and multitude of words which were typical of him". Doña Tomasa then added that she had urged him not to say such things; they could be harmful to him because people would not understand them. At this point she burst into tears, because she felt deeply for Fernando and suddenly realized the potential gravity of his situation.

The Inquisitors made less headway with her husband, Augustín Esteve. Free-spirited artists tended to close ranks at any sign of persecution, and besides, Augustín counted Fernando among his friends. Whether wisely or otherwise, as a Court Painter he did not fear the Inquisition. Moreover, ever since Goya himself had permitted Augustín to paint his portrait, Augustín feared nothing whatsoever. No-one could be as intimidating as Goya, and no-one's judgment could induce greater trembling. Having passed that stern test, of Goya sitting for a portrait and ultimately declaring that he loved the finished painting, Augustín treated the Inquisitors rather brusquely, dismissing them as comparatively minor irritants. When they pressed him about Fernando, he replied that Sor was "a cheerful and amusing young man," and would say no more. So they moved on. But they did not forget this snub by a haughty Court Painter, who temporarily enjoyed the protection of Godoy, and (for all they knew) his taste for lewd art. Once Godoy fell from grace—which would be soon enough, they reckoned—Goya and his libertine circle would be investigated in their turn.

Meanwhile others could always be found who were more forthcoming, including an unidentified eighteen-year-old girl, who told them that Fernando had said "that the Mass was nothing but a dice-game, invented by friars to get money". (This was exactly the kind of utterance that made Doña Tomasa so afraid for him, and not without reason.) Fernando had used the term '*el juego de los cubiletes*', referring to a set of dice and cups favored by hustlers on the Ramblas in Barcelona, but the girl, a young Madrileña, could not have known this. So she described Fernando as "an incomprehensible man, light in the head". The inquisitors scribbled it all down. But, unlike the friar in Moretti's risqué ballad, they did not inquire into the details of young girl's romantic adventures, neither with Fernando nor with anyone else. They were investigating Sor, not her.

The Inquisitors then shifted their attentions to various parish priests, beginning with the one in Casarrubios, who said that he had spoken only once or twice with Fernando, and had detected nothing that suggested anything other than good moral conduct. Then Inquisitors then spoke with the priest of San Luis in Madrid, who said that he knew little or nothing of Sor, because the Russian ambassador had lodged him at his house for months on end, in exchange for playing and arranging house concerts, and giving musical instruction.

This marked a temporary dead end for the Inquisitors, since they had no authority to interrogate a foreign envoy. Even though he was clearly a Russian Orthodox heretic, His Excellency Ivan Matveyevich Muravyov-Apostol had been appointed ambassador to Spain by Tsar Alexander I, and as such enjoyed both diplomatic immunity and the protection of the Spanish Court. An immensely cultured man professing overtly liberal sympathies, Muravyov-Apostol was not only a diplomat but also a statesman, a writer, and a polyglot. He had been sent to Madrid by the Tsar in 1802, to open the very first Russian Embassy to Spain, and to keep a close eye on the political and military situation there. Tsar Alexander was very much aware of Napoleon's Iberian ambitions, and fervently hoped that they would hinder Bonaparte's eventual invasion of Russia, which he regarded as inevitable. So Muravyov-Apostol was Alexander's Iberian watchdog, and a most keen-nosed one. He gleaned more intelligence from card games with Court painters, musicians, and writers—who were inadvertently privy to all kinds of state secrets—than he collected at official functions with Grandees. The more politically important his dinner companions, the less of importance was said. Muravyov-Apostol had hunted several times with Charles IV, and was astounded that His Majesty's conversation never strayed far from the quarry of the day.

For his part, Fernando was delighted to manage the musical affairs of this cultured Russian noble, and had no idea that he was occasionally mentioned in dispatches to Saint Petersburg. At the same time, Fernando frequented Godoy's palace, where he gave regular concerts, as well as the Royal Palace, where he regularly visited Goya, who had taken up residence there following the Duchess of Alba's death. Even so, and notwithstanding Fernando's constant presence in Madrid's innermost and uppermost circles, a command performance for King Charles IV continued to elude him.

Not that Godoy never mentioned him to the King. On the contrary, Godoy could neither refrain from reminding His Royal Majesty about Fernando's astonishing virtuosity, nor restrain himself from recounting Sor's scintillating performance at his latest concert. But to the very end of his reign—which was coming soon—Charles IV remained intransigent. Under the permanently malign influence of his jealous Chief Musician, he insisted on disparaging the guitar as '*frons-frons*', and chided Godoy whenever Fernando's name came up: "Come, come, Chief Minister, first let our Royal Physician purge the wax from your ears, then pray join us on a hunt, where you will hear the clarion cadence of horns, the chorus of baying hounds, and the crescendo of horses' hooves. This is music fit for a discerning ear: never mind the *frons-frons* of Catalan buskers!" And so they batted Sor back and forth, like a metaphorical tennis ball.

Although the Chief Musician's petty jealousy kept Fernando from giving a command performance at the Royal Palace, Queen Maria Luisa's unlimited jealousy drew him into far greater danger. She was constantly wary of Godoy's roving eye, so that any cute young chambermaid upon whom his fleeting glance lingered longer than a heartbeat might find herself suddenly assigned to the laundry of a banana plantation in the Canary Islands. The Queen had attended several of Fernando's monthly concerts at Godoy's palace, and she grew alarmed at the number of ravishing young beauties drawn to his enchanting performances and charming persona. Fernando could scarcely handle them all, and whenever the Queen stole glances at Godoy, she saw him more often pre-occupied with the bevies of beauties than with the performer's virtuosity. So she resolved to get rid of Fernando, thus banishing these rivals at one stroke.

Her plot hatched itself early one evening in 1804, when she found the King in an agreeable mood after a particularly successful hunt.

"My Lord," she importuned in a honeyed tone, "does Godoy still weary you with fables of that Catalan guitarist Fernando Sor?"

"Indeed he does, my Queen. Godoy seems perpetually captivated by the *frons-frons*. It lies beyond our understanding how anyone with such keen political judgment could be so lacking in musical taste. Moreover, that Barcelonan busker seems to have insinuated himself in Madrid's best circles, where his very presence is an affront to our reign."

"May I suggest a way to relieve yourself of this unworthy irritation?"

"Pray, do."

"Your wish is my command, my Lord. It seems that this upstart also enjoys playing at cards, and that he has previous administrative experience in the army."

"And so?" His Majesty blinked obtusely. However expert at following animal tracks, he struggled, as though from congenital disability, to connect political dots.

"My Lord, he is technically on leave from the army. Why not re-instate him by Royal Decree, and appoint him Inspector of the Royal Playing Card factory in Málaga? Let him disintegrate on the beach, like a piece of sodden driftwood, or better yet die of yellow fever, a plague of which has already carried off thousands down there. And should he decline the commission, then fling him into prison him for refusing to do his duty to the Crown, and let him rot in a dank cell instead."

She uttered this last option laced with such venom that His Majesty paused to wonder what Sor had done to cross her.

"A capital idea, my Queen," His Majesty exclaimed. "And so it shall be done... However could we reign without you and Godoy to advise us?" Little did he imagine that, largely thanks to their advice, he would soon reign over nothing, but would nonetheless continue to be advised by them until the end of his muddled days.

Not long afterwards, Fernando duly received a letter from His Majesty, reinstating him in the army at the rank of Captain, with equivalent pay, under the nominal command of General Francisco Javier Castaños (head of the Andalusian forces), and ordering him to report to the Royal Playing Card Factory in Málaga (actually, in nearby Macharaviaya) within a month, where he would assume the duties of Inspector. Like his former appointment at Villafanca, it was a sinecure, which carried virtually no obligations other than his occasional signing of papers or *pro forma* inspection of playing cards. But in effect, it banished him from Madrid.

Upon reading this letter, Fernando recalled the myth of Icarus, and felt as though he, too, had flown too close to the sun, causing the wax on his wings to melt. Plummeting from a great height and drowning in the sea, as did Icarus, seemed an apt metaphor for his present fate: plummeting from the cultural heights of Madrid and drowning in the obscurity of a seaside village (as Málaga was in those days). But little did Fernando suspect, nor could he have reasoned at the time, that this banishment was actually a huge blessing in disguise. A guardian angel still watched over him, and was preparing his future ascent to unimaginably greater heights.

Fernando brought the letter along to his next evening of cards with Goya, in his luxurious quarters at the Royal Palace. They were joined by Moratín as usual, and on this occasion by the Russian envoy, Muravyov-Apostol. As the foursome played whist, drank cognac, and smoked cigars, they endeavored to make sense of Fernando's banishment. Had they asked the merest scullery maid in the palace, she would have immediately intuited the Queen's hand in it, for this is how women's minds work. Guided unerringly by intuition and emotion, they know things without knowing how they know them. Prior to, and even during, Fernando's age, this could easily be mistaken for witchcraft. In contrast men make use of reason, sometimes rightly, at other times wrongly, always knowing how they know, but not always knowing whether they know truly, or falsely. So these men sought a rational political explanation for Sor's situation; and being unusually well-placed men, they soon found one.

"It must be the work of Godoy," surmised Goya. In a most ironic way this was partly correct, of course.

"Indeed," concurred Moratín, "the Prince of Peace is tightening the noose around all Spain's leading liberal necks. El Conde remains secluded in Seville, ostracized by Godoy's Aragonese faction. Jovellanos still languishes in Bellver Castle, imprisoned by Godoy. Now you, Fernando, are banished to Málaga. If not for your immense popularity, you too might have been flung into prison, on some ridiculous trumped-up charge. I feel the rope chafing my neck as well. The Inquisition has been howling to ban my play *The Maidens' Consent*, which is due to be performed next year. One the one hand Godoy still keeps them at bay, since they also dream of confiscating and burning his gallery of nudes, but on the other hand he regularly feeds lesser liberal fishes to these holy sharks, to sate their implacable thirst for blood. For the time being Godoy protects me merely to protect himself, but tomorrow he may just as well betray me, should that protect him better. Yet once he falls, the Royal Library will be purged of its modern collection. Either way, my days as Royal Librarian are numbered... Only you, Francisco, still somehow float beyond the treacherous reach of politics. However do you manage it?"

At this, Goya smiled wryly. "My dear Leandro, I will tell you what I told Fernando when he asked me this: I am posterity's witness, bound to paint what I see. If the powers that be have thus far spared me, it is only because they greatly fear my testimony, and desperately hope to be portrayed in a favorable light."

The company nodded in agreement.

Then Moratín turned to the Russian envoy. "And what do you make of our situation, Excellency Ivan Matveyevich? After all, you are the eyes and ears of Tsar Alexander. Pray enlighten us, from your vast perspective:

are these mad Iberian antics merely what Shakespeare called 'a tale told by an idiot, full of sound and fury, signifying nothing'?"

Now it was Muravyov-Apostol's turn to smile wryly. He had read *Macbeth* in English and, thanks to Moratín, in Spanish as well.

"Your translation of the Bard is surpassingly fine," he commended Moratín. "But know that from where I sit, my dear esteemed artists, events in Iberia signify the very opposite of nothing. That is to say, they signify everything. The fates of Europe and Russia alike will hinge on whatever happens here. This 'Prince of Peace' Godoy deems himself a sly fox, because he has outwitted the indigenous hounds. But soon he must contend with a ferocious Corsican lion, who can dispatch him with one careless swipe of its paw, and barely take notice. This fox professes liberal sympathies, scheming to align himself with the liberating lion. At the same time, he suppresses his fellow liberals, lest they out-maneuver him and make a separate peace with the lion, more favorable to themselves. Either way, this lion's claws will soon rake Iberia, and its fangs will wound her deeply. It is not your leaders, but rather your people, who will determine your fate. If they can withstand this ravening beast, then Iberia, Europe and Russia alike will be saved. If not, then all will be devoured. You, the celebrated artists, must do everything in your power to inspire resistance in the populace; that is, inspire them to resist both the machinations of the fox, and the rapacity of the lion."

No matter how much the company had drunk that evening, the Russian envoy's words exerted a sobering effect on them. In sum and substance, his assessment matched El Conde's, and El Conde was the wisest statesman they knew. Yet Fernando felt somewhat cheered withal, because he realized that while the people could be ruled only from Madrid, they could be inspired (as could he) from anywhere.

And as Fernando made his preparations to depart for Málaga, his many friends conferred fond farewell gifts. Among them, Moratín gave a him a copy of his play *The Maidens' Consent*—destined to become a hit and (as he had foreseen) to land him in trouble. Muravyov-Apostol gave him a letter of introduction to William Kirkpatrick, the influential American Consul, wealthy wine merchant, and redoubtable entrepreneur based in Málaga. This introduction would turn out to be a pearl beyond price. Goya unveiled a superb portrait in oils of the young maestro, guitar in hand, on which he had worked ever since their first meeting in Liria Palace. His was the youngest solo portrait of a non-royal that Goya had ever painted, or would ever paint.

"It is magnificent! How can I ever thank you, Elder Brother?" asked Fernando.

"You already have, Younger Brother, and many times over. Painting your cherubic countenance and good cheer proved contagious; like a tonic, it dispelled my melancholy whenever I worked on it... Perhaps I should paint another," he laughed.

So in early May of 1804, just around the time that Dr. Álvarez was reporting him to the Inquisition, Fernando packed up his goods and chattels, and made the long and dusty journey from Madrid to Málaga. As always, his waking thoughts and dreams alike were a whirl of possibilities.

Chapter 13. Málaga: Idyllic Interlude with the Kirkpatrick Family

As William Kirkpatrick drove his horse and wagon from his stately town home in the hills above the city to his well-provisioned warehouse and busy office in the Port of Málaga, his thoughts too were a whirl of possibilities. Born in 1764 in Scotland, into a prolific clan with sprawling and intertwined branches, William was marked by Providence for greatness. His own daughters, and one granddaughter in particular, would later be marked for destinies greater than greatness. His father, William Kirkpatrick of Conheath, had built a capacious stone house in Glencaple, which his mother, Mary Wilson, filled relentlessly to the rafters with nineteen children. In our age, it is well-nigh incomprehensible how a woman could carry, birth and rear so many offspring, but it seemed normal enough to Mary—save that, against all odds, fifteen of them survived into adulthood. Perhaps it was due to a combination of factors, including hardy parental stock and a healthy rustic lifestyle.

By nature and nurture alike, young William was fond of agriculture and rural life. Yet he was also smitten by wanderlust, and insatiable curiosity about the wider world. He knew, from an early age, that he must escape his convivial if crowded familial confines in order to find his true path. So as a young adolescent he apprenticed to the shipping trade, as a clerk with a customs broker (and cousin) in Dumfries. Here William had his first brush with greatness, in the person of a fellow apprentice, by the name of Robert Burns, destined to become Scotland's most celebrated bard. Soon William moved to a trading house in London, run by yet another cousin. Here he began to come into his own, displaying both initiative and prudence, earning profits not only for the firm, but also, via rapid promotion, for himself. This success prompted a move to Ostend, where he joined a prosperous trading firm operated by an older brother, John. Here William made his first fortune and, desirous of striking out on his own, moved to Málaga, where he blossomed.

William was neither the first Scot, nor even the first Kirkpatrick, to settle in the sunny and somewhat sleepy town of Málaga. In those days it was still a tiny place, and the least-developed port on the Costa del Sol, much smaller than Valencia and Barcelona. Málaga had been the last Muslim stronghold on the coast, boasting not one but two hilltop citadels, Alcazaba and Gibralfaro. The last southern port to be re-conquered, Málaga's development had lagged behind the others. This lag struck foreign entrepreneurs as an opportunity, especially since Málaga was the closest Spanish port to the Straits of Gibraltar—and therefore the first place of haven for ships passing through the straits, against the ravages of the fearsome Barbary corsairs. A number of English, Irish, and Scottish merchants—including several branches of Kirkpatricks—had settled on the Costa del Sol during the seventeenth and early eighteenth centuries, had intermarried with one another and with the local populace, and were well woven into the fabric of the community. William arrived in Málaga in 1788, with his young Belgian wife, Françoise de Grivegnée, daughter of his business partner Henri in Ostend. Just as royal marriages of the day often served the primary purpose of cementing political relations, so marriages between business partners could similarly cement commercial ones.

William's gift for entrepreneurship flowered in Málaga. Among other produce, he exported oranges, saffron, sherries, wines, sea salts, and famed Tyrian purple dyes, made from the local sea-snails. He imported wheat from America, spices from Africa and India, silks from the Orient, and cigars from Cuba. More unusually, he sought to establish vineyards abroad with various grapes from the region, which he exported as far as Australia. He also established a cotton plantation in Adra, and a sugar plantation in Marbella, which occupied moral high ground over their New World counterparts, since William's estates were worked by local wage-earners, and not by African slaves. For William was a liberal supporter of progressive enlightenment values, including anti-slavery, and he believed in practicing what he preached.

At the same time, he was also a hard-nosed Scottish pragmatist, who desired nothing more than to provide abundantly for his family, and make the best possible marriages for his daughters. To accomplish this, his commercial affairs were bound to bend and sway not only with the predictable cycle of tides and trade winds that filled the sails of his merchant ships, but also with the prevailing political tides and anti-trade winds that threatened to drain his coffers. As the British naval blockade of Spain gradually but inexorably throttled his commerce with Spanish colonies in the New World, William had been obliged to diversify his business interests. In the process, he had cultivated an impressive network of political, diplomatic and social connections across Europe and the Americas.

Anyone who questioned the quality of William Kirkpatrick's networking acumen would have had their doubts dispelled by the contents of his wagon as he headed toward the port on that bright May morning of 1804, and by the accompanying letter in his frock pocket. It was addressed to none other than Thomas Jefferson, President of the United States of America, and it read:

Sir

A Vessel offering from hence for Alexandria, at the Opening of our Fruit Season, for the first time, I have taken the Liberty of shipping on board of her, a few of what the Vineyards of my Family produce, to the Care of James Madison Esquire with a request to present them to your Excellency, in my name, as also a Cask cased of the very best Old Mountain or Málaga Wine (being of the Vintage 1747) that my Stores can boast of.

I sincerely hope these trifling Objects may arrive in safety, and be delivered in good Condition to your Excellency, who I flatter myself will do me the Honor to admit of them, as a rarity not to be met with in America.

I profit with much pleasure of this Occasion, to assure your Excellency of the high Esteem with Which I have the Honor to be,

Your Excellency's most obedient & humble Servant

WILLIAM KIRKPATRICK

William had been appointed American Consul by President George Washington himself, on the recommendation of State Senator George Cabot of Massachusetts, who had visited the Costa del Sol on a trade mission in the early 1790s, and who was struck by William's commercial expertise and integrity of character, and the wide repute of his firm, *Messieurs Grivegnée & Co.* This appointment proved prescient indeed, as William's extensive network of diplomatic and business contacts, paid informants, and sympathetic spies paid appreciable dividends to the US government, and especially to Thomas Jefferson's administration's efforts to curtail the havoc wreaked on American shipping by the relentless Barbary pirates. These bold Muslim corsairs, known as the scourge of the Mediterranean, preyed on shipping from innumerable hideaways along half of North Africa's coastline, from Tangier clear to Tripoli. They hijacked vessels, plundered their cargos, and held their crews for ransom, or sold them into slavery. Although every legitimate merchant whose ships plied the Mediterranean sooner or later fell prey to these sea-borne brigands, William's intelligence network combined with American frigates helped keep their incessant piracy somewhat at bay. Thanks to this partnership, the cargo described in William's letter indeed reached the White House in good order. And once Jefferson had sampled the Old Mountain Wine of Málaga, he was bound to agree with his Consul that nothing of its ilk could be found in America.

Also thanks to William's network—in particular, a spy in Godoy's palace—Fernando had no need of the letter of introduction from the

Russian envoy. For William had known Fernando was coming to Málaga even before he left Madrid. Fernando had no idea of his importance to William and his wife Françoise, but would soon find out. It all hinged on their burning ambition, bordering on obsession, to see their daughters marry well. While this may sound normal enough to any parents of daughters, William and Françoise had already gone to extraordinary lengths to prepare the ground. To them, Fernando represented the proverbial icing on the wedding cake.

The couple had three surviving daughters: Maria Manuela, Heniquita, and Catalina Carlota. (Their firstborn and lastborn has died in infancy, like so many of that era.) The eldest, Maria Manuela, had been born on February 24, 1794, and on that joyous day her father immediately initiated the first step to securing a successful matrimony with a noble family. In Spain at this time, sheer wealth was necessary but insufficient to that end. The social chasm that separated the Grandees from everyone else could not be bridged by mere money, but only by blood line. Whereas in England one could simply buy a peerage if wealthy enough, this was not the case in Spain, where titles could be conferred for meritorious service (or for successful treachery), but never for cash on—or by—the barrel. Besides, William's commercial fortunes were already compromised by ongoing foreign conflicts, and would soon be devastated by all-out war in Iberia. Whereas many of his British compatriots had made fortunes on the Costa del Sol in earlier decades, sufficient for their comfortable retirement in Britain, William nursed no such expectations. For better or worse, he had cast his lot on these sunny shores, and would remain here come what may. So while he took pains to convey the impression of wealth, such that his Spanish and French contacts deemed him a multi-millionaire, the true value of his assets remained an undisclosed secret. The English, by contrast, disparaged him as 'a shopkeeper', which only loaned him more cachet on the Continent. But while William was content to foment speculation concerning his wealth, which was actually good for business, he could ill-afford to take chances concerning his social status, which would pre-determine the eligibility of his daughters to marry nobility. To give them the best possible odds, he needed to be certified as a *hidalgo*. While this term translates into English as 'noble', its meaning is closer to that of 'gentleman', as in landed gentry. So on the very day that Maria Manuela drew her first breath, William began to assure her future.

Becoming a certified *hidalgo* was no trivial undertaking, and William spared no expense in rounding up the necessary documentation. He engaged a swarm of solicitors and certifiers and notaries in Britain, to prove (as required) his descent from seven generations of Scottish landowners. Then he engaged a similar swarm in Spain, to translate the mountain of documents, to certify the translations, to certify the British certifiers, and finally to make the formal application itself. William drove this process forward with boundless energy, indomitable spirit, Job-like patience, and regular infusions of cash. Finally, in 1797, the year Catalina Carlota was born, he received word of his application's approval. From that day forward, he and his family held the coveted certificates of *hidalguia*.

Although of decidedly lesser status than Grandees, *hidalgos* still enjoyed certain enviable privileges. For example, their houses, horses, and arms were immune to confiscation for debts, as they themselves were immune to being jailed and tortured for indebtedness. In some cases they could demand satisfaction by fighting duels. In no case could they be condemned to death by insulting means, such as being burned at the stake or carved up by the sword. Nor could they be exiled. In these uncertain and still brutal times, every measure of protection against cruel and unusual punishment had intrinsic value, even for such morally upright and law-abiding persons as the Kirkpatricks. Yet this thought scarcely crossed his mind. William's overarching purpose in becoming a *hidalgo* was to make his daughters eligible to marry nobles.

And their mother, Françoise de Grivegnée Kirkpatrick, was of one and the same mind. She had inherited a sweep of social graces and feminine charms, with which she imbued her daughters from an early age. Combined with William's commercial wealth and political connections, her flair for fashion, decor, and culture made for brilliant luncheons and soirées, and vaulted the family into the stratosphere of Andalusian social circles. They spoke perfect Spanish (among a half-dozen other tongues), and had long since converted to Catholicism. Their *hidalgo* status enabled their daughters, once of age, to mingle socially with Grandees. These doting and dutiful parents harbored great expectations for their children, and they would not be disappointed.

When William broke the news of Fernando's impending arrival in Málaga to Françoise, she was absolutely over the moon with delight.

"This is our happiest news in years! He is a Godsend!" she fairly sang. "You must find him a nearby house, and engage him to direct our concerts. Beyond this, if he proves amenable, perhaps we can prevail upon him to teach Maria Manuela. Everyone says she is a musical prodigy."

"Tongues wag more freely in Málaga than in Madrid," replied William, with his accustomed touch of dour Scottish humor, "because nothing down here impedes the sea breeze ... Even so, we shall see what can be done."

Whenever he uttered those words, as Françoise knew from long experience, he had already made up his mind to see things done. She felt overjoyed, and bursting with excitement. And it made William's heart glad to see her this happy. In her mind's eye, she had already begun to plan Fernando's inaugural concert at their villa in Adra. But on the heels of that scenario, her female brain flew into one of its accustomed panics.

"But I haven't a thing to wear! And neither do the girls!" Françoise insisted.

Not a thing, thought William, except the contents of every overstuffed wardrobe in seemingly every room of their town house in Málaga, and their villa in Adra, not to mention the steamer trunks full of spare nothings stowed in attics and closets. But William held his tongue. When a woman says she has nothing to wear, so experience had taught him, she means she wants something new, and will not settle for less.

"I'm expecting a new shipment of silk and lace this month," he sighed. "As soon as it arrives, you can take your pick from the warehouse."

So Françoise resumed her joyful plans, while William sent messengers to every innkeeper in town, requesting that he be alerted immediately, whenever and wherever Maestro Sor pitched up.

And pitch up he did. One evening around mid-May, Fernando checked into a local inn: not on the row of seedy taverns and brothels that flanked the port, catering to sailors and other rough trade, but across town near a beckoning beach of yellow sand, in a more genteel quarter favored by visiting merchants and miscellaneous gentlemen. After seeing to the stabling of his horse and the stowing of his carriage, Fernando dined on delicious Andalusian fare and a fine local wine—not quite of the vintage sent by William Kirkpatrick to President Jefferson, but potable nonetheless. Then he repaired to a comfortable room with an ocean view, and was soon lulled into deep sleep by a fragrant sea breeze and the gentle rhythm of wavelets lapping the sandy shore.

Fernando awakened early next morning, roused by the shrilling of gulls and the crashing of waves. He immediately took a walk on the beach, imbibing all the wondrous sea sounds, admiring the rolling whitecaps of the incoming tide, meandering in the foam and flotsam, and around the seaweed and shells stranded with each outrushing wave, then transported higher up the beach by the next thrust of the tidal surge. Immersed in the many voices of Neptune's orchestra, he did not hear the approaching footsteps, muffled by the sand and upwind of the breeze.

"Maestro Sor!" a voice called out, and Fernando turned around. "Good morning, Maestro. Please allow me to introduce myself. I am Antonio Jimenez, an assistant to Señor William Kirkpatrick."

"Pleased to meet you," said Fernando. "In my room at the inn, I have a letter of introduction to Señor Kirkpatrick, from the Russian envoy in Madrid."

"You may give it to him personally, Maestro. It will be well received, but it is scarcely required. Your immense reputation has preceded you to Málaga. My master would like to offer his services in finding a suitable house for you. He has already taken the liberty of identifying some commodious properties for rent, which I will be happy to show you after breakfast. If any of them are to your taste, he will arrange the lease without delay. Beyond this, he cordially invites you to dinner with him and his family, once you are settled in your new abode."

"Splendid!" affirmed Fernando. "I am most amenable to, and grateful for, your master's kindness. I shall eagerly await your return after breakfast."

"Excellent," said Antonio. "Shall I come back for you, say, at eleven o'clock?"

"See you then," said Fernando, whereupon Antonio bowed and took his leave.

That very afternoon, Fernando settled on a charming cottage in the hills of the Barrio Alto, on a winding road amidst stands of pine, cork, and almond trees, not far from William Kirkpatrick's town house, overlooking the city and its palm-fringed bay. The cottage had a large veranda, on which Fernando immediately found himself at home. He could sit there for hours on end, playing his guitar while the sun set languidly over the sea, his exquisite music wafting gently down the hill, while the sweet aromas of jasmine and wisteria wafted up to him. "This is a kind of paradise," he thought. "The King has expelled me from Madrid, and into Eden." Fernando's good cheer apparently pervaded every place he inhabited; and moreover, every place he inhabited apparently reinforced his cheerfulness. The whole arrangement was seamless. He was indeed a blessed young man, upon whom still more blessings were about to be conferred.

Once settled in his cottage, and ever dutiful, Fernando rode out to Macharaviaya, to report to the manager of the Royal Playing Card Factory, and officially to take up his post as Inspector. He was welcomed most convivially, and offered a rustic but hearty peasant's lunch, washed down with local wine and regional gossip. The manager understood perfectly well that Fernando's position was a sinecure, and that as such he was not expected to do any actual work—other than making a show of it. So he handed Fernando a deck of cards to inspect. Fernando flipped through them, and said they looked just fine. The manager had also prepared a stack of papers for Fernando to sign after lunch, and to stamp with the Inspector's Seal that had just been made up. Fernando willingly obliged, and the manager apologized for detaining him. The papers would be sent to various bureaucrats, both civilian and military, in Córdoba, Seville and Madrid, with duplicates kept in the factory of course. Fernando wryly inquired as to when his next inspection should be scheduled, and the manager suggested (with a straight face) that, if not too inconvenient, he might return more-or-less on a monthly basis. Fernando agreed, whereupon the manager handed him a small packet of half a dozen decks of cards, which he could further inspect at his leisure, and a purse containing his monthly stipend. They made polite small talk for a while, after the fashion of country folk, who considered city folk rude for all their brusqueness. Then, his duties as Inspector fulfilled, Fernando rode happily home to play his guitar.

As Fernando returned to Macharaviaya each month, and came to know the manager and his top hands better, his visits gradually grew longer. Being a man of the people at heart, he was soon persuaded to play cards with them at lunch—what better way to inspect the factory's product?—and swill carafes of local wine, and sing risqué army ballads. They found him to be a convivial fellow, and he increasingly enjoyed these monthly drinking and gambling parties, which sometimes lasted through the night and into the next day. There were far worse ways, he temporized, to honor a Royal sinecure.

But what Fernando liked best was making music at home, on his veranda, ever enamored of the superb vista. In late afternoons his new housekeeper and cook, Conchita, brought him tapas at regular intervals, while she bustled about the kitchen preparing his evening meal. Conchita had been recommended by Françoise de Grivegnée Kirkpatrick, who employed her older sister Constancia in a similar capacity. These Kirkpatricks made a formidable team, in addition to highly considerate friends. For while William's assistant Antonio had been scouring the neighborhood in search of suitable houses for rent, Françoise had been inventorying her servants for suitable household help for this famous young bachelor.

In fact, he and the Kirkpatricks had hit it off immediately. Fernando and William liked each other at first sight, and had become friends for life during their very first lunch together in the port, within days of his arrival.

"You must come to my home for dinner, one night soon, and meet my family," William had insisted. "My wife and daughters will be thrilled to make your acquaintance." And so he did, and so they were. As it turned out, they formed mutually beneficial relationships on many levels. Notwithstanding William's widespread business and political contacts, and Françoise's elevated social standing in the region, they had never before had as a neighbor and guest at their table an artist of the highest caliber, who moved with such ease among the ruling elites—and yet who remained completely down-to-earth in his humility and congeniality. And their girls, at this time aged ten, eight, and seven, being socially precocious, quick-witted, and flirtatious, were immediately charmed by Fernando's youthful countenance, playful spirit, and perpetual air of innocence. He appeared to them as the very embodiment of a Prince from their favorite fairy-tales. For Fernando's part, it had been a long time since he had last nestled in the bosom of a wholesome and whole happy family: that being his own, before his father's death. The Kirkpatricks provided him with a surrogate familial milieu, in which he could recapture the missing years of his late childhood. For these among other unspoken reasons, they bonded strongly, and deeply.

Needless to say, William and Françoise had swiftly realized that Fernando was also the master key who could unlock the final matrimonial door between their daughters and prospective suitors of nobility. He was a virtual magnet for Grandees: his reputation, compositions and performances would lure them from all corners of Andalusia. The budding natural beauty and carefully cultivated charms of their daughters, along with their *hidalguia* status, would accomplish the rest. For Fernando's part, he had greatly enjoyed directing concerts for the Russian envoy in Madrid, and relished the role. So when William invited him to do the same in Málaga, offering to match the Russian's stipend, Fernando happily agreed.

Their musical relations scarcely ended at that. William introduced Fernando to Jayme Torrens, the composer, organist and choir-master at the cathedral, who had attended Montserrat before Fernando's time there. Mutually inspired, the pair embarked on several fruitful collaborations. Torrens was also giving piano lessons to the Kirkpatricks' eldest daughter, Maria Maneula, and he told Fernando that she had conspicuous musical abilities, including a lovely voice. This piqued his curiosity. And once Fernando became a regular visitor to their household, Françoise asked him whether he might consider giving Maria Manuela singing lessons. Straightaway Fernando invited the ten-year-old to play the piano and sing a song for him. Being not in the least bit shy, and if anything downright extroverted, she performed with such aplomb and musicality that he immediately agreed to become her singing teacher.

While it may seem from these developments that the Kirkpatricks were keenly milking Fernando like some purebred musical cow, nothing could be further from the truth. Remember, William had spent several years in London, while Françoise herself hailed from Belgium. They were both lovers of music among other arts, and found themselves somewhat culture-starved in Málaga. So Fernando would have been a godsend for this reason alone. But because they grew to cherish him as a friend, they eagerly reciprocated acts of friendship, both wittingly and otherwise.

For example, one night over dinner, William asked him "How many languages do you speak?"

"Only three: Catalan, Spanish and French," replied Fernando. "And of course I read and sing Latin."

"Don't forget the most universal language of all: music!" William reminded him. "You are amazingly fluent on many instruments."

Fernando laughed. "And how many do you speak?" he asked William.

"Seven," replied William. "I speak Gaelic, English, Dutch, French, and Spanish fluently, and Portuguese and Arabic tolerably well."

"But that is astounding!" said Fernando. "However do you manage it?"

"Don't ask the centipede how it manages a hundred legs," joked William, "for then it will not be able to walk."

Fernando laughed merrily at that.

"But seriously," continued William, "you play so many instruments, and you can remember a piece of music perfectly after hearing it only once, because you have a special gift. My gift for languages is much more ordinary, but not entirely dissimilar. My linguistic ear partly resembles your musical one: I only have to hear a language spoken, and somehow I can parrot it back and begin to make sense of it. Besides, I have a strong ulterior motive: it is very good for business! The more tongues one can master, the more trade one can generate, and the less likelihood of being misunderstood, or cheated."

"Fair enough," replied Fernando. "So, if I were to learn a new tongue, which one would you recommend?"

"English!" said William emphatically, and without hesitation. "And then, more English!"

"Why such insistence?" asked Fernando.

"Because we are approaching a historical crisis that will affect us all, however things turn out," said William. "If you would fare as well as can be in time of war, learn the language of the victor. In this policy you are already well advanced. Should Catalonia ever regain its independence from Spain, you already speak its tongue. Should Spain retain its independence in the power struggle between France and England, you already speak its tongue. And should France conquer Spain, you already speak its tongue. But should England prevail, you do not yet speak its tongue. Consider then the wisdom, or at least the prudence, of adding English to your repertoire."

"I can see why you are so successful at business," Fernando remarked. "You have a way of couching suggestions in a most attractive light."

"Aye, that I do," agreed William. And then, in a sincere gesture of friendship, he proposed something quite specific: "You should know, Fernando, that I practice what I preach. My own daughters take English lessons, twice every week. The Secretary of the British Consul in Málaga comes to my home to teach them. The British Consul and I are on the best of terms, as quasi-compatriots, even though, as the American Consul, I am a quasi-traitor to the British Crown. At any rate, you are welcome to join the English lessons, that is if you think you can get a word in edgewise among my three talkative daughters."

Fernando was touched by this offer, and he accepted it on the spot. "But why don't you or your good wife teach them English yourselves?" he asked.

"Mainly for two reasons: namely, myself and my good wife. I have a thick Scottish brogue, which would not serve my daughters well to mimic; while Françoise has an even thicker French accent, such that when she speaks English only the French can understand her," he laughed.

So Fernando began to absorb the English language, and even managed to get the odd word in edgewise among three very talkative girls.

His aptitude was such that before long he could converse with William about small matters and, soon after, larger ones. Fernando had no idea just how valuable this gift of the English tongue would prove to be, but he much more swiftly realized the incomparable value of yet another gift bestowed on him—and via him, on countless future guitarists— by this remarkable Kirkpatrick family; namely, the gift of learning to compose studies for guitar students. Like so many great things, this gift manifested unintentionally, in the aftermath of Fernando's inaugural concert for the Kirkpatricks and their well-heeled guests, in their palatial villa at Adra.

Fernando had prepared for the concert with his usual blend of inspiration and perfectionism. By this time, mid-summer of 1804, Fernando was well settled into his new abode. The cottage itself had come equipped with rustic furnishings, regional pottery, and local bric-a-brac. Fernando had added his musical necessities: a small piano, a cello, a violin, his Alonso guitar, and a trunk full of scores. In addition, he had brought along a modest library, and of course an assortment of attire. He had hung Goya's portrait of him in the place of honor, over the hearth in the sitting room.

William stopped by the cottage one evening, to discuss some details about the upcoming concert. He had last visited the place just after Fernando had first moved in, to make sure that all was in order, but by now he found Fernando well settled, and completely unpacked. As Fernando invited his guest to make himself comfortable in the sitting room, and poured him a sherry, William's eye lit upon the Goya portrait, and his jaw dropped to the floor.

"Great God Almighty!" William gasped. (Although a good Catholic by conversion, he was not averse to mouthing an occasional oath.) "Is that a Goya?"

"It is indeed," replied Fernando. "Goya is my friend and, in spirit, my elder brother," he added, with a modest smile, as if to explain how the portrait came to be there.

But William's mind had rapidly shifted itself into high gear. "Look, I've no right to ask you this," he confessed, "but is there any way to convince you to permit me to hang this work in my villa? It deserves to be seen by more eyes than ours alone, and by equally discerning company that will appreciate its magnificence ... I'd be happy to rent it from you, by the month, and have it fully insured of course. Just name your terms."

At this, Fernando was mightily amused. He had rarely seen William so animated, and so vulnerably betraying a deep-seated need.

"Please, my dear friend," Fernando beseeched, "Let us not speak of money. If the portrait means that much to you, then you may simply borrow it, and for as long as you wish. Without a doubt, it is better suited to a villa than to this cottage. And besides, if I wish to behold myself, I can always look in the mirror."

They both laughed at that. Then William grew serious again.

"You have a most generous heart," he observed, "and you have no idea how much this will mean to my family."

That matter settled, they returned to the initial purpose of William's visit, and finalized their plans for the concert.

It took place in late August of 1804, and the date—set by Françoise—had scarcely been chosen at random. Not a few Grandees were still entertaining summer guests in their Andalusian country estates, well within traveling range, while other ladies and gentlemen of condition were summering or touring on the Costa del Sol. Paris too was still empty, as *la rentrée* would not begin for another week, and so the Spanish coast was still sprinkled with distinguished French travelers. Françoise being an exceptionally able socialite, harboring no less ambition for her daughters than did William, for Fernando's concert she had cast a wide net, through whose fine meshes few fishes of consequence swam free. Everyone in the region had heard about the event; no-one of importance had failed to receive an invitation; and anyone with good sense and musical sensibility would have given their eye teeth to attend. No composer and guitarist of Fernando's stature had ever graced Málaga's musical circles, and the Kirkpatricks played on his reputation like virtuosi.

The venue itself was as fitting as the artist and the guest list. The Kirkpatricks' villa in Adra was a colonial-style mansion, sprawling on a gentle rise set well back from the road, and approached on an expansive, tree-lined drive. This splendid abode, which formed the centerpiece of a sizable cotton plantation, was embellished with gardens, orchards, and vineyards that delighted the eye and the palate alike. Anyone who knew

William well enough knew too that, landed gentry or not, *hidalgo* or not, he had sprung from a hardscrabble Scottish lowland farm, and that his parents had needed to sire a platoon of offspring just to wrest a meager livelihood from the grudging ground. So Adra was William's dream come true, for here he could play the Spanish equivalent of the patrician role of a lush plantation owner from the American south (minus the sin of slavery), with none other than Thomas Jefferson as a regular correspondent. Indeed, the very pillars on his Palladian portico were virtual copies of Jefferson's design at Monticello, for which William had paid a pretty penny to Italian quarries and craftsmen to replicate. Although never one to rest on his laurels, at Adra William could at least adorn himself and his family with them, and feel he had justifiably earned them. And never far from his thoughts, nor from those of Françoise, were the matrimonial possibilities afforded their daughters by this idyllic set piece, and the guests now drawn to it by Fernando's incomparable artistry.

On this day, one could scarcely stroll in the garden without tripping over a Grandee. The glittering array included some whom Fernando had met previously in Madrid, and others whose acquaintance would be new to him. As they took their seats in the music room, and awaited the young maestro's entrance, their eyes could not help but light on Goya's portrait of him, which William had hung—with little subtlety but large impact—center stage above the dais. As their host had calculated, the painting raised their expectations of the artist, for most of them were well aware that Goya had never before painted anyone so young in a solo portrait. It also elevated their estimation of the host, for the Costa del Sol was not exactly littered with Goya's works. William sat front and center, flanked by Françoise and their daughters, resplendent in their new dresses sewn of his latest exquisite imported silks.

On their right sat the handsome, and handsomely titled Cipriano de Palafox y Portocarrero, 13th Duke of Peñaranda del Duero, 18th Count of Teba, and 8th Count de Montijo. A dashing young nobleman of twenty, Cipriano de Palafox had short-term soldierly and long-term political ambitions. As a youthful torch-bearer of French Enlightenment values, a promising future lay before him.

Next to him sat the great patriarch Francisco Cabarrús y Lalanne (Conde de Cabarrús), his son Domingo Cabarrus y Galabert, and grandson Domingo Cabarrus y Quilty. Francisco Cabarrús was descended from an exotic tangle of merchant shipbuilders, Basque sea captains, whalers, and assorted adventurers. His financial and economic talents had blossomed under King Charles III, during whose reign he founded the Banco de San Carlos (today's Bank of Spain), built the Canal de Cabarrús that supplied water to Madrid, and initiated many other projects. He was also a fixture of the Spanish Enlightenment, and a close friend of Floridablanca, Jovellanos, and other reformists of his generation. Goya had naturally painted his portrait, which still adorns the head office of the Bank of Spain. But after Charles III's death in 1788, and the ensuing crackdown on liberal sympathizers, he had been flung into prison on the usual trumped-up charges of embezzlement. He was later released and politically resuscitated.

His son Domingo aspired to follow not only in his father's reformist footsteps, but also in the even more revolutionary ones of his celebrated sister, the beautiful and socially influential Parisienne Teresa Cabarrus Galabert, also known as Madame Tallien. She had operated one of the most incendiary salons in Paris during the revolution, and was later instrumental as an organizer of the Thermidorian rebellion that overthrew Robespierre. She had arranged for Theresa and Joséphine de Beauharnais to be released from prison, and had enjoyed a brief flirtation with Napoleon himself. Reveling in scandal, she once appeared at the Paris Opera scantily clad in a translucent sleeveless white silk dress, which also revealed a complete absence of underwear. Talleyrand was overheard to observe "*Il n'est pas possible de s'exposer plus somptueusement!*" ("It is not possible to expose oneself more sumptuously!"). Madame Tallien married a succession of rich and powerful men, and eventually became the Countess of Caraman and Princess of Chimay.

Ambitious as they were for their own daughters, the Kirkpatricks breathed silent sighs of relief that Madame Tallien had *not* joined her father, brother and nephew on this occasion. For Maria Manuela, Heniquita, and Catalina Carlota were already feisty enough, proving to be handfuls even at their tender age, without being exposed to a French woman of world-class salacious repute, notwithstanding her undeniable success.

Next to Françoise sat the Military Governor of Málaga province, General Theodor von Reding, who also commanded the First Division of the Army of Andalusia. Already renowned for his leadership and bravery, he would soon become a hero to all of Spain. Next to von Reding sat Françoise's sister Catherine and her husband, the French diplomat Mathieu Maximilien Prosper, Comte de Lesseps. They had been married in Málaga in 1801, and Catherine was now carrying their third child, Ferdinand, who was destined to become chief engineer of the Suez Canal.

Assorted other members of the Kirkpatrick clan, hailing from up and down the coast, along with other nobles, consuls, diplomats, officials, merchants, and miscellaneous ladies and gentlemen of condition, packed the music room and fell silent with expectation.

Before long Fernando made his entrance with freshly strung Alonso guitar in hand, its soundboard gleaming mirror-like with French polish. He was smartly attired in dark silk breeches, a white silk shirt with frilled and layered collar, and a velour jacket—all done up courtesy of William's latest imports, and Málaga's finest tailor. (Unlike Madame Tallien at the Paris Opera, Fernando wore underwear.)

His performance brought the house down. Even those who had heard him play brilliantly in Madrid insisted that this was his best concert ever. The most acclaimed pieces were his boleros, of distinctively Spanish character yet embellished with unmistakable touches of Haydn and Mozart. For the mandatory encore, he surprised and delighted the audience by welcoming on stage fellow guitarist Dionisio Aguado, now a twenty-year-old virtuoso in his own right, with whom he played several scintillating duets he had composed for the occasion, and dedicated to the Kirkpatricks of Málaga.

When Fernando finally left the stage, bowing and smiling repeatedly to the relentless applause, the audience found themselves looking again at Goya's portrait. In the immediate aftermath of the concert, still reverberating mellifluously in their heads, they suddenly appreciated Goya's rendering of Fernando in a brand-new light: it was so realistic, so well imbued with the guitarist's cherubic countenance and joyful spirit, that they half-expected the likeness to leap out of its frame and play another encore.

In addition to the illustrious company itself, the magic of Fernando's music and persona pervaded and enchanted the subsequent reception. Everyone said it was not only the most memorable concert of the season, but also unparalleled in the musical memory of the region. Moreover, the social bonds that were forged or deepened that day would have momentous consequences for many in attendance, including the Kirkpatrick daughters, who could not then have known that their future husbands were all present.

The after-effects on Fernando were no less long-lasting. Immediately after the concert, Maria Manuela excitedly told her parents that she wished to learn the guitar, with Fernando of course as her teacher. While her progress with piano and singing left them no doubt as to her musical ability, William and Françoise felt some trepidation in approaching the maestro to instruct a rank beginner, and a child no less, on such a challenging instrument. So they procrastinated. But being their parents' daughter—beautiful, bold, and brilliant—Maria Manuela pestered them remorselessly, and without surcease. Whereupon, to their happy amazement, they found Fernando completely amenable. He explained why.

"I first wanted to play the guitar at age five. My mother approved, but my father resisted. Fortunately, my mother prevailed. Of course my father wanted what was best for me, but he could think only in terms of what was best for him. If you truly want what is best for your children, then you must never fail to imagine something better than what is best for you. If Maria Manuela wishes to learn the guitar, then I will teach her without reservation. Our only obstacle is convincing a luthier to make an instrument small enough to accommodate her petite hands."

Given Fernando's fame and William's persuasive purse, that presented no obstacle at all. Joseph Martinez, Málaga's best luthier, built a scaled-down yet sweetly sonorous guitar for her within two months. When William surprised Maria Manuela with it, she shrieked with joy.

The long-lasting effects on Fernando were felt as soon as Maria Manuela started her guitar lessons. He suddenly realized that he needed a method for beginners, and—being virtually self-taught on guitar—had never really developed one. Moretti had published a method in 1799, but it did not accord with Fernando's style. Earlier methods had also been published in 1794 by Le Moine in France, and in 1795 by Light in England, but of these Fernando had not yet heard. So he resolved to develop his own, a project that began with Maria Manuela, his first pupil, and culminated many years and numerous pupils later, with its first publication in 1830. Meanwhile Fernando invented his method by teaching it, starting with body position and technical exercises for both hands, and working its way up to simple pieces. This would lead him to bequeath precious musical gifts to guitarists of generations yet unborn. Like Bach's keyboard pieces written for his students, Sor's studies for guitar were similarly masterpieces: easy enough for beginners to play, yet profound enough for the concert stage.

And something else began to affect Fernando, something deeply personal, as he taught singing and guitar to this vivacious and precocious young girl. He began to wish for a daughter of his very own, a musical prodigy like himself, who would make him as proud of her as William and Françoise were of Maria Manuela. He was now twenty-six, and most men were fathers by then. His day-dreams of a daughter soon led him to dream at night, exclusively of Joaquina. Somehow he knew that she was destined to be the mother of his child; but exactly when and where, and in what circumstances, still eluded him.

And precisely because William and Françoise took Fernando's sage advice to heart, in wanting a better future for their daughters than they themselves could imagine, so it would come to pass.

Catalina Carlota, their youngest, would marry back into the family in 1818, to a distant cousin named Thomas James Kirkpatrick, whose branch was based in Gibraltar. They had first met at Sor's concert, when Thomas was but twelve and Catalina only seven. Their eventual eldest son, Alexander, would one day become British Vice Consul in Málaga. Being the youngest daughter, perhaps Catalina was 'babied' longer than her older sisters, whose spirited independence and audacity no doubt panicked their parents at times. At any rate, and for whatever reasons, her horizons were comfortable but vastly diminished compared with those of her two sisters.

The middle daughter Heniquita could not be constrained, and in late 1817 would marry Domingo Cabarrus y Quilty, grandson of the venerable Count of Cabarrus. They, too, had first met as children, at Fernando's concert. Unfortunately her husband died before his father, Domingo Cabarrus y Galabert, the 2nd Count of Cabarrus, and so he did not become the 3rd Count. But that title was inherited by their daughter, Paulina Cabarrus y Kirkpatrick, who in due course became the 3rd Countess of Cabarrus.

Maria Manuela, the eldest and most high-spirited of the three daughters, would ensconce her father's name in history's boldest typeface. In early 1817 she would marry the dashing Cipriano de Palafox y Portocarrero, 13th Duke of Peñaranda del Duero, 18th Count of Teba, 8th Count de Montijo, and later Marquis de Algava, Duke of Granada, Duke of Peñaranda, and a Grandee of Spain. Like her sisters and their future husbands, she first had met Cipriano at Fernando's concert. But this couple's children's stars would blaze more brightly than her parents could ever have imagined, even in their wildest dreams. She and Cipriano would have two daughters: Maria Francisca (born 1825) and Maria Eugenia (born 1826).

Doña María Francisca de Sales Portocarrero y Kirkpatrick, affectionately known as 'Paca de Alba', would accede to all her father's titles, and thus became the 12th Duchess of Peñaranda de Duero, 10th Marchioness of Valderrábano, 17th Marchioness of Villanueva del Fresno and Barcarrota, 13th Marchioness of la Algaba, 15th Marchioness of La Bañeza, 15th Marchioness of Mirallo, 14th Marchioness of Valdunquillo, 9th Countess of Montijo, 17th Countess of Miranda del Castañar, 18th Countess of Fuentidueña, 13th Countess of Casarrubios del Monte, 20th Countess of San Esteban de Gormaz and 18th Viscountess of Palacios de la Valduerna. These titles would be incorporated into the House of Alba through her future marriage to Jacobo Fitz-James Stuart y Ventimiglia, one of the wealthiest men in all of Europe, and the 15th Duke of Alba.

But her younger sister, Maria Eugenia, would fare even better. Doña María Eugenia Ignacia Augustina de Palafox y KirkPatrick, 16th Countess of Teba and15th Marchioness of Ardales, would go on to marry Louis Napoleon III, nephew of Napoleon, President of the Second Republic, and later Emperor of the Second Empire. She would first meet Prince Louis Napoléon while chaperoned by her mother, at a reception given by the 'prince-president' at the Élysée Palace in 1849. Helplessly attracted by her beauty, Louis Napoleon would immediately try to seduce her, only to find himself rebuffed. Unaccustomed to rejection, he demanded "What is the road to your heart?" "Through the chapel, Sire," Eugenie demurely answered and, irresistibly charmed, he would embark on it, and make her Empress of France.

So, in the autumn of 1804, in the sleepy seaside town of Málaga, Fernando gave guitar lessons to a high-spirited young girl named Maria Manuela Kirkpatrick y Grivegnée, born of Scottish and Belgian merchants. Little could he, or for that matter her parents, imagine that this little girl from Málaga would become the future mother not only of 15th Duchess Consort of Alba but also of the last Empress of France.

But Fernando's idyllic interlude on the Costa del Sol was not to last. The clouds of war were gathering in earnest over Iberia, and their violent storm would soon enough break over all their heads.

Chapter 14. Málaga, and Beyond: Exoneration, and Invasion

Fernando's sunlit sojourn in Málaga gradually lengthened into months, and his fruitful months there likewise elongated, almost imperceptibly, into years. The Mediterranean coast invariably exerts this effect on one's perception of time, seemingly any amount of which runs together like sand through one's fingers, and elapses as if one long day at the beach.

However and all the while, the Inquisition of Fernando Sor moved forward at a calculated pace, silently dogging him like an invisible shadow. When their investigation reached a cul-de-sac in Madrid, the Inquisitors followed him to Málaga, and thence to Macharaviaya, after allowing a sufficient passage of time for any new heresies to be voiced and overheard in those places. Thus they gave him, as the British were wont to say, enough rope to hang himself. And sure enough, their patience would bear fruit, ripe enough to cause Fernando palpable anxiety. Yet this religious tempest would prove a mere squall compared to the political maelstrom that was brewing in France.

It goes without saying that William Kirkpatrick kept his finger daily on a multitude of political and economic pulses, because he knew the worth of Bacon's dictum that 'knowledge is power'. William's livelihood, and thus his family's well-being, hung in the balance of his ability to keep pace with and adjust, as best he could, to current events. Since

Fernando frequented the Kirkpatricks' home in Málaga and their villa in Adra, he too kept abreast of the news.

And lately the news was not good. In December 1804, the First Consul of France had crowned himself Emperor Napoleon I at Notre-Dame de Paris, having snatched the crown from the hands of Pope Pius VII and laid it on his own head. This set off shock waves of disapproval across the Continent, not only from Catholic monarchs who regarded the authority of the Pope as sacrosanct, but also from Enlightenment intellectuals who admired the ideals of the French Revolution and had applauded the former First Consul's secular reforms. These latter reactions were epitomized by Beethoven, who had just dedicated 'The Napoleon Symphony' (his third symphony) to the First Consul. Upon hearing the news, he promptly threw a fit and undedicated it. He crossed out the dedication so violently that he tore right through the cover page of the score, which he renamed 'The Eroica Symphony'. The Emperor was unperturbed. He fully intended to vacate every throne he could lay his hands on, replacing their decadent monarchs with trusted family members or loyal Marshals. As to the artists and intelligentsia, for all he cared they could hold their collective breath until they turned blue, and he would not lose a wink of sleep. He barely slept an hour per night in any case.

The prospects for a peaceful Iberia deteriorated markedly the next year, in October 1805, when the combined fleets of France and Spain—more than thirty ships of the line—were routed by Admiral Nelson's inferior numbers, but superior seamanship and gunnery, at the now-legendary Battle of Trafalgar. Although Nelson was mortally wounded, his victory enabled Britannia to rule the world's waves for the next hundred years, and forced Napoleon—as the political pundits in Iberia had feared—to set armies marching across the Continent. If the French Emperor's destiny could not be fulfilled by sea, it would come to fruition by land.

Wasting little time, Napoleon won a decisive victory in December of that year, at Austerlitz, in 'the battle of the three Emperors'. Turning the tables on Trafalgar, his Grande Armée defeated a much larger force led by Russian Emperor Alexander I and Holy Roman Emperor Francis II.

While the Corsican lion permitted the Russian bear to limp home and lick its wounds, in 1806 Napoleon compelled the abdication of Francis II, abolished the Holy Roman Empire, installed his brother Joseph Bonaparte as King of Naples, and named various family members to other important posts.

Then, in November 1806, Napoleon promulgated the Berlin Decree, which instituted the so-called Continental System, preventing British ships from entering European ports. He mistakenly thought he could weaken Britain's will by inflicting economic hardship on its people. The British responded with a naval blockade of Europe itself, preventing French and their allies' ships from leaving European ports. This only incensed Napoleon further. While these mutual economic sanctions utterly failed to leash the dogs of war, they caused considerable privation and suffering among the general populace, by crippling trade, inducing shortages of foodstuffs and other necessities of life, and putting innumerable merchants out of business.

Late in that fateful month, William described this bleak picture to Fernando over one of their habitual lunches in the port.

"So what will you do now?" Fernando asked his friend.

"Tighten my belt, batten my hatches, and reroute as much of my trade as can still earn a penny. Come to that, I may even have to trade some things at a loss, just to maintain certain otherwise-valuable partnerships."

"But how can you run both blockades?" Fernando wondered.

"Portuguese ports are still open under British control, as long as I can ferry goods to and from them. Naturally, my position as American Consul leaves me in bad odor with England, but business is business. And now I am also obliged to deal with various devils, striking ill-favored bargains with black marketeers and pirates. They will rob me blind, but if I give them steady custom they may see the wisdom of robbing me that much less. Yet this situation cannot last. Now that Napoleon has sent Russia packing, dismantled the Holy Roman Empire, and brought central Europe to heel, he is bound to invade Iberia by land, in his quest to drive the English out of Portugal."

"But what of Spain?" asked Fernando. "Will we not resist him?"

"That, my friend, is the largest question of our times. I only wish I knew the answer."

At that they both fell silent. Then William sensed a further worry in Fernando's countenance, a visible departure from his normal good cheer, even in this darkening hour.

"And what troubles you, my friend? Is it something more immediate than the fate of Spain?"

"Indeed it is," said Fernando in a grave tone. "I am summoned by the Inquisition. They came to my house yesterday, to question me, along with an order to confiscate my books for their scrutiny. Since I was not at home, they took the books, and left the summons with Conchita, whom they also questioned. The poor girl was frightened out of her wits, and remains so terrified that she is praying all day today, for her security and my exoneration. At all events I will report to them tomorrow, and see the matter through."

"Godspeed," said William. "If I can help in any way, do not hesitate to ask. But your concern appears well founded. At least I can still strike bargains with my devils, and haggle over the price of a cargo. But these holy devils will not haggle with you over the price of your soul. May God preserve it from their unholy ministrations!"

And on this solemn note, they parted company and went about their business.

Having bided their time, Inquisition had indeed followed Fernando's trail to Macharaviaya, where he had by now spent enough time drinking and gambling to warrant their investigation. As usual, they began with the parish priest, Don Pedro de Aguirre. The priest told them that he himself had nothing against Sor in matters of religion, but that he had heard someone else claim that Sor had said heretical things. Don Pedro had not taken this seriously, since he deemed Sor merely to have been jesting, as was his wont. When the Inquisitors demanded to know the identity of that person, the priest gave them her name: Maria de Prada. When they interrogated her, she told them some shocking things. One day, in the presence of witnesses, she had asked Fernando whether he had gone to confession. He said yes, and also that he had taken a *torrezno,* and wondered whether it would pass out the next day, at the other end. A *torrezno* is a wafer of fried bacon, sold in packets, by which she understood that he meant the Holy Sacrament. Of course she was utterly scandalized by this heresy. She also told them that he owned books by Voltaire (which were banned of course), and that he had muttered other heresies besides.

So they questioned two of the alleged witnesses named by Maria de Prada, who contradicted her testimony by claiming that they had never heard Sor say such things. At this the Inquisitors temporized. That she may have lied about there being witnesses did prove that she was lying about Sor's heresies. After all, they reasoned, women were notorious liars, but that did not mean that they were completely incapable of telling occasional truths. As usual, they did not inquire into Maria's motives. Perhaps she had flirted with Sor, and he had spurned her. Or perhaps he had merely teased her, 'winding her up' as he was known to do when people took their own piety—or anything else about themselves— too seriously. But Doña Tomasa Esteve had been right all along: it was dangerous to say such things in Spain at this time, to whomever and for whatever reason.

Returning to Málaga, they questioned a local priest, one Don Juan Gonzalez. He told them that Sor was a good Samaritan, who had once gone to the house of a dying friend, and had summoned him (that is, Don Juan) to administer the last rites. When asked about his character, the priest responded that Sor "had a lively and cheerful spirit, amusing, and addicted to the daughters of Adam"—in other words, that he liked women, perhaps too much for his own good.

After careful deliberation, the Inquisitors concluded that there was 'strong evidence' that Sor might be 'a libertine, a materialist, a dogmatizer, and a heretic'. This had prompted their summons.

Following his rather fitful lunch with William, Fernando returned home and wrote up a dutiful plea to the Inquisitors. He begged them to accept his statement "in case it should be that by some incident, some action, or some phrase might possibly have given rise to some malicious interpretation, because the scrupulousness of his Catholic way of thought and his respect for the religion which he professed caused any doubt which might be held about it to be bitter to him and did not allow him to live in tranquility if by some distraction, some heated speech or by some thoughtlessness even the very least suspicion might have been caused to anyone; and if the Tribunal were not completely satisfied or found anything at all which might be considered to be against our religion, he begged them to absolve him from any faults into which against his will or against his reason he might possibly have fallen and which he certainly would detest with all his heart, whatever they might be, so that he might now promptly return to carry out the obligations of his work."

On the next day Fernando reported to the Tribunal. They entered his written statement into the record, and asked him a number of questions, to which he responded forthrightly and solemnly, making sure to excise every iota of levity from his tone. He was particularly careful to refrain from jokes, although he could barely suppress the urge to tell them the one about the Jesuits that he had overheard at Montserrat, after a Benedictine father had dived too deeply into the medicinal brandy:

A Benedictine and a Jesuit were debating which order was more beloved in the sight of God. Since they could not agree, they decided to write to God and ask Him. So they composed a missive, beseeching Him to tell them which He favored more: Benedictines, or Jesuits. Lo and behold, an angel appeared and conveyed their missive on high. Moments later the angel returned, bearing God's response, which read:

"Dear Brethren,

"Know that all orders are equally beloved in My sight.

"I love all, and favor none.

"Yours faithfully,

"God, S.J."

The Benedictines had roared with sinful laughter at this, but the Tribunal would not have been in the slightest amused. Although Fernando was an incorrigible jokester and sometime prankster, he was hardly suicidal, and so he held his tongue. However, he could not refrain from telling himself this joke, even in the midst of the Inquisitors' relentless questioning. Even so, he put on a masterful show of seriosity, betraying not the slightest hint of amusement at the proceedings. After all, he was potentially on trial for his life.

Following what seemed an interminable round of questioning, the Tribunal returned Fernando's books to him, which included works of poetry, mathematics, and fortification, the letters of Abélard and Héloïse (volume 2), some tales by Marmontel in French, various miscellaneous but innocuous works, and (to his credit with them) a *New Testament* and a *Guia de Pecadores*.

But the Tribunal was thorough to a fault, and decided to keep Fernando wriggling a while longer on their zealous hook. They dismissed him for the time being, and said they would recall him once their verdict had been reached. Whereupon they returned to Macharaviaya, and questioned Maria de Prada more closely about Fernando's supposed book by Voltaire, which they had not found in his modest library. How did she know that he owned one? She said it was because he sometimes read a small book that was in French, and he put it aside whenever anyone approached him, and she knew that Voltaire was prohibited and so she had assumed that the book must be by Voltaire. After hearing this flimsy and flighty deduction, the Tribunal dismissed the girl with a dry admonition to devote more time to devotional prayer and less time to logical inference.

Then they re-summoned the local priest, Don Pedro de Aguirre, for a final round of questioning. The priest testified that he never heard Sor say anything that was contrary to the doctrines of the Church, in fact quite the opposite. According to Don Pedro, Sor recited the proper doctrines that he had learned in the school at Montserrat, from the fathers there who taught him, in whose house he had grown up from a child. Then they pressed him more closely, and asked about confession. The priest replied that he had heard confession from Sor only once, but—without violating the sanctity of the confessional—he could say that he found nothing in Sor other than a good Roman Catholic and Apostolic Christian.

At last, in December of 1806, the Tribunal returned to Málaga, and re-summoned Fernando to hear their verdict. To his immense relief, they acquitted him of the charge of heresy. They dismissed him with a maddeningly vague but unmistakably grave warning, that he should detest and abjure anything potentially heretical that had been said about him which might have some basis in it.

Fernando met William for lunch soon after, and shared this good news with his friend, who was delighted to hear it.

"Françoise said all along they would acquit you, no matter what the evidence. She is convinced that a guardian angel watches over you, and now I half-believe her. But I told her to be careful about repeating that persuasion to careless ears, for she herself might have been accused of heresy had the Tribunal convicted you. It is frightfully easy to mistake devils for angels, especially these days."

Fernando nodded in accord. This talk of angels reminded him of the joke about the Benedictines and the Jesuits, which by now he was dying to tell someone. So told it to William, who guffawed with laughter.

"By God, you have the mind of a little devil!" William unwittingly echoed the long-ago words of Father Arredondo.

"Be that as it may," Fernando smiled, "yet the minds of much bigger devils give us both cause for concern. What news do you have from Madrid? And from abroad?

"Alas," said William, "I have too much news: most of it rumor, and all of it contradictory. I can make neither head nor tail of the situation, which seems to vacillate from day to day. Will Spain resist France? Will Spain collaborate with France? And who will decide what Spain will do? There is no coherent answer, either because there are too many competing policies in Madrid, or because there is no policy at all. We can only wait for the proverbial axe to fall. Exactly whose necks it will sever, and how many heads will roll, remains to be seen."

Napoleon would soon see to it that more blood would be shed in Iberia than either William or Fernando could have imagined, but before that the Emperor of Europe had one further mission to accomplish: in this case, a diplomatic one. He needed to secure a treaty with Tsar Alexander, and wean him away from Russia's alliance with England, in order to protect his eastern front before driving the English out of Portugal.

The two Emperors met in Tilsit, in late July 1807, in a tent on a raft, moored exactly in the middle of the Niemen River. They had each been rowed there, to confer alone, while their armies cheered from the opposite banks. Both armies were weary from incessant battle, and both Emperors sought a respite, and they both knew it. At the same time, neither one trusted the other, and each sought to deceive the other, and they both knew that too. Moreover, each one tried to lead the other into believing he had indeed been deceived by the other, the better to probe each other's true intentions. And they both knew that as well.

For his part, Alexander regarded it as inevitable that Napoleon would invade Russia just as soon as he felt strong enough to do so. But by the same token, he needed to buy time to strengthen his own defenses. To his surprise, he found Napoleon rather charming, and thoroughly regal; a far cry from his portrayal by Prussian Junkers, among others who reviled him, as a brash upstart and a coarse bandit. As their rapport deepened, Alexander found it easy to come to terms with him. This was not surprising, as each needed concessions from the other. But Alexander never made the mistake of trusting him to abide by their agreement.

For his part, Napoleon knew full well that Alexander might suspend—but would never completely abandon—his alliance with England, especially in view of their common enemy, Turkey. Despite this, he found the Emperor of Russia a congenial dialogue partner, in whom he had finally met an equal with whom he could talk turkey, as it were. But in truth Alexander remained a cipher to Napoleon. Perhaps that was because the former had been born and bred to rule a vast and long-standing Empire, having learned at the knee of his grandmother, Catherine the Great; while the latter had seized and forged his empire piecemeal and *de nouveau*, through a combination of audacity, instinct, and destiny. In any case, Napoleon had finally met his match, for Alexander could neither be cowed nor bullied, unlike so many of the milquetoast monarchs of decadent Europe.

Their initial meeting in the tent was so mutually agreeable that they continued their dialogue for several days in the town of Tilset, in more commodious surroundings, where fine victuals and rare vintages were much closer to hand. Both emperors had travelled with their imperial chefs and food tasters, along with wagons well stocked with delicacies, both solid and liquid. When their agreements were finalized, and the time came to redraw the maps, they sealed their accord with Petrossian caviar washed down with Prunier cognac, at a price tag that could have kept either army in the field for a week.

They were both well pleased with their agreement. Russia would end her cooperation with England, and participate in France's Continental System. At a stroke, they callously carved up Prussia, and imposed heavy reparations on both the Prussians and the Austrians, to help defray the costs of their wars. By secret treaty, France would give Russia a free hand in Finland and Sweden, while Russia would grant France similar *laissez-faire* in Spain and Portugal.

Both Emperors returned home in triumph: Alexander to the unimaginable opulence of his palace in Saint Petersburg, to plot his next moves carefully amidst the incessant intrigues of the Russian nobility; Napoleon to acclaim in Paris, for having brought peace to a newly expanded empire, along with revenues from defeated enemies. Music played a central role in both Emperors' celebrations. Alexander commissioned imperial composer Dmitry Stepanovich Bortniansky to create a cycle of operas as well as devotional pieces; Parisians commemorated Napoleon's bloodless victory in extravagant French style: with a festival featuring a concert, a ballet, and an opera, followed by a grand reception.

At the same time, in sleepy Málaga, Fernando was preparing to give his next concert, while dreaming of music for his first ballet, and for yet another opera. Little did he know, at the time, that the music of his dreams was destined to be acclaimed by French and Russian ears alike, including those of Emperor Alexander himself. But before those happy days would come to pass, the French Emperor's destiny had unfortunate priority, and would shortly inundate Iberia in a bloodbath.

Scarcely had the final notes of the celebratory Parisian festival reverberated away, and hardly had the images of glittering gowns, gleaming jewels, and pungent perfumes of the gala reception's array of enticing women faded from men's minds, when Napoleon made his fateful move in the west.

In July of 1807, the Emperor commanded the Portuguese government to close its ports to British ships. It refused. Anticipating that, Napoleon had made a secret agreement with Godoy, to march an allied force of French and Spanish armies into Portugal, and dismember her. France would administrate one third; Spain would annex another third; while Godoy would be made a Prince of the remaining third, ruling it as his private principality. This was to be Godoy's reward for convincing Queen Maria Luisa and King Charles IV to accede to this plan, although needless to say Napoleon had not the slightest intention of honoring it. He recalled quite vividly that just one year before, in 1806, an impetuous Godoy had pledged Spain's active friendship in Prussia's war against France. Now Napoleon played skillfully upon Godoy's myopic duplicity and monumental vanity, dangling an imaginary principality to lure Spanish troops into a coalition, adding decisive weight to his hammer blow on Portugal. Indeed, Godoy had committed eight thousand Spanish infantry and three thousand Spanish cavalry to join General Junot's army of twenty thousand Frenchmen, which crossed the Bidasoa River into Spain in the month of October 1807.

As they marched across Spain toward Portugal, word of their invasion rapidly outpaced them to Lisbon, where the Portuguese royal family had no intention of awaiting their arrival, and no armed forces sufficient to repel them. The entire royal court boarded ship and set sail for Brazil, escorted by the British navy. Junot occupied Lisbon without firing a shot. Napoleon then imposed on the Portuguese people an indemnity of one hundred million francs to finance this operation, which he immediately enlarged. He sent three additional armies into Spain under the command of his intrepid Marshal Joaquim Murat, ostensibly in case the British decided to land an expeditionary force, but obviously with the aim of occupying Spain as well as Portugal. Murat stationed these armies strategically around Madrid.

This much accomplished, Napoleon was ready to seize the Spanish throne, but preferred a political pretext rather than a military coup. The discord that now prevailed within the royal family handed him a better excuse than even he could have engineered. It all revolved around the disturbed character of the heir apparent, Ferdinand VII, an angry young man of twenty-three. History had not heard anything from him until this juncture, beyond Goya's tongue-in-cheek portrayal of the royal family some years before, in which when Ferdinand had appeared as an innocuous-looking adolescent. Even in 1800, when Goya had painted him solo, as the Prince of Asturias, he looked like a harmless if somewhat perplexed youth.

But in reality, Ferdinand had been a selfish and spiteful child. He hated his father, whom he deemed despicably weak and unfit to reign. He hated his mother even more, whom he condemned as a trollop for her scandalous affair with Godoy. He hated Godoy several times over: first, for having seduced his mother; second, for having exploited her blind love for him, along with her husband's craven weakness, to usurp the power of the throne; third, for having ruthlessly excluded Ferdinand himself, during his childhood, from every conceivable avenue of grooming for the crown. In his spare time, Ferdinand hated music, literature, and liberal ideas of every kind. While his father hunted beasts of prey, Ferdinand trapped, tortured, and mutilated small animals. In sum, he was a monster, awaiting his appointed time to wreak sadistic havoc on all who fell within his malevolent clutches.

And now, in October 1807, Ferdinand thought his hour had come. Supported by a conservative faction liberally sprinkled with sociopaths, he hatched a plot to overthrow Godoy, to force his father to abdicate, and to place himself on the throne. But Godoy's spies uncovered the plot at the eleventh hour, whereupon Godoy turned the tables: he arrested Ferdinand and his chief advisors, intending to try them for treason. But within a few months, still awaiting the materialization of his promised Portuguese principality, which he now realized had been a Napoleonic ploy, the duped Godoy began to panic. Fearing that Murat would liberate Ferdinand and his inner circle, who would surely and swiftly inflict vengeance on him, Godoy released Ferdinand himself, and made hasty preparations to flee to America with the King and Queen.

Things came to a head on March 17, 1808, a day which proved neither excellent nor serene nor particularly peaceful for His Highness Manuel Godoy, The Most Excellent and Most Serene Prince of Peace. Angered by his wild antics and animated by even wilder rumors, the populace of Madrid rose up against him. An enraged mob stormed Godoy's palace, found him hiding under some carpets in the attic, captured him alive, and flung him into a dungeon. This development thoroughly spoiled

King Charles's hunt, and threw Queen Maria Luisa into a tizzy; whereupon a befuddled Charles IV resigned as monarch, allowing Ferdinand VII to don the crown.

Now Napoleon made his move. On March 23 Murat marched into Madrid and occupied the city. On Napoleon's orders, Murat freed Godoy and refused to recognize Ferdinand as King. Egged on by this turn of events, and at the prompting of Maria Luisa and Godoy, Charles rescinded his abdication. In Paris, Talleyrand urged Napoleon to seize the throne at once, but the Emperor had other plans. Until they unfolded, nothing but confusion reigned in the Spanish capital.

As reports of these wildly fluctuating actions reached Málaga, each new day in Madrid dawning seemingly more confused than the last, Fernando found himself unable to remain in place. Hitherto he had avoided politics, but suddenly he felt called to action. He had long supported the transplantation of French Enlightenment ideals into Spain, but could not for one moment sanction its occupation by French troops. In early April 1808 he wrote to General Castaños, requesting a transfer from his administrative post in Macharaviaya to active service in Madrid. Fernando did not wait for a response. He donned his uniform, packed his belongings, and loaded his carriage. He bade farewell to the Kirkpatrick family, who shared his patriotic passion and fully understood his personal call to duty. At the same time, young Maria Maneula was heartbroken at the departure of her teacher, but Fernando consoled her with kind words of reassurance and encouragement, which she never forgot.

"What about Goya's portrait?" asked William. "Shall I forward it to you in Madrid?"

"Pray let it hang a while longer in Adra," said Fernando. "I shall return once order is restored."

"May God speed your journey, my friend."

"And may God keep you and your family safe, come what may."

The two friends embraced, and with that Fernando departed the still-tranquil Costa del Sol, and rode courageously toward Madrid, and into the emergent chaos.

Part 3. Fernando in War, 1808-1813

Chapter 15. Madrid and Bayonne: El Dos de Mayo

Fernando reached Madrid on April 14, the same day that Napoleon arrived in Bayonne, around twenty miles north of the Spanish-French border. The Emperor had 'invited' (a polite euphemism for 'commanded') King Charles and Queen Maria Luisa on the one hand, and their son Ferdinand on the other, to join him there, to discuss how best to restore an orderly and stable government. 'Discuss' was yet another euphemism, for the next Spanish government would be formed not by these bumbling Bourbons, but rather by the Emperor of Europe and Iberia (or so, at least, the Emperor surmised).

Anxious to plead his case, would-be King Ferdinand VII and his senior advisor, the ambitious but delusional Canon Juan Escóliquiz, went hotfoot to Bayonne. Napoleon dined with them, and after a lengthy dinner conversation he concluded that Ferdinand was too immature, both intellectually and emotionally, to walk the necessary political tightrope of maintaining law and order in Spain, while sustaining subservient allegiance with France. Napoleon did not straightaway inform the youth of his decision, but let him cool his heels pending the arrival of his dawdling parents, accompanied by the inevitable and apparently indestructible Godoy.

Fernando had meanwhile found lodgings on the Gran Via, then went immediately to visit Goya in the Royal Palace.

"Welcome, little brother!" Goya beamed at him, delighted as always to see him.

"Thanks, elder brother!" returned Fernando, unfailingly inspired by Goya's frenetic persona and bustling studio, bursting as usual with works in progress.

As they caught up with one another, Fernando asked about the prevailing political situation.

"No-one is officially in charge," answered Goya. "The King and Queen and Godoy are on their way to Bayonne, to confer with Napoleon. Ferdinand is already there. Murat is meanwhile 'caretaker' of the Royal Palace. The rest of the royal family are still here, but under 'guarded ease'."

"What does that mean?" asked Fernando.

"It means that their every need is met; their every want, satisfied. Nonetheless, they are not free to come and go, and remain under house arrest, albeit in a palace."

"And what of the Spanish army?" Since Fernando was attired in his Captain's uniform, his question was personal and professional as well as political.

"France and Spain are still, at least as of this morning, allies against Portugal and England. The French troops are our honored guests, and thus far they have comported themselves respectfully, and with friendliness. The French are polite to a fault, even when requisitioning local resources. Anyway, since Portugal is footing the cost of their stay in Spain, our economy is happy to absorb them. Our troops are under orders to treat them as welcome allies, and our generals are maintaining that status quo until and unless the political situation changes. That seems to hinge on whatever transpires in Bayonne."

Goya's account put Fernando much more at ease, at least for the time being. He nurtured a flickering flame of hope that somehow the political uncertainties would be resolved peacefully, and that a duly chastened Bourbon monarch—whether father or son—would, under the watchful eye of the French Emperor, usher in renewed reforms in Spain. That was a pious hope, if but a pipe dream. But it did permit Fernando's thoughts to return to music, which after all he lived and breathed.

Napoleon had said that an army marches on its stomach. By now he had sent one hundred thousand troops into Spain, including some forty thousand into Madrid itself, and thus far they were indeed well fed and well quartered. Fernando quickly discovered that the French army also marched with its culture—an array of literati, poets and accomplished musicians were in uniform, along with excellent engineers and brilliant mathematicians. Indeed, under Napoleon's regime the most advanced mathematics could be studied only in the French artillery schools.

Fernando had of course been recognized by the palace staff, and admitted without question to visit Goya. Despite his protracted absence from Madrid, he was still the most famous guitarist in Spain, and a visible celebrity. As word of his presence circulated among the French guards posted by Murat, who were keeping a discreet eye on the royal family but otherwise not interfering with normal palace traffic, Fernando soon discovered the extent of his reputation, if not downright fame, in France. On his way out of the palace, he was approached by a French officer who introduced himself as an adjutant to Lieutenant General Jean-Marie Le Barbier de Tinan. The General, he said, was a fine amateur musician, both a violinist and a guitarist, who greatly admired Sor's compositions, many of which were well-known in Paris. Would Maestro Sor consider accepting an invitation to play for the General, and some of his staff? They would be honored to host his recital in the music room of the Royal Palace itself.

Thus he unwittingly made Fernando an offer he could not refuse. Fernando accepted his invitation with a wry inward grin. It was a kind of poetic justice, he reckoned, that while his own King had never invited him to play in this palace, and indeed had banished him from it, a French General, under the auspices of Emperor Napoleon, had opened that very door. Perhaps this alliance with France was a good thing after all, Fernando mused.

And so it came to pass, within two short weeks of his return to Madrid, that he finally played his guitar to an appreciative audience in the Royal Palace, which did not for an instant mistake his music for '*frons-frons*'. That the audience happened to be French and not Spanish made little difference to him. William Kirkpatrick had been right: music was an international language, and these Frenchmen understood it surpassingly well. During the *après-concert* reception, Fernando had a most congenial conversation with General Le Barbier de Tinan, during which he divined that the General wanted to play for him. Not the guitar—Fernando was an impossible act to follow on that instrument—but rather the violin. So Fernando offered to accompany him on the piano, and they regaled the company with some pieces by Mozart, and Haydn, and Sor himself. The General was indeed a fine musician, and not the only talented amateur to be stationed in Madrid. Toward the close of April 1808, Fernando happily made music with several of them. Their bonhomie and camaraderie, however, was destined to be short-lived, and supplanted by unimaginable horror.

Spain's royal *ménage à trois*, as Napoleon disparagingly thought of them, had by now arrived in Bayonne. One look at them sufficed to tell the Emperor that he was scraping the bottom of the Bourbon barrel. He beheld a cuckolded king too weak to wield the reins of power, a shameless queen who wielded them via purblind love for a rank opportunist, and the conniving upstart himself, who loved only power while feigning affection for the dysfunctional couple that had empowered him. Having deposed virtually every hereditary monarch on the continent, Napoleon had never beheld a sicklier triumvirate than this. "History will thank me," or so he imagined, "for putting this lame menagerie to pasture."

Alas for Napoleon's imagination. Had he invested slightly more energy studying history instead of making it, he would have thought at least twice about sparking the tinderbox of Spain. It was not a secret that the Republic of Rome, thinking itself invincible after its twin defeats of powerful Carthage and mighty Corinth in 146 B.C., came to grief by invading Hispania. There the Romans found themselves bogged down in a quagmire of stubborn resistance and guerilla warfare that slowly but surely bled their demoralized legions white. Then, in 711 A.D., the Umayyad invasion touched off the longest war in human history: almost eight centuries of intermittent yet relentless resistance—the *Reconquista*—that culminated only after every Moor in Iberia was slaughtered, converted, or expelled. But Napoleon seemed oblivious to the perils of occupying the Iberian Peninsula. If it were true, as Tolstoy would later write in *War and Peace*, that "a king is history's slave," then an emperor (as Napoleon had yet to learn) is merely history's concubine.

Determined to clean house, Napoleon sent orders to Murat to escort the rest of the royal family—the king's brother, younger son, and daughter—to Bayonne. But Ferdinand caught wind of this, and dispatched couriers to Madrid to alert his supporters, among them key generals, of Napoleon's intention to terminate the rule of the Spanish Bourbons. These couriers were intercepted in turn by Napoleon, but nevertheless word of the royal family's plight reached Madrid, and spread quickly through the populace.

The morning of May 2, 1808, dawned bright and warm in Madrid, and seemed full of spring's verdant promise. As French soldiers ushered Charles IV's brother, younger son, and daughter into a carriage, preparing to escort them under guard to Bayonne, an angry crowd gathered spontaneously at the Royal Palace, to prevent the princes and princess from being kidnapped. The crowd protested verbally at first, then began throwing stones at the French soldiers, who tried to ignore them and carry out their orders. But the stalwart indifference of the disciplined French troops transformed the incensed crowd into an enraged mob, which—armed with knives, sticks and stones—charged and overwhelmed the small French escort, literally tearing some of them to pieces. The commotion awakened Goya who, from his palace window, witnessed much of what ensued.

Murat responded immediately, dispatching a battalion of grenadiers from the Imperial Guard, along with a detachment of artillery, to the palace. The grenadiers and artillery opened fire on the mob, indiscriminately slaughtering men, women, and children alike, as well as some priests who had joined the throng. The carnage was unspeakable. The palace grounds were soon littered with dead Spaniards, whose twisted and mangled corpses struck macabre poses. Their sightless eyes stared vacuously at nothing; their frozen faces wore expressions of mute horror; their crimson blood left spreading stains on the manicured greenery. Assorted body parts, entrails, and organs, along with mounds of unidentifiable quivering flesh, lay strewn about by cannon-fire. The cries of the wounded and the dying filled the air. At last the survivors dispersed, dragging themselves and their wounded comrades away from these gardens of slaughter.

Goya had witnessed it, and would later paint it. He could scarcely believe his eyes, nor bear what they were seeing, but neither could he tear them away. Worst of all were the screams, which assailed his ears with the full force of the victims' agonies. The screams went on in his head, long after he retreated from the window and, hands shaking with shock, poured himself a stiff drink. Only when his butler came in to check on him did Goya realize that the man was mouthing words he could not hear. Although the screams in his head persisted for several days—and for weeks thereafter in his troubled dreams—Francisco Goya had become stone-deaf. He now perceived the world more clearly than ever by sight, but heard nothing more of it, nor cared to hear any more, for the remainder of his long life.

To Murat's consternation, the insurrection quickly spread to other parts of the city. Everywhere the same sequence of events unfolded: leaderless mobs assembled spontaneously and, armed only with knives, sticks, stones, and pieces of broken glass, confronted French troops wherever they found them. Murat summoned reinforcements, and heavy fighting broke out at the Puerta del Sol and Puerta del Toledo. Hundreds of civilians died in the ensuing street fights, while hundreds more were arrested. Murat declared martial law, and ordered all Spanish troops within the city confined to barracks. His orders were disobeyed by Spanish artillery units at the barracks of Monteleón, where two captains, Luis Daoíz de Torres and Pedro Velarde y Santillán, deployed their forces and joined the uprising. Both officers were killed in the subsequent action, when superior numbers of French troops stormed and obliterated their positions. A monument to their heroism stands to this day outside the Alcazar de Segovia.

As the commotion spilled onto the Gran Via, and as crashing cannonades reverberated through the city, Fernando too was roused from slumber. Initially, he thought it was a thunderstorm. But then, like Goya, he went to his window and witnessed some of the carnage. Also like Goya, he shuddered at the sounds of the screams. The composer in him took charge before the soldier could be mobilized, and—reverting to Catalan— he wrote *Crits de Carrer* (*Screams of the Street*) in response to the cacophony of horrific cries.

While order was finally restored by evening, retribution followed swiftly and harshly. Murat convened a military commission, headed by General Grouchy, which declared that all civilians arrested bearing arms—meaning knives, sticks, stones, or pieces of broken glass—would be summarily shot by firing squads. The public executions began bright and early on May 3, and by that day's end hundreds more corpses—including civilian men, women and even children—lay stacked like cordwood in the city's most prominent squares. Goya witnessed this, and would paint it too. He could no longer hear their cries of anguish, but the horrific images were indelibly engraved in his mind's eye. And as the sharp echoes of the fusillades volleyed through the alleyways, Fernando began to compose patriotic songs.

From the French point of view, these reprisals were entirely justified by the unprovoked insurrection. From the Spanish point of view, they were villainous atrocities. The blood of Madrileños boiled as many were herded into the squares and forced to witness the executions—*pour décourager les autres*— and their hatred of the French knew no bounds. But for the time being they suppressed their fury. Thus Murat, and Napoleon when he heard the reports, thought they had quelled the rebellion. The paucity of their understanding would soon be revealed. For Iberia was a powder keg just waiting to explode, and El Dos de Mayo (The Second of May) had merely lit the fuse.

Back in Bayonne, Napoleon unfolded the next phase of his plan. On May 5 he summoned Charles, Maria Luisa, Godoy, and Ferdinand into his presence, and when they were all gathered the Emperor flew into one of his well-rehearsed rages, berating them mercilessly for having permitted Spain, through their gross incompetence, to fall into such political disarray. Taking his cue, Charles and Maria Luisa then heaped their fair share of verbal abuse on their son, accusing Ferdinand of having plotted parricide. Godoy prudently kept his ears open, and his mouth shut. He had been hoping for a propitious moment to remind the Emperor of his promise of a Portuguese principality, but no such opportunity arose. Napoleon then gave Ferdinand an ultimatum: he had until eleven o'clock that evening to abdicate, or else he would be imprisoned by his parents and tried for treason. The terrified youth capitulated immediately, and restored the scepter to his father. But Charles had no more stomach for the throne; he longed for security and peace rather than power. Maria Luisa and Godoy were instantly dismayed, and had it not been for the cold glare of Napoleon—whose stony gaze alone commanded them to hold their power-hungry tongues—they would have remonstrated with their reluctant monarch.

By now the Emperor had had his fill of this dysfunctional family, and sought to wash his hands of them, once and for all.

"So be it," Napoleon declared. "We shall ourselves take charge of Spain." He said this as though unforeseen circumstances had forced his unwilling hand, whereas of course he had engineered them from the start. No-one could say that this playful Emperor did not enjoy charades.

Then he turned to Ferdinand: "You, and your brother and sister, will receive handsome pensions, and will be commodiously sequestered in guarded ease in Talleyrand's chateau at Valençay." Even this edict concealed a measure of cynical Napoleonic revenge. Charles-Maurice de Talleyrand-Périgord, the 1st Prince of Benevento and the 1st Duke of Talleyrand, was the Emperor's chief diplomat, and right-hand man when it came to making peace. Habitually pre-occupied with Europe, Talleyrand had shown insufficient interest in Iberia to suit Napoleon's liking. So now the Emperor would afflict him with the custody of that peninsula's most troubled and troublesome prince.

At last Napoleon turned to the inseparable triumvirate of Charles, Maria Luisa, and Godoy. "You three will be sent to live in luxury, and guarded ease, in Marseilles's Château d'If."

"Very well, Your Imperial Majesty," assented Charles, who had little choice in the matter. Then, to everyone's surprise including his own, Charles found the temerity to lodge a final pathetic protest, on a matter of gravest concern. "But, if it please Your Imperial Majesty, since the Château d'If perches on a small island in the Bay of Marseilles, whatever, wherever, and whenever may we hunt?"

The Emperor shot him a look so far beneath contempt that no words could possibly describe it, not even in French. Ascending very near the summit of his cynicism, Napoleon replied "Your Majesty may hunt clams, on the beach, at low tide—or if you prefer, at high tide." And with that, he turned on his boot-heel and unceremoniously dismissed the Spanish house of Bourbon, both from his presence, and from their realm.

If Napoleon thought he had made good riddance of them all, he was gravely mistaken—not because he had failed to understand what made them tick, but because he had failed to understand what made Spain topsy-turvy. For one thing, he quickly discovered that its throne had now become a proverbial 'hot potato' that nobody wanted to handle. Having toppled hereditary European monarchs like tenpins, he had replaced them—in the finest traditions of nepotism— with loyal and trusted siblings. While Napoleon himself was Emperor of France and King of Italy, he had installed his older brother Joseph as King of Naples; his younger brother, Louis, as King of Holland; and his youngest brother, Jérôme, as King of Westphalia. First Napoleon offered the throne of Spain to Louis, who flat-out refused it; then to Jérôme, who said he didn't feel quite up to it; and finally to Joseph, who said he preferred to take his chances with Mount Vesuvius, which he prudently deemed less likely to erupt than the Spanish populace. Napoleon's brother-in-law, Joachim Murat, married to his sister Caroline, was actually angling for the throne of Spain, and would have accepted it. But the Emperor had other plans for the intrepid Marshal, in his coming invasion of Russia, and needed him closer to hand. Since Joseph owed Napoleon bigger political favors than the others, the Emperor overruled his objection and simply imposed the Spanish crown on him, while re-assigning the Neapolitan crown to a rather sulky Murat. With that Napoleon rode back from Bayonne to Paris, feeling well pleased with himself. But this was to be short-lived.

Thus Joseph dutifully but reluctantly exchanged a cornucopia of pleasures—every conceivable recreation, gratification, and satisfaction, as well as other pleasures quite inconceivable, save in Italy—that had been his daily fare while kinging it in Naples, for a harvest of intractable problems and a dire dearth of solutions that accompanied his coronation as King of Spain. He brought with him a semi-liberal but hastily hamstrung version of the Code Napoleon, which contained many of the reforms that had made Napoleon the darling of the Enlightenment intelligentsia, but which (on Napoleon's insistence) hedged its bets by recognizing Catholicism as the sole legitimate religion of Spain. But this ploy backfired dismally and, notwithstanding his sincere efforts at being a popular monarch, Joseph's reign was doomed from the outset.

While the Spanish liberals supported him, the suspicious if not hostile nobility kept him at arm's length. Spanish generals followed their private inclinations: some opposed him as devoted patriots; others picked their battles as opportunistic warlords; and not a few behaved like depraved lunatics toward the civilians they were sworn to protect. Worst of all, the clergy condemned Joseph as a Lutheran, a Freemason, and a heretic, thus maintaining popular resentment at the boil. The common people saw only that Napoleon had dethroned their Church-blessed Bourbons, replacing them with a foreign infidel who barely spoke a word of Spanish, and who reigned not by the Grace of God, but rather at the point of a bayonet and through the mouth of a cannon. They declared their undying loyalty to their deposed King Ferdinand VII, whom they regarded as Spain's only legitimate monarch.

And so the insurrection of El Dos de Mayo, temporarily quelled in the capital, spread like an invisible underground wildfire, suddenly flaring up with incendiary violence, and without warning, in scores of localities across Iberia. Since the rebellion erupted with neither pattern nor predictability, no plan sufficed for its prevention. People armed themselves with anything that lay at hand, from sticks to stones to knives; every civilian was potentially a guerilla fighter. Even before Joseph's June 6 coronation, uprisings had taken their tolls in the Sierra Morena and Santa Cruz de Mudela. On the day he was crowned, insurgencies broke out in Barcelona and Valdepenas, and as far away as Porto, Portugal. Columns of French troops were ambushed by guerillas as they marched through unfamiliar terrain; while smaller French units, including scouts and reconnaissance parties, were wiped out if they strayed too far from their encampments. By now some regular Spanish troops had joined the fray, and they, together with the guerillas, overwhelmed undermanned French garrisons in Barcelona, Girona, and Valencia, and broke the first French siege at Zaragoza.

Taking their cue from El Dos de Mayo, the citizens of Zaragoza joined six thousand militia and five hundred regular Spanish troops, repeatedly repulsing vigorous assaults by a French army of ten thousand men and sixty cannon. A national heroine, Agustina Raimunda Maria Saragossa i Domènech, known as the Spanish Joan of Arc, would emerge from this battle. Toting a basket of apples to feed Spanish gunners, she saw to her horror that the French troops had broken through and were bayoneting the Spanish militia left and right. The defenders broke ranks and began to flee. Augustina dropped her apples, raced forward, loaded a cannon, and lit the fuse with French soldiers only yards away. She blasted them to smithereens, thus stalling the assault, and inspiring the defenders in that sector to regroup. Under the overall command of José Rebolledo de Palafox y Melzi, 1st Duke of Saragossa, the Spanish defenders broke the first siege and compelled the French to withdraw. But they would soon return, and with a vengeance.

Meanwhile, in July 1808, a sizeable French force of twenty-one thousand men, under General Pierre Dupont de l'Étang, was dispatched from Madrid to Cádiz, to secure the vital port and protect a French naval squadron lying at anchor. En route he encountered resistance in Córdoba, which he stormed and plundered, but then made the fatal error of pulling back to await reinforcements. None arrived. Having strung his divisions along the banks of the Guadalquivir River, Dupont found himself outmaneuvered and surrounded by the Spanish Army of Andalusia, led by Generals Francisco Castaños and Theodor von Reding. A melée raged for three days, from July 16-19, with much of the decisive action unfolding in and around the village of Bailén, which loaned the historic battle its name. Dupont lost more than twenty-five hundred men before surrendering his remaining army of almost eighteen thousand to what he mistakenly thought to be a vastly larger Spanish force. In fact the victorious Spanish generals had the same number of men as he. Under the terms of the surrender, Dupont's troops were supposed to be repatriated. Instead, only the senior French officers were spared, while the rank and file prisoners of war were shipped to the uninhabited Balearic island of Cabrera, where thousands would die of starvation and disease.

The French invaders soon found themselves at sixes and sevens in Portugal as well. The June uprising in Porto sparked further outbreaks of insurrection, mostly in the north, which culminated in July at Évora, where French General Loison massacred its civilian men, women, and children alike. But this atrocity only intensified Portuguese hatred of the French, and stiffened resistance against them. When word of Évora reached Spain, just after the Battle of Bailén, it exerted the same effect on the Spanish people, who redoubled their efforts to resist the invaders.

The ignominious rout of the French at Bailén had immediate as well as far-reaching consequences not only for Napoleon Bonaparte, but also for Fernando Sor. The Emperor was beside himself with a combination of disgrace and fury. Bailén marked the very first defeat in battle of Napoleon's Grande Armée, thus shattering the aura of French invincibility that had helped him cow Europe into capitulation. Suddenly his traditional enemies, notably Prussia and Austria, beheld by example that armed resistance was not necessarily futile. This sowed the seeds of yet another coalition against him, the Fifth, soon joined by Britain. Coupled with Portuguese insurrection, Bailén held out the same hope to England, namely defeating this monster on *terra firma.* So the British landed an expeditionary force at Portugal's Mondego River, led by the intrepid Sir Arthur Wellesley (the future Duke of Wellington), which was soon joined by bands of Portuguese infantry.

The French commander in Lisbon, General Jean-Andoche Junot, 1st Duke of Abrantès, had allowed himself to be seduced by delusions not dissimilar to Godoy's: he regarded Portugal as his personal satrapy, and envisioned leading a lifestyle of luxury and ease. In consequence, his thirteen thousand conscript troops were ill-prepared against Wellesley's British army reinforced by Portuguese infantry, whose combined strength of nineteen thousand dealt Junot a crippling defeat at the battle of Vimeiro, on August 21. This ended once and for all Napoleon's short-lived occupation of Portugal, and with it his intention to slam the back door of Iberia shut against English incursion.

Another immediate consequence of Bailén, which the Spanish were not slow to realize, was that the road to Madrid now lay wide open and undefended. So the Spanish Army marched toward the capital, gathering strength in the process. Lately-crowned King Joseph had insufficient forces to resist them, and so he was obliged to abandon Madrid and retreat far northward, almost to the Pyrenees, taking up defensive positions along the Ebro river.

The Spanish Army entered Madrid in triumph on August 23, lustily cheered by throngs of overjoyed Madrileños. As the victorious troops marched through the Puerta de Toledo in their thousands, their path strewn with garlands, soldiers and civilians alike gave rousing voice to the most famous patriotic song of the period: *Venid, Vencedores* (*Come, Victors*), with lyrics by the poet Juan Bautista Arriaza, set to music by none other than Fernando Sor. For Fernando had never forgotten El Conde's prophetic injunction, to play the musical role not only of a virtuoso who charmed the nobility, but also of a patriot who inspired the people. The events of El Dos de Mayo—those anguished cries from the street that so painfully wounded Goya's and Fernando's hearts alike—which had rendered Goya deaf, and would soon compel him to paint monsters, had aroused Fernando's voice, and impelled him to make the entire populace sing. He wrote a cycle of patriotic songs, which were soon sung all over Spain. Thus Napoleon's ill-starred invasion unwittingly elevated Fernando to unprecedented popularity, but at the same time drew him into mortal danger.

Chapter 16. Madrid: El Capitan Maestro and the Siege

Napoleon's feelings of disgrace at the defeats of Bailén and Vimeiro soon gave way to rage. Having mistaken Iberia for a somnolent hive of docile bees, from which he could pluck honey at will, the Emperor had instead thrust his hand into a nest of angry hornets, which had stung him painfully and repeatedly. Unaccustomed to such treatment, he had to rethink his plans. His biggest concern was that Tsar Alexander, if egged on by these Iberian setbacks, might abrogate their Tilsit treaty and join the Fifth Coalition against him. Since Napoleon was not yet prepared to wage war against Russia, and moreover was determined to be the first to violate their agreement, he needed to convene another meeting with Alexander, to refresh the Russian Tsar's credence in French invincibility. Whether by bluster or bluff, Napoleon sought reassurance that Russia would neither turn on him (that is, not before he was secretly ready to turn on Russia), nor assist Austria and Prussia in any aggressions. Once reassured, with his eastern flank secure, he could vent his full spleen against those insufferable Spaniards.

So Napoleon invited Alexander to another conference, this time not a private meeting in a tent on a raft, but rather a grand and glittering assembly of every noble European vassal whom Napoleon could cajole, bribe or bully into paying him homage. In addition, he brought along his own family, most of his generals, and their entourages. The Emperor insisted on hosting this conference in newly acquired territory: Erfurt, a German city recently folded into the French empire. He coaxed Talleyrand out of retirement to assist his new foreign minister, Jean-Baptiste de Nompère de Champagny, 1st Duc de Cadore, in making all the arrangements. Talleyrand recorded in his memoirs that the guest list of nobles alone ran to three pages. Among other entertainments, Napoleon instructed August Laurent, the Comte de Rémusat and director of the Comédie-Française, to transport to Erfurt the best actors of the troupe, including the famous François-Joseph Talma. The leading lights of German literature, namely Johann Wolfgang von Goethe and Christoph Martin Wieland, led a literary soirée. The two Emperors hunted at Jena, took in a performance of *La Mort de César* at the Weimar Theatre, and reveled at a gala ball in splendorous surroundings adorned by bevies of glamorous women.

"I wish the Emperor of Russia," Napoleon declared, "to be dazzled by the sight of my power. For there is no negotiation which it could fail to render easier."

The Tsar was dazzled indeed, but not for one instant deceived. While the two foreign ministers and their aides prepared to draw up a renewed alliance, the two Emperors danced with pretended lightness around the weightiest issues at hand. Napoleon nonchalantly agreed not to interfere with Russia's intended annexation of Wallachia and Moldovia, but drew the line when Alexander casually mentioned Turkey. (France could never allow the Russian navy to control the Bosphorus strait, and thus gain unrestricted access to the Mediterranean.) For his part, Alexander could hardly suppress a crocodilian grin when Napoleon asked for reciprocal non-interference in Spain. The Tsar feigned some reluctance—not too much but just enough to be convincing—then granted his *quid pro quo*. He was of course secretly delighted that Napoleon himself planned to cross the Pyrenees at the head of a considerable army, thus sinking even deeper into the quagmire of Spain, and he fervently hoped that the Spanish guerillas would bleed the French white. He would not be disappointed. "God bless Spain," thought the Tsar, while pledging his non-interference as though he were doing Napoleon a favor.

The two Emperors concluded their cynical bargain with empty promises of mutual assistance in case of aggression by enemies. Alexander had not the slightest intention of lifting a finger against England, should it attack Napoleon's forces via Portugal or anywhere else; while Napoleon fully intended to invade Russia himself, so was hardly in a position to help defend Russia against his own attack. So the Emperors parted company and returned to their respective capitals, once again mutually pleased with their renewed accord. They had also agreed to meet again, but history would decree otherwise, for Napoleon's unlimited ambition and unslakable thirst for conquest had by now sown the seeds of his own demise. In the interim, however, Spain's immediate fate was sealed and, along with it, so was Fernando's.

Napoleon's plan to re-invade Spain proved less than popular with his French subjects themselves, who were beginning to weary of their Emperor's incessantly warlike ways, and felt reticence at becoming bogged down in futile foreign escapades. But Napoleon was willing to risk unpopularity for the sake of victory, and he made his intentions clear to posterity: "It was impossible," he later wrote, "to leave the Peninsula a prey to the machinations of the English, the intrigues, hopes and pretensions of the Bourbons." So, deploying sufficient forces in the east to deter an Austrian or Prussian attack (or so he hoped), the Emperor crossed the Pyrenees on October 19, 1808, at the head of one hundred and fifty thousand men of the Grande Armée. He sent ahead strict orders to his brother Joseph, still encamped along Ebro river, to avoid engaging with the approaching Spanish Army, but rather to allow them to advance in an ever-spreading and ever-thinning semicircle. In November, Napoleon's forces smashed the Spanish center near Vitoria, while other French divisions overwhelmed the Spanish flanks at Burgos and Tudela. The Spanish Army scattered hither and yon. Napoleon cleared the last obstacle to Madrid on November 30, at the battle of Somosierra, when an uphill charge of his Polish light cavalry overran the Spanish artillery, capturing the vital mountain pass that separated the provinces of Segovia and Madrid. The road to the Spanish capital now lay wide open.

Militarily, Madrid was indefensible. It had no fortifications, no narrow winding streets, and was overlooked by the Retiro hill, from which it could be mercilessly shelled by cannon fire. The gates to the city were largely ornamental, their main purpose being the collection of duties and tariffs. There were only three thousand Spanish troops in the entire city, but they were reinforced by at least twenty thousand civilians, who once again armed themselves with whatever lay at hand, and vowed to perish rather than surrender. They swiftly constructed a massive but useless wall, made mostly of paving stones, which fragmented when struck by artillery. More defenders were ultimately killed by its shrapnel than by French cannonballs. In their exuberance at building the wall, they also neglected to reinforce their own artillery on the Retiro hill.

When the news of Somosierra reached him, Captain Fernando Sor had reported to the Junta, which was short of officers as well as enlisted men. Fernando was placed under the command of Captain-General Castelar, who assigned him to lead a mixed company of soldiers and civilians, and charged him with the defense of the Puerta de Alcala. Early in the morning of December 2, Fernando deployed his rag-tag company around the gate, and behind some paving slabs hastily piled in front of it, where they resolutely awaited the French attack. He had two dozen infantrymen, mostly new recruits, armed with muskets and bayonets but short on powder and musket-balls—for Joseph had emptied the city's armories and magazines on his way out. Fernando's troops were reinforced by five or six dozen civilians, including several women and a priest. They had armed themselves, as usual, with a pathetic assortment of sticks, stones, knives, and glass shards. The priest brandished a large wooden crucifix, which he apparently intended to utilize as a bludgeon. Fernando could not help but think (but of course he refrained from saying it) that if the long end of the crucifix were sharpened, it would make a better dagger than a club. Muskets as well as ammunition being in short supply, and Fernando being in command of the position, he had only a sword with which to direct fire, and if need be defend himself. Moreover, it was his very first battle, against a far better equipped foe boasting vastly superior numbers. Yet to Fernando's surprise, he felt no trepidation, only anticipation. Heedless of his own fate in the impending action, his main concern was to keep the enemy at bay for as long as possible, and to safeguard the lives of those in his charge, insofar as it might be feasible.

Of course Fernando was instantly recognized by his company, soldiers and civilians alike. They had all sung *Venid, Vencedores* on their jubilant and bloodless retaking of Madrid on sunny and sultry August 23. That celebration having been short-lived, they now shivered under December's slate-gray skies and chill winter wind, hoping to outlive the impending battle. Yet Fernando's very presence buoyed their flagging spirits, and they felt touched and honored to be led by 'El Capitan Maestro', as they fondly called him.

"El Capitan Maestro, will you write a new song for us after we win today's battle?" they asked Fernando, with as much bravado as they could muster. He saw that some of these civilians, gaudily clad *majos* and *majas*, were actually spoiling for a fight. Fernando was deeply moved by their courage—or forlorn hope—against such odds. "At your service, my dear compatriots," he replied. "As soon as victory is ours, my new song will be yours." At this they cheered, and resolved either to win, or else to die defending the gate of Alcala.

Napoleon arrived at the outskirts of the city at noon, hoping that Madrid would surrender without a fight. Not that he harbored the slightest doubt about the outcome of a battle, but he preferred to leave the capital intact rather than lay it to waste. After all, he had come to re-install his brother on a throne, not to deposit him on a heap of rubble. Besides, this was the anniversary of his historic victory at Austerlitz, and such occasions always made the Emperor wax sentimental. But the Junta brusquely rejected his initial demand of surrender, replying that the "people of Madrid were resolved to bury themselves under the ruins of their houses, rather than to permit the French troops to enter their city." So Napoleon sighed, and ordered his gun batteries drawn up before the northern and eastern gates, including Fernando's post at the Alcala. He also ordered Marshal Claude Perrin Victor's division to prepare to storm the Retiro hill, and capture or at least disable the Spanish artillery.

On the morning of December 3 Napoleon issued a second demand to surrender, which was met with a counter-suggestion by Captain-General Castelar for a twelve-hour truce. This transparent ruse, an attempt to buy time for Spanish reinforcements to arrive from the south, was rejected out-of-hand by Napoleon, who then unleashed the main assault on Retiro. He created diversions by ordering his batteries to open fire on the northern and eastern gates, marshaling troops behind them to feign coming attacks, so as to pin their defenders in place.

Fernando and his company stood their ground, ducking for cover as cannonballs smashed their makeshift walls of paving slabs to smithereens, spraying sharp fragments of stone shrapnel in all directions. Several defenders were wounded by these, but none mortally. As expected of officers in the field, who incurred appallingly high casualty rates, Fernando did not flinch. His guardian angel must have been on duty, for neither he did receive a scratch. Angered by the artillery fire which they could not return, and frustrated that the French troops were massed behind the cannons, well out of musket range, Fernando's courageous if motley crew hurled taunts between incoming volleys of cannonballs, daring the French to fight them hand-to-hand. This was a doomsday dare, as the defenders were outnumbered fifteen or twenty to one.

Meanwhile, Napoleon's main assault unfolded on Retiro. Following an intense artillery barrage, which punched holes in the thin defenses, Marshal Victor's division poured through the gaps and overran the hill, capturing most of the Spanish guns before the defenders could spike them. They also began to wheel up their own artillery, to vantages from which they could bombard any quarter of Madrid at will. The French troops then swept into the heart of the city, scattering the defenders before them. Once they had reached the palace of the Duke of Medinaceli, Napoleon called a halt and issued his third and final demand to surrender. By now the Spanish military leaders realized the full futility of continued resistance, which would result only in pointless carnage and collateral destruction, but the populace itself remained suicidally defiant, and determined to fight on. General Castelar sent General Morla to negotiate with Napoleon, who was in no mood to discuss terms. Instead, he issued an ultimatum that unless the Junta capitulated by 6 a.m. next morning, every man, woman, and child under arms would be put to death.

The Junta had no choice but to surrender, and could confidently command their troops to do so. Yet they sincerely doubted their authority over the restive populace, still animated by the spirit of El Dos de Mayo. And because the French had not yet encircled the city completely, a good many armed defenders escaped during the night, deliberately unnoticed by their commanders. They vanished into the countryside, and were able to join other Spanish contingents. Fernando was not among them. He had decided to obey orders, lay down his sword, and remain in Madrid, at least for the time being, to see what would transpire.

Napoleon entered Madrid on December 4, occupying it with a host of troops. When some of his soldiers began to pillage, Napoleon seized the opportunity to prove his benevolent intent to Madrileños, and had two French soldiers publicly executed for looting. While this did not have the endearing effect he had hoped for among the populace, the pillaging stopped at once. He then re-installed his brother Joseph on the throne, and immediately promulgated a number of decrees, which it would be his hapless sibling's duty to implement. When King Joseph read them he groaned inwardly, and longed once more for the carefree and concupiscent kingdom of Naples, instead of this accursed and thorny throne of Spain.

When Fernando read them he could not suppress an inward cheer, for Napoleon had decreed, at one stroke, a slate of reforms that Floridablanca, Jovellanos, and all the champions of the Spanish enlightenment had not achieved in a lifetime of dreaming and striving. This was the Emperor's way. A veritable force of nature, he unfailingly cut with a two-edged sword. Callously disdainful of human life on the battlefield, Napoleon would later say—after running short of adult conscripts and drafting young adolescents—"A boy can stop a bullet as well as a man". Yet on the heels of his blood-soaked conquests, and of all the corollary miseries and tragedies of war that he inflicted in his sanguinary wake, he invariably became a benevolent despot, a liberator of the people, a dutiful 'Son of the Revolution', transforming societies from feudal enslavement to meritocratic modernity.

So while Napoleon the conqueror heavily garrisoned Madrid, and kept it under martial law, Napoleon the reformer gave the Spanish people a new constitution, the like of which they had never seen. It abolished feudalism, along with all feudal monopolies over agricultural lands, commercial enterprises, and hereditary wealth. It abolished the Inquisition, and sequestered its property and assets for redistribution by the state. It reduced the numbers and constituents of monastic orders to one-third of their current size, thus sparing the people the enormous burden of their maintenance, and it consolidated several religious houses to spare further costs of supporting redundant Church bureaucracy. It abolished trade barriers between the Spanish provinces, thus facilitating commerce and engendering economic growth.

Those who knew Napoleon well had reason to believe that he cared not a fig for these liberal policies. Rather, he expediently introduced them to garner popular support from the masses, without which his regime could not have endured the animosity and enmity he provoked from the two received pillars of power—the Roman Church and the hereditary monarchy—which he toppled in Samson-like fashion. Thus Napoleon confronted history with a paradox: was he a dictator, or a liberator? He himself sometimes pondered that very question, although never in moments of self-doubt, which were alien to his unshakeable faith in his own destiny, but only on rare occasions when he allowed himself the luxury of wondering how history would judge him. He had once voiced it aloud, to Rousseau's bust in the National Assembly: "Do you think that mankind would be better off had neither of us been born?" The bust wore an amused expression, but made no answer.

Nonetheless, it was a just question. Both of their places in history had been laid by the French Revolution. Even though Jean-Jacques Rousseau was far better known during his lifetime for his literary works *Émile* and *Héloïse*, and not for *The Social Contract*, he owed the Jacobins profound if posthumous thanks for making his name a mantra that conjured his fatuous myth of the *general will*, a mere slogan for inflaming and manipulating the debased and bestial passions of the mob. That was exactly why Plato had argued so strenuously, in his *Republic*, for censorship of inflammatory works. Even though Rousseau was posthumously lionized in the politically charged Parisian salons of Madame de Staël and Madame Roland, the most celebrated pre-revolutionary literary *salonnière*, namely Marie Anne de Vichy-Chamrond, Marquise du Deffand—who had entertained Voltaire, Montesquieu, and D'Alembert—called Rousseau "a charlatan". Indeed, the rabble that lustily chanted Rousseau's name while pelting aristocrats en route to the guillotine with refuse and night-soil could not have paraphrased a single thought of their supposed political mentor.

Voltaire himself knew better, for Rousseau had sent him a copy of his *Discourse on Inequality* in 1755, and had evinced the temerity to ask for an endorsement. What a grand irony! Voltaire was living in Geneva as a political refugee from France, whereas Rousseau had wandered from Geneva to Paris in search of opportunity. Voltaire's reply was a masterpiece of caustic rebuke, bottled in exquisitely perfumed French politeness:

> *I have received, sir, your new book against the human race, and I thank you for it. You will please people by your manner of telling them the truth about themselves, but you will not alter them. The horrors of that human society—from which in our feebleness and ignorance we expect so many consolations—have never been painted in more striking colors: no one has ever been so witty as you are in trying to turn us into brutes: to read your book makes one long to go about on all fours. Since, however, it is now some sixty years since I gave up the practice, I feel that it is unfortunately impossible for me to resume it.*

Fernando too had read Rousseau's *Discourse*, which needless to say was banned in Spain by the Inquisition, since it fingered ownership of land and property as the greatest source of injustice, and the Church was the largest landowner after the Grandees. Fernando had also read Voltaire's stinging reply—banned in this case because Voltaire was an atheist—which he greatly admired for its wit. He was far too canny to keep such books in his possession, which is why the Inquisition had failed to unearth them when they ransacked his house in Málaga. But Fernando had availed himself of Spain's abundant underground libraries. So he was well aware that Rousseau had not made the French Revolution as much as the French Revolution had made Rousseau and, in its inevitably chaotic aftermath, had made Napoleon's meteoric trajectory possible if not inevitable.

But now Fernando found himself on the horns of a deep dilemma: Napoleon's sweeping constitution contained everything he could have wished for Spain, according to the liberal principles that he himself espoused in his rational mind; yet Napoleon's imposition of these self-same principles on Spain, by naked coercion as a foreign conqueror, was intolerable to the patriotism that welled up in his heart. So although Fernando was unaware of Napoleon's question to Rousseau's bust—"Do you think that mankind would be better off had neither of us been born?"—Fernando would have been obliged to give contradictory answers: "No" with his mind, but "Yes" with his heart. Not better off in principle, but better off in practice.

So El Capitan Maestro Sor surrendered as commanded by the Junta, and laid down his sword. His soldiers grumbled, but mostly followed suit and laid down their muskets. A few refused, and disappeared into alleyways. Fernando made no attempt to stop them. The civilians of Madrid likewise piled their makeshift weapons on the pavements, and sullenly melted away, song-less but alive to fight another day. The priest hung on to his crucifix, and blessed them all. Every last one of them, including Fernando, resolved to find a way to continue the fight. Meanwhile Fernando consoled himself, and assuaged his inner battle between mind and heart, with a new-found revelation: that however many military victories Napoleon might claim in Spain, the Spanish people themselves would never surrender, for their spirit was indomitable.

Napoleon himself had yet to learn this lesson, concerning the invincibility of the Spanish populace, and they were all going to pay dearly for his education. The Emperor now had more than two hundred thousand men in Spain, yet faced a host of problems as proportionately large as his Grande Armée. Although he now held the capital city under martial law, and had defeated and disarmed Spanish troops in the central province of Madrid, there was insurrection in virtually every other region. So he was obliged to dispatch his Marshals and Generals in every direction, to reinforce existing garrisons and establish new ones, to defeat Spanish forces wherever they might be found, and to quell insurgencies wherever they might arise. But this military challenge in itself posed many insuperable problems. For one thing, Spanish roads were generally terrible, and some of the terrain was impassable. For another, although the French army was famous (or rather infamous) for living off the land, Spain's vastly undeveloped tracts and fallow fields offered the troops precisely nothing on which to live. Rural villages were mostly hostile, either hiding their resources or even destroying them, preferring starvation over provisioning the enemy. On top of this, reconnaissance and communication were impeded not only by poor roads and bad terrain, but also by partisans who ambushed and murdered lone couriers or small scouting parties. While Napoleon tackled the military problems with a will, his hapless brother King Joseph could yet do little to implement the Emperor's utopian constitution, and put in place the necessary civil administration. Ultimately, they both needed and wanted to be popular, but popularity was the one prize that would perpetually elude them.

Napoleon had already arranged to sit for a portrait by Goya. With the cries of anguish from the streets of El Dos and El Tres de Mayo still ringing in Goya's now-deaf ears, his portrayal of Napoleon might have been other than imperial. But Goya remained faithful to his mission: as a witness to his era, he would simply paint what he saw. Napoleon was willing to take his chances. Since the era already had his name stamped indelibly on it, he could not resist sitting for Goya's pictorial testimony. Without a doubt it would have been the most important painting in both of their careers, but fate would shortly intervene to prevent it.

For his part, King Joseph had arranged for a coronation concert and ball. Having consulted General Le Barbier de Tinan on which Spanish musicians to feature, thinking thereby to ingratiate himself with the Grandees by showing his appreciation for indigenous talents, he discovered the name of Fernando Sor atop de Tinan's list. But Fernando, at least at this moment, had greater misgivings than Goya. While the Junta's surrender and French martial law had jointly compelled him to remove his uniform, they could not prevent him from hearing the screams that Goya still heard in his mind's ear. The only piece that Fernando was in the mood to play for King Joseph was *Crits de Carrer*, but he was similarly fated never to play for Joseph. History had other plans for them all, and it lost little time unveiling them.

No sooner had Napoleon established his military headquarters in the northern Madrid sector of Chamartin than he learned of the arrival of a British army in Salamanca, consisting of twenty thousand men led by Sir

John Moore. Wellesley had propelled this bold sortie from his stronghold in Portugal, and its target was Marshal Soult's division, presently deployed around Burgos. This news made Napoleon lick his chops in gleeful anticipation of inflicting sweet revenge against the perfidious English. His humiliating naval defeats at the hands of Nelson, both in Alexandria and more recently—and decisively—at Trafalgar, still infuriated the Emperor to the marrow of his bones. But now he had them exactly where he wanted them: on *terra firma*, where they would eat French lead and taste French steel. So he mustered a considerable force and marched northward, planning to sandwich Moore between himself and Soult.

Napoleon's troops had to cross the unforgiving Sierra de Guadarrama, and their midwinter traverse of the Guadarrama pass tested even Napoleon's iron will. The ordeal was worse than his crossing of the Alps in 1800, and his soldiers' sufferings brought them to the verge of mutiny, quelled only because they feared immolation in the furnace of their Emperor's wrath more than they dreaded freezing to death in the frigid winds and jagged ice caps of the Sierra. When Moore caught wind of Napoleon's coming, he sought to escape the trap by wheeling westward, toward Coruña, and the safety of the British fleet. He led Napoleon and Soult on a daunting chase across two hundred and fifty miles of rough, snowed-packed terrain. But by January 2, 1809, Napoleon was snapping at his heels, determined to annihilate every man-jack of Moore's army. Poised to strike his vengeful blow, Napoleon was suddenly halted in his tracks by urgent news from Vienna and Paris.

In Austria, the Archduke Karl Ludwig was mustering an army and preparing for war. And Napoleon's spies in Saint Petersburg informed him that his supposed ally, Tsar Alexander, was not mobilizing as much as a pack-mule to come to France's aid—notwithstanding their pact of mutual assistance. Meanwhile in Paris, the treacherous Talleyrand, who had once idolized Napoleon as a savior but lately deemed him the ruin of France, was hatching a *coup d'état* in cahoots with Fouché, the minister of police. They were planning to dethrone him, and replace him with Murat. So Napoleon was obliged to abandon his pursuit and annihilation of Moore's army, which he left to Marshal Soult, and return hotfoot to Paris, to settle all this newly arisen hash. The Emperor was fated never to revisit to Spain, but thereafter to regret ever having invaded it in the first place.

Marshal Soult lacked Napoleon's burning hatred of England, so he slackened his pace in pursuit of Moore. This permitted Moore's army to reach the port of Coruña, and to begin embarking on English naval vessels, virtually under the noses of Soult's artillery, just a stone's throw out of range. Moore and a contingent of intrepid volunteers fought a heroic rearguard action, keeping the French at bay just long enough for his army to embark and escape annihilation. Moore himself perished in the desperate fray, but his army lived on, to return to Spain and fight another day. One hundred and thirty-one years later, when Britons would celebrate the 'Miracle at Dunkirk', few would recall that the blueprint for this evacuation had been drawn up in Coruña in 1809. As Santayana sagely wrote: "Those who cannot remember the past are condemned to repeat it."

Meanwhile Madrid remained under martial law, and so Fernando remained disarmed but torn by interminable internal conflict. His rational mind still fondly embraced enlightenment values, while his patriotic heart stoutly resisted their imposition by a foreign power. It was the populace of Madrid itself that unwittingly charted his next course, by falling prey to an understandable but unfortunate confusion that would painfully rend the fabric of Spanish history for decades if not centuries to come.

As we have seen, the common people loved their Bourbon monarchs, for better or worse, through thick or thin, even though the worse and the thin had more often prevailed. The power of the Catholic Church, and the depth of the people's religious convictions, served daily to reinforce unquestioned loyalty to their Catholic Kings and Queens, to the point of blind faith. Prior to the French invasion, reformists among the nobility, the high bourgeoisie, and the intelligentsia were routinely denounced by the Church yet generally tolerated if not supported by the people, who after all hoped to hedge their bets and gain a few modest comforts in the mundane City of Man without jeopardizing their passports to the everlasting City of God. And so it was possible for reformists like Floridablanca, Jovellanos, Moratín, Goya, and Sor to enjoy great popular support, even if disapproved by the clergy, for no-one among them ever dreamed of deposing the monarchy itself. In this the reformists and the people remained united, and determined not to follow the infamous example of the French Revolution. They sought to reform the standing order by degrees, and not to decapitate it at one stroke.

But the French invasion ruptured this unity of common cause between the Spanish people and their reformists, once and apparently for all time. It was a topsy-turvy irony, possible only in Spain. While the Spanish people had been horrified by the French rabble that had persecuted and executed their aristocrats, many of these same Spaniards now behaved as a rabble themselves, a populace transformed into a mob, turning on their own reformists with the same murderous zeal. Disarmed by the surrender of their Junta, and prevented by French martial law from mounting further guerilla resistance in the city, roving bands of vigilante Madrileños vented their pent-up fury against a designated enemy from within, whom they despitefully called '*afrancesados*'.

Suddenly, anyone known to espouse, or even suspected of harboring sympathies for enlightenment values, was branded an *afrancesado*, which bore the connotation of apologist for, if not collaborator with, the French invaders. Virtually overnight, Spain's most ardent reformists and celebrated patriots became her most despised *afrancesados* and notorious traitors. The same throngs that had sung resounding choruses of Fernando's *Venid Vencedores* in the streets of Madrid during August 2008 were now apprehending, torturing, and summarily executing *afrancesados* in those very same streets in January 1809—and Fernando now found himself among those most at risk. Goya was also witnessing this gruesome spectacle from his windows, and although he could no longer hear the screams of anguish emanating from the streets, the horrifying images of these latest atrocities were seared into his memory, and his nightmares. In due course, he would paint them for posterity, in horrific etchings such as *El Populacho*.

Desirous above all of casting off the yoke of French occupation, and prudently concerned about being executed by the very populace he was seeking to liberate, Fernando heard that a regiment of volunteers was being recruited in Córdoba. So in early February 1809, he bade farewell to his elder brother Goya, slipped undetected out of Madrid, and headed south toward Andalusia. He and Goya would not see one another again for almost twenty years, and would never meet again in their beloved Spain.

Chapter 17. Córdoba: El Capitan Maestro of the Volunteers

Fernando reached Córdoba without incident, and was warmly welcomed into the regiment of the Córdoban Volunteers, at the rank of Captain. As in Madrid, the troops were overjoyed at beholding him in their midst, and likewise referred to him as 'El Capitan Maestro'. But quite unlike Madrid, whose outnumbered and ill-equipped defenders had been a desperate and rag-tag assortment of green recruits and untrained citizens, the Córdoban volunteers constituted a well-armed and well-drilled corps. Led by Colonel Francisco Carvajal, himself a prominent and popular Córdoban, they were battle-ready and enjoyed the adulation of a spirited populace. This being Andalusia, the regiment boasted numerous musicians, which formed into marching bands and even an orchestra. They gave weekly processions and concerts, playing not only Spanish orchestral scores but also popular tunes, including patriotic songs written by El Capitan Maestro (as they too called him), which he continued to churn out to everyone's delight. It seemed as though the entire citizenry of Córdoba turned out for these musical occasions, cheering wildly and singing along with the soldiers. Fernando's stirring tenor rose above even this din, as did the throngs' applause for him as he marched by. Yet these festivities soon enough gave way to battles, in anticipation of which the Córdoban volunteers began to gird their loins, and write potentially their last letters home. Fernando too wrote to his family, and to Joaquina.

His dear mother Isabella was maintaining herself well enough in Barcelona, all things considered. With increasingly good cause, she fretted day and night over the welfare of her sons, both of whom were now exposed to mortal combat. Still attached to the army of General Vives, Carlos Sor had risen, like his elder brother Fernando, to the rank of Captain. And Carlos had recently survived a devastating Spanish defeat at the hands of French General Laurent Gouvion Saint-Cyr, at the battle of Cardedeu.

In early December of 1809, Vives had besieged the small French garrison in Barcelona with his Catalan army of twenty-four thousand men. But just in the nick of time, Napoleon had dispatched Saint-Cyr with an army of twenty-three thousand, to relieve the garrison. Seeking to outmaneuver Vives, Saint Cyr feigned a siege of the fortress of Girona, which had thus far repulsed two French attacks. Leaving his artillery and most of his supplies deployed around the fortress, Vives's spies were deceived by this feint. Meanwhile Saint-Cyr quick-marched sixteen thousand infantry through the mountains in the dead of night, toward Barcelona, gambling that he would catch Vives by surprise. He did. Vives, whose army was deployed in the encirclement of Barcelona itself, managed to free up only nine thousand men to block the approach of Saint-Cyr. Vives's troops, Carlos Sor among them, took up their positions on high ground, but were swiftly overrun by the French. Of their nine thousand men, the Catalans lost twenty-five hundred dead or wounded, while Saint-Cyr's force of sixteen thousand lost only six hundred. To add insult to injury, Saint-Cyr captured five of Vives's cannons. Thus the French garrison in Barcelona was relieved, while Vives was obliged to retreat. Vives was then relieved of his command by the Catalan Junta, and replaced by Theodor von Reding.

Captain Carlos Sor himself survived the debacle unscathed, though he saw many comrades mown down by volleys of musket balls, or run through at close quarters by savage thrusts of bayonets. When Isabella finally received a letter from him, smuggled to her by guerillas, she literally wept for joy, profusely thanked the Holy Virgin for watching over Carlos, and solemnly prayed for the salvation of the souls of the fallen. When she received a letter from Fernando around the same time, recounting the siege of Madrid, Isabella wept, thanked, and prayed anew. She allowed herself precious little room for relief that her two sons were thus far spared by these horrible events. As mothers will, she fretted constantly. She worried without surcease about what *could* have befallen them, or about what *might* befall them in battles yet to come. So when she received Fernando's latest letter, from Córdoba, Isabella renewed her interminable rounds of daily and nightly anxiety.

Yet Isabella was fortunate that Barcelona was merely occupied, and not reduced to rubble—an unhappy fate that would befall not a few Spanish cities. To be sure, the occupying French army had to be provisioned, and this made foodstuffs scarce for the Barcelonans, many of whom would starve to death. The prices on the inevitable black market—even of eggs, cheese, and ham—made such staples well-nigh unaffordable to the mainstream populace, which subsisted mainly on bread, potatoes, olives, and salted fish. Even wine was in short supply. But thanks to the dutiful love of both her sons, who had never failed to send money to her monthly ever since they first left home, Isabella had amassed sufficient savings to tide her through the austerities of occupation. She happily shared her good fortune with Sofia and Joaquina, and also shared with them the latest news from Fernando and Carlos.

Joaquina herself had also received letters from both brothers, ordinary love-letters from Carlos and extraordinary ones from Fernando, but she kept them secreted away from the prying eyes of both mothers. Her poor heart was still unbearably torn between them, and was scarcely mended by each brother begging that, should he be killed or taken prisoner, then she must marry the other.

Isabella and her incessant maternal worries were primarily why Fernando had enlisted in Córdoba and not Villafranca. For he had pondered the unthinkable: what if two brothers serving in the same theatre of war were both killed in the same battle? Even one of their deaths would be devastating to their dear mother; both would be ghastly beyond imagination. Although this matter doubtless lay in the hands of inscrutable Providence, Fernando had hedged his bets by electing to serve in Andalusia instead of Catalonia.

If another truth be told, he had grown to love Andalusia as well. While Catalonia would always be his home, and Castile y Leon the perennial grand stage of power, politics, and intrigue, Fernando had grown deeply fond of Andalusia's magical light, delectable victuals, fine wines, and musical spirit. Even now, as the long shadow of war fell on Córdoba, and the Volunteers prepared for battle, their weekly processions and concerts continued unabated. Fernando realized that music not only stirred the patriotic fervor of the populace, but also animated the steadfast march of the army, even if their synchronized steps were to prove a dance of death.

At the same time, Fernando's extraordinary love for Joaquina, and hers for him, somehow blossomed amidst the withering horrors of war. Andalusia being a land of dreams, he began to dream of her anew in Córdoba, just as he had dreamed of her repeatedly in Málaga. And these dreams revealed a near-future reality to him: that he and Joaquina would marry just as soon as this war was over, no matter who emerged victorious. And so he wrote to her:

My Dearest Joaquina,
If against all commonsense and sound reason you still love me as madly as I do you, and if your patience yet endures my uncommon and unreasonable absence of so many unforgiving years, then know this in your precious heart: The very moment the war ends, and come what may, our wedding bells will chime. You have my solemn and everlasting promise before God. Know too, that if our long and seemingly endless ordeal of being apart commits you to a different course, a better man, and a happier life, then go with my devout blessing, undying affection, and imperishable desire for your happiness.
I beg to remain,
Your most ardent suitor, and eternal admirer,
Fernando

As Joaquina read these words, she wept until her tears stained the paper. Then she clasped the letter to her bosom, trying desperately but impossibly to embrace him through it, and lost all track of time. When she recovered her senses a while later, she wrote back to him:

My Dearest Fernando,

Know that I have always loved you, love you still, and will love you forever. If this be madness, then may sanity remain eternally a stranger. Know too that since there has never been any transgression, so there is nothing to forgive. I will await you, my husband-to-be, until this war ends, or until the Second Coming if it pleases God. My heart is in your safekeeping, until you return it to me. May our blessed Mother Mary watch over you until that happy day.

I beg to remain,

Your most patient, devoted, and loving bride-to-be,

Joaquina

When Fernando read these words, he kissed the scented paper they were written on, carefully re-folded it, and placed it in the breast pocket of his tunic, like a shield over his heart. And with that, he made ready for battle.

Still under Colonel Francisco Carvajal's command, the Córdoban Volunteers were now assimilated into a much larger Andalusian force, called the Army of La Mancha, led by General José de Urbina y Urbina, 3rd Conde de Cartaojal. Their patriotic mission and sacred duty was to prevent a French army, led by General Horace François Bastien Sébastiani de La Porta, a Corsican compatriot and long-time supporter of Napoleon, from conquering Andalusia. General Sébastiani's army headed south from Madrid in March 1809, while General Cartaojal's army moved north from Córdoba to confront them.

On the foggy night of March 24, a regiment of six hundred lancers from General Valance's Polish Division, led by Colonel Jan Kanopka, were vulnerably encamped in the village of Los Yébenes. Unbeknownst to them, more than four thousand cavalry and a thousand militia of the army of La Mancha had crept up on their exposed position, undetected in the fog. Only when the Spaniards attacked did the Polish lancers suddenly realize their plight. A savage melée ensued, in which only the ferocity of Kanopka's desperate counter-attack, combined with the lack of a coherent battle plan by General Cartaojal, prevented a massacre. The badly outnumbered but frenzied lancers hacked and hewed their way through the now-astonished Spanish force, losing nearly one hundred of their six hundred horsemen in the process. Adding insult to injury, they also lost their supply wagons, one of which contained their regimental banners, gifted to them by Josephina de Beauharnais, Napoleon's wife and first Empress of France. This marked the only defeat of the Polish lancers during the entire Peninsular War, and word of it spread rapidly through Spain. But to the French in general and the Poles in particular, the capture of their colors was a greater stain on their honor, which they thirsted madly to avenge. They would do so a mere three days later, in a much bigger battle, in which Fernando found himself immersed.

On March 27, more sizeable contingents of the French and Spanish armies faced one another just south of Ciudad Real, arrayed on opposite banks of the Guadiana River, whose sole bridge in the region was defended by the Spanish, blocking the French advance toward Puertollano, and thence into Andalusia. Once again the French found themselves outnumbered. General Sébastiani's Imperial troops, reinforced by Colonel Kanopka's Legion of the Vistula, amounted to some nine thousand men. Arrayed against them were twelve thousand troops from General Cartaojal's army of La Mancha, including Colonel Carvajal's Córdoban Volunteers. General Sébastiani noted well that General Cartoajal had stretched his troops along the river bank on both sides of the bridge, intending to foil any French attempt to ford the Guadiana and gain a foothold on either Spanish flank. Indeed, the Córdoban volunteers were dug in along the river bank flanking the right-hand side of the bridge, and Fernando could plainly see a French artillery regiment lining up their cannons on the other side, massing cavalry and infantry behind the guns. This deployment, however, proved to be a feint.

Having stretched his army too thinly along the river bank, and having counted on his numerically superior forces to repulse a frontal assault on the bridge itself, General Cartaojal then committed a final and ultimately fatal error. He had failed to absorb the recent lessons of Los Yébenes; namely, that the Polish lancers could slice their way through numbers much greater than their own, and moreover that they were desperate to erase the dishonor of having seen their regimental colors captured by the very General whom they now faced again, this time in broad daylight.

As the artillery batteries fired opening salvos from both sides of the river, cannonballs blasted opposing earthworks to smithereens, occasionally obliterating a gun and its crew, but more frequently whistling overhead and smashing into assembled ranks of cavalry or infantry, reducing them to unidentifiable heaps of dismembered and mangled body parts, and drenching the earth with blood. This was the first real battle that Fernando had ever witnessed, and what he would remember more than its ghastly scenes from Hell—not surprisingly, in his case—were its infernal sounds: the explosive cacophony of cannon fire, the horrible screams of wounded and dying men and horses, and soon enough the thundering of hooves, the sharp cracks of muskets, the zinging clashes of steel, and the barking of officers' commands, including his own. These horrific sounds of battle embedded themselves in Fernando's auditory memory, and later he would write music to reflect them. Meanwhile the melée raged around him.

The exchange of artillery salvos along the banks kept the Spanish lines extended, and diverted their attention from the unthinkable French assault on the bridge itself, which suddenly exploded across it. Riding hell for leather, Colonel Kanopka's Polish lancers pierced the wall of defenders on the Spanish side, while right behind them a tide of Imperial infantry surged through this central gap in the Spanish lines, cutting the army of La Mancha in half. Then the lancers themselves divided, sweeping around both halves and encircling them from behind, while the swelling tide of Imperial infantry engaged both halves from the front. Before General Cartaojal could react and reform his lines, panic began to spread among the Spanish troops, especially those on the left-hand flank of the bridge. Hundreds then thousands broke ranks and dispersed toward the hills, and many were shot down or run through, or else trampled or captured, during their disorderly retreat.

The right-hand Spanish flank, including the Córdoban Volunteers, stood their ground far better. Under the cool command of Colonel Carvajal, the infantry formed vaunted squares that repulsed Kanopka's horsemen, and poured concentrated fire into them and the approaching

Imperial troops. El Capitan Maestro Sor remained unflinchingly at his post, in the middle of a side of one such square, his saber glinting in the sun as he directed his two ranks of men—one kneeling, the other standing—to alternate volleys of fire and reload, while a third rank of men behind them calmly awaited their turns to replace the fallen. Men struck by French musket balls toppled to Fernando's left and right, including a man standing next him shot straight through the heart. At that El Capitan Maestro touched his own breast pocket, and felt Joaquina's letter inside. Whether shielded by her love, or by the grace of God, Fernando himself remained unscathed, except for his memory of the battle's horror.

While the discipline and valor of several Spanish regiments kept the French attackers at bay for a time, the result of the battle itself had already been decided in its earliest moments, when the Polish lancers stormed the bridge and split the Spanish army in twain. Thus a battle that many on both sides thought beforehand would be fought for days was over in a matter of four hours. The Spanish regiments that had maintained their discipline and stood their ground were able to effect an orderly retreat, but losses among those who had panicked and dispersed were appalling. General Cartaojal's army of nineteen thousand men lost two thousand killed and wounded, and a like number taken prisoner, while General Sébastiani's force of twelve thousand sustained only light casualties—numbers so small that French history did not record them.

What Spanish history did record, in the aftermath of this debacle, was General Cartaojal's immediate dismissal by the Central Junta for gross incompetence, and his replacement by General Francisco Javier Venegas de Saavedra y Ramínez de Arenzana, a man of fewer words and a lengthier name, but not altogether better judgment. For his conspicuous valor, Colonel Carvajal was promoted to Brigadier. Thus Fernando learned a valuable lesson from the battle of Ciudad Real: that military victories were won by able leadership, not superior numbers. Those Spanish troops who had panicked and dispersed were badly led but were not bad soldiers, Fernando thought, for those among them who had managed to escape death or evade capture would return to fight another day. And so Fernando's dilemma returned to haunt him: even though he proudly wore the uniform of a Spanish Captain, laying his life literally on the line to fight against foreign occupation, yet he also recognized the virtue of Napoleon's meritocracy as compared with the decadence of Spain's aristocracy. In Spain, an incompetent man could be promoted to General by means of social connections or political favors alone; whereas in France a man could rise to that rank only by sheer ability and naught else. So Fernando continued staunchly both to resist the French invaders, and yet to admire their ideals. Thousands of his Spanish compatriots likewise shared this view and, being branded *afrancesados* and therefore traitors for espousing it, would soon enough share the fate to which it was inexorably leading.

On the day after the debacle at Ciudad Real, so Fernando would soon learn, the Spanish suffered an even worse defeat at Medellin, under another notoriously incompetent commander: General Gregorio García de la Cuesta y Fernández de Celis. Following El Dos de Mayo, General Cuesta had proved so reluctant to lead the insurgency in Valladolid that the local populace erected a gallows in front of his house and threatened to lynch him unless he assumed command. Lurching from one near-disaster to another, Cuesta was eventually appointed commander of the army of Extremadura by the Central Junta, with orders to prevent the French from occupying southern Spain. When General Arthur Wellesley led the British expeditionary army from Portugal into Spain, General Cuesta was ordered to coordinate with him, but proved so dangerously unreliable that Wellesley petitioned the Central Junta to remove him, to no avail.

At Medellin, on March 28, Cuesta's army of twenty-four thousand infantry and thirty-five hundred cavalry faced a much smaller French army, under Marshal Victor, of thirteen thousand infantry and forty-five hundred cavalry. Cuesta ordered his infantry to advance across open terrain, which became a shooting gallery for the French. The Spanish suffered eight thousand dead and two thousand taken prisoner, with twenty of their thirty cannons captured to boot. By contrast, French casualties amounted to one thousand dead or wounded. British historian Sir Charles Oman described General Cuesta as "a criminal maniac".

Even so, Sir George Jackson, a British officer seconded to Cuesta's command, observed at Medellin what Fernando had also witnessed earlier at Ciudad Real, namely the indomitable courage of the ill-equipped, poorly armed, and often badly led Spanish infantry. Jackson wrote that these ordinary foot soldiers "... behaved nobly. Though great numbers were without shoes and almost without clothing, they advanced with a coolness and resolution that would have done credit to veteran troops." This touched the essence of the topsy-turvy Peninsular War, in which, over and over again, common Spanish soldiers and militia exhibited nobility, and were slaughtered, while their aristocratic generals displayed degeneracy, and were rewarded. It made Fernando despair for the fate of Spain.

Meanwhile, back in France, Napoleon busied himself suppressing a rash of seditious plots hatched against him, seemingly from all quarters. Jacobins and Royalists alike, although mortal enemies of one another, were apprehended for plotting treason against the Emperor, and several from both camps were executed by firing squad. Royalists put to death included Armand de Chateaubriand, brother of René, the most celebrated author in France. Louis-Marcelin de Fontanes, Grand Master of the University of Paris, discreetly voiced his growing discontent, while many members of the Imperial government expressed theirs openly. Count Denis Decrès, Minister of the Navy, declared "The Emperor is mad, completely mad; he will bring ruin upon himself, and upon us all."

Yet Napoleon was also hoist with his own meritocratic petard. As absolute dictator, he could execute anyone on a whim. But because he needed able men to help him manage his empire, he was obliged to exercise forbearance if not forgiveness toward some of his most competent traitors. He both bullied and cajoled Fouché in order to regain his Minister of Police's loyalty, then threw a calculated temper-tantrum upon seeing Talleyrand in the Council of State. Berating his Vice-Grand Elector of the Empire at considerable length for both duplicity and treachery, Napoleon shouted "You are ordure in a silk stocking," swiveled on his boot-heel, and left the room. His consummate French priorities in place, Talleyrand remarked to the Councilors "What a pity that that so great a man should have such bad manners." Yet Napoleon retained Talleyrand's services, and privately commended him as his most capable minister. Talleyrand himself would lose no time devoting his capacities to hastening the Emperor's downfall.

His own house restored to a semblance of order for the time being, Napoleon set about settling Austria's hash. He levied an enormous army, now conscripting boys to compensate his growing shortage of men, and led them eastward. He crossed the Danube during the night of July 4, 1809, at the head of one hundred sixty thousand troops and more than six hundred guns. The next day, at Wagram, he attacked Archduke Karl's army of one hundred seventy thousand troops and more than four hundred guns. Wagram became the bloodiest battle to date in European history, with more than eighty thousand overall killed, wounded or missing. Even so, the Emperor won a decisive victory, compelling the Archduke of Austria to sue for peace, and thus collapsing the Fifth Coalition against the Empire.

Secretly advised by the treacherous Talleyrand, Tsar Alexander of Russia had not lifted a finger, neither to help Napoleon against Austria (as their own secret treaty obliged him to so) nor to help Austria against Napoleon (as he privately wished to do). Instead, the Tsar patiently bided his time, deriving consolation from the steep blood-price of Napoleon's victory at Wagram. Every French soldier killed outside Russia was one French soldier less with which Napoleon could invade Russia, as Alexander believed he would sooner or later do, a belief which Talleyrand shared.

But the consequences of Wagram were not so good for Spain, as Napoleon now had more troops at his disposal. Having quelled the threat in the east, the Emperor marched reinforcements westward, to help subdue the stubborn Spaniards. Yet even before these troops could pour across the Pyrenees, two major battles in Spain would deepen the plights of all parties to that conflict, including Fernando's.

King Joseph badly needed reinforcements, and could hardly wait for them to arrive. In addition to the incessant insurgencies of guerillas and partisans throughout the land, he still had to contend with two main Spanish forces: General Cuesta's army of the Extremadura, now joined by Wellesley's expeditionary force, and General Venegas's army of La Mancha. Catalonia's main army had been defeated by Saint-Cyr at the battle of Valls in February of that year, in which the courageous Von Reding had sustained wounds of which he died in April. The remainder of Catalonia's defenders, led by General Enrique José O'Donnell y Anatar, Conde de La Bisbal, were heavily besieged in the near-impregnable fortress of Girona, which would not succumb for months to come. But at least they were removed from the field.

Had Cuesta, Wellesley, and Venegas been able to coordinate their strategies and movements, they might have been able to force Sébastiani to retreat, and to dislodge Joseph from Madrid. But that was a mere pipe-dream of incurably romantic strategists, rendered impossible by realities on the ground. For one thing, communications were far too unreliable even to coordinate movements perfectly within one army, let alone among three. For another, Spanish generals were more often concerned with competing against each other for glory than with uniting to defeat the French. To make matters even worse, some Spanish generals viewed the English not as allies, but rather as invaders in their own right, and sought to pit them against the French without committing their own troops to battle. This infuriated Wellesley among other English commanders, and strained political relations no end. All these factors came to a head in the summer of 1809, at Talavera and Almonacid.

In late July, King Joseph Bonaparte and Marshal Jean-Baptiste Jourdan led forty-six thousand troops and eighty guns, including Sébastiani's army, against a combined force of twenty thousand English troops and thirty guns led by Wellesley, and thirty-five thousand Spanish troops and thirty guns led by Cuesta. The resulting battle of Talavera, fought on July 27-28, was a tactical but Pyrrhic Anglo-Spanish victory, and ultimately a strategic French success. The French suffered more than seven thousand casualties, a very high number for them thus far in their set-piece Iberian battles. When Napoleon heard this news in Vienna, he was actually impressed by the English commander, and remarked "*Il parait que c'est un homme, ce Wellesley*". ("It seems that this is a man [to reckon with], this Wellesley.") Napoleon would send more than enough reinforcements to make good this loss. But the English, who had done most of the fighting for the allies, endured more than six thousand casualties, amounting to almost one third of those engaged in the battle, and one quarter of Wellesley's total expeditionary force. The Spanish lost only twelve hundred men, because the treacherous Cuesta had withheld his assault while Wellesley's men were being slaughtered at an appalling rate. While King Joseph and Marshal Jourdan were first to withdraw from the field, thus allowing the allies to proclaim victory, in fact both sides retreated to lick their wounds.

Critically, the aftermath of Talavera also gave Sébastiani time to block Venegas's path to Madrid. Venegas had dawdled during late July, his troops comfortably encamped along the Tagus river, swimming and sunbathing in the hot Spanish summer. Both Wellesley and Cuesta had dispatched urgent messages, exhorting him to seize the opportunity to retake Madrid before Sébastiani could disengage from Talavera, but to no avail. Venegas disregarded Wellesley, despised Cuesta, and refused to budge. By the time he decided to march on the capital, it was too late. He was encouraged to do so neither by the sound advice of his English ally nor by that of his compatriot Spanish general whom he hated, but rather by a French ruse. Sébastiani had probed his defenses by sending small parties across the Tagus river to feign attacks. Repulsing these French probes, Venegas wrongly concluded that the French forces were weak enough to be overrun. So he finally gave orders to advance.

On August 11, Sébastiani's army awaited him, fully deployed near Almonacid. The army of La Mancha was in fact outnumbered: Venegas's twenty-three thousand infantry, three thousand cavalry, and twenty-nine guns faced Sébastiani's twenty-six thousand infantry, four thousand cavalry, and forty guns. The French attacked immediately, losing dozens of officers in the process but swiftly wreaking havoc on the Spanish army. Once again, as at Ciudad Real, the Córdoban regiment under Brigadier Carvajal distinguished itself against superior numbers, holding its ground with discipline and fortitude. As before, El Capitan Maestro Sor bravely directed fire from his infantry command, emerging unscathed from the fray. But the bulk of Venegas's army did not fare as well. Spanish losses at Almonacid amounted to thirty-five hundred killed or wounded, another two thousand taken prisoner, and the capture of twenty of their twenty-nine guns. Total French losses were twenty-four hundred men.

As Venegas retreated from Almonacid in disarray, thousands of his troops melted away into the hills, or dispersed across the countryside. The army of La Mancha had been battered, and soon after—along with the Córdoban regiment—was mostly disbanded. Spanish resistance hardly ended there, but rather transformed itself into a myriad of ongoing guerilla and partisan actions against the French invaders. Fernando was decommissioned in Córdoba, and for the first time in his life he knew neither where to go, nor what to do next. He remained in Córdoba for some months, long enough to taste the chaos to which the entire country was now succumbing, as the invasion and occupation intensified, and to despair at the unspeakable atrocities committed by all parties as the madness of full-scale conflict gripped Spain like a vise. Moreover, and so contrary to his natural cheerfulness, Fernando became increasingly dismayed by the bitter internal rivalries among Spanish political and military leaders, now exacerbated to a fevered pitch by bloody battles, and depressingly disheartened by their chronic unwillingness or inability to unite against a common foe.

Chapter 18. Córdoba and Málaga: The Darkness Deepens

Fernando's uncharacteristic despair was unfortunately justified by subsequent events that autumn of 1809 and, unbeknownst to him, was echoed in even more pessimistic tones by Sir Arthur Wellesley, who was in a position to know many things that Fernando was hypothetically happier not to know, even if he merely intuited them.

For one thing, the Central Junta was preparing to launch a new offensive campaign that autumn, based almost entirely on poor estimates of French troop strength and false rumors of French strategic retreats. They still held out the delirious hope of recapturing Madrid. They sacked General Venegas, replacing him with Juan Carlos de Aréizaga, and ordered Aréizaga to begin re-organizing the Army of La Mancha. They also sacked General Cuesta, transferring the remnants of his army of Extramadura to Aréizaga's command. That formed one prong of their intended two-pronged offensive. To form the second prong, they combined the armies of Galicia and Asturias, placing them under the command of Vicente María Cañas y Portocarrero, 7th Duke Del Parque. This was called the Army of the Left.

But the Central Junta itself faced growing opposition from the people for its mishandling of the war thus far. It was pressured to convene a Cortes (that is, a parliament), which would not assemble until 1810. Meanwhile the Junta hoped to regain the people's confidence with their new campaign, in which they tried but failed to embroil Wellesley. For one thing, his estimates of French strength were larger than theirs—around one hundred and thirty thousand, or so he reckoned—while in fact there were by now one hundred and eighty thousand French troops in Spain, with more pouring across the Pyrenees every day. For another, Wellesley's own political frustrations with the Junta, and the lack of military coordination with and among Spanish generals, made him chary of renewing the offensive prematurely. Instead, Wellesley withdrew to Badajoz—one of the few fortresses still in Allied hands—and gave orders for the construction of new defensive lines in Portugal, which he felt sure the French would re-invade. His judgment would prove sound on all accounts.

As to the Junta itself, Wellesley sent a sobering and also somewhat perplexing dispatch to London:

> *The Supreme Central Junta is neither an adequate representation of the crown, nor of the aristocracy, nor of the people, nor does it comprise any useful quality either of an executive council, or of a deliberative assembly, while it combines many defects which tend to disturb both deliberation and action ... its strange and anomalous constitution unites the contradictory inconveniences of every known form of government without possessing the advantages of any ... it is not an instrument of sufficient power to accomplish the purposes for which it was formed, nor can it ever acquire sufficient force or influence to bring into action the resources of the country and the spirit of the people with that degree of vigor and alacrity which might ... repel a foreign invader.*

While Wellesley's political masters grasped all too well the military implications of his report—that it would take considerably more time, effort, and investment by the English and their allies to drive the French out of Spain—they were utterly baffled by its political assessment. It lay beyond their experience, understanding, and imagination that any government could somehow manage to represent no-one whatsoever, not even itself.

But this was because they made the fundamental mistake, which Napoleon had also made and would continue to make at fatal cost, of assuming that Spain was a singular nation to begin with, in the same sense that England, Portugal, France, Austria, Russia, and all the other nations of Europe conceived themselves to be. Had Spain been a singular nation like the rest, then virtually any known form of government could have represented it, at least in some credible way. But precisely because Spain was neither a singular nation, nor even a pluralistic one, no known form of government could represent it at all, except in incredible ways. This was Spain's topsy-turvy political paradox. And while Wellesley's shrewd political intelligence, coupled with his experience on the ground, had enabled him (among very few foreigners) to identify the enigma, no-one on earth had the power to solve it, save perhaps the Spanish people themselves, in the ripeness of a future time.

As Muñoz Torrero—priest, former president of the University of Salamanca, and soon-to-be chair of the committee that wrote the Cadiz Constitution—would declare to the Cortes itself: "If a foreigner were to come here who did not know us he would say that there are six or seven nations." Indeed, there was Catalonia, Aragon, Andalusia, Galicia, Castile y Leon, the Basque country, and more. While Spain may have been the sum of them, yet none of them conceived itself as Spanish. The same could be said of the social classes: there was the monarchy, the aristocracy, the church, the military, the civil service, the intelligentsia, the *hidalgos*, the bourgeoisie, the *majos* and *majas*, the peasants—yet each of them likewise had different conceptions of Spain. Ultimately, as Fernando would soon realize and express in an epic lament, Spain was not a nation at all, and not even a conception of a nation; rather, it was a congeries of conflicting and often incoherent conceptions of a nation. It was a future nation, awaiting its own formation, yet incognizant of exactly who would form it, of precisely when this would occur, and of conceivably which form it would take. In other words, at the present time, Spain was the name of nothing other than a tapestry of dreams, all clashing perfectly in unison.

Yet this was the very secret of Spain's invincibility, and her saving grace. While a nation can be invaded and conquered, no-one can invade and conquer a dream. This was the crux of Napoleon's error, as it had been the Moorish error before him, and the Roman error before them.

Napoleon's conquests were all based on a single formula: defeating a nation's army in a decisive battle led swiftly and surely to that nation's political subjugation. Napoleon had conquered Austria by winning the battle of Ulm. Napoleon had dissolved the Holy Roman Empire by winning the battle of Austerlitz. By the same token, the British had mastered the world's sea-lanes by winning the battle of Trafalgar. Now, according to these lights, Napoleon sought to conquer Spain by winning a decisive battle there. But this formula would prove his undoing, for no matter how many battles he won, he could never subjugate an imaginary polity.

If Spain's armies were defeated, then the populace would resist. If its cities were devastated and the populace subdued, then guerillas would arise. If the guerillas were executed, then women, children and priests would attack from the rubble. If every single human being were annihilated, then bears, wolves and boars would maul, bite and gore. If the beasts were all hunted down, the rats would swarm from the ports and urban gutters. If the rats were all poisoned, the fleas they carried would infest the invaders and infect them with disease. And if the invaders recovered from disease, they would starve to death unless they abandoned this hostile land and returned whence they came. The very land itself might be reduced to scorched earth, but the dream that was Spain could not be conquered, except perhaps in futile hallucinations.

But as Napoleon's invasion of the dream that was Spain intensified, life itself became a waking nightmare, and for all concerned. The Emperor had never waged a war like this one, and so he sank even deeper into the Iberian quagmire. Wellesley—who had fought in Europe, India, and Scandinavia—had never engaged in a war like this either, but was determined somehow to unite his Spanish and Portuguese allies with his English troops, and drive the French back to France, where they belonged. Fernando had never fought in a war at all before this one, but however imaginary Spain might be, the sufferings of its people became increasingly horrific, and all too real.

Moreover, Fernando suffered three times over: first, for the hardships and privations that war was imposing on him and his family (although he never complained on his own account); second, for the immense toll of death, injury and destruction that the war was inflicting on the people themselves, from whom he never felt far removed, and whose sufferings afflicted his very soul; and third, for the complex internal conflicts caused by his growing love-hate relationship with both the French and the English.

As we have seen, Fernando continued to love the ideals of the Enlightenment, which in his own way—once he had shed enough blood—Napoleon also espoused. Then again, Fernando hated despotism, and even unwilling despots like King Joseph rankled him, having been imposed by a bigger tyrant in the guise of a liberator. If this were not complex enough, Fernando experienced a parallel conflict over the English. Of course he loved his English ally for seeking to liberate Spain from the French invaders. How could he not revere them for this? After all, standing shoulder-to-shoulder in combat, they were shedding the same red blood as his compatriots in this noble cause. Then again, he hated his English ally on account of Wellesley's political mission. For Wellesley had not come purely to liberate Spain from French occupation; that—as Fernando understood perfectly well—was merely Wellesley's strategic aim. But England's political goal in Spain, which Fernando reviled to the marrow of his bones, was to root out democracy itself, making sure it would never take hold in Iberia.

In this matter William Kirkpatrick had instructed Fernando thoroughly, explaining that English Tories still smarted from having lost their American colonies in the populist Revolutionary War, and would not forsake this opportunity to take their revenge against democracy wherever they could, in this case using Spain as their whipping-boy. Indeed, the dyed-in-the-wool conservative Wellesley would soon write to Lord Bathurst, British Secretary for War, inquiring "whether, if I should find a fair opportunity of striking at the democracy, the government would approve of my doing it". And the English government, as Kirkpatrick had foreseen, was delighted at the possibility. Bathurst would reply "You may be assured that if you can strike a blow at the democracy in Spain, your conduct will be much approved here."

So Fernando was emotionally torn by his love-hate relationships with the French and the English alike, combined with his love for the Spanish people and their imaginary nation, and his growing anguish over their unrelieved sufferings from the agonies of all-out war. His despair only deepened during November of 1809, when the desperate Central Junta made a last-ditch effort to salvage its sinking legitimacy by launching a two-pronged attack, in an ill-starred attempt to retake Madrid. Wellesley had been prudent to refrain from joining this offensive, as it turned into a complete debacle.

Notwithstanding the growing numbers of French troops in Spain, the Grande Armée was still spread relatively thinly, owing to civilian rebellions that continued to flare up far and wide. While sufficiently large French garrisons were not attacked by guerillas or partisans, smaller ones—along with supply lines, scouting parties and dispatch riders—were under constant threat of ambush and massacre. Thus the Spanish resistance tied down large numbers of French troops, merely to maintain law and order in one place, only to see insurgency erupt in another.

And notwithstanding the Central Junta's countless and irremediable defects, so ably catalogued by Wellesley, their November offensive initially caught the French by surprise. Aréizaga's newly formed Army of La Mancha had forged swiftly northward. He led a substantial force of forty-five thousand infantry, seven thousand cavalry, and sixty guns. By November 9 Aréizaga had reached Ocaña unopposed, only thirty-five miles from Madrid. There he encountered a few token French divisions, amounting to some seven thousand troops. But instead of attacking immediately, Aréizaga apparently lost his nerve and halted. He then engaged in a series of pointless maneuvers for several days, allowing the French sufficient time to summon reinforcements. When the armies finally clashed on November 19, King Joseph and Marshal Soult still had only twenty-four thousand infantry, five thousand cavalry, and fifty guns at their disposal.

Nonetheless, General Aréizaga proved to be as inept a tactician as he was a strategist. In spite of their superior numbers, the Army of La Mancha was virtually destroyed at Ocaña, losing five thousand killed or wounded, more than twenty thousand captured, along with the loss of forty-five of their sixty guns; while French casualties amounted to a mere two thousand killed or wounded. Needless to say, many thousands of Aréizaga's infantry were raw recruits: barely clothed, hardly shod, poorly armed, and badly trained. And with correspondingly few seasoned

Spanish offers to led them in battle, it was perhaps inevitable that, in spite of their superior numbers, they could not maintain discipline under fire.

The other prong of the offensive, attacking from the north, fared no better. The Duke del Parque's Army of the Left comprised some thirty-two thousand men and eighteen guns. The French commander, François Étienne de Kellermann, 2nd Duc de Valmy, had only sixteen thousand troops and twelve guns. Even so, on November 26, at Alba de Tormes, Kellerman caught Del Parque's army in the midst of trying to ford the Tormes river, and attacked immediately. Del Parque lost three thousand men and half his guns in the battle, against negligible French losses of five hundred men. The Army of the Left then retreated under cover of darkness, where thousands more melted away into the hills, utterly deserting the cause. Del Parque and the remnants of his army made their winter headquarters in the remote mountain village of San Martín de Trevejo in the Sierra de Gata, where freezing cold weather and meager provisions would oblige them to subsist, like squirrels, on acorns. By January 1810, nine thousand more would die of illness or starvation.

Thus the November offensive became an unmitigated disaster, in whose aftermath the Central Junta lost every trace of credibility to which it had so forlornly clung, while Andalusia herself now lay undefended, and wide open to wholesale French occupation. The Central Junta made ready to flee from Seville to Cádiz, still under Spanish control, and there convene a Cortes, becoming in effect a government in exile. Neither did Fernando await the coming French occupation of Córdoba; immediately after learning of the fiasco at Ocaña he rode south to Málaga, to confer with William Kirkpatrick. For although Fernando had witnessed El Dos del Mayo and the short-lived siege of Madrid, and even though he had been in combat with the Army of La Mancha at Ciudad Real and Almonacid, he needed to understand the bigger military and political picture, instead of struggling to keep afloat on the raging torrent of rumors, half-truths, misinformation, and outright lies which swept everyone away during times of war. If anyone had credible knowledge of the overall situation it would be William, whose life and livelihood depended on his networks of reliable intelligence. Besides which, Fernando missed his dear friend in Málaga, along with the whole Kirkpatrick family, into whose bosom he had been made so welcome during those last and ever-so-precious years of peace.

Busy as usual in his cluttered office at the port, William was no less happy to see Fernando. He leapt up from behind his desk, warmly shook Fernando's hand, embraced him, and insisted on bringing him home for lunch. Françoise and the girls jumped for joy at the sight of him—especially Maria Manuela, who let out a shriek of pure delight. Fernando noticed at once that they were all thinner and even somewhat gaunt, and that their clothing, while not exactly threadbare, hung on them more loosely, a far cry from their usual finery.

"These days, it is much safer not to appear prosperous," said William, noting Fernando's look of surprise. "Besides which," he added after a modest lunch, when they repaired to his library for man-to-man palaver, "our prosperity now hangs by a thread. Málaga has not yet been occupied, looted, and pillaged, but that dark day may soon arrive. No-one has enough to eat, for the war has devastated agriculture and destroyed commerce. The Spanish army has requisitioned most of our stores, and the French will soon strip us bare. Even the wine cellars stand close to empty, which will only incense the French further. Thank God we can still find fishes in the sea. Yet we are only eighteen months into this war, and I am already approaching the brink of ruin. I fear greatly for my wife and daughters, and resolve to do all in my power to protect them."

Fernando beheld the deep consternation that knitted William's features and furrowed his brow, and his heart went out to him. "It must be impossibly worrisome to maintain the welfare of one's family during such trying times."

"Aye, that it is," acknowledged William. "And no less difficult to sustain close friendships," he added rather cryptically.

"Whatever do you mean?" asked Fernando, detecting a note of sudden desperation in William's voice.

"My dear Fernando," explained William, "I now owe you a debt that can never be repaid, no matter what the outcome of this wretched war."

Fernando raised a quizzical eyebrow.

"As you well know," continued William, "Spanish agriculture is a stagnant tale of wasted capacity, shamelessly lingering decades if not centuries behind Europe, hopelessly awaiting the enactment of long-overdue land reform. On top of this, Spain must now find a way of feeding not merely one, but three large armies—the Spanish, the Anglo-Portuguese, and the French—all bent on living off that very land. The countryside is being stripped bare (at this Fernando nodded from his own experience), and when starving soldiers enter a town or a city, they cannot be prevented from going on a rampage."

Fernando understood this well enough, but could not yet divine any connection between all this, and William owing him a debt. So he continued to listen patiently as his friend unburdened himself.

"Immediately after Ocaña, Marshal Soult dispatched commissary officers from his general staff into Andalusia, to begin making arrangements to provision his army. Unfortunately, my reputation as a successful merchant and trader led French officers straight to my door. I met with them several times. The French offered to protect my supply chains, by land and along the Mediterranean coast, in exchange for my help in acquiring and distributing provisions among other things. Although they are masters of politeness, their seemingly genteel offer thinly veiled a sinister threat—both to Málaga in general, and to my family in particular."

"Monsieur Querquepatrique," they said, "sadly, you know that atrocities can and do occur in wartime. Unfortunately, soldiers—even French soldiers—are capable of committing heinous crimes against defenseless civilians. The plunder and rapine that took place in northern Portugal, for example, were regrettable but unavoidable, since our troops were practically starving for want of adequate victuals. But if you can assist in provisioning the French army that will shortly occupy Andalusia, we can assure you that the citizens of Málaga—including your beautiful wife and charming young daughters of course—will be protected by troops that might otherwise take liberties with their possessions and their persons... So will you kindly render us your every assistance? The Emperor would be eternally grateful."

"They left me little choice, Fernando," William continued, "for I had already heard horror stories about the French troops in Portugal. Have you any inkling of what transpired there?"

Of course Fernando had witnessed the brutally violent uprising of El Dos de Mayo, and the merciless executions of Madrileños by French firing squads in its aftermath. Moreover, he had seen men die violently in battle: blown to pieces by cannonballs or mutilated by canister shrapnel, shot by musket balls or run through by bayonets. He had seen wounded soldiers dying in agony on the battlefield, or wasting away from illness on long marches. But he had neither witnessed nor heard tell of the atrocities committed by the French in Portugal, which William now described to him.

"To begin with, both the English and the French were utterly scandalized by the living conditions of ordinary Portuguese people. Everyone who sails into Lisbon is at first charmed by views from afar, as this city of glistening white stone sparkles like diamonds set in a blue sapphire bay against an azure sky. But once they land in port, they are overcome by the stench of raw sewage running ankle-deep in the streets, not to mention the rotting garbage and vermin-infested hovels that line its narrow streets, from which filthy, emaciated and rag-clad citizens emerge every morning to sit on their wretched stoops and pick lice off each other. One English officer described them as 'positively not a degree above savages'. Every soldier billeted more than a few days in Lisbon falls ill with dysentery, or succumbs to outbreaks of cholera or typhus, or carries away some pernicious pox that rots him from the inside out.

"English contempt for the Portuguese extends to the Spanish as well, for most English officers being Anglicans, they despise what they deem the abysmal ignorance and sordid superstitions of Roman Catholics. As to the French invaders, their contumely for Iberians comes naturally to them: the French are so full of themselves that they hold all foreigners in contempt by default.

"When the French retreated from Portugal, they ransacked, looted, and pillaged everything in their path—from hardscrabble farms to fine houses of *hidalgos*. A business associate of mine in Oporto saw his home destroyed: furniture ruined or carted away, rugs and paintings removed, cutlery and jewelry stolen, finely carved balustrades smashed, mirrors and chandeliers shattered, wallpaper torn or defaced. Yet he was lucky. One of his neighbors, an upright Portuguese gentleman, had his brains blown out by one of Soult's officers because he refused to permit the assassin to borrow his daughter to gratify his lust. He raped the girl anyway, right next to her father's dead body.

"In retaliation for these among many such outrages, mobs of Portuguese civilians caught and nailed French stragglers to barn doors or trees, cut off their genitals, and stuffed them in their mouths. They also demanded that the English turn French prisoners over to them, for similar vengeance.

"Fernando, I would do anything in my modest power to avert such atrocities in Málaga."

Fernando nodded in complete understanding.

"But when local guerillas found out that I was talking to Marshal Soult's commissary officers, they branded me an *afrancesado*, and razed my cotton plantation to the ground, along with the villa."

"I am truly sorry," said Fernando, "for Adra was an enchanting abode."

"Thank you, my friend. But my sorrow is mostly *not* for Adra—after all, homes can be rebuilt, crops can be replanted—but to my everlasting regret, Goya's magnificent portrait of you was also consumed by the flames. How can I ever repay you for that irreplaceable loss?"

At this Fernando smiled wryly, catching William completely by surprise. Notwithstanding the deep bond between these two friends, William was after all grounded in the material world, from which he made his living and based his lofty aspirations for his daughters; while Fernando was an utterly ethereal being, attached above all to music, which fire could not burn.

"The loss of a painting is nothing beside the loss of peace, prosperity, good will, and human life in this horrible condition of war. Let us rather give bountiful thanks to our Lord and Savior for preserving our loved ones, who are truly irreplaceable, and pray to the Virgin Mary to watch over them, day and night, until this time of madness passes. Meanwhile, there is nothing to repay; let us rather rejoice at the renewal of our friendship."

"Amen to that," said William, his eyes misting over ever so slightly. Had he been a more sentimental man, he would have shed tears of relief at Fernando's magnanimity of spirit.

Françoise and the girls were so cheered by Fernando's presence—which bathed them in rays of inextinguishable light that pierced the gloomy and foreboding fog of war—that they insisted he remain as their houseguest for as long as he wished, or at least until the fog lifted enough for his path to become clear. For his part, Fernando did not need much persuasion. Absorbed into the wholeness and wholesomeness of the Kirkpatrick family, he began to recover from the traumas inflicted on him by total immersion in the previous twenty months of war. Late in 1809 he dedicated a composition to them—*The Bells Will Not Toll*—a somewhat cryptic title suggesting, perhaps, that they were mired so deep in limbo that they could neither celebrate nor mourn.

General Sébastiani's army occupied Córdoba, unopposed, in January 1810. Soon after, French troops swarmed the rest of Andalusia, and laid siege to Cádiz, preventing the Cortes from convening. It would take many months for its far-flung representatives make their hazardous ways from all parts of Spain, by hook or by crook through French lines, to join the first freely elected Spanish government in three hundred years. But with topsy-turvy Spanish irony, they now governed nothing but an idea, if not a dream, as the land itself lay trampled under the heels of Napoleon's boots.

And as Fernando heard the reports that streamed to William from his expansive networks, far and wide, his gloom could only deepen.

Chapter 19. Jerez: El Capitan Maestro of the Police: Traitor or Patriot?

Outwardly, Fernando still appeared his usual cheerful self, radiating congenital joy and causing others in his presence to feel joyful themselves, even in these terrible and troubled times. But inwardly, he felt increasingly tormented by the monstrosity of war, and by all the hideous atrocities, injustices and sufferings it so callously inflicted on so many, be they innocent bystanders or willing accomplices. The reports he heard from William's networks heaped horror upon horror: the monstrousness seemed to feed on its own monstrosity, yet no-one could slay the monster itself. Fernando longed to slay it, had already risked his life to slay it, and would have gladly given his life to slay it, but was powerless even to wound it. Instead, it wounded him, and deeply; not his body, but his very soul. He recalled an etching that Goya had once shown him, made in response to the Jacobin terror of the 1790s. Goya had titled it *The Sleep of Reason Produces Monsters*. Fernando shuddered as he wondered what monstrous works would now emerge from Goya's boiling brain. The long sleep of reason in Spain had lately produced hellish monsters of nightmarish proportions, and this was a nightmare from which nobody had the power to awaken. For the first time in his life, Fernando felt crushed by an interminably long and utterly dark night of the soul. And every report seemed to deepen the darkness.

Fernando learned that the French army was not alone in its looting, pillaging, and plundering. Wellesley was massing yet more English troops in Portugal, preparing to reinvade Spain with a vengeance, and among them were many unwilling conscripts, including criminals and ne'er-do-wells who had been snatched off the streets, out of alleys, or straight from pubs. They too committed outrages in Portugal, and some were killed in retaliation by furious Portuguese mobs. Wellesley himself complained "The army behave terribly ill. They are a rabble ... they plunder in all directions." One English soldier, in search of firewood as they crossed back into Spain, entered a church and saw a coffin lying in the vault. He profanely tipped the body onto the floor and used the coffin to fuel their campfire. While disregard for human life is the daily bread of war, disrespect for the dead is indigestible, and cannot be stomached by the living. Indeed, an English officer named Thomas Browne observed "The common soldiers appeared to me to become daily more ferocious and less fit to return to the duties of citizens, and I sometimes apprehended that when they should be disbanded in England after the restoration of peace, the country would be overrun with pilferers and marauders of every description." So much for the ordinary conduct of Spain's English ally.

From one end of Spain to the other, and regardless of which 'side' they were on, the soldiers' behaviors were the same. Towns and villages were half-burned; women and girls raped; houses ransacked and churches looted; farm animals killed or stolen; wooden tools and implements used for firewood; everything remotely edible consumed; inhabitants left to starve. As one of Marshal Ney's *aides-de-camp* lamented: "This is no longer a campaign that we are conducting; it is rather a devastation by bandits in uniform."

Even more disturbing to Fernando were reports of the lawless bands of Spanish guerillas who roamed far and wide, terrorizing their own people, scavenging what precious little remained after marauding armies had stripped everything bare. These guerillas robbed even the scanty baggage-wagons of their own famished troops. It particularly wounded his heart to hear of the *somaténes* in Catalonia, in theory a patriotic citizens' militia attached to the regular Spanish army, but in practice a feckless array of deserters, outlaws, thieves, swindlers and smugglers. Needless to say, the *somaténes* were completely unreliable for military purposes, yet could always be relied on to commit every imaginable crime, especially against hapless civilians. As one Spanish officer, transferred from the defunct Army of Andalusia to Catalonia, lamented: "Every day I hate these people more: they have no other God than money... The whole of the much-vaunted Army of Catalonia is composed of bands of thieves who under the name of *somaténes* enter the towns and villages in almost the same manner as the French... the only difference being that they are rather more skilful at robbing them."

As if this were not enough, the collapse of the Central Junta was followed by a mushrooming of new Juntas in towns and villages across the land, adding further confusion to the existing hostile competition among the main Juntas in the larger cities. Incessant jostling over jurisdictions even led some Juntas to the brink of declaring war upon others, as if Spain were not already drowning in a bloodbath of chaotic conflict. Needless to say, each Junta backed its favorite general and, as we have seen, the generals themselves spent more time plotting against one another and leaving their English allies in the lurch than they did cooperating against the common foe.

So by early 1810, as these among other horrific reports filtered into Málaga, Fernando found himself near his wits' end. He had to do something, but what could possibly be done? He prayed to God for guidance, and mercifully received it: neither from priests nor patrons, neither from friends nor fellow musicians. Guidance came ultimately from the people themselves, to whom his heart had gone out time and again, and for whom it had bled so copiously in this seemingly interminable strife.

King Joseph had decided to make a desperate bid for popular support, and to woo the people's hearts from supporting the British, who promised to 'liberate' them from French tyranny but who openly recognized the young Bourbon tyrant-in-exile, Ferdinand VII, as the rightful monarch of Spain. So King Joseph commanded his army to prepare to parade, in all their finery, through the main cities and towns of Andalusia, where he himself would lead a series of royal processions. Concerned for his safety, and worried about assassination attempts by insurgents, some of his military commanders objected, but he overruled them. "If we are truly to rule Spain," he declared, "then we must be seen by our subjects to be truly ruling Spain." Notwithstanding the palpable security risks, his logic was irrefutable. And so preparations were duly made.

To the immense relief of those charged with protecting him, these royal processions proved popular even beyond King Joseph's wildest expectations. One of those who had fretted most, namely General Bigarré, the King's *aide-de-camp*, was astounded by the jubilant and reverent mood of the people everywhere on Joseph's route: in Ecija, in Jerez, in Santa Maria, in Ronda, in Granada, in Jaen ... and Fernando witnessed it for himself in Málaga. As Bigarré recorded in his memoirs,

> *In every town, the nobility, formed up as a guard of honor, came to congratulate him on his happy arrival, and swore to extend to him their unlimited devotion. They even embraced his feet and his knees ... Following their example, the people kissed his horse and prostrated themselves on the ground, crying 'Long live King Joseph!', whilst I saw women of the lower classes begging him to do them the honor of riding over their bodies.*

While some parties to this glowing reception were undoubtedly play-acting out of mere prudence, it seemed to Fernando that the vast majority were relieved and overjoyed to have a King again at last. They saw the monarch as a symbol of peace, security, and unity which—out of desperation borne of devastation—they allowed themselves to believe would be immediately if not magically restored in the wake of his procession. Witnessing their adulation as if at the arrival of the Savior, Fernando not only forgave their flood-tide of naivety but also permitted himself to be swept away by it. The momentary respite from unremitting conflict afforded by this spectacle could be prolonged indefinitely, or so he allowed himself to imagine, if only all the people of Spain accepted Joseph as their rightful ruler. It was a logical, if impossible, flight of fancy into a realm of peace. But it provided Fernando with a profoundly welcome sense of relief from his own desperation. For ever since El Dos de Mayo, he had inhabited just the opposite: a completely illogical but all-too-possible world of war.

Once the King's procession had passed through Málaga, and Joseph's civil administration began to assume their daily functions, Fernando did what thousands upon thousands of his compatriots similarly felt compelled to do. He calmly walked into City Hall, and declared that he wished to swear his allegiance to King Joseph. He requested an administrative post in the civil service. Under no circumstances, he emphasized, would he ever bear arms against his own people; rather, he would help restore civility, law, and order to a hopelessly war-torn country.

After ascertaining his administrative experience in Catalonia and Macharaviaya (Fernando tactfully neglected to mention his combat with the Córdoban Volunteers, and the French politely neglected to ask), the authorities appointed Fernando a Captain of Police, and assigned him to the precinct in Jerez. Thus Fernando became a Josefino, an *afrancesado* not only by ideological persuasion, but also and quite unmistakably by quotidian appearance, in full-blown French uniform, albeit civil and not military. Yet although he now appeared as a French officer rather than a Spanish one, El Capitan Maestro's political convictions had not deviated one iota, and remained exactly the same as before. Those who are wont to judge reality by mere appearances among other shallow perceptions—just like the captives chained to the wall of Plato's cave—deemed Fernando a traitor for pledging his fealty to a foreign King. But those who saw deeper into the matter—like the captives who become liberated from their shackles and emerge from the cave into the bright light of reality and understanding—realized that Fernando wanted something for Spain that Spain could not yet provide for itself: amity and nationhood instead of enmity and chaos. Better to capitulate to a power that can forge Spain into a single harmonious nation, or so he reasoned, than to persist in a futile struggle that can only shatter her into agonized shards, more painfully splintered with each passing day.

Uncounted thousands shared Fernando's conviction and vision—among them artists, intellectuals, businessmen, politicians, nobles, and hordes of common folk like those who had celebrated King Joseph's processions—and deemed submission to this bearer of Enlightenment ideals the most elevated form of Spanish patriotism, or at least the surest way to staunch the bloodshed. Yet a majority of Spaniards still reviled the French, and preferred instead to perpetuate the conflict and carnage, to cling to the reactionary Church, to reinstate the stagnant Bourbons. On their stubborn lips, '*afrancesado*' became an everlasting synonym for 'traitor'.

Uncounted thousands more shared Fernando's conviction and vision yet continued the struggle as before, unwilling to change their uniforms yet unable to avert their steady march into the slaughterhouse that Spain had become. Carlos Sor was one of these. He remained a steadfast Captain in the remnants of the Army of Catalonia, abhorring the banditry of so many regular troops and *somaténes* alike. Yet in his heart he wished that peace could be restored by an enlightened monarch, and in his mind he knew that Joseph was a better bet that Ferdinand VII. Thus the only apparent difference between the Sor brothers was the color of their coats. Politically, they were in complete agreement. But practically, Carlos sensed that he and his Catalan comrades-in-arms were somnambulating toward an abyss, into which they might well plunge before they awoke.

For his part, Fernando had tried to awaken. But as the sordid reality of his new and daily duties in Jerez sank in, and as reports of unremitting hostilities now reached him through French channels, he realized that things were getting worse before they got better. His French commanders respected his vow not to bear arms against his fellow Spaniards—be they soldiers, civilians, or guerillas—so they handed him a shovel instead, and ordered him to bury the dead. They placed a squad of policemen under his command, all similarly equipped, and assigned them to burial details throughout the precinct. When Fernando later recalled this period in his autobiography, he tersely summarized it as "two years alternating shovelfuls of sand and lime". There were so many dead and dying that they could barely keep up.

By day he buried the dead; by night he composed an epic poem, which of course he set to music. Called *Adonde vas, Fernando incauto*? (*Where are you going, unwary Fernando?*), it was a personal chronicle of anguish, protest, condemnation, lamentation, and aspiration. It crystallized while he shoveled sand and lime, spanning the outbreak of the war and incorporating his response to horrific current events, as breaking news continued to reach his ear between 1810 and 1812. Its twelve stanzas reveal not only Fernando's state of mind during this time, but also some of the terrible tragedies that were playing out across Spain, as the war increasingly commingled desperate patriotic struggles with pitiless internecine quarrels.

Where are you going, unwary Fernando? Do not leave your country. See how your people, who adore you, know who Napoleon is; flee from the trap which he has laid for you, and foil his scheme and his intention—But he won, and they captured Ferdinand and the House of Bourbon.

But as a good man judges others according to his own noble heart, Ferdinand judged treachery to be incompatible with a crown. He who had no experience of deceit, could not doubt the truth of his friendship; he imposed silence on his servants and followed his own path.

The innocent one arrived at Bayonne; and instead of the reward which he had expected for his excessive trust, he found humiliation; he who had called himself his friend and offered him his protection, robbed him of his crown and imprisoned him in a castle.

While these stanzas accurately depict Napoleon as a duplicitous crown-robber, Fernando could only guess at the events in Bayonne. So he decided to romanticize the people's feelings for a supposedly 'innocent' Ferdinand VII, whereas we, with the benefit of hindsight, have seen what more truly transpired. In due course this 'innocent' will regain the throne, and history will remember him, without a trace of adoration, as the worst king that Spain has ever known, the monstrous product of a dysfunctional family that had become unfit to rule. Meanwhile the poem continued:

The Spaniards, angry at such atrocious perfidy, swore to avenge their monarch and to honor the name of Spain. All at once the cry of vengeance resounded throughout Spain, and everyone took for this device his King, his country and his religion.

Here, of course, Fernando alludes to El Dos de Mayo, and to the spread far and wide of the insurrection it had sparked. Now he speaks as a witness, and his words carry the full force of truth.

> *The young, the brave and the strong, set out to face the champion, who had already arrived as far as Córdoba with his sacrilegious army. At the first encounter, victory crowned such a noble endeavor, and every Frenchman who did not die at Bailén was taken prisoner.*

Here Fernando begins to reveal his own inner conflict, as both a good Catholic and a proponent of Enlightenment ideals. As we have seen, Bailén indeed debunked the myth of French invincibility, and inspired renewed resistance to Napoleon in Europe. But it is interesting that Fernando deems the French invaders 'sacrilegious' for espousing secular values to which he and his Spanish Enlightenment peers likewise subscribed.

> *The people of Zaragoza and Valencia defended themselves valiantly; but their valor and fortitude in the end yielded to misfortune. Tarragona resisted attacks tenaciously but in vain, because he who could save her was a mere spectator.*

We have seen somewhat of the courageous yet ultimately futile resistance of Zaragoza, which finally succumbed to relentless French sieges at a horrific cost in civilian lives, and a virtual demolition of the city. Historic and beautiful Valencia suffered a similar conquest. But for Tarragona an even crueler fate was reserved—not by the French, but by him who could indeed have saved her, and moreover whose sworn duty it was to save her. This 'spectator' to whom Fernando alludes was the Spanish General Marquis de Campoverde, commander of Tarragona's defenders. He had abandoned his post when General Louis Gabriel Suchet besieged the city in May 1811, leaving its garrison in the hands of his second-in-command, Lieutenant General Juan Senen de Contreras. A normal government would have executed or at least demoted Campoverde for desertion, but the topsy-turvy Junta in Cádiz instead entrusted him with the command of an army to break the siege. Napoleon desperately wanted to capture this Catalan city and its useful port, so he dangled a coveted Marshal's baton as the prize for General Suchet's success. This spurred Suchet to pursue his attacks with vigorous brutality.

Meanwhile, Campoverde busied his army with absurd maneuvers in the hills, and at the last moment arranged his own escape by sea—accompanied by the wealthiest elites of Tarragona. Those with money enough to bribe their way to the port and pay Campoverde's exorbitant fee for passage escaped with their lives. The common people of Tarragona meanwhile refused to surrender, and were massacred in their thousands when the city was finally stormed. In fact, Suchet had ordered his troops to spare Spanish soldiers, but to show no mercy toward civilians, who had offered the fiercest resistance. This, among so many calamities, had filled Fernando's heart with anguish as he shoveled sand and lime.

> *The armies of the ambitious one overrun Spanish soil, and their inhuman commanders lend their consent to crimes; every soldier is a tyrant to property and to honor, and repays with desolation the hospitality which he receives.*

Of course Fernando recalls the earliest days of the French army's entry into Spain, prior to El Dos de Mayo, when they were welcomed hospitably, as allies against the English and Portuguese. But he has since witnessed the descent into total war and ruthless criminality, and he accuses of inhumanity those whose very uniform he himself now wears.

> *Wicked men, a blotch upon the name of Spain, give themselves over to assassination, theft and devastation. They commit as many crimes as the imagination can conceive, and the name of Ferdinand serves for impunity from aggression.*

With equal anguish, Fernando cannot help but heap his share of condemnation upon those among his own compatriots, those whose moral sensibilities have been swept away by the riptides of turpitude. He is speaking not merely of deserters, *somaténes*, outlaws, bandits, and opportunists of the common variety; and not only of the populace, which at any time or place could degenerate into a savage mob and turn against its own; but also of the more illustrious but not less criminal aristocrats: the Campoverdes and their ilk. We have already seen, and Fernando also knew, of the scandalous antics of General Cuesta at Medellin, and General Aréizaga at Ocaña. In Medina de Rioseco, Generals Cuesta and Joaquin Blake refused to join forces because of personal disagreements, and each watched as the other's troops were beaten separately by the French. In Cádiz, besieged by a French army seventy thousand strong, a British sortie to break the siege was supposed to have been reinforced by Spanish General Manuel Lapeña, who stood idly by and watched instead. British General Thomas Graham was so incensed at this betrayal that he swore never again to collaborate with Spanish commanders.

Adding to Fernando's outrage were the honors with which these treacherous men were showered. As we have seen, after Medellin Cuesta was promoted to Captain General, while Campoverde enriched himself by desertion. General Lapeña's inaction at Cádiz was rewarded with the Great Cross of Charles III. The Spanish people or the troops themselves often resorted to bringing their criminally incompetent leaders to swift justice: they put to death Captain General Filanghieri in Galicia; the Marquis of Socorro in Andalusia; the Duke de la Torre del Fresno in Extremadura. As they had done with Cuesta in Valladolid, the people raised a gallows in the atrium of the Captain General of Castilla la Nueva, to elicit his patriotism; while the people of Zaragoza imprisoned the Captain General of Aragon.

By 1811 the Spanish people were starving, yet these criminals among other 'spectators' stuffed themselves with food. Goya had skewered them with withering mockery in *Los Caprichos*, among other surrealistic etchings that poured from his feverish brain, now forming a shocking series called 'The Disasters of War'. Goya no longer needed to seek inspiration in prisons and lunatic asylums; he merely had to look out his window. Although now incommunicado, he and Fernando spoke with one voice in condemning these horrors. And so Fernando's poem continued:

> *Spaniards are divided in their opinion on this matter. Those who want to avoid ruin, are in favor of submission; they judge so obstinate a resistance*

to be useless, even disastrous, and that to continue the fight will complete the destruction of Spain.

"Divided in their opinion" is Fernando's rendition of British understatement. Every stratum of Spanish society was at war, either for or against either the French or the English, or indeed against both, and pitted moreover against every other stratum of Spanish society, including itself. Spain was indeed poised on the brink of complete destruction, and submission was the only way Fernando saw to end the madness. In rebuttal of naysayers, he continued:

Those who believe that the country can find its salvation in other ways, go off to the remotest parts. One abandons his father, another his wife and his house, another perhaps some innocent, the unhappy fruit of a marriage.

Here Fernando alludes in general to the cruel dislocations and separations imposed by war. Whether men served in the army (as he himself had done), or took to the hills as partisans, or became deserters and outlaws, there was no telling where they might end up. The toll this took on families was steep. More particularly, "the remotest parts" refers to the Central Junta, which had fled to the Isla de Leon, just off the coast of Cádiz, where it was cornered and besieged. As we have seen, it convened a Cortes in 1809, which could not even assemble until late 1810, owing to ubiquitous hazards of cross-country travel encountered by its would-be delegates. The Cortes eventually hammered out a liberal constitution in 1812, which it was utterly impotent to implement. When he wrote about the Peninsular War and the Cortes, Karl Marx would say that "Spain was divided into two parts. At the Isla de Leon, ideas without action—in the rest of Spain, action without ideas." It was against this pointless action without ideas, and the internecine strife it fomented, which brought only misery in its train, that Fernando's poem railed.

Sad Spain has become the scene of the most atrocious unhappiness; behold her sons divided! Oh, how great a misfortune! One calls another a fool, and in his turn he is called a traitor; may a bad end come to the ambitious one who caused this division.

As Fernando has witnessed, the Peninsular War in turn provoked a bitter civil war, which he experiences as a dagger through his heart. He had composed patriotic songs for Spain, not for himself. He had volunteered and fought for Spain, not for himself. He had submitted to Joseph for the sake of Spain, not for himself. Even though he is now wearing the uniform of a French police captain, he had donned it to douse the flames of hell burning pell-mell across Spain, not to fan them. No man alive was a greater patriot than Fernando, yet those committed to interminable conflict, crime, quarrel, and corruption now branded him a traitor. He silently mouthed the words of Jesus on the cross: "Forgive them Father, for they know not what they do." Yet being imperfectly human himself, he had to vent his fury and frustration somehow. So he hurled imprecations at Napoleon, whose ambitions had unquestionably fuelled the invasion, which has now turned brother against brother. Fernando's final stanza petitions the Lord in prayer:

O immense God, who reading in the hearts of men, knows what are my own feelings and hopes, unite the votes of Spain; bring an end to this fierce dissension; let us all live together as brothers, for this is how a nation prospers.

Sunk deep in despondency, Fernando is convinced that only God wields the power to make peace, to establish brotherhood, to forge nationhood. Fernando has seen enough to know that men unaided by providence have dismally failed this noble quest, and are unequal to its challenge. The Central Junta and the Cortes would have made Floridablanca president of their imaginary republic, but alas, this great statesman and father of the Spanish Enlightenment was eighty years old when El Dos del Mayo erupted, and far too frail for political office. El Conde had died in December of that year, passing out of possibility and into history.

And what of El Conde's great protégé, Jovellanos? King Joseph had released him from Bellver Castle, where Godoy had imprisoned him in

1801. Joseph offered him the sun and moon to serve as his Prime Minister, but Jovellanos steadfastly refused every title, bribe, and appurtenance of office proffered by this foreign king. Instead, he joined the Central Junta, and helped reorganize the Cortes. Like Fernando, he imagined Spain as a nation. But Jovellanos's dream was shattered when the Junta itself was discredited by the very Cortes it had formed; and so he wielded his failing pen, and expended his final energies, defending the former against the latter. He succumbed to a delirium in 1811, no longer writing but rather raving against the evils that had befallen his beloved Spain: "My nephew ... Central Junta ... France ... the nation without a head ... o woe is me!"

Fernando had nowhere else to turn but to God, as the very best men he knew, among them the noblest and ablest sons of Spain, had failed to make of her a nation. So he shoveled sand and lime, and wondered when and how the madness would end. His despair was so dark, and the conflicts within and without so intractable, that his vision could not penetrate the gloom. Thus he could not yet see that his prayer was about to be answered: not yet for the nation's destiny, but rather for his own. Even though Fernando had composed, fought, submitted, and prayed for the nation and not for himself, inscrutable providence was about to illuminate his path, and answer his prayer for the bad end of the ambitious one, the namesake of this bloodthirsty era and source of its unspeakable carnage.

Chapter 20. Farewell Spain: Valencia, Barcelona, and Exile

While Fernando shoveled sand and lime, the ambitious one in Paris alternated between episodes of sullen pouting and violent temper tantrums. He rained curses daily on the Iberian peninsula, unable to conceive, even in French, of a suitably dire metaphor to describe his predicament there. In early 1812, Marshal Louis Suchet's successful siege of Valencia had decimated yet another Spanish army of defenders, commanded by Captain General Joaquin Blake. Suchet lost two thousand killed or wounded among his French troops, but took sixteen thousand Spanish troops prisoner, killed or wounded four thousand more, and captured 371 guns. But notwithstanding this seemingly endless string of apparently decisive French victories, year after year in battle after battle, the Spaniards somehow resisted subjugation. Napoleon now had three hundred thousand troops tied down in Spain, led by a hundred generals, and still it was not enough. He would later call Spain 'an ulcer' and 'a cancer' that ultimately sapped the strength of his armies and the resolve of their commanders, dooming his larger ambitions to defeat. Indeed, the conquest of Valencia would prove the high-water mark of Napoleon's invasion of Iberia, after which the tide of his fortunes there would ebb inexorably toward retreat.

By 1812, the ambitious one had not only failed to subjugate Spain, but had also succeeded in renewing the ardor of Austria and Russia likewise to rise against him. Never one to await being attacked, he habitually retained his initiative by taking the fight to the enemy, at a time and place of his choosing. So Napoleon felt he had no option but to invade Russia, before Russia invaded Europe. While he did not lack the will to launch such a bold campaign, he unquestionably lacked sufficient manpower. So he levied yet another unpopular wave of conscription in France, mustered his groaning Polish ally, and began to pull troops out of Spain, thinning and weakening his Iberian lines to the breaking point. Even the remaining thousands could scarcely be counted on at face value, for at least half were debilitated by wounds, illnesses, malnutrition, and inadequate equipment. Napoleon inevitably pulled his strongest contingents out of Spain, leaving the weaker ones behind.

At the same time, the English were growing stronger: not only by dint of more of their own boots on the ground, but also because General Wellesley had been placed in overall command of the allied forces, notwithstanding predictable objections by disgruntled Portuguese and Spanish generals. The Cortes too had called for a new mobilization, levying an additional one hundred thousand Spanish soldiers, although this was also a species of fiction, as perhaps only a third of that number were willing and able to serve. Nonetheless, the scales now were tipping against the French, and it would not take long for the English and their allies to realize just how diminished the presence of the invaders had become.

Fernando felt it, too. His safety in Jerez became increasingly precarious, as bands of guerillas and vigilante mobs continued to prey upon French troops and Josefinos alike, with growing gusto. And as the French army began to melt away from the province of Cádiz, Fernando's sense of personal jeopardy heightened. For the Portuguese and English armies that forced the French retreat from Andalusia were no less gangs of robbers and murderers. Among the English, continual breaches of discipline saw waves of soldiers break off engagements with retreating French troops in order to plunder their baggage-wagons, causing an enraged General Wellesley to complain to the Earl of Bathurst: "We have in the service the scum of the earth as common soldiers." The Portuguese were no less prone to misdeeds, even against their supposed allies. An English officer wrote that the Portuguese "considered it no greater crime to kill a British subject than one of their dogs. They generally carried a large knife concealed up the sleeve of their coat, and be assured they knew how to handle it."

Fortunately for Fernando, and for musical history, he was spared the utter lawlessness that descended on Andalusia that summer of 1812. The French still had a stronghold in Aragon, and their Governor of Valencia—Count Louis Mazzuchelli—was both an army General and a connoisseur of music. Knowing of Sor's captaincy of the now-vulnerable police precinct of Jerez, he summoned Fernando to Valencia and bade him compose some music. It was like throwing a life-preserver to a drowning man.

"And what kind of music would your Excellency wish to hear?" Fernando asked him. (He was ready to compose anything under the sun, and there was plenty of sun in Valencia.)

"Speaking personally, Maestro, I am honored and delighted to hear anything that you are moved to write," the Count replied, with the usual hyperbolic French politeness. "But on this occasion my request is made on behalf of Madame Honorine Anthoine de Saint-Joseph, the wife of Marshal Suchet. She is also a niece of Queen Consort Julie Clary, the wife of King Joseph Bonaparte. Madame de Saint-Joseph is a talented amateur soprano, and has come to Valencia to enjoy a summer on the Spanish Mediterranean. Can you compose a cantata in the French style, for her to sing with accompaniment? It will be a surprise gift for her, from the Marshal himself."

Needless to say, this was an offer Fernando could not refuse. It was like a ray of light that pierced the darkness of the war, touching his soul with a gladness he had not known since Málaga.

"It will be my singular honor, Excellency, to compose such a piece for Madame."

"Thank you, Maestro. She and the Marshal will be eternally grateful."

At this juncture, it was Fernando who felt gratitude. Relieved at last of the depressing burden of shoveling sand and lime into mass graves, he picked up a quill, and joyfully shoveled notes into the staves of his musical score. The resulting cantata—for soloists, four-part chorus, strings, and winds—was a great success, so much so that Madame Honorine Anthoine de Saint-Joseph, soon-to-be the Duchess of Albufera, became

Fernando's life-long admirer. His penchant for charming royalty, and royalty-to-be, had not become a casualty of the otherwise tragic Peninsular War. Far from it. In fact, Madame de Saint-Joseph was so enchanted with Fernando's cantata that she entreated her aunt Julie, wife of King Joseph, to likewise commission Fernando. Had these Bonapartes remained a little longer on the throne of Spain, this and more commissions like it would have come to pass.

But history had other plans. Even before Fernando was summoned to Valencia, renewed allied campaigns by Wellington's rejuvenated armies won bloody battles against the French at Ciudad Real, Badajoz, and Salamanca. These victories rendered Madrid indefensible, and in August 1812 King Joseph abandoned the capital and took refuge in Suchet's stronghold of Valencia itself. But by then his court was in no mood for music. Joseph busily and desperately planned a counter-offensive, intending to retake the capital, and his throne, that autumn.

Newly ensconced as the liberator of Madrid, and elevated to the title of Earl of Wellington for his victory, Wellesley straightaway summoned Goya and commissioned a portrait. As a faithful witness to this historic power-shift, Goya naturally obliged. His portrayal marked the turning tide of the times, depicting Wellington's forthright countenance, proud chest, jutting chin, stiff upper lip, and wide-open orbs, gazing with anticipation and determination at the immediate horizon. He saw what Wellington's eyes beheld, and preserved their reflection for posterity. While Goya set to work painting this rising English star, Napoleon's sun was about to flare into a supernova, a prelude to its inevitable self-destruction.

Prior to September 1812, the little town of Borodino was known for precisely nothing. It had nestled quietly in rolling bucolic hills, one hundred and thirty kilometers west of Moscow. It was about to become the most blood-soaked ground, to date, of the sanguinary Napoleonic Wars. The French Emperor's Grande Armée, with an estimated strength of one hundred and seventy thousand men, plus another eighteen thousand troops of the Imperial Guard, had swept though eastern Europe and into Russia, trampling everything in its path. The Russian Imperial Army, commanded by Field Marshal Prince Mikhail Kutuzov and numbering a hundred and sixty thousand men, made its stand at Borodino. When the acrid dust had settled on the crimsoned hills, and the saturated earth could absorb not another drop of blood, the French had won a tactical but utterly pyrrhic victory. Napoleon had lost thirty-five thousand men killed, wounded, or captured, including forty-seven generals; while Kutuzov's losses were even greater: forty-five thousand dead, wounded or captured, including twenty-three generals. When the Russians made a tactical retreat, the road to Moscow lay wide open, and Napoleon urged his staggering army forward.

But the wily Tsar Alexander had two mighty allies in reserve, which now leapt to the defense of his Motherland. His first ally was the monumental size of Russia: the world's largest country, it could not be conquered by a mere invading army of men, any more than by an invading stream of ants. Alexander gave orders to abandon Moscow and raze it to the ground, while the troops and the populace alike packed up their scanty necessities and retreated further eastward, deeper into Russia's fathomless hinterland. When Napoleon's army reached Moscow, they found it a smoldering ruin, devoid of food, depleted of fuel, and denuded of shelter. That set the stage for Alexander's second ally, namely the frigid Russian winter.

Napoleon realized that he had neither the manpower nor the logistical resources to pursue the retreating Russian army. Once again, and soon repeatedly, he cursed the stubborn Spanish resistance, which even then was still tying down some two hundred thousand French troops. As his Grande Armée shivered and starved in Moscow's chilly September rain, with nothing to eat but scorched earth, unable even to light campfires from the now-sodden ashes of the burned city, the Emperor knew they had to beat an ignominious retreat back to France, before the harsh Russian winter set in. So sure had Napoleon been of a swift and bountiful conquest, that he had not equipped his men with winter clothing, nor his horses with padded blankets. That decision would shortly prove catastrophic.

Tsar Alexander's second ally arrived early that year, and in frigid force. Napoleon's shattered Grande Armée struggled westward against bitter winds, driving snow, and freezing cold. Uncounted thousands perished of exposure, illness, and starvation, leaving a long trail of corpses which could not be buried in the frozen earth. With coffins of threadbare uniforms and shrouds of drifting snow, the vacant eyes of the dead stared up at the sullen sky, eyeballs frozen solid with silent wonder at their cruel fates. In December 1812, Napoleon at last reached home with the tattered and exhausted remnants of his once-invincible army. Even these so-called survivors kept the surgeons busy amputating frost-bitten fingers and toes and ears and noses (if they were fortunate), or arms and legs wholesale. Among them, uncounted thousands died of gangrene, induced either by rotting thawed flesh, or unsterilized surgical implements. An entire generation of amputees would become beggars on the mean streets of Paris, huddled on its indifferent pavements, their tin cups rattling with pathetic centimes, deformed monuments to the hubris of a man who had mistaken himself for a god.

Tsar Alexander, who did not confuse himself with a deity, gave boundless thanks to the Almighty for sparing Mother Russia, and abundant thanks to the brave bull of Spain, for incessantly goring and eventually bleeding the French monster white, dooming its attempt to subdue the Russian bear. So deeply was Napoleon's debacle embedded in the Russian psyche that decades later (in 1880) Tchaikovsky would commemorate it with his resounding *1812 Overture*.

Meanwhile, King Joseph's desperate sortie from Valencia, reinforced by Marshal Suchet's remaining strength, caught Wellington by surprise, obliging him to make a strategic retreat back to Portugal, where he wintered and prepared a decisive spring offensive to scour Spain of the French invaders, once and for all. Joseph re-entered Madrid in November 1812, for the very last time, but not for long.

Fernando wintered in Valencia, waiting for the English axe to fall, knowing that his—among thousands of Josefinos'—days in Spain were likewise numbered. It fell in the spring of 1813. Wellington re-emerged from Portugal refreshed, re-enforced, re-armed and re-purposed. His allied armies forced French retreats from every province, including Aragon and Catalonia. Napoleon, himself busy fighting rear-guard actions against encroaching Sixth Coalition armies in Europe, could not help his brother's cause. A retreating

King Joseph girded his loins and gathered his troops for one last stand in the Pyrenees. On June 21, 1813, Wellington's allied armies fought and won a decisive battle at Vitoria, precipitating the end of the French occupation of Spain.

In England, Wellington's political masters promoted him to Field Marshal, and all Europe's eyes were upon him too—including Ludwig van Beethoven's. The immortal German composer wrote *Wellington's Victory* (sometimes called *The Battle Symphony*) to commemorate Vitoria, and premiered it in Vienna that December, at a benefit concert for Austrian and Bavarian soldiers wounded at the battle of Hanau. The other piece premiered on that program, and conducted by Beethoven himself, was his brilliant Seventh Symphony. Playing cello in that orchestra was a young Italian prodigy—guitarist, cellist, composer and singer—named Mauro Giuliani. He would soon elevate the guitar to great prominence in Italy, and leave a copious legacy of compositions for the instrument. But it was Giuliani's fate to play second fiddle to Fernando as the outstanding guitarist of the age. In any case, such was the tenor of the times that Beethoven's Seventh Symphony was overshadowed by his Battle Symphony, which proved an instant hit, earning him substantial income during Napoleon's demise. At the same time, on December 11, 1813, King Joseph finally abdicated the Spanish throne, signaling the official French relinquishment of Spain.

But in fact, the French armies did not wait that long; they began to evacuate Spain in earnest after the battle of Vitoria. Fernando was necessarily caught up in their evacuation; it would have been perilous for him to remain, as Josefinos were prime targets for vengeful mobs. But now that the end of Joseph's reign was nigh, Fernando's immediate path had suddenly become illuminated. In June 1813 he made his way up the coast, without incident, from Valencia to Barcelona, heading for one of the most bittersweet moments of his life. He rode homeward as if in a dream, not impelled by the internal workings of an imperfect moral compass, but rather propelled by the external hand of unerring destiny. He was returning home not only to claim his long-suffering bride, if she would accept him at this latest of stages, but also to bid farewell to his beloved family, and to their dear homeland, and to take her into exile in France, if only she would accompany him. Fernando still had no inkling that his fate was to become the Beethoven of the guitar, and that he must leave Spain to fulfill it. He knew only that he must leave Spain—with or without Joaquina.

Fernando reached the Dry Quarter one hot evening in early July, and knocked on the door of his mother's house. His brother Carlos opened it, and they both recoiled a step in mute surprise, mutually unable to believe their eyes. Then they warmly embraced, for neither had been sure of seeing the other alive again.

"Who is it?" called Isabella from the dining table, where she and Carlos had just sat down to share a meager supper.

Still a Captain in what remained of the Army of Catalonia, Carlos was on leave, while his commanders decided whether to pursue the French troops that were pouring over the Pyrenees, day and night, desperate to escape the hell-world of Spain and reach their homes in France by autumn.

"It is Fernando, mother!" replied Carlos.

"Fernando!" cried Isabella, her voice overflowing with joy. She fairly leapt from the supper table and charged into the anteroom, where the brothers stood side-by-side. "My beloved Fernando!" she cried again, hugging him tightly, as tears ran down her cheeks and onto his coat, which she tried to dab with a handkerchief. Then she stepped back to take a closer look at him, and suddenly noticed that his coat was blue, and not white like his brother's. Then it dawned on her that his uniform was French, not Spanish, and that her two sons were clad as mutual enemies, and not as loving brothers.

"But what can this mean?" their poor mother asked, now beside herself with confusion and despair. "This terrible war has destroyed Spain. Has it destroyed our family too?" Her frantic tone pleaded for reassurance, despite what her eyes were seeing.

Fernando did his best to reassure her.

"Dearest mother, pray do not be misled by mere appearances. Carlos and I have always loved each other, and always will. We both want exactly the same things for Spain—peace, prosperity, unity, nationhood—but lately we have sought to attain these ends by different means. Despite the rift implied by our costumes, our hearts are forever united."

At this the bothers embraced again, and Isabella felt somewhat mollified. So Fernando explained himself further.

"I am only a captain of police, and not a soldier. Never would I bear arms against my compatriots. But I did bear arms against the French during El Dos de Mayo, and in my service with the Córdoban volunteers, until I understood that it was futile. I will spare you the unspeakable horrors that I have witnessed and heard, as I am sure that Carlos has likewise spared you for his part."

At this Carlos silently nodded his corroboration.

Fernando continued: "And so I came to despair over what had befallen Spain, and hoped with all my heart that King Joseph would make of us a nation, which the Bourbons could not."

At this Carlos nodded his reluctant agreement.

Then Fernando produced a tattered copy of his poem, and gave it to Isabella and Carlos to read. They did so silently, and tears ran down their cheeks. When they had finished reading, they understood why Fernando had donned the blue coat.

"But what will you do now?" Isabella asked him, afraid of her own question and in dread of his inevitable answer.

"I am a branded Josefino," said Fernando, "and have no choice but to join the French exodus. *Afrancesados* who remain in Spain court imprisonment or death."

This too she understood. And now Isabella realized that he had come home only to say goodbye, and that she might never see him again. She broke down and wept uncontrollably, and both brothers tried in vain to comfort her.

Then Fernando took a different tack. Not without trepidation, he asked his mother "And what of Sofia and Joaquina? Are they well?"

"As well as can be," she replied, drying her tears. "Sofia and I have helped each other survive these catastrophic times, thanks in no small part to our lifelong friendship, and to the monies that you and Carlos have unfailingly and dutifully sent home. A mother could not be more blessed... Yet I have worried so much for you and Carlos, every minute of every day, knowing that you have been in mortal combat. And Sofia worries no less for Joaquina, but in a womanly fashion. The poor girl has pined and wasted away, such that no-one knows what will become of her. Still unmarried at twenty-eight, she will soon reach an age when most women are grandmothers."

"That might be speedily remedied," said Fernando, "for Joaquina and I have long-since pledged our troth, and we have been waiting for this horrible war to end. Now it has finally ended, and I have come to claim my bride."

Carlos had known that this day would arrive. The pain of the dagger in his heart had been numbed by the horrors of war, but suddenly he felt it twist anew, and sink deeper, as his brother was about to carry off their one true love. At least, Carlos silently temporized, she would be finally out of sight, and so perhaps also out of mind.

For her part, Isabella felt momentarily overjoyed by these tidings, but immediately sank into sadness, as she realized that Fernando would take Joaquina away to France. How would she and Sofia ever cuddle their own grandchildren?

Fernando had foreseen that his homecoming and farewell would be bittersweet for all concerned, and now that his mother and brother had each tasted its flavor, it was time for Joaquina and Sofia to sample it too.

"Dearest mother, dearest brother, please excuse me for a short while. I must go see Joaquina and Sofia now."

"Go with God, dearest Fernando," said Isabella and Carlos with one voice. "And bring them back here with you, for supper."

Fernando went resolutely down the street, and knocked on their door. Joaquina opened it, and they both stood stock still. Their eyes locked, and misted over, and they remained like this, seemingly frozen, beholding one another across a still-impassable gulf, incapable of speech or movement, for what seemed to them both an eternity. But then the unbridgeable chasm of impossible time, imposed between them so cruelly and for so long by fate, finally dissolved. In the next moment they fell deliriously into each other's arms, embracing wordlessly, sobbing with joy and relief, then thrilling with happiness, that their long-awaited hour had finally arrived.

Fernando was the first to regain his voice. "Dearest Joaquina, will you come away with me to France? We can make a life in Paris, until it is safe to return to Spain."

"Dearest Fernando, I will follow you anywhere, be it to Paris, or to the very ends of the earth."

Oblivious to everything but their all-encompassing embrace, and mutual commitment to exile, they did not even notice that Sofia had followed Joaquina to the door, sensing that something extraordinary was unfolding. From a discreet distance she had wordlessly witnessed their intensely tender reunion, and tears of joy and sadness alike now ran silently down checks as well. Sofia felt overjoyed that her daughter would wed at last, and marry this famous maestro no less—but in the same instant she noticed that Fernando was wearing a French uniform, and realized in a flash that he would carry her precious daughter away with him, to France. To a woman like herself, who never had never left Barcelona, Paris may as well have been the far side of the moon.

At last the star-crossed lovers relaxed their mutual embrace, at least long enough to observe Sofia watching them with an admixture of joy and sadness. Fernando did not even manage to ask for Sofia's hand—in any case their marriage was already a foregone conclusion—because Joaquina was the first to speak.

"Mama, will you still let me wear your wedding dress?" she asked Sofia.

"Of course, my child," her mother replied, and ran off at once to fetch it from a trunk, so they would not see that she was crying anew. Her tears were bittersweet, as Fernando knew they would be. His keen ears had heard her suppress an involuntary sob, and he only hoped that her happiness would outweigh her sorrow.

Meanwhile he fished a small velour-covered box from a concealed inner pocket, containing an exquisite Georgian engagement ring made of a sparkling rose-cut diamond, more than a carat in weight, set artfully in 14-carat gold. Fernando had acquired it on a whim, from William, before leaving Málaga for Jerez in 1810. We may recall his ardent desire for a daughter of his own, stirred by giving guitar lessons to his first pupil, Maria Manuela. This desire having been sealed by his commitment to Joaquina as the mother of their future children, it had prompted Fernando to ask William if he knew of any reputable jewelers in Málaga. William had grinned, and replied that he knew one in particular, and added that Fernando was presently conversing with him. It did not surprise Fernando that, when it came to trade, William could get his hands on just about anything, for that was his métier. But it did surprise Fernando that, once William ascertained that he sought an engagement ring, he had made a gift of this very fine piece, refusing to accept a maravedie for it.

"A token of my best wishes for your marriage," he had said, in both overt affection as well as covert relief at being able to do anything, however miniscule by comparison, to offset the loss of the Goya portrait. "And who's the lucky lady?" William could not forebear from asking.

"For now, her identity remains confidential," said Fernando, not realizing just how secret it would remain, owing to the vicissitudes of the coming times, and to bafflement of future historians.

"I admire a man who can retain a confidence," said William.

Fernando recalled this delightful incident as he slipped the ring onto Joaquina's finger. She felt giddy with happiness, and almost swooned from dizziness as the diamond scintillated brightly, flashing with a spectrum of colors even in the candlelight.

By this time Sofia had returned with the wedding dress, bundled in a rough jute sack, and the threesome made their way back to Isabella's house for supper. It was to be their last meal together, and this unvoiced thought lurked furtively among them, tingeing their bittersweet celebration with apprehensive sadness.

Isabella meanwhile raided the remains of her larder, sifted through her cellar and bustled about her pantry, trying desperately to assemble a credible if hasty feast for the occasion. In fact they were all gaunt and emaciated, for (as we have seen) victuals had been in ever-shorter supply as the war years had lengthened. But since they were all in the same condition, and not one of them looked well-fed by comparison, malnutrition had become a kind of norm. They were all habitually grateful for whatever stray morsels one might round up at any time, let alone at meal-time.

While Isabella prepared their modest repast, Carlos readied the horses—Joaquina's, Fernando's, and his own—for imminent departure. For Carlos knew better than any of them the immediate danger that Fernando was in. Irregular contingents of Spanish troops, including *somaténes* among other bandits, were hunting French stragglers all the way to the frontier, and even across it, robbing and killing them without a second thought. The cities and towns were no safer, as mobs of civilian vigilantes vented their fury on known or even suspected *afrancesados*, apparently reluctant to miss any opportunity to fatten the catalogue of atrocities wrought by this war. And no Josefino was better known than Fernando. This made Carlos fear for his brother's life, though he refrained from saying so in order to spare the women additional anxiety.

But by the time they all sat down to their last supper together, Isabella and Sofia had realized there would be no minutely planned and indulgently fussed-over wedding in Barcelona. On the contrary, they understood that Fernando and Joaquina would have to ride posthaste for France, and hope to make it safely across the border. Being loving mothers to the bittersweet end, they showered the couple with blessings. And Carlos too revealed his magnanimous heart, by insisting that he accompany them to the frontier.

"My uniform may shield you from Spanish miscreants," he said, "as yours may shield me from French ones. Riding together, we can better protect our beloved Joaquina—your precious bride-to-be—as well as one another, until you both reach safety."

Fernando could neither dispute the logic of his brother's plan, nor conceive of a greater fraternal love than that now displayed by his gallant sibling.

As they sat together at the table, devouring the scraps that Isabella had cobbled into a farewell feast, it seemed to them the most delectable repast they could remember since this disastrous war had begun. Fernando contributed a bottle of Jerez's choicest sherry, which the French had been quick to confiscate by the case. They emptied it with copious toasts. They could not help but recall more innocently giddy times at this table—such as their meal that had been so deliriously interrupted by Fernando's invitation from the Duchess of Alba, back in 1799. What whirlwind had swept away these fourteen years, as if in an instant?

Deeply reluctant to bid farewell to his mother, Fernando suddenly recalled how their initial parting had not troubled him at all, when she had delivered him to Montserrat so long ago. Yet mindful of the urgency of the moment, and aware that a full moon would light the way, Fernando knew it was best to set off without further ado. So he arose from the table, but his voice suddenly choked, and he could not find words to speak.

His mother helped him. "My dearest Fernando, you and Joaquina must take your leave. It is not safe for you to tarry in Barcelona, nor indeed to remain in Spain. May Mother Mary watch over you both, as she has always done. God willing, we will meet again soon. Remember, when you were but a little boy, a gypsy woman foretold that you would travel far and wide, like a wandering star, and everywhere meet with great acclaim. Go now and fulfill your magnificent destiny! Know that your mother is more proud of you than mere words can express, and loves you more than life itself. Come, let me embrace you as if for the very last time."

Sofia and Joaquina exchanged similar if more tearful good-byes. "Go with God, my sweet child," her mother said.

"Dearest mother, I will return to you soon," replied Joaquina, "God willing, along with your first grandchild. But meanwhile," she added with a note of caution, "if anyone inquires after me, say only that I have professed vows, and entered a convent. You must protect yourself from those who would stoop so low as to persecute the mother of an *afrancesada*. And I am afraid, in these dark days, that many would betray their own mothers for a crust of stale bread or a dubious political favor."

With that, the same whirlwind that had swept Fernando to fame and fortune in Madrid now carried him and Joaquina toward the Pyrenees, and beyond them to yet unknown fates in Paris. Carlos led the way northeast out of Barcelona, and into the forested hills surrounding Girona. They camped concealed in the woods by day, and rode by night. Heading due north past Girona, they skirted Figueres and made for the French border.

They halted in the barrio of Els Limits, in the Spanish quarter of the border town of El Pertus. There they found a small chapel, called the Sanctuary of Our Lady of Fatima, and in it Joaquina and Fernando were wed, with Carlos as witness. She wore her mother's wedding dress for the occasion; while Fernando and Carlos, as best they could, spruced up their Captains' uniforms.

If the priest found anything strange in the conflicting attire of the groom and the witness, he gave no sign of it. In fact, he was only too happy to officiate and sanctify the betrothed couple's marriage vows. For even this tiny barrio had been overrun by war. The retreating French troops were not only harried by allied attacks, but also obliged to turn and make defensive stands at their own borders. Wellington himself had despaired as uncontrollable Spanish units crossed into France and wreaked havoc in the frontier towns, taking nominal revenge for French atrocities against Spanish civilians, while attracted by the prospects of engaging in similar rapine and plunder themselves. The priest had grown accustomed to being summoned at all hours, to administer the last rites to the horribly maimed and mortally wounded on his side of the border, as well as to bury the lucky ones who had simply been shot dead, thus spared pointless suffering.

So this beleaguered priest was relieved and overjoyed to celebrate a wedding, for a change, and he neither knew nor cared that Joaquina had entered a fictitious name—Julia Cardona—on the marriage certificate. Fernando had insisted on this beforehand, for her own protection, and her mother's. As a fire later destroyed the parish records, historians never learned the assumed identity of Fernando's first wife, and would need more than two centuries to ferret out her real one. Thus the ruse protected Joaquina, and Sofia, even more thoroughly than originally intended. While Fernando would always call her Joaquina in private—which she loved—she would thereafter be introduced and known, in France, as Madame Julia Sor.

The ceremony concluded, Joaquina once again donned her riding clothes, while Carlos prepared to part company with the newlyweds.

"Beloved brother, dearest sister-in-law, I must leave you here and return to Barcelona. The border is but a stone's throw away." He gestured in its direction. "If Spain recovers its senses, your return home will be most ardently welcomed. If not, then I may join you soon enough in exile. Either way, may God keep you safe until, by His Grace, we meet again."

Carlos and Fernando made a farewell embrace, as only loving brothers can. Joaquina too embraced Carlos, and tears of sisterly love and gratitude streamed down her cheeks and stained his jacket. By escorting her and Fernando safely to the frontier, and by solemnly witnessing their marriage, Carlos had revealed a heart of purest gold. She knew that he still loved her, but no longer in an ordinary way; and moreover, she suddenly realized that she still loved him, but likewise no longer in an ordinary way. Their love had been transformed by his golden heart, into something neither mundanely ordinary nor dangerously extraordinary; rather, into the boundlessly unselfish love of siblings.

While alchemists perennially sought the so-called philosopher's stone, which could reputedly transmute base metals into gold, Carlos Sor's golden heart had transmuted ordinary infatuation into familial adoration. Joaquina and Carlos had become sister- and brother-in law, now sharing an incorruptible bond that only death could sunder.

And so the threesome parted company. Fueled by their extraordinary love, and propelled by the political chaos that prevailed in Spain, Joaquina and Fernando crossed the border into France, and exile.

Fernando: Beethoven of the Guitar

End of Book I

Appendix 1: Bibliography

A. Britten, 2013. The Guitar and the Bristol School of Artists. *Early Music*, Volume 41, Number 4, 585-594.

Richard D.E. Burton, 1994. *The Flaneur and His City: Patterns of Daily Life in Paris 1815-1851.* University of Durham.

Colin Carlin, 2011. *William Kirkpatrick of Málaga.* Glasgow: The Grimsay Press.

Salvador Garcia Casteñada , 2010. *The Spanish Emigrés and the London Literary Scene (1814-1834).* London: Spanish Embassy of London.

Curtis Cate, 2004. *Russia 1812: The Duel Between Napoleon and Alexander.* New York: Pimlico (Random House).

Gilbert Chase, 1941. *The Music of Spain.* New York: W.W. Norton & Company.

Evelyne Diebolt, 2013. The Beginnings of the Nursing Profession: The Complementary Relationship Between Secular Caregivers and Hospital Nuns in France in the 17th and 18th Centuries. *Récherche en soins infirmiers*, 113, 6-18. https://pubmed.ncbi.nlm.nih.gov/23923734/

Fyodor Dostoyevsky, 1995 (1880). *The Brothers Karamazov.* Translated by David McDuff. London: Penguin Books.

Will and Ariel Durant, 1967. *The Story of Civilization, Part X: Rousseau and Revolution.* New York: Simon and Schuster.

Will and Ariel Durant, 1975. *The Story of Civilization, Part XI: The Age of Napoleon.* New York: Simon and Schuster.

Katharine Ellis, 2005. *Interpreting the Musical Past: Early Music in Nineteenth-Century France.* Oxford University Press.

Alfredo Escande, 2012 (2009). *Don Andrés and Paquita.* Translated by Charles Postlewate and Maria Herrera Postlewate. Milwaukee, WI: Amadeus Press.

Charles Esdaile, 2015. *The Peninsular War: A New History.* New York: St. Martin's Press.

Maria Fairweather, 2005. *Madame de Stael.* London: Constable.

Fernando Ferandiere, 1799. *Arte de Tocar la Guitarra Española por Música.* Complete facsimile edition with an introduction, English translation, and transcription of the music by Brian Jeffery. London: Tecla Editions 2013 (1977).

Juan Francisco Fuentes y Pilar Garí, 2015. *Amazonas de la libertad: Mujeres liberales contra Fernando VII.* Marcial Pons Ediciones de Historia.

David Gates, 2001 (1986). *The Spanish Ulcer. A History of the Peninsular War.* Cambridge, MA: De Capo Press. Perseus Books.

Johann Wolfgang Von Goethe, 1959 (1790). *Faust, Part One.* Translated by Philip Wayne. New York, Penguin Books.

Nikolai Gogol, 2004 (1842). *Dead Souls.* Translated by Robert A. Maguire. London: Penguin Classics.

Wenonah Milton Govea, 1995. *Nineteenth- and Twentieth-century Harpists: A Bio-critical Sourcebook.* Westport, CT: Greenwood.

Juan van Halen, 1830. *Memoirs of Don Juan van Halen, in Two Volumes.* London: Henry Colburn and Richard Bentley.

T.F. Heck, 2004. Fernando Sor, Composer-Guitarist. *Early Music,* Volume 32, Part 1, 148-150.

Robert Hughes, 2003. *Goya.* London: The Harvill Press.

Daisaku Ikeda, 2005. *Goya: A Discussion of the Life of a Great Spanish Artist.* Kuala Lumpur. Soka Gakkai Malaysia.

Mijndert Jape, 2014. *Fernando Sor: A Bibliography of Published Literature and Music.* Hillsdale, NY: Pendragon Press.

Brian Jeffery, 2020 (1994, 1977). *Fernando Sor: Composer and Guitarist.* London: Tecla Editions. The 2020 edition is an e-book only, available at www.tecla.com

Brian Jeffery, 2012. Sor in Trouble with the Spanish Inquisition, 1803-1806. *Soundboard,* Volume 38, Number 3, 15-19.

F.D. Klingender, 1968. *Goya in the Democratic Tradition.* New York: Schocken Books.

Alexandre de Laborde, 1813. *Voyage Pittoresque et Historiqu et Description de la Principauté de Catalogne.* Paris: L'Imprimerie de Mame.

Adolphe Ledhuy and Henri Bertini (editors), 1835. *Encyclopédie pittoresque de la musique.* Paris: H. Delloye.

Josep María Mangado, 2019 (1998). *La Guitarra en Cataluña.* London: Tecla Editions. The 2019 edition is an e-book only, available at www.tecla.com

Josep María Mangado, 2020. *Fernando Sor (1778-1839), volumen 2: documentos inéditos, reflexiones e hipótesis.* E-book only, available at www.tecla.com

Josep María Mangado, 2020. *Fernando Sor (1778-1839), volumen 3: la actividad guitarrística en París (1825-1839).* E-book only, available at www.tecla.com

Allen McConnell, 1970. *Tsar Alexander I: Paternalistic Reformer.* New York: Thomas Y. Crowell Company.

Gordon H. McNeil, 1945. The Cult of Rousseau and the French Revolution. *Journal of the History of Ideas,* Vol. 6, No. 2, 197-212.

Wolf Moser, 2014. *Fernando Sor: The Unwritten Autobiography Including his Reflexions on the Guitar.* València: Piles, Editorial de Música.

Luise Mühlbach, 1898. *The Empress Josephine: An Historical Sketch of the Days of Napoleon.* Translated by W. Binet. New York: D. Appleton and Company.

Emili Olcina i Aya, 1993. *Apuntes sobre Ferran Sors y la creación romántica en la España de Goya.* Barcelona: Laertes editorial, S.L.

Charles Oman, 2014 (1908). *A History of the Peninsular War, Volume III: September 1809 to December 1810.* Auckland: Pickle Partners Publishing.

George Orwell, 1938. *Homage to Catalonia.* London: Secker & Warburg.

Christopher Page, 2014. New Light on the London Years of Fernando Sor, 1815-1822. *Early Music,* Volume 41, Number 4, 557-569.

Boris Pasternak, 2010 (1957). *Doctor Zhivago.* Translated by Richard Pevear and Larissa Volokhonsky. New York: Pantheon Books.

Reinhard G. Pauly, 1965. *Music in the Classical Period.* Englewood Cliffs, NJ: Prentice-Hall, Inc.

Vladimir E. Pavlov, 2009. Agustin Betancourt in Russia. *Quaderns d'Historia de l'Enginyeria*, X, 169-183.

Bernard Piris, 1989. *Fernando Sor: une guitare à l'orée du romantisme.* Paris: Aubier.

Otto von Pivka (text) and Michael Roffe (photos), 1975. *Spanish Armies of the Napoleonic Wars.* London: Osprey Publishing.

Piotor Rafalski (text), Jan Morek (photos), 1985. *Warzawa.* Warsaw: Interpress.

Marie-Pierre Rey, 2012. *The Tsar Who Defeated Napoleon.* Translated by Susan Emanuel. DeKalb, IL: NIU Press.

Elizabeth Ripley, 1956. *Goya.* New York: Oxford University Press.

Manuel Rocamora, 1957. *Fernando Sor. Ensayo Biográfico.* Barcelona: Enrique Tobella.

Wendy Rosslyn and Alessandra Tosi, editors, 2012. *Women in Nineteenth-Century Russia: Lives and Culture.* Cambridge: Open Book Publishers.

George Santayana, 1905. *The Life of Reason: Reason in Common Sense.* New York: Scribner's.

Susanne Schmid, 2013. *British Literary Salons of the Late Eighteenth and Early Nineteenth Centuries.* Palgrave MacMillan.

Fr. Josep M. Soler i Canals (text), Salvador Gonzalez Solé, Marc Linares, Mario Sarrià, and FISA-ESCUDO de Oro archive (photos), 2011. *All Montserrat.* Montserrat: Escudo de Oro.

Fernando Sor, 1945. *Twenty Studies for the Guitar.* Revised and edited by Andres Segovia. Edward B. Marks Music Corporation.

Fernando Sor, 1996 (1982). *The Complete Works for Guitar Solo and Guitar Duet.* In nine volumes. Reprints of the original editions with notes and commentaries by Brian Jeffery. London: Tecla Editions.

Fernando Sor, 2007 (1830). *Sor's Method for the Spanish Guitar.* Translated by A. Merrick. Mineola, NY: Dover Publications, Inc.

Lewis Spence, 1994. *Spain: Myth and Legends.* London: George G. Harrap & Co. Ltd.

Jules Stewart, 2015 (2012). *Madrid: The History.* London & New York: I.B. Tauris.

Richard Stites, 2008. *Serfdom, Society, and the Arts in Imperial Russia: The Pleasure and the Power.* New Haven, CT: Yale University Press.

Jane T. Stoddart, 1906. *The Life of the Empress Eugenie.* New York: E.P. Dutton & Co.

Leo Tolstoy, 1984 (1868-9). *War and Peace.* Translated by Louise and Aylmer Maude. London: Guild Publishing.

Henriette-Lucy, Marquise de la Tour du Pin, 1979. *Escape from the Terror.* Translated and edited by Felice Harcourt. London: The Folio Society.

Giles Tremlett, 2006. *Ghosts of Spain.* New York: Walker & Company.

Harvey Turnbull, 1976. *The Guitar from the Renaissance to the Present Day.* London: Batsford.

Graham Wade, 1980. *Traditions of the Classical Guitar.* London: Calder.

Alan Walker 1987 (1983). *Franz Liszt: The Virtuoso Years* (1811-1847). Ithaca, NY: Cornell University Press.

Walter Hayle Walshe, 1946 (1850). *The Nature and Treatment of Cancer.* London: Taylor & Walton.

Joseph Blanco White, 1825. *Letters from Spain.* London: Henry Colburn.

Walt Whitman 1945 (1891-2). Leaves of Grass. New York: Modern Library.

Appendix 2. Filmography

Amadeus (Miloš Forman, 1984).
Barry Lyndon (Stanley Kubrick, 1975).
Dr. Zhivago (David Lean, 1965).
Goya in Bordeaux (Carlos Saura, 2000).
Immortal Beloved (David Rose, 1994).

Appendix 3: Webography

Adam Kazimierz Czartoryski – Wikipedia
https://en.wikipedia.org/wiki/Adam_Kazimierz_Czartoryski

Afrancesado – Wikipedia
https://en.wikipedia.org/wiki/Afrancesado

Agustín Argüelles – Wikipedia
https://en.wikipedia.org/wiki/Agust%C3%ADn_Arg%C3%BCelles

Agustín de Betancourt – Wikipedia
https://en.wikipedia.org/wiki/Agust%C3%ADn_de_Betancourt

Alexander I of Russia – Wikipedia
https://en.wikipedia.org/wiki/Alexander_I_of_Russia

Alexander Palace – Wikipedia
https://en.wikipedia.org/wiki/Alexander_Palace

Alexander Pushkin – Wikipedia
https://en.wikipedia.org/wiki/Alexander_Pushkin

Alexander von Benckendorff – Wikipedia
https://en.wikipedia.org/wiki/Alexander_von_Benckendorff

Alexandre Dubuque – Wikipedia
https://en.wikipedia.org/wiki/Alexandre_Dubuque

Anatole (dancer): French ballet dancer – Biography and Life
https://peoplepill.com/people/anatole/

Andrés Segovia – Wikipedia
https://en.wikipedia.org/wiki/Andr%C3%A9s_Segovia

Andrés Segovia Biography
http://www.maestros-of-the-guitar.com/segovia1.html

Andres Segovia, Virtuoso of Solo Guitar, Dies at 94 – Los Angeles Times
https://www.latimes.com/archives/la-xpm-1987-06-04-mn-4748-story.html

Angelica Catalani – Wikipedia
https://en.wikipedia.org/wiki/Angelica_Catalani

Antoine Beauvilliers – Wikipedia
https://en.wikipedia.org/wiki/Antoine_Beauvilliers

Antonio Alcalá Galiano – Wikipedia
https://en.wikipedia.org/wiki/Antonio_Alcal%C3%A1_Galiano

Apostolic Nunciature to France – Wikipedia
https://en.wikipedia.org/wiki/Apostolic_Nunciature_to_France

Armand Trousseau – Wikipedia
https://en.wikipedia.org/wiki/Armand_Trousseau

Arthur Wellesley, 1st Duke of Wellington – Wikipedia
https://en.wikipedia.org/wiki/Arthur_Wellesley,_1st_Duke_of_Wellington

Auguste Mathieu Panseron – Wikipedia
https://en.wikipedia.org/wiki/Auguste_Mathieu_Panseron

Baker's Biographical Dictionary of Musicians
https://archive.org/stream/bakersbiographi00bakegoog#page/n118/mode/1up

Battle of Alba de Tormes – Wikipedia
https://en.wikipedia.org/wiki/Battle_of_Alba_de_Tormes

Battle of Almonacid – Wikipedia
https://en.wikipedia.org/wiki/Battle_of_Almonacid

Battle of Bailén – Wikipedia
https://en.wikipedia.org/wiki/Battle_of_Bail%C3%A9n

Battle of Borodino
https://en.wikipedia.org/wiki/Battle_of_Borodino

Battle of Ciudad Real – Wikipedia
https://en.wikipedia.org/wiki/Battle_of_Ciudad_Real

Battle of Leipzig – Wikipedia
https://en.wikipedia.org/wiki/Battle_of_Leipzig

Battle of Medellín – Wikipedia
https://en.wikipedia.org/wiki/Battle_of_Medell%C3%ADn

Battle of Navarino – Wikipedia
https://en.wikipedia.org/wiki/Battle_of_Navarino

Battle of Ocaña – Wikipedia
https://en.wikipedia.org/wiki/Battle_of_Oca%C3%B1a

Battle of Paris (1814) – Wikipedia
https://en.wikipedia.org/wiki/Battle_of_Paris_%281814%29

Battle of Talavera – Wikipedia
https://en.wikipedia.org/wiki/Battle_of_Talavera

Battle of Wagram – Wikipedia
https://en.wikipedia.org/wiki/Battle_of_Wagram

Battle of Waterloo – Wikipedia
https://en.wikipedia.org/wiki/Battle_of_Waterloo

Before and after: How Moscow looked in the 19th century and today (PHOTOS) – Russia Beyond
https://www.rbth.com/history/328734-moscow-19century-before-after

Behind the French Menu: Tournedos Rossini, after 150 years still the most famous of all steak dishes. Tournedos Rossini and Gioacchino Rossini.
https://behind-the-french-menu.blogspot.com/2012/06/tournedos-rossini-after-150-years-still.html

Benoît-Joseph Marsollier – Wikipedia
https://en.wikipedia.org/wiki/Beno%C3%AEt-Joseph_Marsollier

Berlin Palace – Wikipedia
https://en.wikipedia.org/wiki/Berlin_Palace

Berlin State Opera – Wikipedia
https://en.wikipedia.org/wiki/Berlin_State_Opera

Bibliografía | FernandoSor.es
https://fernandosor.es/bibliografia-general/

Biographical and pictorial chronology of Goya
https://goya.unizar.es/InfoGoya/Life/Cronologia.html

Bolshoi Ballet – Wikipedia
https://en.wikipedia.org/wiki/Bolshoi_Ballet

Bolshoi Theatre – Wikipedia
https://en.wikipedia.org/wiki/Bolshoi_Theatre

Bolshoi Theatre Symphony Orchestra (Orchestra) – OperaAndBallet.com
https://operaandballet.com/?play_person_cod=bol_th_symph_orch

Bronzelettern Sanssouci – Sanssouci – Wikipedia
https://en.wikipedia.org/wiki/Sanssouci#/media/File:Bronzelettern_Sanssouci.jpg

Carlo Andrea Pozzo di Borgo – Wikipedia
https://en.wikipedia.org/wiki/Carlo_Andrea_Pozzo_di_Borgo

Carlsbad Decrees | German history | Britannica
https://www.britannica.com/topic/Carlsbad-Decrees

Carlton House – Wikipedia
https://en.wikipedia.org/wiki/Carlton_House

Cayetano Valdés y Flores – Wikipedia
https://en.wikipedia.org/wiki/Cayetano_Vald%C3%A9s_y_Flores

Charles IV of Spain – Wikipedia
https://en.wikipedia.org/wiki/Charles_IV_of_Spain

Charles IV of Spain and His Family – Wikipedia
https://en.wikipedia.org/wiki/Charles_IV_of_Spain_and_His_Family

CHARLES X IN THE ROLE OF THE GREAT NUTCRACKER – Charles X of France – Wikipedia https://en.wikipedia.org/wiki/Charles_X_of_France#/media/File:CHARLES_X_IN_THE_ROLE_OF_THE_GREAT_NUTCRACKER.jpg

Charles X of France – Wikipedia
https://en.wikipedia.org/wiki/Charles_X_of_France

Charlottenburg Palace – Wikipedia
https://en.wikipedia.org/wiki/Charlottenburg_Palace

Château de Saint-Cloud – Wikipedia
https://en.wikipedia.org/wiki/Ch%C3%A2teau_de_Saint-Cloud

Chernigov Regiment revolt – Wikipedia
https://en.wikipedia.org/wiki/Chernigov_Regiment_revolt

Christian Günther von Bernstorff – Wikipedia
https://en.wikipedia.org/wiki/Christian_G%C3%BCnther_von_Bernstorff

Christoph von Lieven – Wikipedia
https://en.wikipedia.org/wiki/Christoph_von_Lieven

Cologne Cathedral – Wikipedia
https://en.wikipedia.org/wiki/Cologne_Cathedral

Concierto de Aranjuez – Wikipedia
https://en.wikipedia.org/wiki/Concierto_de_Aranjuez

Congress of Vienna – Wikipedia
https://en.wikipedia.org/wiki/Congress_of_Vienna

Congress Poland – Wikipedia
https://en.wikipedia.org/wiki/Congress_Poland

Constitution, Education and Research – eerj.2013.12.1.34
https://journals.sagepub.com/doi/pdf/10.2304/eerj.2013.12.1.34

Constructing Paris Medicine – Google Books

Coronation of the Russian monarch – Wikipedia
https://en.wikipedia.org/wiki/Coronation_of_the_Russian_monarch

Decembrist revolt – Wikipedia
https://en.wikipedia.org/wiki/Decembrist_revolt

Der-Denkerclub 1819 – Carlsbad Decrees – Wikipedia
https://en.wikipedia.org/wiki/Carlsbad_Decrees#/media/File:Der-Denkerclub_1819.jpg

Did tsar Alexander I leave his throne for a solitary life in Siberia? – Russia Beyond
https://www.rbth.com/politics_and_society/2017/08/23/did-tsar-alexander-i-leave-his-throne-for-a-solitary-life-in-siberia_827382

Dionisio Aguado Biography
http://www.maestros-of-the-guitar.com/dionisioaguado.html

Dmitry Bortniansky – Wikipedia
https://en.wikipedia.org/wiki/Dmitry_Bortniansky

Dmitry Golitsyn – Wikipedia
https://en.wikipedia.org/wiki/Dmitry_Golitsyn

Elena Andreianova – Wikipedia
https://en.wikipedia.org/wiki/Elena_Andreianova

Elizabeth Alexeievna (Louise of Baden) – Wikipedia
https://en.wikipedia.org/wiki/Elizabeth_Alexeievna_(Louise_of_Baden)

Émilie Bigottini – Wikipedia
https://en.wikipedia.org/wiki/%C3%89milie_Bigottini

Enlightenment in Spain – Wikipedia
https://en.wikipedia.org/wiki/Enlightenment_in_Spain

Enrique O'Donnell, Conde de La Bisbal – Wikipedia
https://en.wikipedia.org/wiki/Enrique_O%27Donnell,_Conde_de_La_Bisbal

Étienne Méhul – Wikipedia
https://en.wikipedia.org/wiki/%C3%89tienne_M%C3%A9hul

Eugène Delacroix – Wikipedia
https://en.wikipedia.org/wiki/Eug%C3%A8ne_Delacroix

Facts about Andrés Segovia that you might not know | Guitar news on Veojam.com
https://www.veojam.com/news/archives/190/andres-segovia-interesting-facts

Félicité Hullin-Sor — Wikipédia
https://fr.wikipedia.org/wiki/F%C3%A9licit%C3%A9_Hullin-Sor

Ferdinand VII of Spain – Wikipedia
https://en.wikipedia.org/wiki/Ferdinand_VII_of_Spain

Fernando Sor – Wikipedia
https://en.wikipedia.org/wiki/Fernando_Sor

Fernando Sor | Encyclopedia.com
https://www.encyclopedia.com/people/history/historians-miscellaneous-biographies/fernando-sor

Fernando Sor Biography
http://www.maestros-of-the-guitar.com/fernandosor.html

First Barbary War – Wikipedia
https://en.wikipedia.org/wiki/First_Barbary_War

First Carlist War – Wikipedia
https://en.wikipedia.org/wiki/First_Carlist_War

Francis II, Holy Roman Emperor – Wikipedia
https://en.wikipedia.org/wiki/Francis_II,_Holy_Roman_Emperor

Francisco de Borja Álvarez de Toledo, 12th Marquis of Villafranca – Wikipedia
https://en.wikipedia.org/wiki/Francisco_de_Borja_%C3%81lvarez_de_Toledo,_12th_Marquis_of_Villafranca

Francisco Goya – Wikipedia
https://en.wikipedia.org/wiki/Francisco_Goya

Francisco Goya: bulls, milkmaids and a lasting presence in Bordeaux – Invisible Bordeaux
http://invisiblebordeaux.blogspot.com/2012/06/francisco-goya-bulls-milkmaids-and.html

Francisco Javier Castaños, 1st Duke of Bailén – Wikipedia
https://en.wikipedia.org/wiki/Francisco_Javier_Casta%C3%B1os,_1st_Duke_of_Bail%C3%A9n

Francisco Tárrega – Wikipedia
https://en.wikipedia.org/wiki/Francisco_T%C3%A1rrega

François Cabarrus – Wikipedia
https://en.wikipedia.org/wiki/Fran%C3%A7ois_Cabarrus

François-Joseph Fétis – Wikipedia
https://en.wikipedia.org/wiki/Fran%C3%A7ois-Joseph_F%C3%A9tis

Franz Liszt – Wikipedia
https://en.wikipedia.org/wiki/Franz_Liszt

Franz Schubert – Wikipedia
https://en.wikipedia.org/wiki/Franz_Schubert

Frédéric Chopin – Wikipedia
https://en.wikipedia.org/wiki/Fr%C3%A9d%C3%A9ric_Chopin

Frederick the Great – Wikipedia
https://en.wikipedia.org/wiki/Frederick_the_Great

Frederick William II of Prussia – Wikipedia
https://en.wikipedia.org/wiki/Frederick_William_II_of_Prussia

Frederick William III of Prussia – Wikipedia
https://en.wikipedia.org/wiki/Frederick_William_III_of_Prussia

Friedrich Kalkbrenner – Wikipedia
https://en.wikipedia.org/wiki/Friedrich_Kalkbrenner

Gaspar Melchor de Jovellanos – Wikipedia
https://en.wikipedia.org/wiki/Gaspar_Melchor_de_Jovellanos

Gaspare Spontini – Wikipedia
https://en.wikipedia.org/wiki/Gaspare_Spontini

George Cavendish, 1st Earl of Burlington – Wikipedia
https://en.wikipedia.org/wiki/George_Cavendish,_1st_Earl_of_Burlington

George III of the United Kingdom – Wikipedia
https://en.wikipedia.org/wiki/George_III_of_the_United_Kingdom

George IV of the United Kingdom – Wikipedia
https://en.wikipedia.org/wiki/George_IV_of_the_United_Kingdom

George Sand – Wikipedia
https://en.wikipedia.org/wiki/George_Sand

George Santayana – Wikipedia
https://en.wikipedia.org/wiki/George_Santayana

German Confederation – Wikipedia
https://en.wikipedia.org/wiki/German_Confederation

Giacomo Giustiniani – Wikipedia
https://en.wikipedia.org/wiki/Giacomo_Giustiniani

Girolamo Crescentini – Wikipedia
https://en.wikipedia.org/wiki/Girolamo_Crescentini

Gohlis – Wikipedia
https://en.wikipedia.org/wiki/Gohlis

Goya's Last Works | Yale University Press
https://yalebooks.yale.edu/book/9780300117677/goyas-last-works

Grand Duchess Maria Pavlovna of Russia (1786–1859) – Wikipedia
https://en.wikipedia.org/wiki/Grand_Duchess_Maria_Pavlovna_of_Russia_(1786%E2%80%931859)

Grand Theatre, Warsaw – Wikipedia
https://en.wikipedia.org/wiki/Grand_Theatre,_Warsaw

Guitar Quotes | this is classical guitar
http://www.thisisclassicalguitar.com/guitar-quotes/

Güllen Sor, Felicata
https://clever-geek.github.io/articles/2723917/index.html

Hector Berlioz – Wikipedia
https://en.wikipedia.org/wiki/Hector_Berlioz

Heinrich Heine – Wikipedia
https://en.wikipedia.org/wiki/Heinrich_Heine

Henri Bertini – Wikipedia
https://en.wikipedia.org/wiki/Henri_Bertini

Henri-Montan Berton – Wikipedi
https://en.wikipedia.org/wiki/Henri-Montan_Berton

History of Poland – Wikipedia
https://en.wikipedia.org/wiki/History_of_Poland#Reforms_and_loss_of_statehood_(1764%E2%80%931795)

Homage to Catalonia – Wikipedia
https://en.wikipedia.org/wiki/Homage_to_Catalonia

Hôtel Beauharnais – Wikipedia
https://en.wikipedia.org/wiki/H%C3%B4tel_Beauharnais

Hôtel d'Estrées – Wikipedia
https://en.wikipedia.org/wiki/H%C3%B4tel_d%27Estr%C3%A9es

House of Golitsyn – Wikipedia
https://en.wikipedia.org/wiki/House_of_Golitsyn

How bears really walked the streets in Russia – Russia Beyond
https://www.rbth.com/history/328668-how-bears-really-walked-streets-russia

Hundred Days – Wikipedia
https://en.wikipedia.org/wiki/Hundred_Days

Hundred Thousand Sons of Saint Louis – Wikipedia
https://en.wikipedia.org/wiki/Hundred_Thousand_Sons_of_Saint_Louis

Ignaz Pleyel – Wikipedia
https://en.wikipedia.org/wiki/Ignaz_Pleyel

Imperial Theatres – Wikipedia
https://en.wikipedia.org/wiki/Imperial_Theatres

Isabella Colbran – Wikipedia
https://en.wikipedia.org/wiki/Isabella_Colbran

Ivan Muravyov-Apostol – Wikipedia
https://en.wikipedia.org/wiki/Ivan_Muravyov-Apostol

James Duff, 4th Earl Fife – Wikipedia
https://en.wikipedia.org/wiki/James_Duff,_4th_Earl_Fife

Jean Antoine Meissonnier – Wikipedia
https://de.wikipedia.org/wiki/Jean_Antoine_Meissonnier

Jean-Baptiste Bouillaud – Wikipedia
https://en.wikipedia.org/wiki/Jean-Baptiste_Bouillaud

Joachim Murat – Wikipedia
https://en.wikipedia.org/wiki/Joachim_Murat

Joaquín María Ferrer – Wikipedia, la enciclopedia libre
https://es.wikipedia.org/wiki/Joaqu%C3%ADn_Mar%C3%ADa_Ferrer

Johann Baptist Cramer – Wikipedia
https://en.wikipedia.org/wiki/Johann_Baptist_Cramer

Johann Sebastian Bach – Wikipedia
https://en.wikipedia.org/wiki/Johann_Sebastian_Bach

Johann Wilhelm Hertel – Wikipedia
https://en.wikipedia.org/wiki/Johann_Wilhelm_Hertel

Johann Wolfgang von Goethe – Sturm und Drang (1770–76) | Britannica
https://www.britannica.com/biography/Johann-Wolfgang-von-Goethe/Friendship-with-Schiller-1794-1805

Johann Wolfgang von Goethe – Wikipedia
https://en.wikipedia.org/wiki/Johann_Wolfgang_von_Goethe#Details_of_selected_works

Johann Wolfgang von Goethe | Biography, Works, & Facts | Britannica
https://www.britannica.com/biography/Johann-Wolfgang-von-Goethe

John Field (composer) – Wikipedia
https://en.wikipedia.org/wiki/John_Field_(composer)

José Fernando Macario Sor Montadas | Real Academia de la Historia
http://dbe.rah.es/biografias/8386/jose-fernando-macario-sor-montadas

José María de Torrijos y Uriarte – Wikipedia
https://en.wikipedia.org/wiki/Jos%C3%A9_Mar%C3%ADa_de_Torrijos_y_Uriarte

José Miguel de Carvajal-Vargas, 2nd Duke of San Carlos – Wikipedia
https://en.wikipedia.org/wiki/Jos%C3%A9_Miguel_de_Carvajal-Vargas,_2nd_Duke_of_San_Carlos

José Moñino, 1st Count of Floridablanca – Wikipedia
https://en.wikipedia.org/wiki/Jos%C3%A9_Mo%C3%B1ino,_1st_Count_of_Floridablanca

Joseph Meissonnier – Wikipedia
https://en.wikipedia.org/wiki/Joseph_Meissonnier

Józef Elsner – Wikipedia
https://en.wikipedia.org/wiki/J%C3%B3zef_Elsner

Józef Zajączek – Wikipedia
https://en.wikipedia.org/wiki/J%C3%B3zef_Zaj%C4%85czek

Juan Escoiquiz – Wikipedia
https://en.wikipedia.org/wiki/Juan_Escoiquiz

Juan Miguel de Vives y Feliu – Wikipedia
https://en.wikipedia.org/wiki/Juan_Miguel_de_Vives_y_Feliu

Juan Van Halen – Wikipedia
https://en.wikipedia.org/wiki/Juan_Van_Halen

July Revolution – Wikipedia
https://en.wikipedia.org/wiki/July_Revolution

Jus exclusivae – Wikipedia
https://en.wikipedia.org/wiki/Jus_exclusivae

Karl Nesselrode – Wikipedia
https://en.wikipedia.org/wiki/Karl_Nesselrode

Krakowskie Przedmieście – Wikipedia
https://en.wikipedia.org/wiki/Krakowskie_Przedmie%C5%9Bcie

L'irato – Wikipedia
https://en.wikipedia.org/wiki/L%27irato

La Chapelle-Hullin — Wikipédia
https://fr.wikipedia.org/wiki/La_Chapelle-Hullin

La guitarra es la protagonista del I Festival Ferran Sor | Barcelona Cultura
https://www.barcelona.cat/barcelonacultura/es/recomanem/festival-ferran-sor-guitarra

La Leocadia – Wikipedia
https://en.wikipedia.org/wiki/La_Leocadia

Leandro Fernández de Moratín – Wikipedia
https://en.wikipedia.org/wiki/Leandro_Fern%C3%A1ndez_de_Morat%C3%ADn

Leipzig – Wikipedia
https://en.wikipedia.org/wiki/Leipzig#Notable_residents

Leipzig Opera – Wikipedia
https://en.wikipedia.org/wiki/Leipzig_Opera

Liria Palace – Wikipedia
https://en.wikipedia.org/wiki/Liria_Palace

Lise Noblet – Wikipedia
https://en.wikipedia.org/wiki/Lise_Noblet

List of ambassadors of Russia to the United Kingdom – Wikipedia
https://en.wikipedia.org/wiki/List_of_ambassadors_of_Russia_to_the_United_Kingdom

List of Champagne houses – Wikipedia
https://en.wikipedia.org/wiki/List_of_Champagne_houses

List of compositions by Fernando Sor – Wikipedia
https://en.wikipedia.org/wiki/List_of_compositions_by_Fernando_Sor

List of music students by teacher: C to F – Wikipedia
https://en.wikipedia.org/wiki/List_of_music_students_by_teacher:_C_to_F#John_Field

List of Spanish general officers (Peninsular War) – Wikipedia
https://en.wikipedia.org/wiki/List_of_Spanish_general_officers_(Peninsular_War)

List of works by Francisco Goya – Wikipedia
https://en.wikipedia.org/wiki/List_of_works_by_Francisco_Goya

Lord Byron – Wikipedia
https://en.wikipedia.org/wiki/Lord_Byron

Louis Philippe I – Wikipedia
https://en.wikipedia.org/wiki/Louis_Philippe_I

Louis XVIII – Wikipedia
https://en.wikipedia.org/wiki/Louis_XVIII

Louis XVIII of France – Wikipedia
https://en.wikipedia.org/wiki/Louis_XVIII_of_France#Bourbon_Restoration

Louise of Mecklenburg-Strelitz – Wikipedia
https://en.wikipedia.org/wiki/Louise_of_Mecklenburg-Strelitz

Ludwig van Beethoven – Wikipedia
https://en.wikipedia.org/wiki/Ludwig_van_Beethoven

Luigi Cherubini – Wikipedia
https://en.wikipedia.org/wiki/Luigi_Cherubini

Madame Anatole – Wikipedia
https://en.wikipedia.org/wiki/Madame_Anatole

Maison dorée (Paris) – Wikipedia
https://en.wikipedia.org/wiki/Maison_dor%C3%A9e_(Paris)

Manuel Godoy – Wikipedia
https://en.wikipedia.org/wiki/Manuel_Godoy

Marcelino Calero y Portocarrero – Wikipedia, la enciclopedia libre
https://es.wikipedia.org/wiki/Marcelino_Calero_y_Portocarrero

Maria Amalia of Naples and Sicily – Wikipedia
https://en.wikipedia.org/wiki/Maria_Amalia_of_Naples_and_Sicily

María Cayetana de Silva, 13th Duchess of Alba | Revolvy
https://www.revolvy.com/page/Mar%C3%ADa-Cayetana-de-Silva%2C-13th-Duchess-of-Alba

Maria Feodorovna (Sophie Dorothea of Württemberg) – Wikipedia
https://en.wikipedia.org/wiki/Maria_Feodorovna_(Sophie_Dorothea_of_W%C3%BCrttemberg)

María Manuela Kirkpatrick – Wikipedia
https://en.wikipedia.org/wiki/Mar%C3%ADa_Manuela_Kirkpatrick

María Manuela Kirkpatrick de Grevignée – Wikipedia
https://en.wikipedia.org/wiki/Mar%C3%ADa_Manuela_Kirkpatrick_de_Grevign%C3%A9e

Mariánské Lázně – Wikipedia
https://en.wikipedia.org/wiki/Mari%C3%A1nsk%C3%A9_L%C3%A1zn%C4%9B#Notable_people

Marienbad Elegy – Wikipedia
https://en.wikipedia.org/wiki/Marienbad_Elegy

Martín Zurbano – Wikipedia
https://en.wikipedia.org/wiki/Mart%C3%ADn_Zurbano

Matvey Dmitriev-Mamonov – Wikipedia
https://en.wikipedia.org/wiki/Matvey_Dmitriev-Mamonov

Mauro Giuliani – Wikipedia
https://en.wikipedia.org/wiki/Mauro_Giuliani

Military mobilisation during the Hundred Days – Wikipedia
https://en.wikipedia.org/wiki/Military_mobilisation_during_the_Hundred_Days

Montmartre Cemetery – Wikipedia
https://en.wikipedia.org/wiki/Montmartre_Cemetery

Moscow Kremlin Museums: – Architectural ensemble of the Moscow Kremlin
https://www.kreml.ru/en-Us/visit-to-kremlin/what-to-see/sobornaya-ploschad/

Moscow State Academy of Choreography – Wikipedia
https://en.wikipedia.org/wiki/Moscow_State_Academy_of_Choreography

Muzio Clementi – Wikipedia
https://en.wikipedia.org/wiki/Muzio_Clementi#Move_to_England

Napoléon Coste – Wikipedia
https://en.wikipedia.org/wiki/Napol%C3%A9on_Coste

Napoleon III – Wikipedia
https://en.wikipedia.org/wiki/Napoleon_III#Early_life

Nathan Mayer Rothschild – Wikipedia
https://en.wikipedia.org/wiki/Nathan_Mayer_Rothschild

National Theatre, Warsaw – Wikipedia
https://en.wikipedia.org/wiki/National_Theatre,_Warsaw

Niccolò Paganini – Wikipedia
https://en.wikipedia.org/wiki/Niccol%C3%B2_Paganini

Nicholas I | Biography, Facts, & Accomplishments | Britannica
https://www.britannica.com/biography/Nicholas-I-tsar-of-Russia/Ascent-to-the-throne

Nicholas I of Russia – Wikipedia
https://en.wikipedia.org/wiki/Nicholas_I_of_Russia

Nicholas Palace – Wikipedia
https://en.wikipedia.org/wiki/Nicholas_Palace

Nikolai Borisovich Galitzine – Wikipedia
https://en.wikipedia.org/wiki/Nikolai_Borisovich_Galitzine

Nikolaus II, Prince Esterházy – Wikipedia
https://en.wikipedia.org/wiki/Nikolaus_II,_Prince_Esterh%C3%A1zy

Orlov Trotter – Wikipedia
https://en.wikipedia.org/wiki/Orlov_Trotter

Orlowski podrozny – Troika (driving) – Wikipedia
https://en.wikipedia.org/wiki/Troika_(driving)#/media/File:Orlowski_podrozny.jpg

Palace of Facets – Wikipedia
https://en.wikipedia.org/wiki/Palace_of_Facets

Paris Opera Ballet – Wikipedia
https://en.wikipedia.org/wiki/Paris_Opera_Ballet

Pas de deux – Wikipedia
https://en.wikipedia.org/wiki/Pas_de_deux

Peninsular War – Wikipedia
https://en.wikipedia.org/wiki/Peninsular_War

Peredelkino – Wikipedia
https://en.wikipedia.org/wiki/Peredelkino

Philaret (Drozdov) of Moscow – OrthodoxWiki
https://orthodoxwiki.org/Philaret_(Drozdov)_of_Moscow

Pierre Baillot – Wikipedia
https://en.wikipedia.org/wiki/Pierre_Baillot

Pope Gregory XVI – Wikipedia
https://en.wikipedia.org/wiki/Pope_Gregory_XVI

Pragmatic Sanction of King Ferdinand VII | Spanish history | Britannica
https://www.britannica.com/topic/Pragmatic-Sanction-of-King-Ferdinand-VII

Preobrazhensky Guards | Russian military unit | Britannica
https://www.britannica.com/topic/Preobrazhensky-Guards

Preobrazhensky Regiment – Wikipedia
https://en.wikipedia.org/wiki/Preobrazhensky_Regiment#Uniforms

Presidential Palace, Warsaw – Wikipedia
https://en.wikipedia.org/wiki/Presidential_Palace,_Warsaw

Prince Augustus Frederick, Duke of Sussex – Wikipedia
https://en.wikipedia.org/wiki/Prince_Augustus_Frederick,_Duke_of_Sussex

Quinta del Sordo – Wikipedia
https://en.wikipedia.org/wiki/Quinta_del_Sordo

Rafael del Riego – Wikipedia
https://en.wikipedia.org/wiki/Rafael_del_Riego

Reform Act 1832 – Wikipedia
https://en.wikipedia.org/wiki/Reform_Act_1832

Regency History: The Argyll Rooms in Regency London
https://www.regencyhistory.net/2017/09/the-argyll-rooms-in-regency-london.html

Revolutions of 1830 | European history | Britannica
https://www.britannica.com/event/Revolutions-of-1830

Rochefort, Charente-Maritime – Wikipedia
https://en.wikipedia.org/wiki/Rochefort,_Charente-Maritime

Rosario Weiss Zorrilla – Wikipedia
https://en.wikipedia.org/wiki/Rosario_Weiss_Zorrilla

Royal Ballet School – Wikipedia
https://en.wikipedia.org/wiki/Royal_Ballet_School

Royal Palace of Brussels | The Belgian Monarchy
https://www.monarchie.be/en/heritage/royal-palace-of-brussels

Russian ballet – Wikipedia
https://en.wikipedia.org/wiki/Russian_ballet

Russian guitar – Wikipedia
https://en.wikipedia.org/wiki/Russian_guitar

Saints Peter and Paul Cathedral, Saint Petersburg – Wikipedia
https://en.wikipedia.org/wiki/Saints_Peter_and_Paul_Cathedral,_
Saint_Petersburg

Salle Le Peletier – Wikipedia
https://en.wikipedia.org/wiki/Salle_Le_Peletier

Salvador de Madariaga – Wikipedia
https://en.wikipedia.org/wiki/Salvador_de_Madariaga

Sanssouci – Wikipedia
https://en.wikipedia.org/wiki/Sanssouci

Saxon Palace – Wikipedia
https://en.wikipedia.org/wiki/Saxon_Palace

Segovia and Politics | Francisco Franco | Spain
https://www.scribd.com/document/209056582/Segovia-and-
Politics

Siberian fur trade – Wikipedia
https://en.wikipedia.org/wiki/Siberian_fur_trade

Siege of Madrid, 1-4 December 1808
http://www.historyofwar.org/articles/siege_madrid_1808.html

Siege of Valencia (1812) – Wikipedia
https://en.wikipedia.org/wiki/Siege_of_Valencia_(1812)

Sor, Fernando (1778-1839) | The Hispanic-Anglosphere ...
https://hispanic-anglosphere.com/individuals/sor-fernando-1778-1839/

Spanish Inquisition – Wikipedia
https://en.wikipedia.org/wiki/Spanish_Inquisition#End_of_the_Inquisition

States of the German Confederation – Wikipedia
https://en.wikipedia.org/wiki/States_of_the_German_Confederation

Stepan Stepanovich Apraksin – Wikipedia
https://en.wikipedia.org/wiki/Stepan_Stepanovich_Apraksin

Stroganov family – Wikipedia
https://en.wikipedia.org/wiki/Stroganov_family

Symphony guide: Hector Berlioz's Symphonie Fantastique | Music | The Guardian
https://www.theguardian.com/music/tomserviceblog/2014/aug/19/symphony-guide-hector-berliozs-symphonie-fantastique

Terem Palace – Wikipedia
https://en.wikipedia.org/wiki/Terem_Palace

Terpsichore – Wikipedia
https://en.wikipedia.org/wiki/Terpsichore

The Bose House | Bach-Archiv Leipzig
https://www.bach-leipzig.de/en/neutral/bose-house

The Cholera Epidemic of 1832
https://www.thoughtco.com/the-cholera-epidemic-1773767

The Congress of Vienna | Boundless World History
https://courses.lumenlearning.com/boundless-worldhistory/chapter/the-congress-of-vienna/

The Governess: Caught Between Children and Adults
http://web.utk.edu/~gerard/romanticpolitics/governess.html

The Great House of the Golitsyn Mansion | izi.TRAVEL
https://izi.travel/en/149b-the-great-house-of-the-golitsyn-mansion/en

The opening of the Estates General May 5, 1789 in the Salle des Menus Plaisirs in Versailles Stock Photo: 217013876 – Alamy
https://www.alamy.com/the-opening-of-the-estates-general-may-5-1789-in-the-salle-des-menus-plaisirs-in-versailles-image217013876.html

The Prayer of Russians – Wikipedia
https://en.wikipedia.org/wiki/The_Prayer_of_Russians

The Restaurateur: Dining in Paris in the Early 19th Century | Shannon Selin
https://shannonselin.com/2019/02/restaurateur-dining-paris-19th-century/

The Second World Cholera Pandemic (1826-1849) in the Kingdom of the Two Sicilies with Special Reference to the Towns of San Prisco and Forio d'Ischia. – PubMed – NCBI
https://www.ncbi.nlm.nih.gov/pubmed/26377228

The story of the Grand Véfour
http://www.grand-vefour.com/en/legrandvefour/thehistory.html

Thérésa Tallien – Wikipedia
https://en.wikipedia.org/wiki/Th%C3%A9r%C3%A9sa_Tallien

Third Carlist War – Wikipedia
https://en.wikipedia.org/wiki/Third_Carlist_War

Three Popular Palais-Royal Restaurants of the 1800s – Geri Walton
https://www.geriwalton.com/three-popular-palais-royal-restaurants-1800s/

Timeline of the life of Francisco de Goya y Lucientes
https://eeweems.com/goya/timeline-of-the-life-of-goya.php

To Russia with Love! Fernando Sor and Félicité Hullin : Interlude.hk
https://interlude.hk/to-russia-with-love/

To Thomas Jefferson from William Kirkpatrick, 23 September 1803
https://founders.archives.gov/documents/Jefferson/01-41-02-0313

Troika (driving) – Wikipedia
https://en.wikipedia.org/wiki/Troika_(driving)

Tuileries Palace – Wikipedia
https://en.wikipedia.org/wiki/Tuileries_Palace

Victor Hugo – Wikipedia
https://en.wikipedia.org/wiki/Victor_Hugo

Walter Scott – Wikipedia
https://en.wikipedia.org/wiki/Walter_Scott

Wet nurse – Wikipedia
https://en.wikipedia.org/wiki/Wet_nurse

Wilhelm Würfel – Wikipedia
https://en.wikipedia.org/wiki/Wilhelm_W%C3%BCrfel

William I of the Netherlands – Wikipedia
https://en.wikipedia.org/wiki/William_I_of_the_Netherlands

William IV of the United Kingdom – Wikipedia
https://en.wikipedia.org/wiki/William_IV_of_the_United_Kingdom

Winter Palace – Wikipedia
https://en.wikipedia.org/wiki/Winter_Palace

Wit: Voltaire and Frederick the Great | Hannibal and Me: life lessons from history
https://andreaskluth.org/2008/11/23/wit-voltaire-and-frederick-the-great/

Wojciech Bogusławski – Wikipedia
https://en.wikipedia.org/wiki/Wojciech_Bogus%C5%82awski

www.ingramcontent.com/pod-product-compliance
Lightning Source LLC
Chambersburg PA
CBHW020220260626
47156CB00002B/471

* 9 7 8 1 9 5 4 9 6 8 0 6 6 *